MADAM

PHOEBE WYNNE

QUERCUS

First published in Great Britain in 2021
This paperback edition published in 2022 by

QUERCUS

An imprint of

Quercus Editions Ltd
Carmelite House
50 Victoria Embankment
London EC4Y 0DZ

An Hachette UK company

A CIP catalogue record for this book is available from the British Library

PB ISBN 978 1 52940 876 8

10 9 8 7 6 5 4 3 2 1

Typeset by CC Book Production

Printed and bound in Great Britain by Clays Ltd, Elcograf S.p.A.

MIX
Paper from responsible sources
FSC
www.fsc.org
FSC® C104740

Papers used by Quercus are from well-managed forests and other responsible sources.

Phoebe Wynne worked in education for eight years, teaching Classics in the UK and English Language and Literature in Paris. She left the classroom to focus on her writing and went on to hone her craft in Los Angeles and in London. *Madam* is her first novel. She is both British and French, and currently spends her time between France and England.

Praise for *Madam*

'*Rebecca* meets *The Secret History*. Gloriously dark, gloriously gothic'
Sara Collins, author of *The Confessions of Frannie Langton*

'The simmering menace and mystery kept me absolutely gripped. It gave me the same feeling as when I read *The Secret History*. . . This was a smouldering slow burn of a novel that I could not put down'
Jennifer Saint, author of *Ariadne*

'Imagine if Donna Tartt and Margaret Atwood got together to write a creepy, suspenseful novel about a school for young women in the Scottish Highlands. . . Brooding and unsettling, Wynne paints a gorgeous picture that only serves to camouflage the dark secrets she's hidden within'
Chandler Baker, author of *Whisper Network*

'I ripped through it and thoroughly enjoyed the ride. . . A highly entertaining and atmospheric read'
Kate Sawyer, author of *The Stranding*

'Chilling, eerie and very clever. I devoured it'
Polly Crosby, author of *The Illustrated Child*

'A thrilling debut, reminiscent of Du Maurier. The narrative, written in precise prose with beautifully crafted characters, barrels along at pace, leaving us breathless at each twist and turn. A truly wonderful read'
Nydia Hetherington, author of *A Girl Made of Air*

'Brooding, creepy and suspenseful. . . Perfect for fans of *The Handmaid's Tale*'
Woman & Home

'A dazzling slice of dark, Gothic feminism'
Heat

'A wonderful, refreshing, beautifully written novel, and I cannot wait to read Wynne's next'
Louise Fein, author of *People Like Us*

'Strange, dark, and utterly consuming. . . I loved it'
Katie Lowe, author of *The Furies*

'Chilling, unsettling with strong messages about femininity, *Madam* shocks as it builds from subtle hits to its big satisfying crescendo . . . An interesting mix of modern gothic, the anticipation of a thriller and a strong female voice'
My Weekly

'Thick with Gothic intrigue and menace, this is also a novel with a feminist heart'
Daily Mail

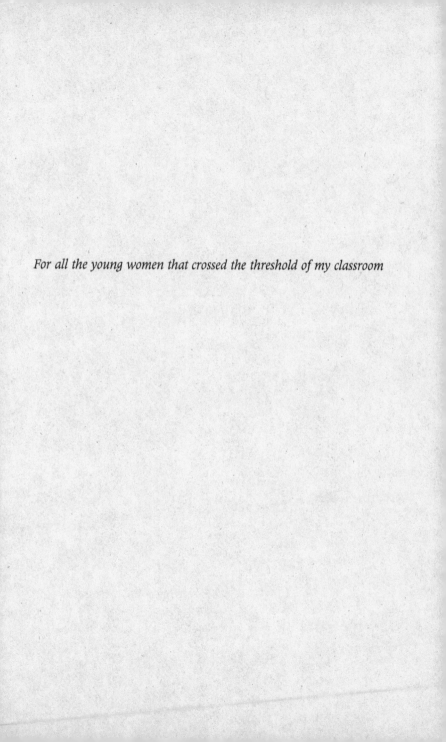

For all the young women that crossed the threshold of my classroom

'Courage calls to courage everywhere'

Dame Millicent Fawcett

Πῦρ γυνὴ καὶ θάλασσα, δυνατὰ τρία

'Fire, woman and sea, the mighty three'

Aesop

PROLOGUE

Summer 1993

The merriment of moments before had dissolved into panic; chairs were dragged back, wine glasses tumbled to the floor. Soft silk dresses moved quickly as the wall of smoke drew nearer, thick with heat and tails of flame.

Slim girlish arms pressed urgently at the wide door frame as others streamed past in an attempt to escape. But the main passageway had already given itself up to the fire, the scorched wood and stone falling away beneath their feet. Dazed parents were grasping at any girl, whether their daughter or not; other guests pushed forward in a bold effort to save themselves. Teachers dispersed among the others, losing their grip on authority, reality, sanity – searching for a plan of escape on the Headmaster's shocked face.

The hall's windows shattered into hot shards; the cool sweet air of the night swirled high above them as if in mockery.

A voice cried out, 'Who did this?'

Another rasped, 'Why was there no alarm?'

The person at the door was missing. Everybody was out of place but somehow, that empty spot read as a particular betrayal.

A few passages away in a smaller hall, the windows shattered too

– this time by force, in a small boarding house where escape seemed likely, and where the waking girls were more alert than those at the party. Heavy doors had been forced closed against the smoke while small hands punched at windows, using the curtains to push around the glass.

In another part of the school, younger girls in pyjamas hurried about, while their housemistresses and matrons slept soundly above.

The school building felt none of this urgency, standing firm despite its burning injury, holding fast as it was eaten from the inside out.

The cold black seawater danced all around the peninsula. Lapping waves flashed red with complacency as the reflected fire burned. A wreck of seabirds flew away, silently and very fast.

From the office of the Headmaster

PUELLAE MUNDI

Caldonbrae Hall
Est. 1842

Friday, 8th May 1992

Dear Jane,

Further to our meeting last week and a discussion with the board of governors, we have concluded that your employment at Caldonbrae Hall must be terminated.

Your final lessons have now been taught and you must depart from the school's premises by Sunday, 17th May. You will be required to vacate your classroom, the Classics office and your apartment. As per the terms of your contract, after this date you will be banned from the school's premises, and from contacting its occupants, particularly any girls you have taught. May I also remind you of the terms that forbid you from discussing the school anywhere outside its grounds, and the severe repercussions should you do so.

Considering the value of the twelve years' service you have given the school, and due to the short notice of this termination, you are assured that both I and the governors will see to your future professional and personal situations. Caldonbrae Hall will always be by your side.

We shall be searching for a replacement head of Classics, without the need for your involvement.

Yours,

Headmaster

Summer 1992

Rose leaned on the wall behind her and spoke in a rush. 'Mum, I had to phone you. Sorry, I know it's a bad time, but . . . the thing is, I got the job.'

'At Caldonbrae?' Her mother was breathless; Rose didn't know if it was from disbelief or the illness.

'Yes, I got a letter,' Rose insisted. 'I can't believe they've offered it to me.'

'That's excellent.' Her mother heaved an elated sigh. 'Exactly what we needed.'

'I knew you'd be pleased.' Rose bit her lip, wanting to tear the words back as soon as she'd spoken them.

'When would you start?'

'Really soon. September.'

There was a cough. 'Yes.'

Rose frowned. 'You don't sound too good today.'

'I'm fine, contrary to what the nurse tells me. Just some tingling in my hands.'

Rose could hear an echo behind her mother's voice; she wondered which room they'd put her in. 'They *do* know best, Mum.'

'Not here they don't. You can put me up in a proper place, now that you're moving up in the world.'

Rose winced as she continued: 'I don't know about accepting it, though . . . I've only been teaching a few years, and the other staff will probably be at least twenty years older than me. I'm not sure if I can really—'

'Nonsense, child. They've chosen you. Your record is outstanding.'

'Yes, maybe, but the school's so . . . grand. It's a boarding school, Mum, and it's all girls.' Rose looked out at the glow of a street lamp in the rain; it was darker than it should have been on this low June evening. She hadn't switched on any of the lights in the flat – she'd been too astonished after spotting the letter on the doormat, tearing it open and rushing to the phone. Her flatmate was obviously still out. No one to celebrate with except her sickening mother at the other end of the line.

'Caldonbrae Hall *is* grand. It's what we deserve, you just have to get on with it.' Her mother's hoarse voice rang with victory. 'I've fought for things like this all my life. This is excellent for us.'

For me, Mum, Rose pleaded inwardly. 'I still don't know . . .'

'Sorry?'

'It's just mad, really,' she carried on, 'coming through that recommendation from a colleague. Then their visit here and the interview – strange to think I haven't even been to the school at all.'

Rose remembered how the two impossibly stuffy and elegant women in their late forties had shuffled into her messy Portakabin of a classroom: the deputy head, Vivien, and another Classics teacher, Emma. Rose wondered at the time why *she* hadn't been given the head of department role – Emma had been at the school for more than a decade. After they'd left, Rose felt certain she'd never hear from anyone at Caldonbrae again. 'They haven't hired anyone externally for years, apparently. It seems so weird – they've barely seen me teach.'

'Well,' her mother's voice was strong, 'the recommendation was enough. Clearly that's how they do things. Besides, nepotism is how Britain is run, so why shouldn't we benefit from it?'

Rose frowned again, twisting the curled cord of the phone around her fingers; it pulled at the unit on the side table.

'But I don't like that. And you've always argued against—'

'Times have changed,' her mother said coolly. 'Open your eyes, dear.'

'It's just overwhelming!' Rose sputtered out. 'And it's so far away, such a huge change from everything I have here.'

'You have nothing here but me, Rose.'

Rose felt a rush of heat in her cheeks. 'That's a bit harsh, Mum. *And* it's not true.'

Her mother heaved a heroic breath in response. 'You're right that Caldonbrae Hall is far, no more of your weekend visits. I'll come and visit you instead, with a carer. You'll pay for it, of course.'

'Oh, well . . .' Rose leaned against the side table. 'I don't know whether that's—'

'A palatial establishment like that? Of course I will.' Rose glared into the phone as her mother continued. 'Will they give you somewhere to live?'

'Yes, they do that for all the staff apparently,' Rose replied, relieved at the change of subject. 'The letter says they'll give me a flat above one of the boarding houses.' She took a moment to squint across the dark sitting room, scanning her few bits of furniture and slotting them out in her mind from the ones her flatmate owned.

'Well, lucky you. Once you're in, they'll take proper care of you. My Rose.' Her mother's voice lifted with emotion, and something like pride. 'Head of Classics, at one of the most famous schools in England, in *our* family.'

'It's in Scotland.'

'None of that, please,' her mother rasped, coughing again. 'Listen to me, Rose. This is the best thing that has ever happened to us. I can't wait to tell the others here. Stop dawdling and accept the job!'

Rose cast her eyes over the letter; the school's emblem seemed to catch the dim light of the street lamp through the window.

'I suppose . . .' Rose's tongue danced on the words before she spoke them, 'Dad would have been pleased, wouldn't he?'

There was a difficult silence before her mother answered: 'You are exhausting. Call them now.'

Rose dropped the receiver onto the phone unit and picked up her letter again, searching for something to soothe her trepidation. She traced her finger over the emblem, reading the neat ribbon of Latin beneath it. *PUELLAE MUNDI – girls of the world.*

The ancient words were calling to her and she nodded back.

Scotland was far, more than five hundred miles from here in Kent. She wouldn't be paying for her mother to visit – the woman could revel in her gushing satisfaction where she was.

Rose dared to wonder whether five hundred miles was far enough for the ties between her and her mother to stretch tight and finally snap.

MICHAELMAS TERM

Caldonbrae Hall's four traditional guiding qualities are:
confidence, courteousness, charm and courage.

Caldonbrae Hall prospectus, 150th anniversary edition

1.

Rose dragged a finger under one eye; the slam of the train doors and the yell of a guard jogged her forward. She held her suitcase close to her, nudging her handbag to the side, pulling her dark hair into a thick twist before tucking it into the collar of her tweed jacket. The warmth and stench of the station was suddenly invigorating; she was grateful for it.

As the train had slowed for its entry into Edinburgh, she'd glimpsed the sloping hilltop of Arthur's Seat, surprisingly soft-looking and uneven, as if Zeus himself had pushed and moulded the hills with his enormous hands. The carriage had been warm with the late summer sunshine and Rose's eyes had wavered along with the train's long mechanical trundle. She'd kept her hand as a bookmark in the pages of the school's heavy prospectus, and given up on the Cat Stevens tape in her Walkman. The headphones given to her by a friend were no good – the ear pads were so thin that Rose worried about the other people in the carriage hearing her music.

The prospectus had arrived a week before, attached to a letter with a few kind words from the Headmaster. *For Miss Christie, the first new member of teaching staff in over a decade – congratulations!* It was the newest edition, since Caldonbrae Hall had just celebrated its 150-year anniversary. The pages already scoured, she'd simply spent the journey gazing at the shining photographs, hoping to imprint them on her brain. An aerial view of the stretch of peninsula, the particular bend of the land, the brilliant sea, the rocky beach, the ruddy cliffs, and the school's majestic structure perched above. It sat at the furthest end of the peninsula's finger, like an extraordinary grey wedding cake; halls and towers and rows of turrets added like great ornaments, with outlines of flying buttresses to decorate. There were more photographs of sculpted stone cloisters, a greenish quad, a close-up of a merman-like gargoyle. And then inside: wood-panelled walls, the stained-glass chapel window, a library with books stacked to the ceiling. Rose blinked at the sunny pictures of the students: a tall dark-haired beauty shaking hands with the Headmaster; a very fair red-haired girl laughing with her friends on a hockey pitch; other girls filling an art studio, or set like a tableau across a theatre stage. The opening pages read:

> Established in 1842 by Lord William Hope, a baron and a prominent Whig within the Victorian peers. Owing to the formation of the United Kingdom of Great Britain and Ireland, the lands and title were granted to Lord Hope's father by King George III. Upon inheritance Lord Hope had the castle fortress rebuilt in the Scottish Baronial style, and fitted it out as a dame school suitable for his six daughters, one of the first of its kind in Great Britain.

A well-dressed man in the seat opposite Rose had stared down at the prospectus, his eyes burning into the pages as the sun slid across his face. Avoiding his gaze, she'd nudged the prospectus deeper into her lap and kicked her legs over her suitcase for security.

But now the prospectus lay idle in her handbag, heavy over the rest of her things. Rose's anticipation urged her forward as she dragged her suitcase towards the station's concourse. She was in desperate need of a cup of tea.

The square hall of the concourse was full of people looking harried and hurrying in all directions, while a row of taxis shunted past on the other side of the wide doors. Pulling her jacket tighter around her, Rose spotted a cafe bar in the corner, a spread of chairs and tables in front. The jacket was slightly too big for her, thanks to the tweed's boxy shoulders. She'd found it in a charity shop and loved it instantly; it reminded her of Clarice Starling's in *The Silence of the Lambs*. It was definitely too hot to wear in early September, but she wanted to look impressive when she first arrived, and hoped it might boost her confidence. Queuing behind a young family, Rose glanced over a row of newspapers clamped in stands next to the bar. A few of them flashed the same lurid picture – Princess Diana wearing a brilliant new dress, chatting to some man other than her husband. Rose frowned in sympathy: she liked Diana, even if her mother didn't.

At the front of the queue Rose trawled her eyes down the menu, even though she already knew what she wanted. When it was her turn she smiled at the pink-faced woman.

'Earl Grey, please, thanks.' She cleared her throat. 'Teabag in.'

'Milk, dear?'

'No thanks.'

A cross-looking man hovered behind the woman, pulling a glass bottle out of a small fridge. Rose's eyes lingered over a row of flapjacks.

'You're far from home,' said the woman.

Rose looked back at her; the woman's face was creased in kindness. 'Yes, I am.'

'What brings you to Edinburgh?'

Ed-in-bu-rruh. Rose wanted to imitate the woman's pronunciation, to roll her tongue around those round consonants, against the harshness of her English accent.

'I'm on my way further up north-east. To—'

'Caldonbrae.' The man was standing straight now, frowning at Rose.

'Yes. How did you know?' Rose half laughed in surprise and the man glanced down at the prospectus peeking out from her bag. 'I love the way you say it, with your accent. It sounds terrible the way I say it. Do you know of it, then?'

'You're never a student?' he answered with thinly veiled contempt. Rose checked the hardness in his eyes, the draw of his face.

'No, I'm a new teacher there.'

'Ach,' he scowled. 'You're awful young.'

'I am older than I look. I've been teaching for four years now, including training,' Rose answered firmly.

'That's no' Scotland, that place.'

'Well,' the woman came in brightly, 'how lucky those girls will be, to have you teaching them. I'll bet they've got a load of old cranks up there.'

'Best of luck on your journey.' The man turned back to the fridge as his wife smiled at Rose.

'Will you be wanting anything else?'

'No thanks,' Rose answered flatly, preparing the change from her purse. 'Just the tea.'

'Here you are.' The woman passed over the styrofoam cup.

She shrugged a shoulder at her husband and gave Rose a comforting pat. 'Never mind him.' Rose glanced down at the woman's small hand over her own.

She took a seat at the furthest edge of the cafe's tables, her back to the couple. There, she pulled her suitcase into alignment with her feet.

Rose didn't like being separated from her things. Only a few favourite books and a pile of her smartest outfits were stuffed into this shabby suitcase. The rest of Rose's belongings – old volumes, clothes, bits of furniture – were packed in a small crate and would follow her, days later, to fill her new flat. Her first all to herself. The school had organised it, like they had organised her journey, her arrival, her new life.

She'd managed to stuff one goodbye card from her former pupils into her suitcase, though it was probably creased in all the wrong places now. An over-large piece of card, full of their untidy scrawl, half-correct phrases in Latin, small affectionate doodles. They'd even drawn a version of her head as a Roman bust on the front; she'd blinked with tears and laughter when they'd presented it to her at the end of last term. Well, she wanted to bring that little piece of evidence of her previous life into this new one – some soothing proof of her own capability. And inside that card she'd stuffed the treasured postcards that had decorated her old classroom. Places she'd visited, places her mother had saved up for them to see together, places she'd saved up for alone: Pompeii, Rome, Athens, Ephesus. A view here, a theatre there; a mosaic here, a sculpture there: *to expand her mind, expand her horizons* – one of her mother's favourite phrases. And now these were places she was going to talk about, share with her new students and their fresh set of eager faces.

Rose didn't yet have her timetable, but the Headmaster's letter had informed her of seven classes of girls, one from each of the year groups, aged eleven to eighteen – just what Rose had been used to, and had trained for. At Caldonbrae Hall there were three 'Junior' years: the Firsts, Seconds and Thirds; then two 'Intermediate' years: the Fourths and Fifths; and finally the sixth-form's seventeen and eighteen year-olds: the Lower and Upper Sixth. Rose knew that boarding schools usually had schedules busy with house duties and sports activities, but she'd been told that she'd settle in better with a lighter timetable for her first term.

Rose pressed the cup to her lips but the hot tea burned her mouth, dashing down her throat with a slip of pain.

She knew she would miss her old students just as much as she'd miss her old colleagues and their regular pub evenings or cinema trips. Last term, she and an Art teacher had watched *Thelma and Louise* on the big screen every Friday night for a month. It had been a nice life, and Rose knew that she'd think of them often, down in the sunnier south: even the white prefab of the squat school buildings, the concrete scrap of the courtyards, the shout of the students hurtling down the corridors.

The memories squeezed at her heart and she looked away.

Lucky, her old colleagues had insisted, picked out by an amazing school like Caldonbrae Hall, her career apparently speeding on ahead. Rose couldn't have turned down this opportunity – the regret would have pursued her through her career. Now she'd have to learn to absorb the pride others had in her, to puff up this depleted balloon of self-worth inside her chest. Plus, her mother was right, Rose's salary would cover the care she needed and more; and Rose could pay her back for all the things she'd done for her growing up, especially after her father had died. Rose smiled wistfully; perhaps in her own small way she was carrying on his academic legacy – not in his full lecture halls, but through short lessons in a brightly lit classroom in some tall building in Scotland.

A mechanical voice broke through her thoughts, calling over the tannoy, informing her of her delayed train.

Rose's face flushed with alarm. By how long? The numbers flipped and Rose watched them change. Thirty minutes or more. But, she thought desperately, she wanted to see the place in daylight. It was already so late. Late in the day, late in the holiday. Term would start in two days – Rose needed more than that to settle herself in. But of course, she'd had no say in the matter. She worried about cutting it so fine – as if at any moment the school might turn around and send her away, tell her she wasn't good enough; that it was all a mistake, just some cruel joke.

Rose hoped the car organised at the other end would be aware of any delay; she didn't want to keep them waiting.

The sodden teabag slapped her mouth unkindly as she took another sip. It was lukewarm now and too strong – she flinched before swallowing the mouthful. Rose wondered whether she could ask the woman for a top-up of boiling water. Come to think of it, she needed the loo too. Maybe the woman could watch her suitcase while she went. Yes, she thought, she could even thrust the school's prospectus in the front pocket and have it stare back boldly at the woman's husband, just to taunt him.

*

A few hours later Rose arrived. Barely able to acknowledge the driver and his help with her suitcase, she fell into the back seat and into the final leg of the journey.

Once the car pulled through the gates and trundled up the long drive, Rose stretched out to catch her first glances of Caldonbrae Hall – her new home. But it was only passing shadows that touched her eyes through the glass, a night fog of steeples and turrets moving high above the car windows. She thought of the pictures in the prospectus, trying to fit the grey wedding cake of the photograph onto the hulking black mass that actually met her gaze.

'Are we here?' Rose asked the driver, although she already knew the answer.

He said nothing. She felt only the gentle push of the car rolling forward, around and towards the front entrance of the school. There Rose looked up for the relief of light from several windows – but her sight deceived her still, with sharp corners and two half-faced gargoyles bathed in shadow.

'Good luck,' the driver said as he dropped Rose's suitcase heavily at her feet; he slammed the boot of the car with such force that she flinched.

The following morning Rose tried a walk along the peninsula, but the cold was tearing through her clothes, her jacket, nipping at the nape of her bare neck. She thought mournfully of the warm things she hadn't packed: her knit cardigan, her favourite green blanket, at least one scarf. Even her dark hair taunted her by whipping around her face. Yes, the summer was certainly over, but the first days of September up here in Scotland were colder than she'd expected.

The night before Rose had been met by the porters and an

apologetic note from the Headmaster: complicated circumstances meant that he was unable to greet her that weekend. A band of three gruff but helpful men took her across the dim light of the entrance hall through corridors and passageways, handling her single suitcase between them as they mounted the stairs to her new flat. At the door, they stood in her way. One porter handed over a brass ring of keys, her own singled out. Glimmering with nerves, Rose thanked them, stepping aside to slip into the low-ceilinged rooms; the floor creaked as she crossed the threshold. The porters watched her curiously until she thanked them again with the close of her new front door.

Rose felt along the wall for the light switch. In the small kitchen a hamper was laden with food: a loaf of bread, butter, wrapped cheeses and meats, a box of eggs, a bottle of milk and a few tins of soup. Rose had bent to find the fridge, feeling her way around the cupboards, her heart beating with gladness at the generous and expensive gesture. In the basket was a note from Vivien, the deputy head: another kind apology at the unforeseen circumstances, a promise of the Headmaster's introduction at assembly on Monday, and a full tour of the school led by Rose's colleague Emma that first afternoon. The dining hall would open the first morning of term, so the food was to be enjoyed until then. A lonely beginning, she'd thought, but a welcome one. The porters would show Rose her new classroom the next day, and she'd hope to find Emma wandering about – in the Classics office, perhaps. She'd have to wear her tweed jacket again, for any potential first introductions.

But the next morning she hadn't found Emma, or anyone of importance. The school was hauntingly empty, so she'd ventured outside into the bleary afternoon. She crossed ribboned playing fields, tennis courts, a pale green stretch of land interrupted by a long white pavilion. She peered over the furthest edge of the peninsula, the very tip of the broken finger and its rocky outcrops beyond. There were no others enjoying the grounds, but plenty of seabirds embedded in the ragged rock. Rose wasn't used to that unexpected blue of the sea, the ruddy threat of the cliff – nothing at all like the bleached white cliffs and laughing sunlight of the south of England.

Pushing her hair out of her face, Rose couldn't help but marvel now at the great monster of the school building, as if at any moment it might hoist itself up on its hind legs and unfurl, with thick turrets as black scales down its back, and crawl heavily into the waters below.

Inside its walls she could barely navigate from the wide entrance hall, the sweep of the double Great Stairs with a glass dome ceiling above. She wondered how she would learn all those corridors, those passageways, the rows of classrooms piled up on top of each other. Some dug out of the cliff below like dungeons, and others – like her own – high up and lofty with a fine view of the sea. Then the sudden caverns of the dining hall, the theatre, the chapel, a sports hall. All interconnected, sealed and folded into each other like dark tumours.

Rose was nervous, running through the lines of her speech she'd had to write for Monday morning's assembly, a particular request from by the Headmaster. A speech about knowledge and the ancient world, he'd advised, to introduce her to the girls. Rose didn't want to consider how unusual the request was – a test of nerve in front of the whole school on her first day, perhaps – and by now her printed speech was soft from the damp sea air.

The wind blasted at Rose again and she recoiled at the faint scream from the seabirds. She wanted to go back to her flat, somewhere in that mass of grey brick – her own new spot of warmth. She moved across the pitches, back towards the front entrance of the school, the grand swirl of the driveway and the majestic doors held wide open.

Open for the girls.

Rose stopped. She'd been outside long enough to miss the slow build of sleek black cars, backing far down the drive in a chain leading up to the front, depositing groups of girls and their trunks. There were squeals of laughter as the girls clasped each other before running into the building.

Rose watched them from her distant position, shaking with cold in her tweed jacket. She ought to have donned the old raincoat she'd seen hanging up in an alcove cupboard in her flat – from a previous resident, perhaps – but she hadn't dared. The page of her speech shook too, its paper coming apart, the typed words blurring as she folded it smaller.

Beside the double doors one girl was standing still, separate from the movement of drivers and porters busy around her. She was a blur of dark hair and staring eyes, turned in Rose's direction. Rose looked away, and was hit again by the cold blast of the wind.

Others soon crowded the main doors and the girl was lost among them, as was Rose's only way back into the school. She didn't want her students to see her like this for the first time. Could she get to the rocky beach near the headland, or even wander down to the gatehouse of the peninsula? But then, she'd have to follow the driveway, passing each car and many pairs of young eyes. Rose resolutely turned around, held in that position by some strange force, her ears full of the furious turn of the sea.

When she looked back at the school again – was it minutes, hours later? – the last of the black cars had slipped away from the main doors, now firmly closed.

2.

The next morning, Rose was the centre of attention in the great throat of Founder's Hall. She fixed her eyes on the page in front of her, trying to ignore the mess of young faces beyond the platform where she now stood, all waiting for her to speak.

'. . . Greece has been touched by heroes, gods and Titans, and its mythology leaves marks even today.' The scrawl of her handwriting was unforgiving, her original version of the speech torn apart by yesterday's damp wind. Last night she'd hurriedly rewritten it, remembering extra bits just before she stood to speak. 'One such place is Delphi, where oracles were told . . .'

Three short rows of staff sat in a semicircle behind her on the platform. Rose could see the Headmaster – a surprisingly short man, she'd discovered when he'd introduced himself earlier – nodding along as she continued. But the animated words fell flat against her own ears.

Earlier that morning she'd knotted her unruly hair into a thick plait, before scrubbing her teeth and her face with the same anxious vigour. But along the main corridor she'd seen her mistake – Rose's hairstyle matched the uniformity of the Junior girls'. They wore twists of pigtails or slim plaits down to their waists, tied with silver ribbons that matched the bows at their necks, which in turn finished off prettily their white cotton dresses, long-sleeved and full, buttoned at the wrist and down the back. They looked clean and pressed, just out of a storybook, for their first day back at school.

Rose needn't have worried about finding Founder's Hall for that Monday assembly, she only had to follow the swarm of girls filtering up the Great Stairs, along the first-floor corridor, up and around again towards the surprise of this gaping hall. There had been a short stream of Asian girls, too, one of whom tittered with amusement when she saw Rose stumbling with unfamiliarity towards the front platform.

Now, as Rose spoke, several of the Intermediate girls in the middle rows shuffled in their seats. They were an older but awkward upgrade to the Juniors, in the same high-necked white dresses with tight bodices holding in their adolescence. Cropped grey blazers were fastened around their shoulders; they wore no silver bows, their hair flowing free. But even the Intermediate girls were thoroughly outdone by the sixth-formers lining the back rows. These older girls gave a splendid array of pastel colours, each dress individual and seemingly bespoke. Long-sleeved and long-skirted, the designs played with narrow waists, a high neck or a collarless one, sleeves buttoned or finished with embroidery. Rose had gazed at the delightful picture they all made, touching her own blazer with a tinge of shame. Her favourite outfit, a dark cotton shirt-dress under a second-hand blazer with brass buttons, was nothing compared to these silk and lace creations she saw in front of her.

Rose ended her speech abruptly. A clap from behind infected the rest of the hall with a smattering of applause. She stepped backwards to a nod from the Headmaster, now beside her.

'Thank you, Madam.'

Here again the Headmaster's movements were small and perfectly balanced, gesturing at Rose to resume her seat. He smiled with his mouth, but his brown eyes were sharp and analytical. They matched the brown of his hair, which shone in the light, the shoulders of his frame soft and slight.

'Ladies, what a wonderful introduction from our new head of Classics. Please welcome her warmly according to our Caldonbrae tradition. Thank you, Madam, we hope you will continue to delight us all for many years to come.'

Rose tried to smile, but worried that her face might crack as the hall now split into another ordered applause, a few young faces ducking in amongst each other to share a remark. The tall and angular deputy head, Vivien, took Rose's place at the Headmaster's side, a haughty expression fixed on her severe face. Stepping back to her seat, Rose wondered vaguely why the Headmaster hadn't used her surname, and stuck only to this anonymous 'Madam' label.

To distract her pacing anxiety, Rose sat down and cast her eyes over the large hall. The long, high-walled gallery was set with heavy canvasses including several portraits of aging men – previous Headmasters, she assumed. Rose blinked at an over-large map of the British Empire; its coloured spread across patches of the world reminded her of a Roman Empire poster from one of her old teacher training classrooms. The most prominent portrait was of the Founder, who gazed over the entire hall with disapproval; his grey curled sideburns as thick as his eyebrows, one arm touching a pile of books and the other pressed firmly against his heart. Above him the hammer-beam ceiling was knotted with a darker wood, and around it the hall's upper edge was marked with square windows. The soft morning glow would have been soothing if Rose's nerves hadn't been so frayed.

The deputy head was speaking now, her voice fluid and smoothly assured, somehow matching the curls of her steel-grey short hair.

'And now we will say the school grace, read by the younger sister of Hope's most recent head girl, Vanessa Saville-Vye.' A small girl peeled herself away from an Intermediate row and strode towards the lectern, tripping up the few steps, her face screwed up with distress. Rose stood up with the rest of the staff. The Headmaster and his deputy stepped back to the edge of the platform, their heads bowed in respect.

From what Rose could see the girl was a pale thing, with a wisp of blonde hair around her head. A few of the teachers near Rose clasped their hands together as she grabbed hold of the lectern.

'May we be truly thankful for –'

Rose could hear the girl's thin voice tremor.

'May we be truly thankful for –' She halted. 'No.'

Rose looked up. The girl, Vanessa, was almost vibrating with nerves.

'May we—'

From his large portrait, the school's Founder seemed to glower at her contemptuously.

'I'm sorry, I can't remem –' Vanessa turned her head, presumably to search the rows of girls below, who stared back indifferently. 'Is it thankful . . . or grateful?'

Near the front, a few Junior girls giggled. But a red-haired girl on the edge of a middle row was leaning forward and looking thunder at Vanessa. Rose couldn't tell if it was in repugnance or in support. Vanessa's question still hung in the air; she slowly turned her head towards the Headmaster, who stared at the floor, his eyes bright. Vanessa put one hand to her mouth as the other gripped at the stand. She hitched forward.

Rose almost mirrored the girl's movement. The teacher beside her moved his head with distaste.

'Shouldn't we help her?' Rose whispered.

The teacher's lips were pressed together resolutely.

'It's not our place, dear.' A woman on the other side of Rose shook her head. 'She has to get it right.'

'She'll learn,' the male teacher nodded. 'That one's always been such a disappointment, so unlike her older sister.'

Something burned in Rose's chest.

'Headmaster is dealing with it,' the woman finished.

Sure enough, the Headmaster's eyes were now fixed on the lectern, his face firm as he strode towards the girl. Vanessa stood aside for him awkwardly, and he took the lectern for himself.

'Not to worry, Vanessa. This year's head girl, Clarissa Bray, will continue the grace.'

At the far end of the hall Rose saw a back row of sixth-formers break apart. One girl marched out, a brilliant smile tearing across her face. She wore a green velvet headband across her auburn curls, which tossed across her shoulders and the green of her dress as she strode towards the lectern. The pride in her face seemed to draw the light of the room, but Rose's eyes followed the Headmaster's arm as it hooked over Vanessa's shoulder, drawing the younger girl down the steps, along the front aisle and out of sight.

'What's going to happen to that other girl? Vanessa?' Rose asked the woman beside her.

'Oh, they all go through it, more or less,' she answered, shuffling forward in her seat. 'She's only an Intermediate.'

'Where has he taken her?'

The woman turned to face Rose with a frown. 'Are you always going to be asking so many questions?'

Rose fell back into silence as Clarissa finished the grace.

After the deputy head dismissed the assembly, rows of quiet girls started to filter out from the back, guided by a line of boarding house staff settled there. Rose's own semicircle of staff stood and ruptured into a swell of chatter.

Rose checked her watch; they were well into the first period of the day. She'd planned her first lesson meticulously, with name cards dotted along the desks – cards she'd now have to remove, rewrite and rearrange for the following class.

A woman hooked the crook of Rose's elbow, drawing her forward; Rose nodded with grateful recognition at her Classics colleague, Emma.

'Rose, lovely speech, well done. Sophocles would have been thrilled.'

'Thanks, Emma. I was so nervous.'

A thick curtain of grey-brown hair fell past Emma's shoulder before she tucked it behind an ear, touching the edge of her horn-rimmed glasses. She turned to a group of teachers behind Rose.

'Nice to see you all. Good term!'

'Good term to you too, Emma.'

Rose gave them all a quick nod, before turning her face back to the Founder's painting. At the foot of the portrait the school's coat of arms curled in wrought metal, bold against the shine of the polished wood. Rose took in the bright shield and the ornate ivy that surrounded the image: a dove taking flight with a collar around its neck, lifting off with its wings outstretched.

*

Rose wasn't sure whether her first lesson was a symptom of her first day in a new school, or an example of what she should expect from her future at Caldonbrae. The terror of meeting classes for the first time was something Rose had learned to deal with while she was training – knowing how to gauge the bubbling dynamic of children, how to navigate their vigour and assert her own control – but somehow the power of Caldonbrae Hall pinned Rose against its walls, choking her own courage. And on that Monday the new teacher's vulnerability held itself like a delicious mist for the girls to feed on.

The little Juniors arrived in rows, ordered and obedient to the seating plan. Their energy was like a hot hairdryer, which Rose had to fight even from the first register and rule-giving moments. Rose handed out the textbooks; a few of the girls already carried one, with torn pages or scrawled-over images, the plastic cover split. Those were exchanged with better versions from a pile on Rose's bureau. The exercise books Rose had selected were apparently the wrong size, so she found herself hopping up and down the short staircase to swap them for the larger ones in the Classics office directly below, the girls brimming with smirks as she did so. Rose tried to draw the strings of their previous knowledge together, but their answers were vacuous, punctured with the odd half-remembered Latin word. Her picture activity fell flat, the sequences of images suddenly muddled up or the papers folded and disappearing into a pocket. Rose saw one girl pass a note to another, keeping her eyes pointed at the teacher with an unfazed smile.

After lunch the traditional first staff meeting was cancelled so Rose went on to her tour of the building with Emma, nodding as the labyrinthine pattern of rooms and corridors around the school mapped themselves out in her mind's eye.

Emma swept through the floors at such a pace that Rose felt dizzy with the clanging of keys and the slamming of doors. Emma ignored Founder's Hall – Rose having already seen it that morning – and the rest of the north wing, insisting that there was nothing to interest Rose in that part of the school.

She tried to console herself by considering the shambled first hour as only her first lesson; the next would surely be an improvement. And yet in the following days the classes on her sparse timetable became a continuous spin of grinning faces, ditsy nicknames and offhand comments, rows of girls linked together via seating plans. Rose arranged her features carefully, trying to keep her thoughts as cool as a Roman general, preparing to hit the girls back with her own blast of teaching energy that would ricochet all the way up to the vaulted ceiling of her classroom.

By Thursday morning Rose was waiting to meet the last class on her timetable, the only group she hadn't yet met. Name cards were placed along the desks and she gripped the seating plan in her hand, along with a register.

Rose's classroom was a little battered after the first days of teaching. Her mosaic of postcards remained around the blackboard, but the classical film posters on the wall were tatty in the corners where the Seconds had thumbed at them. At the arched window a ceramic owl watched over the classroom in small homage to the goddess Athene; on top of the bookcase there was a chunk of rock Rose had taken from a walk up Mount Vesuvius.

She caught the owl's wide glassy eyes for a quiet moment, before looking past the gabled roofs and turrets of the massive school building, straight out to the North Sea.

Hearing the sixteen girls trundling up the short staircase, Rose dared to hope that perhaps this last group – Intermediates, Fourths – would be different from all the others. Defiantly, she held on to her smile.

But their elephantine noise hit her like a wall; she drew herself back along the wooden desks to her bureau.

'Oh look, she's tried to decorate,' was the first comment Rose caught. Some of the other girls glanced around with smirks. 'Oh yes, she has.'

The girls chucked their bags across the tables, sending a flutter of name cards to the floor. A few girls had halted at finding their names in undesired places and were now tutting crossly as they moved around each other. Many threw off their cropped grey blazers and dangled them on the backs of the chairs, rearranging their white dresses as they sat down. A girl in the middle row puffed out her chest with bad temper. Rose stepped along the front, bending to replace the scatter of wayward name cards back on their desks.

'Right,' she called out. 'Good morning, ladies! Nice to meet you.' Rose waited for her own silent regoverning of the room before taking them all in. Fourteen was a difficult age, she thought as she moved from face to face, their puberty seething out of them. None of the girls seemed to fit properly in their white dresses, their bodies tightening underneath the stitched cotton. Shining skin, awkward hair, even worse teeth. Rose struggled to find her compassion in the face of their mute disdain.

She gave out her classroom rules, tracing her finger down the list. 'It's my job to talk. It's your job to listen – to me, and to each other. Respect goes both ways, ladies.' They were watching her carefully. 'Take care. Contribute. Always ask.'

Rose checked each name for attendance, nodding at their individual faces and curving her mouth around their names. A girl in the back row was studying Rose, her dark eyes like bullets.

'Ladies, let's start with,' Rose took a pile of paper from her bureau, 'the curriculum for this year.'

A girl at the front spoke up with her clipped accent: 'Yes, this is all very well. But, Madam, who actually cares about Latin?'

Laughter rolled around the swoop of desks and Rose felt a rush of warmth in her cheeks. The girl had Pre-Raphaelite hair that fell red around her broad shoulders and matched her ivory features. These were overtaken by her very animated face, which was the most alarming thing about her.

'Latin is a subject of refinement and excellence,' Rose shot back, handing out the pages, 'and it's very valuable to universities and employers. You'll see –' she checked her seating plan, 'Frederica. And to answer your question, *I* care enough for all of you right now.'

A few girls in the middle tittered as the red-haired girl glared up at Rose. 'It's Freddie, Madam. *Not* Frederica.'

'Oh.' Rose looked down at her seating plan. 'I see.'

'And Latin *is* too hard, Madam,' continued Freddie. 'None of us are any good at it. Don't bother us with it.'

'Does that mean you are going to start testing us, Madam?' said a small blonde girl next to Freddie. With slight shock, Rose recognised her as the unfortunate creature who had failed so spectacularly with the grace during Monday's assembly.

'Don't *suggest* it to her, Nessa.' Freddie turned her pale face towards the blonde girl accusingly.

'Were you not tested before?' Rose demanded. 'Vanessa, isn't it?'

'Nessa, Madam, if you please,' the blonde girl answered softly.

Rose studied her; close up she had a little button nose and a smattering of freckles. 'Nessa, all right.'

'No, Madam,' sighed Freddie. 'We weren't tested at all last year, and we're just fine, thanks.'

'Yes, Madam. We got rid of the one before you – that was easy enough,' the girl at the very back called out. 'I'm sure you'll be no different.' From her deep voice and her narrowed beetle-black eyes, Rose knew she'd been the one that made the unkind comment about the classroom decoration. Rose checked her list again: Josephine.

'No, I reckon this one's half decent.'

'I like your lipstick, Madam.'

'Yes, me too.'

Rose blinked at the sudden array of voices dotted around the classroom. She touched her fingers to her mouth; lipstick was Rose's warpaint.

'Bethany got rid of the other Madam,' said Nessa quietly, 'not us.'

'Well,' interrupted Josephine from the back, 'you look completely different from the previous Latin Madam, anyway.'

'Girls, can we stop interrupting like this.' Rose strengthened her voice. 'Tell me, Josephine, did your—'

'It's Josie, Madam.'

'Oh,' Rose said crossly. 'Does anyone keep to their given names, or do I need to update my seating plan?'

'I'm Daisy, Madam.' A tall girl in the middle row near the window raised her hand; the many badges on the lapel of her blazer shook with the movement. Her long sheet of dark hair framed her square jaw and almond-shaped eyes.

'Okay, Daisy, thank you,' Rose answered as the rest of the class shared a laughing look in Daisy's direction.

At the front, Nessa was deep in thought. 'The old Madam had her favourites, but I wasn't one of them. I'm glad to have a new one.'

'Madam, will you be at Movie Night?' Freddie ignored Nessa, shaking her gold-red curls behind her shoulders. 'You look like the kind of person that would sneak in sweets.'

'But hopefully not eat them all,' Josie interjected smoothly, 'like the last Madam did.'

'Yes,' Freddie continued. 'She was as wide as our great-great-grandmother in the family Rembrandt.'

Rose didn't say anything. She was already weary and it was only a few minutes into the lesson. She looked down at her pile of handouts to muster some resolve. 'Let's have a look at these, shall we?'

'You're a lot younger, too,' pushed Freddie. 'How old are you, Madam?'

Rose answered without looking up: 'That's none of your business.'

'Yes. Why is someone like *you* working somewhere like this?' Josie called out.

'Don't forget, ladies,' laughed Freddie, leaning back in her chair, 'this is one of the best schools in Britain. Top of the league tables, five years in a row now.'

The class erupted with hilarity and Rose looked at Freddie, who seemed so alive that she commanded the attention of the room. Rose felt a throb of urgency. She didn't want to talk about her predecessor, she didn't want to bounce around their throwaway comments – she needed to get on with the lesson.

'Girls,' Rose checked the clock and lifted her voice, 'your literature this year is going to be the *Aeneid* Book Four.'

'Enid? Like Enid in the year above?' Nessa tried.

'No, Nessa, the Ae-ne-id,' Rose said carefully. 'So you've had no introduction to this?'

'No. The previous Latin Madam,' Daisy contributed merrily from her side of the classroom, 'wasn't really interested towards the end.'

'She was upset.'

'No she wasn't, Nessa!' Josie barked out from the back. 'You never know what you're talking about.'

'Hang on.' Rose looked at Nessa and addressed the class. 'Respect each other, please. Josie, I'll thank you not to criticise your peers.'

Josie pushed her chair back from her desk and crossed her arms with a scoff. Rose saw Nessa sneak in a small smile at the front.

'Okay, well,' Rose continued, meandering around the last few desks with her handouts, 'the *Aeneid* is about the Trojan hero Aeneas. He fled from the Trojan War. Have we heard of that?'

'Of course, Madam.'

'Thank goodness.'

'We've got exercise books from last year, Madam, full of nonsense.' Freddie was sifting through her things. 'Did you know?'

'No interrupting, thank you, Freddie.' Rose hesitated near the back row. 'But yes, I'll have to take them all in eventually, to see where you left off.'

'Books aren't for learning, Madam,' interjected Nessa. 'Books are for posture.'

Rose opened her mouth, but couldn't quite frame her

response. She returned to the front and tried again. 'Girls, please look at your handout. We'll be studying the section where Aeneas the Trojan hero lands in a foreign country, a city called Carthage, and meets Queen Dido—'

'Oh, but Madam,' Freddie's eyes widened across the page, 'you're not seriously expecting us to cover of all of this, are you?'

'Yes, Freddie,' Rose said firmly. 'I am.'

'Really? My goodness.' Freddie was still staring at the page. 'Latin Language *and* Literature?'

The rest of the class followed her example and looked through the curriculum list, while Josie tried to slide the page off the desk with her elbow. Rose watched her during the brief pause.

'As long as I do all right in the tests, I'm okay,' Nessa added quietly.

'We'll take it one step at a time,' Rose announced to the class. 'All right?'

'But . . . doesn't being in Scotland absolve us from learning Latin, Madam?'

'Ooh, *absolve,*' Josie piped up, her dark eyebrows knitted together. 'Glad you're getting into big words, Nessa.'

Freddie turned around before Rose could speak. 'Shut up, Josie. That was rude.'

Suddenly Rose realised that it was Freddie who had stared so forcefully at Vanessa – with encouragement, she now understood – during Monday's assembly.

'Ladies, please.' Rose's voice was louder than she expected as she moved towards her bureau. 'We *will* learn respect. Please stop speaking out of turn, all of you. Vanessa, tell me why you think being in Scotland makes a difference?'

'It's *Nessa,* Madam. Didn't the Scots hate the Romans?' Nessa spoke timidly, not looking at Rose. 'Didn't they, you know, kick them out?'

'Yes, the Celts did.' Rose was pleased for the first time that day. 'Hadrian's Wall was supposedly built to keep the Scots out of the Roman grip on Britain. Well done.'

'Yes, I thought so!' Nessa glanced around her. 'See, I *do* know things.'

'But it's not really Scotland on our peninsula, anyway,' Daisy added from the side, throwing her sheet of black hair behind her shoulders. 'Headmaster always says we have our own little glorious England right here at Hope.'

Rose surveyed the class as a few of them nodded. 'Does he?'

'Yes.'

A girl in the middle smiled beatifically, and a few others near her smiled too. Rose couldn't help but look across at her ceramic owl for support.

'And is "Hope" a nickname for Caldonbrae Hall?'

'Yes, Madam,' Daisy chimed in thoughtfully. 'You know, we don't ever get new teachers. You should know that things don't change here. This is a place of tradition.'

'Daisy,' Nessa wrinkled her freckled nose, 'sometimes you actually *sound* like the prospectus.'

'So are we supposed to look up to you, then, Madam?' Freddie leaned forward, her tawny eyes flashing at Rose. 'Is there something you've got to teach us?'

'Yes, Madam. Tell us, what have you got that we need?' added Josie in her deep voice.

Rose felt her chest stir as her cheeks burned at this barrage of words and challenges, questions she couldn't possibly answer. Every day there were fresh lashings of persecution. But she answered, 'I would have thought that you could trust your Headmaster's judgement in choosing me.'

'Yes, but, Madam,' Freddie's eyes stayed on Rose, 'he doesn't have to sit here and translate Latin for an hour each week.'

Rose looked at Freddie for a moment.

'Okay then, girls. You want to know a little bit about me. That's fine.' Rose didn't trip over the words this time; after this, she hoped she'd no longer have to repeat her short biography: 'Caldonbrae Hall is my second school. I taught in a state school before this, and trained in two others. I'm originally from Kent, I've studied in London and in Rome. Your Headmaster and the governors chose me.' Her cheeks flushed again. 'And I can tell you, there aren't many young female teachers out there as dedicated or as passionate as me.'

Rose wheeled around to the blackboard, hearing a slow murmur of surprise from the room behind her. She started to write. Her vain hope that this lot would be any better than her other classes seemed laughable now.

'Yes, but, I mean, are you even married?' asked Daisy.

Rose called out cheerfully from the blackboard, 'Not at all.'

'Oh, really?' Nessa asked. 'Then why have they sent you to teach us?'

'Let's find out, shall we?' Rose turned to face the room, continuing to write without looking. 'For now, though, silence. And copy this down.'

She nodded at them, before glancing at the books on her bureau: Sophocles' *Oedipus*, Euripides' *Medea*, Homer's *Iliad*. One way or another someone was going to get eaten alive here, Rose realised. She'd be damned if it was her.

3.

Later that morning, Rose could sense the girl following her as she paced along the main corridor. Empty but for the two of them, the corridor was endlessly long, guttered with stone and lined with oak wainscoting that in turn presented decorative noticeboards or doors to classrooms and offices. Its ceiling was cavernously high; any footsteps and voices disappeared up into its tall reaches.

Rose focused on the space in front of her. Behind was the same girl that had stared at Rose at the main doors days before – but that stare now seemed daring, accusatory. She had been continually hovering behind Rose every day this week.

Rose had just left the staff common room after a difficult conversation with one of the senior teachers. She'd mentioned her predecessor – who was she, and more importantly, why had she left the department in such disarray? The paperwork, the classes, even the piles of textbooks? But the dismissive woman had cut Rose short, and Rose had left, shamed by the very thing she didn't understand.

Since then the girl had resumed her place behind Rose, seemingly tethered by an invisible bind. She was a sixth-former – Rose could tell by the soft blue dress drawn tightly over her tall, gaunt figure. Her hair wasn't as coiffed as the others'; instead, it hung straggly beyond the bony ripple of her shoulders, her face sallow underneath the decoration of her make-up.

Every time Rose had turned to challenge her, the girl whipped herself away. She hadn't yet followed Rose up to the classroom, though. Rose knew she had more to worry about than one girl's peculiarities, but those translucent eyes, the dark shadows stamped beneath them, made her heart stammer.

At the corridor's halfway point, the entrance hall, Rose's gaze was drawn up to the glass dome of the ceiling above the Great Stairs. The silent scrutiny of that strange eye, twisted with metal and mottled glass, was better than the curious gapes of the staff in the common room, or the hanging shadow of the girl behind her.

The bell rang.

Rose stopped at the foot of the stairs, taking a long look at the Headmaster's study door across the hallway. Her fourth day, and she still hadn't been invited in.

A muddled crowd of Junior girls bumped past her, identical in their white pinafore dresses and pretty silver-ribboned plaits. Rose gripped the dark oak of the bannister as a scuffle of voices came from the stairs.

'Isn't that *her*?'

'Look at her messy hair!'

'Hardly any bosom at all!'

Stepping higher past them, Rose glanced down at her chest in spite of herself. Not much there, she had to admit. She'd never minded – at their age she'd been forced to attend rallies burning other people's bras, her mother shouting her on.

'Harriet!' an adult voice called out behind Rose. 'Remember your manners. This is our new member of staff.' Rose turned to see the deputy head scrutinising the girls as they hopped down the steps.

'Of course. Good morning, Madam!' One of the small girls turned to smile up at Rose, showing all her teeth.

'Well done, Harriet.' Vivien's handsome face was severe as the girls swung around the bannister at the bottom of the stairs. 'As for the rest of you – heads up, backs straight or I'll get the books. What's that?'

Vivien bent her slim figure over two of them, frowning as a blonde-haired girl clutched at her watery-eyed friend, muttering in the deputy head's ear.

'Homesick? For heaven's sake, it's only been a few days. Tell her to stop weeping or she'll cry all the lovely blue out of her eyes.'

Rose turned to climb higher up the stairs.

'Good morning, Madam,' Vivien called over as the Junior girls moved away. 'I trust your first week is going well. We'll have to find a moment to see how you are.'

'Good morning, Vivien,' Rose replied sheepishly. 'I'd really like that. I was hoping to see the Headmaster for an introductory meeting.'

Vivien's face seemed to tighten. 'That's all very good. But please don't address me in that manner in front of the girls. It's "Madam" for every female teacher here.'

Rose opened her mouth to apologise. But Vivien's head had tilted – she'd spotted Rose's quiet follower, frozen in place on the bottom step. Vivien's face flitted from the student to Rose, before dragging her eyes back to the girl with a steely stare.

'Bethany,' she said quietly, 'come with me.' The ice in

Vivien's voice gave Rose an involuntary shudder as the sixth-form girl drew towards the deputy head. They moved away in the next moment.

Bethany, Rose said to herself.

On the middle landing she halted at the library's carved double doors; behind her the Great Stairs split into an extravagant double sweep to the floor above. Rose stayed where she was, still thinking, relieved to be free of her follower. She pushed through the library doors with surprising force.

Shafts of dusty light fell on the bookcases like a blessing. The place had been empty all week and was fast becoming her favourite spot. Rose adored the symmetry of the space: the wealth of books that lined the walls up to the tall oak ceiling, the long window seat that overlooked a quad, the mezzanine floor that ran around the entire shape of the room, the two symmetrical spiral staircases that led the readers up.

But today Rose moved away from the books, past the desks and armchairs to stand in front of the expansive wall opposite, where a huge map was inked across a large spread of parchment. *Hope*, it decreed. Rough at the edges despite the vast glass casement, it revealed the misshapen enormity of the school. With her eyes she followed the blueprint's lines and squares to make out the chapel in the south wing, close to the long dining hall and opposite four wide boarding houses labelled Verity, Temperance, Prudence and Clemency. Then the scattered multitude of classrooms throughout, threaded by corridors and passageways. The northern section of the school held a sports hall, a theatre, and two more boarding houses – Honour and Chastity – embedded within the north wing. Founder's Hall was neatly ensconced there too, like an abscess buried just above the heart of the school.

There was a date at the bottom of the map, but Rose couldn't quite make it out.

She frowned up at the massive spread of parchment. *Speak to me,* she thought. *Let me learn how to live here.*

Later that afternoon, Rose slammed down a pile of books as she entered the Classics office. Emma was bent over her own work against the wall opposite. She looked over.

'Anything wrong?'

'Well, yes.' Rose's brass ring of keys slid from her pile to the wooden desk with a metallic clunk. Her veneer of calm was slipping now that she was alone with her colleague.

'What's happened?' Emma asked cautiously, turning towards Rose and lifting her glasses off her face.

'Where's my Upper Sixth class? I've only seen them once, and apparently they're not here tomorrow.'

'Oh, they've gone to London. They always go in September.'

'London?'

'To be presented, yes. It's an initiation sort of thing, to start off their final year. It's tradition.' Emma waved her comment away with her hand. 'Not to worry, you'll have to excuse them.'

Rose was aghast. 'But what about their lessons?'

Emma answered steadily. 'There are some who would say that the ceremony in London is more important. The girls get a lot out of it.'

'And would *you*? Say it's more important?'

Emma looked disconcerted for a moment, then said, 'Every school has their traditions.'

Rose sat down and glared at the mess on her desk. 'It doesn't set a very good precedent, does it? I haven't got through any of my lesson plans this week.'

'Ah, yes.' Emma gave a wry smile. 'I don't think I've written a lesson plan in years.' She swung back to her work, hooking her glasses back on her face.

Rose couldn't keep the sharpness from her voice. 'I'm so surprised by all of this, Emma. I've met all my classes, now, and the girls are—'

'What?'

Rose blurted out, 'They don't seem to want to learn.'

Emma didn't turn around as the statement hung in the air. 'Of course the girls want to learn, Rose. But they *are* teenagers. You have to win them over, play along a bit. That's what we're paid for, after all. And of course, our young ladies,' Emma nodded, her eyes still on her work, 'are extremely busy.'

'Busy?'

'And I suppose the teaching in the department has been a bit lacklustre in the past . . .'

'Yes, what did happen to my predecessor?' Rose's voice lifted higher. 'What was her name?'

'Jane was her name.' Emma looked up this time; she passed her glasses over her thick skirt, rubbing them on the fabric. 'You're right. She wasn't up to it. *We* always got on very well, but she was troubled and became very unhappy here. She – she couldn't really stay.'

Rose squinted at Emma. 'Oh, come on. You're going to have to give me more details than that.'

'Well.' Emma tilted her head. 'Hope is rather remote, the system is unique . . . we all live here together. It is a lifestyle choice – it needs dedication. Things got badly out of hand for Jane. She simply had to go.'

Rose checked the view outside the long mullioned window. The light was already fading, the wild sea turning grey with the gloom. Leaning forward cautiously, she tried again. 'Can't you tell me why?'

Emma placed her glasses back on her nose.

'It's confidential, I'm afraid.'

'Is this why I was recruited so quickly?'

'You were an extraordinary candidate. Highly recommended. Our first new teacher in over a decade, and a fine choice. Your father, too, was a prominent academic.' Emma reeled off the words as if she'd learned them by heart, then added, 'Vivien and I liked you immensely when we visited your previous school for the interview.'

Rose didn't take the compliment. 'Why didn't *you* take the head of department role? You're much more qualified than I am.'

'Oh goodness, no.' Emma turned back to her work. 'I need to limit my academic responsibilities. I was once considered for a housemistress role, which would have been fabulous. But I can't do too much.'

'Why not?'

'Well,' Emma huffed, and Rose wondered if she was pushing it too far, 'I do a good deal of pastoral work, outside the curriculum, in the boarding houses, in the afternoons.' Emma shook out her shoulders. 'Your timetable will change, once you've settled in and passed the probationary period.'

'Yes, I've been told.' Rose kneed her desk in a frustrated movement. 'Next term, then?'

'Should be, yes,' Emma nodded. 'That's how it was for me, back in the day.'

But Rose wasn't listening. Her knee had loosened a stiff drawer she'd been trying to open a few days before. She waited for Emma to go back to her work before tugging it out and checking the contents. First was a pile of marking, pages of unreturned translations with frayed, yellowed edges, a teacher's spidery writing scrawled over the students' mistakes. But there was something underneath – a flattened, stained handkerchief, its edge stitched in blue, the corner bent out of shape. Rose traced her finger over the initials 'BdV'. No 'J' then, for Jane?

Rose dropped the handkerchief and shunted the drawer closed, feeling her beating heart in the tips of her fingers.

'That reminds me, Rose,' Emma asked suddenly. 'Have you had a proper meeting with the Headmaster?'

Rose breathed out quickly. 'Oh. No, not properly.'

'Well, he's away with the Upper Sixth now. We've got the staff meeting Monday lunchtime, he'll introduce you properly then. But you ought to see him privately. Incidentally,' Emma sat back in her seat with a triumphant look, 'isn't it wonderful news about your mother?'

Rose's quivering heartbeat seemed to reach her throat. 'My mother? What . . . news?'

'Moving to a private clinic, of course.'

'*What* private clinic?'

'Oh, haven't you been informed?' Emma's face fell a little. 'HR should have told you in a memo. They're moving her. She'll have her own dedicated nurses, her own private room, everything.'

Rose choked out, 'How do you know about my mother?'

'It's in your dossier,' replied Emma nonchalantly, turning away, 'and I think you mentioned her when Vivien and I interviewed you. If you don't mind my saying, it's very unfair that you had to sell your family home to cover her treatment . . . but then there are some things that the NHS doesn't—'

'Emma,' Rose couldn't hide her mortification, 'what do you mean she's been moved? She was fine where she was.'

'I'd ask one of the secretaries if I were you. It's all been arranged. One of the perks of being here.'

'Perks?' Rose snapped back.

'Well, look at me.' Emma splayed out her hands. 'Hope certainly takes care of my husband – he's in our family home while I'm here during term-time. The governors, too, arranged for my two boys' private schooling,' she added proudly, 'and entry to their respective universities.'

Rose shook her head in amazement. 'But – no, I don't want them to take care of my mother. That's *my* job.'

'Oh Rose, you are funny.' Emma gave her a renewed smile. 'In order for you to do your job, you need to have no distractions. Surely knowing your mother is in the best possible place will ease your mind? That's the beauty of Caldonbrae. That's the extent of its reach. You should be grateful. I know I am.'

Rose pressed her lips together and touched her hot cheeks with one hand. She wanted to tear out of the office and scream down the stairs, rush into the main office and interrogate the secretaries. She was almost certain she'd never mentioned her mother, or the financial burden of her care, to Emma or to the deputy head when they'd visited her for their interview. But had she intimated something? Even so, how on earth did they find out she'd sold their house? What right did they have to move her mother without informing Rose?

A knock at the office door interrupted the tangle of Rose's thoughts. The door pushed open with such force that it slammed into a pile of old textbooks. Emma bolted upright; Rose flinched at the woman's sudden movement.

'Frances!' Emma exclaimed. 'So good to see you.'

Frances seemed to invade the space with her height and her confidence. Her white-blonde hair was wiry against her broad cheekbones; the stretch of her mauve dress suggested an athlete's figure. Rose stood up to mirror the other two.

'Yes, good to see you, Emma,' said Frances at once. 'Sorry for any absences. I was late to arrive, and I've been keeping my head down, but I'm here now.'

'Ah, Frances, this is Rose,' Emma announced loudly.

Frances thrust out her arm to shake Rose's hand. Her demeanour reminded Rose of Susan Sarandon's Louise – older and more competent than her friend Thelma.

'Welcome, Rose,' Frances said seriously, her clear blue eyes peering through a messy, frazzled fringe. 'I'm head of the Languages faculty. I'm the one you go to for academic things.'

'Oh, does Classics come under Languages here, then? Not Humanities?'

'Yes, Rose.' Emma said, interrupting the handshake and facing them both. 'Frances will be dealing with most of your departmental duties during your probationary period, until you really settle in.'

Frances nodded. 'That's exactly right.'

'Thank you.' Rose attempted a smile. 'I'm looking forward to taking over properly.'

'All in good time, Rose.' Emma continued: 'We've just been discussing a few things, Frances – the absence of the Upper Sixth for one.'

'Yes, that's always an unwelcome interruption.' Frances stretched out a sarcastic smile. 'One of many things sent to torment us here.'

Rose replied darkly, 'There's a lot that I don't really understand.'

'I don't doubt it for a second,' Frances said, her eyes fixed on Rose.

'Also, regarding my mother—'

'Look, I understand there is a lot to take in, but don't panic, Rose,' Emma insisted, resuming her seat. 'You are awfully young; you just need time to get your bearings.'

Frances held Rose's gaze. 'But I expect they're wanting to see how you'll do,' she said, almost rolling her eyes. 'Well, Rose, you can always talk to me.'

'Thank you,' Rose said uncertainly. 'That's good to know.'

'Let's arrange a meeting next week,' Frances suggested. Emma dropped her pen on top of her paperwork before drawing herself up with a haughty pose. 'Let's go and have a cup of tea together now. Frances, do you have a free period?'

'Yes, I'll join you. My Lower Sixth are only learning vocabulary.'

Rose glanced at her pile of work before following the other two. As they left the Classics office, Rose asked, 'What languages do you teach, Frances?'

'Take your blazer with you, Rose,' Emma called out. 'We must always wear some sort of smart jacket when we go downstairs, equal to the men in their suits. School rules.'

'Oh yes, sorry.' Rose doubled back to unhook her blazer from her chair, wondering if she'd ever be able to hold all the new rules in her head.

'To answer your question, Rose,' Frances smiled as she waited, 'I teach Modern Languages – German and Russian. Not that the girls absorb any of it. Perhaps you'll inject me with your vigour! Perhaps we'll all suddenly become more academic.'

'I thought we already were.' Rose pulled on her blazer with

exasperation. 'Haven't you seen the prospectus? It glows with academia. Talks about the school's *"greater function in society"*.'

'Those things are never realistic.' Emma waved her hand in the air, walking slightly ahead of the other two.

The second-floor corridor was empty, and felt somehow longer to Rose as she travelled along with Frances and Emma. Noise bubbled behind every classroom door they passed; Rose was both relieved and dismayed to know that every other teacher might suffer the same classroom experience as her.

In the lower passageway the three women passed a line of Sixths, silent and walking in single file, their footsteps ticking together across the flagstone floor. None of the girls greeted the teachers. Rose felt boosted by her colleagues' company in the corridors, unwitting guardians against these graceful yet unpredictable young women.

Emma called after one of the girls and Frances took the opportunity to turn to Rose. Her voice was kind but filled with urgency as she leaned her arm on the corridor wall, blocking the way forward.

'Rose, how did you find this place?'

Rose was surprised. 'You mean, apart from it being really famous?'

A fractious look crossed Frances's face, so Rose answered quickly, 'One of my old colleagues knows one of yours here. He recommended me.'

Frances's blue eyes seared into Rose's for a moment. Then she said, 'I can't believe he let you come here.'

'What?' Rose replied in bewilderment, but Frances suddenly turned away to descend the stairs to the staff common room. 'Frances, what do you mean?'

Emma appeared behind. 'What's happened, ladies?'

Rose ignored Emma and followed Frances down the stairs, still stuck in the clouded air of her comment. The heavy door of the common room had closed behind Frances, so Rose pushed at it, hard. But the woman's back was already disappearing into the crowd of teachers.

Rose hesitated. She still wasn't used to the heaviness of the common room, buried deep in the bowels of the school. If Rose's classroom was high up, then the common room seemed just as far below; dug out from the rocky cliff foundations, and stone-walled into being. It was always too warm, lit with dim lamps that lined the walls and led the path to the raging fireplace at the far end.

Rose stayed in line with Emma as they wandered over to the coffee and tea service. Frances seemed to have dissolved into the spread of cushioned armchairs and sofas, set out in pockets of conviviality. Old and worn rugs were arranged across the slatted floor, and a long table was laid with cakes and biscuits for an afternoon break. As Rose eyed a slice of lemon drizzle cake, Emma passed her a brimming teacup and saucer.

'I'll take a mug actually.' Rose turned to Emma. 'The cups are too dainty for me.'

'Rose! You are funny,' said Emma, nudging the saucer into Rose's hand. The touch of the porcelain burned Rose's fingers, and the cup clattered into its saucer, the brown liquid sloshing from side to side.

Frances reappeared beside Emma. 'Ladies, I hear that Vivien's on her way. Rose, I did want to talk properly, but I really shouldn't have left my Sixth. I'd better go back.' She gave a broad, apologetic smile which Rose didn't return.

'Oh, what a shame.' Emma sounded oddly relieved as she drew her teacup to her lips.

'It's been good to meet you, Rose. Welcome.' Frances shook Rose's hand again, and when Rose pulled her hand away this time there were red marks across her fingers.

'Don't mind Frances, Rose,' Emma said with a hint of nastiness as Frances moved off. 'She sometimes has her little moods. I never know how I'm going to find her from one day to the next.'

Rose's thoughts prickled with confused dismay as she turned away from Emma. She needed to understand Frances's strange comment. She needed to speak to the secretaries in the main office to check about her mother. She needed to find the curriculum covered in her classes last year. She needed to write all of this down to keep track of it, understand it, get on top of it. Her teacup wobbled again in its saucer; she wished she had a mug.

Rose looked up at the noticeboard mounted on the wall in front of her, teeming with frayed papers. A resulting mess of the first week, she supposed. A glossy poster announced *The Caldonbrae Hall Carol Service,* a holiday spectacular and the highlight of the school term, due to take place in December in the chapel. *A bit early to be thinking about Christmas,* Rose thought. Her eyes roved over an advertised competition with the School Rifle Association, to a formal-looking page decorated with the school's crest. *Demotion,* it read. A girl had moved down to House Clemency, and her progress was being monitored. Beneath the girl's name were four other names of Intermediate girls who were being 'considered' for movement between Houses Temperance, Prudence and Clemency. One of the names was Nessa's, the small blonde girl from Rose's Fourths that very morning; Rose was surprised to find her heart beat with sympathy. A short list of their misdemeanours were labelled as abbreviations: *V-2, D-5, S+1*. Rose narrowed her eyes just as Emma touched her shoulder.

'You've left the teabag in – your tea is black, Rose.'

'That's how I like it.'

'Not very ladylike, is it?' Emma gave a squinting smile. 'Surely you must know there is such a thing as etiquette, Rose. Lord Hope would've been appalled!'

'Oh,' Rose answered, taken aback. She'd never been criticised for the way she took her tea.

The heavy door of the common room shuddered open as another crowd of teachers entered the room, but Emma was already steering Rose to a collection of armchairs. 'Have you spoken to Vivien since you arrived?'

'Just a few words on the stairs earlier, actually.' Rose anxiously tugged at her loose strands of hair, before patting them into some sort of order.

'There's a hairdresser that visits twice a term, you know, for a few days,' Emma said kindly. 'You ought to make an appointment.'

'Sorry? A hairdresser?'

'Yes, he's very good.'

'It's always been unruly, I normally plait it back,' Rose blustered out. 'But couldn't I just go somewhere in the village?'

'Heavens, no! Not amongst the riff-raff in Kennenhaven.'

Rose wanted to laugh at Emma's joke, but realised from her expression that it wasn't meant as one. Emma's eyes skated past Rose's shoulder.

'Vivien's at the tea service with the others. I'll give her a minute before I interrupt her.'

The fire crackled suddenly in the grate. The long black funnel of the chimney sucked up the slim flames. There were no windows in the common room, and Rose wondered vaguely if the meticulous linenfold wood of the walls glamorised a sort of hideous dungeon.

'Okay, let's try now,' said Emma suddenly, sweeping Rose up from her seat. And there Vivien was, as if Emma had conjured her up out of thin air. She was standing tall over another colleague, a withered man folded back into his seat, leaning one arm on the high peak of his armchair.

Vivien hooked her head over her shoulder to smile at Emma and Rose. 'Oh look, John, it's the Classics department here to talk to us.'

Emma spoke on cue: 'Vivien, you remember Rose from our visit in the early summer?'

'Of course I do, Emma.' Vivien's smile crept further across her face. 'Indeed, we spoke earlier this morning. Wonderful to have you here, my dear.' She gave a little laugh. 'We've certainly rescued you from that *desperate* little place.'

'I'm very happy to be here,' Rose heard herself saying.

'And you're on . . .' Vivien turned from Rose to Emma, 'she *is* on a restricted timetable?'

'Yes,' Emma answered. 'Until the end of the probationary period.'

'Of course. And Rose – that wretched girl, she hasn't been saying anything to you, has she?'

'Who do you mean?' asked Rose earnestly, knowing exactly whom Vivien meant.

'Well, never mind her.' Rose heard Vivien's cut-glass accent, so similar to many of the girls'. 'John's been telling me about his trips to the golf club in the village – *so* funny.'

John's face was straight as he surveyed Rose.

'Well, Rose, as I said this morning, do come to me with

anything you need.' Vivien extended her arm like a gorgeous cat. 'I'm mostly pastoral, but still. Complaints about staff – just between us! Need more chalk? The stationery cupboard is in the ink room. We ought to draw you a map, or at least copy that enormous blueprint in the library.' She turned to John. 'I've been saying that for years, haven't I, John? Copy it out for the Firsts when they arrive.'

'Yes, you have.'

'And John's been here longer than any of us.'

'I haven't used chalk in years,' he said in a splintered voice. 'Can't bear the dust.'

'Oh, really?' Rose asked him. 'What have you been using instead?'

The man didn't respond.

'Rose.' Vivien pressed her lips together and placed a hand on Rose's arm. 'I can't tell you how pleased we are to have acquired you – I couldn't believe your references. It's so good to have some fresh blood in the place. You are our new *ingénue*.' Vivien's voice hardened. 'Between you and I, it's always right to get rid of bad eggs, and that's exactly what your predecessor was.'

Emma stood straighter next to Rose.

'Incidentally,' Rose tried to muster some kind of nerve, 'I had a few questions about the academic side of things. I'm not entirely familiar—'

'This is something you can discuss with Frances,' Vivien continued. 'I saw her in the passage just now.'

'And of course, you've got me,' Emma added in a clear voice. 'Rose and I have discussed a few things between ourselves, Vivien.'

'Of course, Emma, that's brilliant.' Rose's arm stiffened under Vivien's grip as the deputy head continued mirthfully.

'I keep hearing about your very serious lessons, Rose, long excruciating Latin sentences you're forcing the girls to translate – already! Well, you *were* recommended for your academic credentials, after all. Why not have Anthony as a mentor? A fellow head of department – History. He's so brilliant at what he does, the girls absolutely adore him.'

'I don't think I've met him yet,' said Rose. 'Although, isn't he the one connected to my old colleague, Frank Thorpe?'

'Yes, it's thanks to him that we got you.' Vivien dropped her arm and Rose staggered back a little, still holding her teacup. 'And now, thanks to us, you'll be taken care of.'

The next day was Friday and the promised end to Rose's first week. She dashed down the Great Stairs in the special muffled silence of mid-lesson time, away from that staring oculus set into the high ceiling. The pallor of the morning had now fallen into a stormy midday, the rain lashing against the thick glass, drowning out the tick of the Roman clock set into the wall above the library doors.

Rose was glad to be out of the Classics office. Her two morning lessons had been no better than her first attempts earlier that week, and then an old copy of Sophocles she'd picked up revealed again that spidery handwriting scrawled in the margins. At the front, in thick black ink that had bled through the page, she had read:

Miss Jane Farrier, Classics 1.
House Prudence

Alarmed, Rose had dropped the book, and left the office.

She berated herself as she strode along the main corridor

– imagine being upset over her predecessor's book? Her old marking, too, in that drawer, with that handkerchief? It was nothing, really. But Rose had to admit that some of the girls' comments were crowding into her anxieties: *The other Madam didn't seem to mind, Oh, how different you are, Madam,* and the worst, *Oh dear, Madam, that's not how it's done at all.* Of course, it was normal for the students to compare Rose to their old teacher, but this place seemed so stuck in the past, so wayward and foreign in its manners that Rose felt as though she was treading behind steep, unflinching footprints.

She hadn't yet dared to challenge the secretaries regarding her mother, either; Rose just wanted her first week to end. Only one Junior afternoon lesson remained on her scant timetable, and it was an activity. But there were so many more weeks ahead; weeks lining up like Roman soldiers ready to be picked off and overcome. But the Romans were the conquerors, Rose frowned, so which was it? Was she the savage, then, and the girls the civilised ones?

Civilised by their strict uniforms, perhaps. Even though she'd seen glimpses of it in the school's prospectus, it was odd to see the uniform every day – like some elaborate joke, or a Victorian fancy dress party. Perhaps the uniforms hadn't changed since the founding of the school. Rose knew that institutions had their extravagances and eccentricities – one of the inexplicable entitlements of the British ruling classes. It was something her mother used to rant about, and her father dismiss as 'just the way things are'.

And the Sixth seemed more civilised still. They moved differently and were much better put together than Rose could ever hope to be – even if she was several years older, she was closer to them in age than to the youngest of the staff.

The general spread of white faces made Rose uncomfortable, despite the small handful of Asian girls that seemed to group together. This lack of diversity leaked across the staff, too – not at all appropriate or modern for the nineties, she thought.

Along the main corridor Rose took in the wide noticeboards from each department: posters of Shakespeare quotes; prints of Elizabeth I's powdered white face; a map of Jerusalem; a satirical poster describing 'Deportment' next to an historical cartoon mockery of the Suffragettes.

A set of double doors was falling closed as Rose approached. She nudged one door and pushed the other open. In her swift movement she collided with another figure: tall, thin, her lank dark hair crossing Rose's shoulder. Rose looked up to see the sallow-faced girl staring, frightened, into her eyes.

Bethany.

'I'm so sorry, are you all right?' Rose asked. 'Did I hurt you?'

The girl's sunken eyes seemed to contract as she pulled her hand across her chest defensively.

'Bethany, isn't it?' Rose looked straight at the girl, whose mouth twisted furiously.

'Not to worry, Madam. You can let go of the door,' a male voice said behind Rose. He held the door with his arm above her head. 'I've got you.'

Rose kept her eyes on Bethany, who stalked away, half limping.

'Madam?'

Rose turned and pushed herself away from the panel of the door. 'Sorry, thanks. You didn't need to hold the door. That girl, I'm not sure—'

'A relic of old chivalry, if you like. Gentlemen *should* open the door for ladies.' The man touched the small of Rose's back with his hand and ushered her forward. She darted out of the way, and looked at him properly. 'I should introduce myself.' He halted, a deep crease set in his forehead. 'I'm Anthony, head of History. My office is just along from yours.'

'Oh. Were you the one to recommend me?' Rose asked, her eyes lingering on his handsome face. 'For the job here, I mean?'

'Oh, yes, good old Frank Thorpe.' Anthony passed a hand through a thatch of sandy-coloured hair. His other hand held a clutch of files across his chest. 'He's a great friend of mine, we trained together. We needed someone to step in and he spoke well of you. Your credentials are excellent, exactly what we're looking for here at Hope.'

At that, Rose was silent.

'Are you going this way?' Anthony gestured.

Rose nodded before speaking up. 'Actually, do you mind if I ask – where does "Hope" come from?'

'It's an affectionate nickname. After our Founder, William Hope. It's his school, his system.'

'I see,' Rose said after a pause. 'So many things to learn.'

'Well now,' Anthony nodded, 'you've almost done a full week. That's cause for celebration, isn't it?'

'I suppose so, Anthony. Although—'

'Oh.' He paused briefly. 'Do please call me "Sir" in the corridors, in front of the girls.'

'Oh, yes.' Rose rolled her eyes as she trailed after him. 'I keep forgetting, all these new rules. I apologise.'

'And you're "Madam", of course.'

'Actually,' Rose said hotly, 'I hate that. Why can't they use our surnames? I'd rather be Miss Christie than "Madam".'

Anthony gave an amiable smile. 'Much grander this way. We love our traditions here – you'll get used to it in time.'

Rose pressed her lips together. 'I suppose so. You're not free now by any chance, are you?'

'Sadly not. I'm very late for a cover lesson,' said Anthony regretfully, stopping at an unknown door and gesturing with his armful. 'But let's do it another time. This is me.' He smiled at her again as he heaved the door open. The wave of raucous classroom noise hit Rose as she smiled back. 'Let's meet properly in the next few days and I'll answer all those questions of yours.'

Many cries of 'Sir!' embraced Anthony before the door closed and Rose was once again alone in the corridor.

That afternoon in the Classics office, Emma was frowning over Rose's final timetabled activity after Rose had asked for directions. It was labelled *D/Conversation* on her schedule and Emma held on to the folded piece of paper, even when Rose tried to tug it away.

'I'm just not *sure*,' Emma's forehead wrinkled, 'that you should have that activity . . . in the Rec classrooms . . .'.

'Well, it's on my timetable.' Rose almost tore it out of Emma's hands. 'I've got to go, haven't I?'

'You could ask the secretaries,' Emma hoisted her arm up to check her watch, '. . . but there's not really time.'

'I'll just go.' Rose hesitated. 'What's "Conversation", anyway?'

Emma's frown wore through her oval face. 'Oh, it's skills, you know, like debating. Didn't you say you'd led the debating team to victory at your last school? Perhaps . . . they're thinking of that.'

Rose didn't have time to worry about it. She followed Emma's directions down a floor and along two corridors, towards what seemed like a separate part of the fortress-like building, with its low ceiling and stony walls. She eventually found a wonky doorway, open and leading to a narrow passageway at the same height as her own classroom.

Rose put her keys away gratefully, biting her lip at her lateness. Pushing on towards 'Rec 5', she hurried past an empty classroom, with red-slicked walls and satin cushions piled up in one corner. The next open classroom door produced a cacophony of girlish laughter, where a group of Junior girls were enjoying balancing books on their heads, alongside an elderly smiling Madam.

Her designated classroom was thankfully two more along.

'Ah, Madam.' A slim woman with enormous spectacles blinked at Rose. 'Well, I suppose you'll do. The girls are just getting on with an exercise.'

'Sorry I'm late.' Rose spoke in a rush as she looked around her. 'It's my first week.'

It was another classroom quite unlike Rose's own, smaller and completely wood-lined. There was a smattering of old-fashioned desks, with raised lids at a slant and a hole for the ink pot – much older than the flat double desks Rose had in her own bright classroom. At the teacher's desk, a nobbled cane was notched to the side; beyond that, a list of school rules had been painted into the long panel beside the blackboard:

Your hands will be clean. Your nails will be clean. All writing will be done with your right hand. Any offence against common sense or good morals is an offence against school rules.

Rose stared at the list in small astonishment.

'We were expecting the Languages Madam.' The teacher's silver hair was combed back and shining, the same colour as the girls' ribbons. 'It's a shame she's not here to showcase her talents. Are you sure you're supposed to be here?'

Rose searched the woman's face, not recognising her at all from the common room. She must have been a member of house staff. 'Well,' Rose attempted, 'it's on my timetable. Perhaps there's been a mix-up, if you say that Frances—'

'No first names, Madam,' the woman almost sang at Rose. 'Madams only.'

'Oh, sorry.' Rose checked the blackboard with slight exasperation. Above it was a young portrait of the Queen, a small tiara perched on her head.

'Now, girls,' the woman addressed the class, ignoring Rose. 'We are on our second point – finding a connection. This leads to a deeper understanding of your subject. You have already led with a compliment.'

Rose hovered near the desk, immobile as the girls copied down some lines from the board. She turned to the woman with a quiet voice. 'Well, since I'm here, could you tell me what exactly . . . ?'

'If you insist.' The woman cleared her throat. 'This is one of the Discipline lessons with the Seconds . . .' She touched Rose's forearm with her slim, veined hand. 'Are you sure you are quite ready for this, dear?'

Rose couldn't answer. Instead she said, 'So it's nothing to do with debating?'

'Debating, dear? No.'

'I'd rather just teach debating as an activity,' Rose added stupidly. 'Or perhaps Greek club?'

'Ah, well.' The woman's thin eyebrows were rising higher than the top of her spectacles. 'Perhaps you should leave us to it.'

'Oh.' Rose felt strangely relieved by the woman's finality. 'Yes, perhaps there's been some mistake. I'll just . . .'

The girls didn't stir as Rose left the room. But beyond the door, she slammed into a tall figure. Rose recoiled, looking up into Bethany's face.

'Yes,' Bethany's voice was rasping and thin, it was the first time Rose had heard it, 'there *has* been some mistake. You don't belong here.'

Rose didn't speak, her body tight with shock. The vision of the girl was too alarming, too surreal, there in that dark passageway, in that part of the school. She pushed past her and hurried down the corridor, away from the strange crack of Bethany's dry, harsh voice.

Rose's shock and worry finally drove her into the secretaries' office. Every stamp down the stairs, every tick of the clock fell in time with the beat of her heart and the echo of Bethany's words. *You don't belong here.* So far, her first week was proving it. Rose's sense of failure was such that she didn't dare report Bethany for what had to be inappropriate behaviour towards a teacher – in case it made Rose sound like the lunatic.

Even the secretaries' office unnerved her: the rows of docile, smiling women bent over their work, the uniformed strictness to their shoulders that matched the buzz of their computers. The secretary at the foremost desk had a tight, suspicious mouth, which slackened into a smile as Rose approached.

'Good afternoon, Madam.' She stopped typing and faced Rose entirely. 'Thank you for coming down to see us. We can't apologise enough for the oversight on your timetable.'

Rose couldn't gather herself for a moment. 'But how . . . I've only just come from there.'

The secretary's face didn't change. 'We're on top of everything here at Hope.'

'Just not my timetable?'

The secretary's smile flickered and Rose immediately regretted her remark. The woman glanced at her computer screen. 'Please give us a moment to print you out an updated timetable with your Friday afternoon amended.'

'Yes, of course. Thank you.' Rose waited a moment before continuing. 'But that's actually not why I'm here.'

'Oh?' The secretary looked up, her mouth tightening again.

'I wanted to check about my mother,' Rose said. 'Apparently she's been moved to a new clinic? I was told yesterday.'

'Ah, yes. Mrs Christie, is it?' The secretary glanced towards her filing cabinet as she spoke. 'We were advised by the board of governors to improve her situation now that you've been taken on.' She nodded up at Rose. 'I assure you all the proper research was done regarding the healthcare professionals.'

'Okay, but why?' Rose's voice grew more courageous. 'She was perfectly fine where she was. Where is she now?'

The secretary shared a look with her neighbouring colleague who then lifted her face to Rose. 'Are we to understand that you want her to be *returned* to her previous situation?'

'No, no,' Rose said forcefully as she looked around the room at the other secretaries. 'I just don't understand why . . .'

'It was in the terms of your contract that any dependants would be cared for by the school.'

Rose scanned her memory but couldn't recall that line from the contract she'd signed – or had she thought that 'dependants' only related to children? 'Yes,' Rose allowed, 'but why wasn't I consulted?'

The first secretary nodded vigorously this time. 'Your mother was consulted. I spoke with her myself.'

'Yourself? But . . .' Rose tried again. 'Surely *I* should have been asked before the decision was made? Or at least notified once it was?'

'I see.' The second secretary tilted her head over-politely. 'And would you like to be consulted on every matter concerning your mother's care?'

'Of course!' Rose shot back. 'I should be the first point of contact!'

'That will certainly be a first for Hope,' continued the first secretary as her other colleagues glanced up at Rose curiously. 'With the staff schedule so busy, *we* usually deal with these sorts of things.' The two secretaries nodded significantly at each other, but Rose was too angry, too much of an outsider to try to understand their private communication. 'Clearly we shall have to make an exception until you are properly settled in.'

'So, can you tell me where she is?'

'Certainly, Madam,' the second secretary said acidly. 'I will have all the details sent up to your office in the next hour.'

Rose nodded, willing herself to remain calm as the first secretary finished with, 'And are we right in thinking that you have no other dependants for us to manage?'

'No, none at all.'

'And is that all, Miss Christie?' A third secretary was standing now. With the whir of the office printer she swiped out a piece of paper, passing Rose the new version of her timetable. The page wavered in the air between them as Rose looked at it.

'Yes, that's all.' Rose took the piece of paper and kept her eyes low. 'Thank you.'

'No, no, Madam, thank *you*.'

But Friday wasn't finished with Rose yet. She was immersed in last year's results – she found easily the GCSE grades from last year's Fifths, but was dismayed to find nothing from the Sixths' A levels. She was trying to make sense of it when Emma suggested dinner in the dining hall together, before Movie Night later that evening. Rose stood up mid-spreadsheet; she was grateful to have the offer of company, but wanted nothing less than to talk through the disaster of her first week. She hoped she could steer Emma into lighter conversations.

'You need your blazer, Rose, to go downstairs.' Rose could hear the exasperation in Emma's voice.

'Yes.' Rose touched the tight leather back of her chair. 'Where is it? I had it here. It must be somewhere.' Her eyes narrowed at the dimness of her desk; the faint evening light outside was no help.

'Is it in your classroom?'

'No, I haven't been up there since lunch.'

'For heaven's *sake*, Rose.' Emma pushed her chair under her desk briskly. 'You can't go downstairs without it.'

'Well,' Rose closed her eyes for a moment to gather herself, 'I definitely had it in the first place, or I wouldn't have come up here. Can I run back to my flat to get another?'

'We're not supposed to go back to our flats until we've finished for the day.'

'I know we're not supposed to.' Rose bit her lip, shaking her head with regret and confusion. She was always careful with her things; what was wrong with her? Emma's frustration certainly didn't bode well for any dinner together. 'Never mind,' Rose said bracingly, 'I'll just go up then and eat at my flat. I've got a tinned soup. Thanks all the same.'

'Well, if you're sure,' Emma said curtly, moving towards the door. 'But you'll need a jacket for Movie Night later.'

'Yes, I know. Thanks.'

Time was shorter than Rose realised, though, so she gulped down the hot soup and grabbed another blazer from her cupboard before hurrying to Movie Night, resenting the misplacement of her favourite one with the brass buttons.

The Friday night activity was a special treat for every girl from Junior First to Lower Sixth, with the eldest year being away. Rose wasn't on duty officially, but was expected to take part as a new member of staff.

Founder's Hall looked entirely different from Monday's formal opening assembly. The imposing portraits were now shadows behind the projector's bright electric beam, which in turn lit up an enormous white sheet strung up at the end of the hall.

Rose watched the boarding house staff bellow at the pyjamaed girls as they handed out cushions and told them where to lie down. Several Juniors from House Verity had brought their duvets, which apparently wasn't permitted, and were told to take them back. This task fell to one girl, who left the hall piled with layers of soft duvets high above her head. Rose watched her walk into the wide door frame of the hall as her peers laughed mirthlessly. She turned to the matron standing next to her.

'Does she need a hand?'

'No, Madam. Let her struggle. The girls will've chosen her for a reason.'

Rose moved away at that remark, towards Frances. Despite her strange comment the afternoon before, there was an aura of competency to Frances that Rose wanted to draw near, and eventually learn from.

The Intermediate girls started to file in and take up their spots, barging the little Juniors out of the way, before the Lower Sixth arrived and demanded that the whole layout be reordered. A task soon fell to Rose to hand out three boiled sweets per girl. A group of Juniors in the front row had undone their hair, and let it flow out so the tendrils threaded together in an array of chestnut, black and blonde. Their feet were stretched out against the front of the platform so that the row of legs looked like an oddly arranged piano keyboard. After the sticky-handed Juniors and Intermediates, Rose halted at the spread of Sixth, none of them taking their allocated sweets, preferring to ignore her entirely. One did hesitate, before raising her eyes to dismiss Rose, touching her head self-consciously. She had a short, boyish haircut, but was no less beautiful than any of the others. Rose resumed her place at the back with Frances; the girls' heads shallow moons and their knees soft peaks in the half-light of the projector.

'I thought the movie was *Beauty and the Beast*?' Rose asked Frances as a black and white film began to whir.

'Yes, the 1950s version. The Jean Cocteau.'

'Oh.' Rose had presumed it would be the new Disney release, one that perhaps a well-connected parent had procured. 'My God, how cultured.'

French words were scrawled across the white sheet as the film started to play out.

'Can the girls translate this?'

'The Sixth should,' Frances whispered.

Rose didn't say much after that. Chaotic orchestral music took over, with the shrill of choral voices. After half an hour she couldn't hold back: 'Is this really a treat? I mean . . .' Rose's eyes widened at the theatricality of the beast. 'There have been so many great movies out recently. *Batman Returns*? The girls would love Catwoman in that, I reckon. Some of them might find a role model in her.' Rose chuckled heartily. 'And *Alien 3* just came out. The first one was really brilliant – we could get that for the projector, it came out a while ago.'

'Hush, please.' It was the matron behind them.

'Your taste is so odd, Rose,' Frances murmured sideways. 'Aliens and comic book heroes?'

'No, really.' Rose turned her face to Frances. 'Didn't you see those movies? They were brilliant.'

The film reeled out in front of Rose's eyes; the stiff tableau of each scene and the schoolboy-Shakespeare costumes bothered her intensely. The girls might have felt the same way: they started to mutter cross words here and there, yawning and unpeeling themselves from each other with ruffled hair.

'No, you can't lie here. Go away.'

'I can't see.'

'Bethany, can you stop moving your head!'

Rose stiffened at that.

'You're blocking the light.'

'Oh, for heaven's sake!' barked a louder voice. '*Why* do you always do this?'

Sure enough, the film's perfect rectangle of light was interrupted by a round-shouldered shadow. A glowing face had turned away from the film, twisted with concentration and staring straight at Rose.

Rose gasped and moved towards Frances. 'Look, look at her.'

'Look at what?'

'She's staring at me, that girl Bethany. She's always staring at me.'

Behind Bethany's shadow the black and white figures spoke gushing French.

'No,' Frances answered, 'she's just trying to annoy the others – she's troublesome, that one. She ought to be in London with the other girls.'

Bethany stood up and blocked a large portion of the view, which produced furious exclamations from the girls. To Rose's horror, she was moving towards them, like a spectre, the silhouette of her long-haired figure growing closer.

She went to one of the matrons and said something to her, close, so that the matron had to lean in to hear. Rose couldn't concentrate on the film; she could only feel Bethany's long and electric stare. Rose set her jaw and turned to Frances. 'What do you mean – Bethany ought to be in London?'

Frances waited a long moment before she answered; she leaned in so that Rose could feel her breath on her neck. 'She's in the Upper Sixth, but there are always a few left behind. Those who aren't fully performing, as it were.'

'Is she not?' Rose stiffened. 'Shouldn't everyone be included?'

'London is only a formality.'

Rose asked before she could stop herself. 'What *is* London, though?'

'Oh,' said Frances, delicately. 'It's an introductory ceremonial thing, very old-fashioned, livery companies and that sort of thing.'

'Where do they all stay?'

'Hope owns quite a few houses in London, near Regent's Park.'

Rose didn't want to admit that she didn't get it; more eccentricities that were beyond her, perhaps. But something else pushed at her more urgently. 'Frances, why did you say yesterday that my old colleague Frank shouldn't have let me come here?' She garbled it out, flushing red as she did so, unnoticed in the shadows.

Frances gave a distant, apologetic grin. 'Oh, that? I was having a bad day, Rose. You'll have to excuse my little tantrums. I lash out sometimes. I can say the oddest things – pay them no heed. I apologise!'

'It's fine,' Rose answered, unconvinced.

She was too anxious to say anything else, as Bethany wandered back to her place, passing in front of the projector and producing a second round of fury from her peers. Rose felt a broad pang of homesickness, feeling further away from anyone in that room than she'd felt before. Her heart quivered in her chest for the duration of the strange black and white film as she concentrated instead on the hard outline of Bethany's head staring back at her.

ANTIGONE

Ἀντιγόνη

οὔτοι συνέχθειν, ἀλλὰ συμφιλεῖν ἔφυν.

Κρέων

κάτω νυν ἐλθοῦσ', εἰ φιλητέον, φίλει

κείνους: ἐμοῦ δὲ ζῶντος οὐκ ἄρξει γυνή.

Antigone

I was born to lead with love, not hate – that is my nature.

Creon

Then go down to hell and love them if you must.

But while I'm alive, no woman will ever rule.

(Sophocles' *Antigone*, 523–525, written 441BC)

Antigone's greatest strength was her youthful impertinence – or, seen in another light, her certainty of what was right by the gods. She'd always known her family was cursed, and ignored others' disdain when she cared for her dying father, the exiled Oedipus, in his last days. At home in Thebes, her uncle Creon was regent king, until her elder brother was old enough to rule. But his inheritance was challenged by her younger brother, and in a fierce battle over the kingship they killed each other.

King Creon now declared that Antigone's elder brother would

be buried with honours, while the younger – the usurper – would be left to rot outside the city walls. Creon announced a new decree: if any man were to try to bury the usurper, he would be condemned to death by stoning. But the gods' law spoke louder to Antigone, and her self-righteousness drove her forward. Grieving and burial ritual was a woman's duty, after all.

She couldn't persuade her sister Ismene to join her, so Antigone set out alone, under the cover of night, to carry out the burial. Her arms grew filthy from the dirt as she whispered the chants to set free her brother's spirit.

But the king's guards caught Antigone, and dragged her in front of her astonished uncle. He was even more confounded by her lack of remorse. What gave Creon, Antigone cried, such moral authority? With her parents dead, she could never have another brother. All souls deserved to be put to rest – what did it matter how they died? Creon rounded on Antigone imperiously. How could his own niece dare to disobey his law so publicly? Did she care more for the dead than the living? Did she want to join her brothers? Would she forsake his son, her betrothed, Haemon? When Antigone still failed to express regret, the king nodded – he must keep to his newly declared law. Antigone would be walled up in a cave, and starved to death. There, at least, her death would be unseen, and the king's hands would not be stained by his niece's blood.

But as soon as Antigone was sent to her fate, the bad omens began: rotten body parts rained over the city, flocks of birds hovered over the palace. The people appealed to Creon, as did his son Haemon, begging for Antigone's life. Even the city's aged prophet approached the king, speaking of the gods' displeasure, warning him of the need for mercy.

The king's resolve began to waver, and he followed his son to Antigone's stone prison. In the bosom of the cave, though, the young girl had pulled her own bed wrappings around her neck and hanged herself. Haemon clutched her lifeless body to him, sobbing, before charging at his father. At the last moment, the young man flinched, and turned his dagger on himself. Haemon's mother soon heard the news, and in agonised grief she followed her son into suicide.

Remembering Antigone's faith in the gods' law, Creon was forced to acknowledge the flaw in his own man-made authority. The king was left with his crown intact, but with an empty heart and an empty home.

The [illegible] ... [illegible]
[illegible] up in the [illegible]
[illegible]
[illegible]
[illegible] before [illegible]
[illegible]
[illegible]
[illegible]
[illegible]
[illegible] the [illegible]
[illegible] The [illegible]
[illegible]

4.

On the Monday of the second week the Upper Sixth had returned, buoyant and enthralled by their time in London. The Headmaster had shaken each returning girl's hand during a special assembly; a Science teacher next to Rose had nodded along with each ascent to the platform.

'Good to see them back, not quite right without them,' he'd said.

A few hours later, Rose was pleased to let in her class of five. They arrived before the bell rang, and filtered gracefully along the desks in a beautiful front row of styled hair and tight silk dresses. Rose's own copy of Sophocles was ready on the desk, not Jane's. *The Three Theban Plays,* she repeated to herself; Rose was surprised at her tripping nerves. She stared at her students as if she were seeing them for the first time.

'So you've already read *Oedipus the King,* with my predecessor,' Rose hesitated, 'and now we're talking about *Antigone.*'

'Yes, Madam,' one girl answered.

'It's a shame because *Oedipus* is one of my favourites,' Rose continued fluidly, turning her book over in her hands. 'It's an amazing play. Did you girls like it?' Not hearing any response, Rose cleared her throat. 'So, we've read the opening of *Antigone.*' She focused on the girl in the middle wearing lilac. 'What did you think, Dulcie?'

'I don't know, Madam. Shall we tell you about London?'

'I'd rather get on with the work, Dulcie, since we missed two lessons last week.'

'Lauren curtseyed to the wrong person!' The girl on Dulcie's right was bursting with glee. 'Can you believe it!'

'Curtseyed?' Rose looked at Lauren, the American girl at the end of the row, whose face was sullen. Rose reacted swiftly. 'I don't want to hear about that, I'm sure you all did brilliantly in whatever it was you were doing.'

'It's true, though!'

'The other Madam used to love hearing about all the final-year preparations,' Dulcie said coyly.

'She and I are not the same,' Rose said firmly.

'No, indeed!'

'And I'm afraid, Dulcie, that you can't have her back, you're stuck with me.'

Dulcie raised her eyebrows. 'We don't want her back, Madam, neither would *you* if you knew what happened to her.'

'Okay,' Rose pushed on, despite the clench in her throat. 'So I asked you to think about the opening of the play. What was Antigone talking about with her sister?'

The five girls were silent; only Dulcie held her gaze.

'Something about their brothers' deaths?' started Rose, impatiently. 'There was a problem there, what was it?'

'Was it about Oedipus being their dad?' suggested the girl on the end, nearest the window. Her dress was a pale yellow, one sleeve dazzling in the bright light.

'No, Alexandra.' Rose stared down at the page, willing it to speak to her instead. 'Their brothers were at war—'

'It's Lex, Madam.'

'Oh, stop this.' Dulcie pulled a face at the girl, her small pointed nose wrinkling. 'You're ridiculous, Alexandra – as *if* we'll call you "Lex". What on earth happened to you over the summer?'

Alexandra touched the mousy curls at the back of her neck and kept her eyes on the page.

'If that's what you prefer, Lex,' Rose said carefully, 'it's fine with me.'

Dulcie's incredulous face rounded on Rose, whose voice breezed over the class, 'So, girls, the two sisters were discussing burying their younger brother. Do you remember?'

'The brothers fought over the throne. The older one was buried normally,' Lauren said methodically in her American accent. 'The younger one who challenged the kingship was called a traitor. Their uncle said he couldn't be buried.'

'Yes, Lauren,' Rose nodded gratefully. 'Do they bury their "traitor" brother? That's what the play is about. Honouring the dead, whether they've done right or wrong in life. Doing right by the gods, going against your uncle. Man's law or gods' law? Write that down.'

The girls buried their manicured fingernails in their pencil cases while Lex glanced up at Rose. 'Madam, where do you want us to write this?'

'In your books.'

'Which book?'

'The book you're holding, Lex. The play. Write all over it. Underline, highlight, pull it apart.'

The girls reacted with surprise. Lauren added, 'Madam, are you sure?'

'Of course, how will you really get into it otherwise?'

'Madam,' Lex rested a hand on the sleeve of her yellow dress, tilting her face, 'I don't want to waste my new highlighter.'

'I think Sophocles deserves your fancy pens, Lex. So what did Antigone want to do? Bury or not bury?'

The girl sandwiched between Dulcie and Lex was a head shorter than the other girls; her soft, serene face was staring out of the arched window. Rose's eyes narrowed.

'Tash?'

The short girl's head snapped back to Rose as her cheeks spotted with embarrassment. 'Beg your pardon, Madam?'

'Antigone wanted to . . .'

Tash's eyes hovered over Lex's notes next to her. 'Um. Antigone wanted to bury her brother and defy her uncle.'

'Yes.' Rose sat down in her chair and tried a different tack. 'You know, girls, Antigone is basically the same age as you.'

'Oh,' Lex answered. 'Really?'

'Anyone got a sister here?'

The girls looked at one another, shaking their heads. Rose frowned. 'Really? None of you?'

'I have a brother back home?' Lauren tried.

Rose seized upon it. 'Yes, Lauren. And would you do anything for him?'

The girl shrugged and a thread of hair fell from her blonde chignon.

'Even if your uncle, or your parents, or the traditional "head of your family" told you to reject him? Would you disobey and do what you thought was right?'

'Disobedience was pretty risky in those times,' Lauren said quietly, 'wasn't it, Madam?'

'Yes, indeed. Particularly for women and slaves.'

'Well,' Dulcie's voice came in firm, 'obedience is one of

the key values we're taught, Madam, so you're saying that Antigone is going against the rules.'

'Yes!' Rose stepped forward abruptly, startling the five girls in front of her. 'She is! And we need to discuss it.'

'But surely there's no question, Madam,' Dulcie continued, her sharp eyes darting around. 'The obedience and submission of the inferior is the cornerstone of any healthy relationship. We all know that.'

'Er . . . I'm not sure I would agree with you, Dulcie,' said Rose, suddenly bewildered. 'But this play is more complicated than that – and according to the Greeks, we're all inferior to the gods.'

'You've lost me, Madam,' Tash said with a frown, looking across at the window again.

'There's no God here, Madam,' Lex called out across Tash. 'Headmaster got rid of the chaplain.'

'The gods, Lex. Not *God*,' Rose said firmly. 'You know, girls, I was taught this play by a man, when I was your age, and he taught us that Antigone was a rebel, a scourge on the city. I believed him because he was my teacher. But then at university I studied the play again, and I saw that the message is very different – just the final chorus is enough to tell you that. So, ladies,' Rose added warily, 'it's important to pay attention, but also to think for yourselves.'

'Goodness, Madam,' Dulcie laughed from the middle of the row, 'you're not one of those feminist hippies, are you?'

Lex tittered, checking Dulcie's face. 'Oh Madam, have you burned all your bras and smashed shop windows and grown out your underarm hair?'

'Have you read all of what's her name,' Dulcie continued with a sneer, 'Germaine Geer?'

'Greer,' Rose corrected quickly. 'And no. I am not.'

'You are funny, Madam.' Lex gave a small smile.

'Anyway,' Dulcie tossed her book on the desk. 'My father says that it's the nineties now, and it's high time we buried that hippy nonsense. He's always right.'

Rose turned her back on the little group and gazed blindly at the blackboard for a moment.

'Does the Headmaster know that you're teaching us this, Madam?'

Rose stiffened, turning around. 'Of course, Dulcie, it's one of the texts for your A level exam, why do you—'

'Madam, if you think women are so brilliant,' interrupted Tash with a certain longing in her voice, 'don't you just love Princess Diana?'

'We're talking about Antigone.' Rose rounded on Tash, whose gaze was as dreamy as her tone. Rose softened. 'But, yes, Diana's all right. She seems different from the others—'

'Tash has a crush on Diana,' Dulcie interrupted. 'She carries a little picture of her wherever she goes. In her pencil case, in her—'

'Shut up, Dulce,' Tash cried, her mouth slack. 'It's a newspaper cut-out, it's not—'

'We're not allowed crushes.' Dulcie shrugged her lilac shoulders. 'My father says—'

'And what,' it was Rose's turn to interrupt, 'does your *mother* say, Dulcie?'

Four girls glanced quickly at Dulcie and Rose immediately regretted her question.

'My mother,' Dulcie drew herself up, 'only ever worries about her chrysanthemums, Madam.'

'I apologise, I shouldn't have mentioned it,' Rose said delicately. 'Let's get on.'

'Anyway, Tash,' Lex leaned towards her neighbour, 'you should drop that crush nonsense. You're in E Pathway, after all. You need to get a grip or you'll mess it up. You don't want to become a C.'

Rose glanced between the two of them and made a mental note to read, scour, ingest the *Staff Handbook*, even if only to understand the terminology the girls continually used in her lessons.

'There were six of us, Madam, before,' Dulcie began with a mean glint in her eye, 'did you know? A girl left. She's a C now.'

'Well, she only left the *class*, not the school. On account of the previous Madam.' Lex was nodding her head.

Dulcie added, 'She said you gave her a shove last week.'

Rose looked up. 'Gave whom a shove?'

'Bethany, Madam. In the corridor.'

'What are you talking about?' Rose said quickly, hoping she wasn't hearing what she most dreaded. 'Bethany?'

'I wouldn't worry, Madam, she's always making a fuss over nothing.' Tash rolled her eyes. 'We're on your side.'

'Do you –' Rose seemed to lose her breath. 'Does anyone need to be on a side?'

Dulcie looked at Rose with the ghost of a smile. 'Of course, Madam.'

Rose froze as she re-entered the Classics office. Her favourite blazer, missing since Friday, was there. It had been tugged over the back of the chair untidily, dark against the leather seat, its brass buttons shining.

As she lifted it off the chair for closer examination, something caught her eye in the light from the window. It was a thick strand of hair. Long and black, not frizzled like Rose's hair, but slick and straight.

In a rapid movement Rose held the blazer away from her. It had been touched, worn, God knew what else. *Bethany.* Rose wanted to throw it out of the window. *There has been some mistake,* she could hear in her mind. *You don't belong here.* Here in this place, she thought; famous, world-renowned and extreme. Here, and so privileged to teach this long line of ladies from the wealthiest families in Britain. No, she didn't belong – she was as wrong as this soiled and misplaced blazer. Rose dropped it to the floor.

It was everything Rose could do not to rush back to her flat, her bedroom, squash her face against the sheets and cry away her anxieties. But it was only Monday morning; the day was moving forward, and she was expected downstairs.

Rose found herself staring at the bronze plaque emblazoned with the Headmaster's name. She could see her own distorted face glaring back at her through the yellow metal on his study door.

Behind her, the iron clock above the Great Stairs showed the correct time for her appointment. She'd seen the Headmaster at the staff meeting over an hour earlier, but this appointment would be private.

'Madam?'

'Me?' Rose pulled at her fingers anxiously. 'Yes.'

The girl was close to her. Rose looked at her white dress and grey blazer, her blonde hair a halo of frizz around her forehead. 'The Headmaster isn't able to see you. Something unfortunate has prevented him.' The girl spoke in perfect recitation, frowning at Rose. 'And he hopes you will accept his apologies.'

'Oh. Thanks. Of course,' Rose said awkwardly.

The girl returned to her group of friends, who seemed to glower at Rose before they carried on up the stairs.

Rose faced the plaque again, as if the Headmaster might appear at that moment, swing his door open and invite her in. To offer her some justification for her own existence there, in this job, in his school.

But then Rose heard it, a muffled laugh on the other side.

Should she bang on the door? Go opposite to the secretaries' office to check? What was she planning to say to him, anyway – thank you for employing me? Thank you for taking over my mother's care? Did she really want to suck up to this new boss of hers, who seemed to hold the strange power of this eccentric place in his small, quick hands? No, Rose thought, she would keep this painful rejection to herself.

At the lunchtime staff meeting he had introduced her to them all in the formality of a lower conference room. The chairs had been laid out in sombre rows, just like at a funeral. The Headmaster had stood at the front in an exquisite suit of thick linen, cut precisely around his slim shoulders, Vivien poker-straight by his side. Rose had been presented as the new head of Classics; the Headmaster spoke about her teaching experience in north Kent, her first-class degree, her studies in Rome and her teacher training. A broken smile on her face, Rose had fixed her gaze on the empty fireplace bedecked with an enormous stag's head and two crossed rifles. The Headmaster reminded the group of Rose's probationary period; pointing out that all being well, she would be welcomed into the tight community at Hope, and would become a fantastic model for growth and expansion. There had been a dash of applause and Rose had felt a beat of gratitude towards the jovial faces looking up at her.

The staff had been exactly as she had seen in the common room – the stiff and aging men were numerous but dominated by women, who were mostly over fifty, and as boarding staff, dressed less formally than the teachers. Sirs and Madams that Rose didn't yet know; she wondered if she ever would with those impersonal labels. Regardless of the Headmaster's words, Rose had felt inexperienced and young. In fact, Frances was probably the nearest to Rose's age, or Anthony perhaps, and both were more than ten years older than her.

Hesitating near the Great Stairs, however, Rose's thoughts were interrupted.

'I say, you're a fine specimen.' A man with grey hair and a wide belly was smiling at Rose. His thick tie was clipped back by a gold clasp. He reminded her of an overgrown schoolboy that had suddenly evolved into an old man.

'Now, now, Ashley,' said Anthony, appearing behind the older man, 'we're not allowed to talk to the female staff like that, you've been told.'

'Oh, nonsense, Anthony, they love it. Besides, there haven't been any as young as this. She's absolutely fresh as a daisy. Head of Classics, what?'

'Yes, Ashley,' insisted Anthony, his hand on the older man's arm. 'You know perfectly well.'

Alarm thrummed through Rose's chest. 'There's no need to talk about me in the third person,' she said haughtily. 'I am right in front of you.'

'Goodness, she's got gumption,' Ashley muttered to Anthony as if discussing an exhibit in one of their History cabinets. 'I like that. Do you know what you've let yourself in for, young lady?'

'Don't worry yourself about anything Ashley says, Rose,' Anthony said quickly, just as the older man shook his arm free. 'He's been here so long he's become part of the furniture.'

'Bit young for a Classicist, aren't you?' added Ashley, regarding her with a teasing eye.

'Not really,' Rose replied firmly, 'but I hear that a lot.'

'Indeed. We're History.' Ashley swung his belly towards her again; his buttons pressed against the white of his shirt. 'Listen. This school in North Kent that Headmaster mentioned earlier – not a state school, was it?'

'Yes, it was. And yes, I was state-educated. Grammar.'

'Dearie me, what about university – Cambridge? I'm a Cambridge man myself, so's the Headmaster.'

Rose couldn't suppress her small smile. 'No, a London university, I'm afraid. More libraries, even better museums.'

'Museums that Hope's benefactors probably donate to regularly. What goes around comes around, my dear! And,' Ashley's wiry eyebrows bent together, 'what does your father do?'

'He was an educator, just like you and I.' Rose paused. 'Please excuse me, Sir, it was nice to speak to you, but I must go back upstairs.'

'Good, good. Onward,' gestured Ashley with his thick hand.

But she didn't have the chance. 'Madam?' A different voice was calling to Rose across the entrance hall. It was Vivien. 'I gather you were to meet the Headmaster, but there's something more pressing you and I need to discuss. Shall we?'

*

Vivien's study wasn't nearly as grand as Rose was expecting. It stood next to the secretaries' office on the northern side of the main corridor, opposite the Headmaster's. It had no proper view of its own, just a dim courtyard. The room was busy with trinkets and ornaments littering the desk and the long shelves – Rose noticed a model of the Trevi Fountain next to an exquisite antique perfume blower. There were two bouquets on the long windowsill and another at the conference table, purple-blue blooms that gave out a sickly sweet smell, echoing the woman herself in her plum velvet jacket.

'I'm glad I've caught you, Rose, we've only got a few minutes. What I have to tell you is this.' Vivien leaned forward in her chair. 'There's been a very serious allegation made against you.'

Rose blinked, horrified. 'An allegation?'

'Yes.'

'But . . . it's only the second week?'

'Now, here at Hope we deal with allegations properly,' Vivien continued in her crisp voice. 'Apparently there was an incident where you grabbed a student in the corridor and she claims that you have been harassing her since the first day.'

'No, no. This can't be.' Rose's voice was frantic as she sat forward. 'I'm innocent. There's this girl who has been following me around. Bethany. I think she even took my blazer. You saw her too—'

'It is, of course, important to hear your version of events, and they will be recorded, but please understand that we do give the girls the benefit of the doubt.' Vivien's eyes bored into Rose. 'She does have bruises, and gives quite a compelling account.'

'Bruises?' Rose shook her head vigorously. 'No, no, this is a simple mistake!'

Vivien raised her eyebrows. 'I assure you there's nothing simple about it.'

'It's Bethany, isn't it?' Rose's voice lifted with panic. 'You *saw* her on the stairs.'

'Bethany deVere?'

'Yes.' Rose hesitated. 'Is that her last name?'

Vivien didn't answer; instead she made a note on a sheet of paper on her desk. Rose hardly noticed. She could only see in her mind's eye that stained handkerchief with its 'BdV'.

'Bethany has had past difficulties – her mother passed away some years ago.' Vivien's eyes wavered over Rose as she thought about it. 'And last year, she formed an attachment to a previous member of staff, which was not at all appropriate.'

'I see,' said Rose, trying to piece these scraps of information together.

'We cannot have the same consequences here.'

'I absolutely agree. There's no attachment, I don't even teach her.' Rose shook her head again, shuffling in her seat. 'I have no need to associate with her. I just wish she would stop following me around,' Rose added loudly. 'I can't have this on me, either.'

'Even so,' Vivien's features grew tense and her eyes didn't leave Rose's face, 'this allegation is serious and will be investigated. Formal notices will go up in the common room. We will have to let the governors know, as well as the parents in the monthly newsletter. We will review the case fully after half-term.'

'But why tell everyone?' Rose's cheeks burned. 'I am totally innocent of this!'

'We may have to collect a statement from you. The local constable—'

'The police? Surely not?'

Vivien paused. 'Surely you understand, Rose. This is a very grave matter within an educational establishment. This allegation comes under "grievous bodily harm", not to mention "abuse of power".'

Rose's voice was now hoarse with fear. 'I haven't done anything wrong.'

'In the meantime, please do not speak to the girl or approach her. It will stand against you.'

'Will this go on my record?'

'Yes, it will, along with the eventual results of the investigation.' Vivien nodded, to herself more than to Rose.

'But surely,' Rose said desperately, 'my reputation, my name . . .' She stared at the model of the Trevi Fountain, an incongruous friend watching her from the other side of the room. 'I've only just got here. And the way it's going—'

'Nonsense, I won't hear that.' Vivien was standing up, her velvet jacket tight around her shoulders. 'The girls are enjoying having some fresh blood in the place.'

'But,' Rose spluttered, 'how can you say that when you've just told me I'm being investigated?'

Vivien stood over her. 'Time will tell. Teenage girls have their peculiarities, as we *all* do.' Rose couldn't help but breathe in Vivien's perfume, floral but overblown. 'We shall get to the bottom of this.'

Rose nodded mutely as Vivien continued. 'Incidentally, there's another item I have to speak to you about. You were privy to a Discipline lesson last Friday. This was an error, and the relevant people have been reprimanded for it. I apologise for the oversight. It will not happen again.'

'Oh,' Rose muttered, 'there's no need to—'

'Indeed, there is.' Vivien nodded sincerely and took Rose's hand, drawing her out of the chair and opening the door.

'Will I need to speak to the Headmaster about this?' Rose asked before her dismissal was complete.

'Not at this point. We will keep you informed. I am sure you understand.'

But Rose understood nothing as the study door closed on her.

DIDO

ille dies primus leti primusque malorum
causa fuit; neque enim specie famave movetur,
nec iam furtivum Dido meditatur amorem:
coniugium vocat; hoc praetexit nomine culpam.

That was the day of death, the source of woe.
For Dido didn't care about her honour nor her appearance;
She thought no longer of a secret love
But called it marriage. Under that name, she hid her misdeed.

(Virgil's *Aeneid* 4.169–172, written 19BC)

Dido was a tender heroine, resilient and impressive until her final moments, when she was used as a plaything for the gods.

At home in Tyre, her well-loved and rich husband Sychaeus was killed by her brother, the king, who had coveted his wealth. That very night, the ghost of Sychaeus appeared to Dido in a dream, telling her of her brother's crime, and commanding her to leave the city with their shared riches and as many loyal attendants as she could find. Dido managed it well; she and her band of Tyrians endured a long meandering journey over land. Eventually they arrived in North Africa, where Dido hoped to start anew.

But tribal kings inhabited those lands, and were reluctant to welcome foreigners. They tried to trick Dido, by offering her as much land as an ox hide could cover. Dido was cleverer than they expected: she cut the hide into long fine strips, and spread them around a nearby hill, to earn herself enough land to found a city. That city became Carthage, which grew and prospered so brilliantly that she was declared queen. One of the tribal kings, Iarbas, demanded that she marry him to prevent the threat of regional war, but Dido insisted that she was faithful to her first husband, Sychaeus, and wished to honour him by remaining a widow.

Several Trojan war refugees landed in Carthage, desolate after the destruction of their celebrated city. Aeneas, the Trojan prince and a son of Venus, led the group of comrades. His escape from Troy had been predestined by Jupiter: for his future lay in Italy, in the founding of the Roman race, and later, his descendants' founding of Rome. Carthage could grant him rest in the meantime. Aeneas's mother, Venus, wanted to ensure that he would be welcome there, so she ordered her immortal son, Cupid, to breathe love and desire into Queen Dido's heart. For the gods always have other plans, and merely use mortals to implement them. Dido and Aeneas consummated their union, and the Trojan refugees enjoyed their respite in this new city. Dido allowed Aeneas to sleep in her palace and stand by her side, for all the neighbouring kings to see.

But Aeneas's departure was soon overdue, and Mercury was sent down by Jupiter to hurry him along. Aeneas moved quickly, giving his men the orders, readying the ships. He did not speak to Dido, who instead heard the news through rumour. In distress she tore at her hair, her chest, her eyes.

But her desperate pleas fell against his deaf ears – Aeneas *would* go, continue his journey, and leave her behind. He refused her wishes to leave her pregnant with a child to inherit her city, he refused to linger one more day. He had been summoned by the gods.

Without Aeneas, Dido saw the mounting threat of the tribal kings around Carthage. Alone and desperate, the queen had no choice. As Aeneas's boats sailed away, she commanded a pyre to be built from his abandoned things: his weapons, his clothes, their bridal bed now stained with betrayal. Then, before it was set alight, she ignored the cries of her sister and climbed to the top. There, she took out a dagger and stabbed herself.

Dido is a lesson in perseverance and courage. Her greatest days were spent standing alone, as queen of her well-loved city, without the need of another.

[illegible] pieces of [illegible] [illegible] [illegible] [illegible] [illegible] [illegible] [illegible] [illegible] [illegible] [illegible] [illegible] [illegible] [illegible] [illegible] [illegible] [illegible] [illegible]

[illegible] herself.

[illegible] [illegible] [illegible] [illegible] [illegible] [illegible] [illegible] [illegible] [illegible]

5.

By the beginning of Rose's third week she'd learned to focus her eyes just above the swarm of heads in the main corridor, hoping that her feet would guide her forward, past the many snide looks turned her way. She fixed an Athene-like stoicism to her features, and carried on.

In the common room there was that promised notice, emblazoned with Rose's good name and the details of the allegation for all to see. Emma thought it highly unfair and had said so in a loud voice when she and Rose were alone, but soon after joined the throng of raised eyebrows amongst the staff. There had been many dripping comments in the common room, particularly from the row of three women that sat near the fire, aged and gnarled in their circle of unkind gossip. Each resembled the gargoyles notched onto the outer walls of the school building. Rose had nicknamed them the Moirai, the three blind mythological Fate-sisters who fought over one all-seeing eyeball; spirits of the same miseries that Macbeth consulted, to his detriment. Rose didn't know which subjects the women taught, but one of them had a chemical stain on her woollen jacket.

There'd been no glimpse of Bethany since Rose's conversation with Vivien the week before. Rose wondered whether the bite of this allegation had relieved the girl temporarily. She didn't miss those translucent eyes stamped with horror – but she did wonder what Bethany was busying herself with now.

Rose wanted desperately to sneak up to the safety of her flat between lessons. The Saturday before, her things had finally arrived and stood, sopping wet, in the darkness of her little hallway. The porters' damp feet had tramped dirt along the floorboards, but Rose had been too anxious to care, or clean up after the men had left. She was only glad that it was past the girls' bedtimes and none of them would see her shabby belongings.

In the light of Sunday morning, Rose's armchair and table had seemed disconnected from these particularly old-fashioned rooms, tight and contemporary against the smart bits of scarred furniture that the flat had already provided. She resisted an urge to hurry back to the porters, order her things back downstairs, back onto the crate that was no longer there, rush them away – to what? To where?

Instead Rose had unpacked everything carefully. She'd held each treasured book, each photo frame and set them around the flat in an effort to fill the space and somehow make it hers. But should she have bothered? What if this allegation got her fired, even before half-term?

Rose walked faster down the main corridor. Tonight, she'd call her mother and tell her how well it was going, and hear all about her new clinic. A dedicated nurse, Rose hoped, an upgrade of fellow patients. She would only contribute self-constructed unrealities during the call, knowing that her mother's rush of gratitude to the Headmaster would trump Rose's shock at their interference. Even Rose had to admit that the school's taking on the financial burden was an enormous relief to her. Surely that boded well for the long term?

'Oh, hi, Madam, how's the Latin?' a girl asked Rose, tossing her red curls behind her shoulder. Rose looked across at Freddie, one of three girls in white dresses, waiting for her response.

'Hi, girls,' Rose answered cautiously. Nessa was by Freddie's side, pale and listless, wearing a blazer too big for her. Dark-haired Josie stood next to her. Rose was mildly surprised to see Josie there; she hadn't connected the three of them together in that way. In Rose's Fourths class, Josie had taken to arching her thick eyebrows as she yelled out the wrong answers from the back of the room, while Nessa sat self-absorbed at the front, and Freddie challenged Rose at any opportunity.

'How's the Latin, Madam?' Freddie repeated, her honey-coloured eyes lit with purpose.

Rose's voice was stronger this time. 'Sorry – how is *my* Latin?'

'Don't say "sorry", say "pardon"!' Josie sang out.

'Well, you don't do anything other than Latin,' Freddie rolled her eyes, 'do you, Madam?'

'Are you dreaming about Aeneas, Madam?' Josie attempted, her black eyes scouring Rose's face. 'Do you want to give him a shove, too?'

'Okay, ladies.' Rose bristled. 'That's enough.'

'Come on, guys,' Nessa said quietly, turning away from the others and pulling the blazer over her shoulders.

'We're being interviewed about your lessons, Madam.' Josie gave a smirk. 'And whether you're nice to us. So, are you?'

Rose focused her gaze on a spot somewhere beyond the three girls. 'That's for you to say, Josie. I hope you tell the truth.'

'No, but Madam, seriously.' Freddie stepped forward as a flow of younger girls filtered past. 'These interviews—'

'Blazers on, girls!' called a male teacher sauntering down the corridor. He looked with concern to Rose. 'Come on, Madam. Keep to the rules.'

'Blazer's at house, Sir, we're on our way,' Josie answered, as Rose's cheeks flushed. 'Not very good at your job, are you, Madam?'

'Don't be rude, Josie,' Freddie commanded.

As Josie shrugged, Rose saw something wriggle underneath the girl's hair, loose at her neck. Whatever it was ran along the back of her white dress and shimmied down her sleeve. Rose pulled her hand to her mouth as she shrank back against the wall.

'Oh Madam! It's only Ronald. Fancy being scared of *him*.'

Rose drew both her hands into fists as Josie lifted her wrist to show the small face of a grey rat, its pinkish nose and dotted eyes poking out of her sleeve.

'Say hello, Madam.'

Rose took a breath. 'No thank you, Josie.'

'Madam, you are mean!' Josie retorted. 'Headmaster says that it's healthy to have something small to love.'

Nessa had separated herself from the other two. She sighed heavily, and her thin frame shifted inside the weight of her blazer.

'Suit yourself. Poor Ronald.' Josie went to kiss her sleeve. 'Latin Madam hates you. We'll see about that, won't we? Matron will give you a treat to make up for it.'

The rat disappeared up Josie's sleeve and Rose stiffened again. Freddie shook out her curls and straightened her shoulders. 'Come on then, let's go.'

Rose watched the girls stalk down the corridor. Touching the back of her neck, she shivered at the thought of that rat, and remembered something Frances had said earlier that day.

'Piles of marking, I see.' Frances had been standing over Rose's desk, glancing at the mass of work.

'It's only classwork, not homework. Still fighting over that one.'

'Well done, all the same.'

'This stupid allegation.' Rose widened her eyes with frustration. 'I have to prove myself somehow.'

'I'm terribly angry about it.'

'Are you?' Rose looked up at Frances with something like gladness.

'Of course. I can't believe they're even giving that girl's story any oxygen. You mustn't worry.'

'How can I not worry? And you can't be angrier than I am.'

'I am, and I've already spoken to Vivien about it.'

'Oh.' Rose hesitated. 'Thank you.'

'Anyway,' Frances huffed, lifting off the first page on Rose's pile, 'is this the Fourths? Daisy, Caroline, Nessa – I have that same class. Some good girls in there.'

'Really?'

'Yes.'

Rose was doubtful. 'But Frances . . . they fight me. At every turn.'

'Of course they do.' Something steely crossed Frances's face. 'They're busy.'

'Busy?'

Rose often wondered where the girls went in the afternoon, lunchtimes or any space that wasn't in between lessons. The school was so tidy, with and without them. They weren't wandering the grounds, admiring the bash of the sea, or even basking in the rare September sun on the green lawns. Rose's old students had once teased her that she wasn't a real person and only appeared out of a cupboard to teach their lessons. Maybe it was that way for her now – the girls weren't real, existing only to trick her, trip her up, upset her.

'Yes, busy. In training for life,' Frances answered with a smile.

Frances was full of curious answers or non-answers; Rose had let that one go. She was still too uneasy to really push for clarity, afraid of what she might find.

The following afternoon Anthony appeared at the door, supporting a cup and saucer in his hand. The wind was bursting at the windows and Rose couldn't help but welcome his warm, sympathetic figure as she looked up from her work.

'I've brought you a cup of tea. Black, isn't it?'

'Oh.' Rose's eyes checked Emma's empty chair. 'Thank you.'

'Earl Grey, yes?' Anthony smiled. 'No milk or sugar?'

'Yes. Th-thanks so much. Come in, of course.' Rose realised she didn't seem very grateful. She stood up, leaning on her desk.

'No need to stand, I'll come to you.'

In one movement Anthony nudged the cup and saucer into Rose's hand and swung Emma's chair towards her desk. 'I'm sorry not to've been able to speak properly until now.' He sat down opposite her.

Rose glanced at him as his face met the daylight from the window. She looked away; Anthony didn't.

'Terrible weather,' Rose tried, touching the edge of her teacup.

'Yes, that's Scotland, I'm afraid.'

Rose faced him. 'It's very wild, outside, isn't it? The sea really crashes against the rocks. Seems quite dangerous.' She bit her lip; she couldn't believe she was talking about the weather.

'Yes, let's hope we don't drown, the porters will have to save us.' Anthony waited as Rose laughed lightly. 'No, it's supposed to be sunnier at the weekend.'

'Oh great,' Rose said genuinely. 'I'd love to get out and go for a walk . . .'

'Rose.' Anthony leaned an elbow on her desk. 'I wondered whether you wanted to go through your class lists. I could talk you through each of your students? It really helps to know a little bit about the girls.'

'Oh,' Rose answered, touched. 'That's kind of you. Really?'

'It might help you settle in a bit more.'

Rose nodded, avoiding the hazel of Anthony's eyes. 'Yes, it's not been . . .'

'I mean to say, this place would be a challenge for any new member of staff. But one as young as yourself . . .' Anthony drew a hand through his sandy-coloured hair. 'The girls love to torture one another, and I'm sure they're torturing you, too. They haven't had anything new to look at for years.'

'Oh dear,' Rose laughed, with slight bitterness this time. 'That sounds—'

'And you mustn't worry about this allegation, Rose,' Anthony said firmly. 'Everybody knows we're very lucky to have you.'

Rose stared into her teacup. 'Do they?'

'Perhaps I should have brought a glass of wine rather than a cup of tea.' Anthony sat back. 'Wrong time of day, I'm afraid.'

'Yes.' Rose lifted her face. 'What a shame.'

Anthony laughed. Then he said, 'Tell me why you chose Classics, Rose.'

'Really?' Rose tried to sit back, too. 'As opposed to History, you mean?'

'Oh no. Classics is far richer than History, and you know it.'

'I'll tell the girls you said that.'

'Please don't,' he smiled.

'Well, Classics . . .' Rose searched the room. 'I think it chose me. I kept trying to give up Latin at school, but I was better at it than anything else.'

Anthony scratched his stubbled chin. 'Was it all those scandals, Roman emperors' daughters sleeping with gladiators and all of that?' He pressed his tie against his chest. 'The love poetry, the drunken symposiums?'

Rose hesitated. 'You're teasing me again. Of course not.'

'Ashley, my colleague, would be disappointed to hear that.'

Rose laughed, glancing at Anthony uncertainly. 'Not at all. Classics is more than language – more than history, literature and society. It's an entire culture and philosophy . . . a civilisation that we still continue to imitate today, without even realising it.' She faced him properly. 'It's the study of people. And sometimes, I understand the Greek and Roman civilisations more than I do our own. So as a teacher it's fun to look at that with my students and ask – have we advanced or not? Who are we, actually, and how far have we come, you know?' Rose added sheepishly. 'Of course, it would help if I understood the culture of Caldonbrae a little better.'

'Ah.' Anthony smiled again. 'Your passion and respect for the past will serve you well here. Hope is a traditional place, and it will make sense to you soon. Give it time, Rose.'

He stretched out an arm to tug at Rose's planner. She

watched him sift through the exposed pages; the comments in her handwriting, her plans and notes on every hour of the past fortnight, written and recorded. In the final pages Anthony found the class lists.

'Here we are,' he nodded kindly. 'Let's start with the Sixth and make our way down.'

That weekend Rose did treat herself to a walk. She wrapped up well, a heavy knit scarf knotted around her neck, a sturdy coat over her woollen jumper. Her head was bare and the wind whipped her dark hair off her face like a punishment. The air stung her nose and ears, she sucked at her teeth as her eyes began to stream. It felt good, though, to feel something that could match the turbulence thrumming in her chest.

A flock of birds was swooping above her head now, drawing Rose on her way. They followed her across the green rectangles of playing fields and tennis courts. Girls were darting with their hockey sticks along various pitches, a ball dancing between them, yells muffled by the wind. Rose walked far beyond the long white pavilion, around which several broad-shouldered men moved. She dashed down the school drive that ran parallel to the rocky line of the peninsula, rutted by skeletal trees and bushes blown scraggy by the brutal sea wind.

Rose bit her lip with regret, remembering two afternoons before, when she hadn't been able to avoid the common room and that notice carrying her name. Emma had tried to draw Rose into a conversation with Deirdre, a polite and attractive Geography teacher in her fifties, who distracted Rose from a discussion about GCSE results by offering her cake, and laughed at Rose's mention of her previous school's subscription to *National Geographic*, insisting that a state school could never have afforded it.

But then, a shrill cry had come from a cluster of armchairs.

'Paula, calm down.'

One of the housemistresses was standing up and arguing in the direction of a tall armchair. 'She's not meeting the expectation?'

'She isn't, I'm afraid.' The clipped voice replied evenly.

'Then we can help her, there's no need to send her down a house.'

'Paula, it's already been decided.'

Rose sat further back in her chair, having recognised the second voice as Vivien's.

'I contest it,' cried the housemistress. 'She deserves better than House Clemency. I'll tell the Headmaster.'

'I wouldn't do that, Paula,' said Vivien carefully.

'We've always been able to fix girls like her!'

Rose turned her head fast and caught Emma and Deirdre's shocked faces.

'Not always,' Vivien had finished sternly. 'But I'm sure it won't go that far with this one.'

Rose had replayed the scene in her mind many times, and again now on her walk, but she was no wiser now than she had been then.

She concentrated on the view in front of her. The sea was an incredible blue today, and there was the mainland now in plain view. It sat far beyond the school, at the bottom of a slight slope. To the villagers, the people of the harbour, Caldonbrae Hall must look like that very monster she had imagined: high up, separate and self-sufficient – its very own jagged kingdom.

At the end of the drive were the heavy-looking school gates,

They were attached to a small, crumbling gatehouse lodge – it was so battered that Rose wondered whether the salty sea air had taken out clawing handfuls. Rose stopped abruptly at the bolted gates, her heart still beating with the rhythm of her walking. She looked up at the wrought-iron railings extending above her head; there was no way to climb over. Rose kicked at the curled metal with her booted foot, but her Doc Martens made little impact.

The door of the lodge swung open. A man with a thunderous weather-beaten face appeared, wearing a green uniform and a green stitched beanie hat over his tangle of greyish hair. Guided by the wind, he moved quickly.

'Here, no! Lassie!' he called over. 'You can't get through. You have to go back.'

The man had a thick Scottish accent; Rose frowned to understand him. 'Hello. Why not?'

'I'm not permitted to let anyone out on foot.'

'What?' Rose wanted to laugh. 'On foot, why not?'

'Are you a student?'

'No,' she answered crossly, 'I'm a teacher.'

'I'm not permitted to let anyone out on foot.'

'Don't be daft.' Rose did laugh this time. 'It's barely a mile to the village.'

'Ach!' He frowned at Rose through his thick eyebrows. 'Typical.'

Rose looked at the groundsman. Both his thick green puffer coat and his hat were stitched with the school's emblem.

'Can't I just go through and you look the other way?'

''Course not!' he almost shouted. 'They're recording everything.'

'But –' She looked around her. 'Really?'

The groundsman snorted. Rose looked longingly at the mainland, the ribboned greens of the shallow hills and the long spattering of houses on the harbour. There was probably a pub there, too.

'You must be new.'

'Yes, I am.'

'Thought I hadn't seen your face before. Are you English?'

'Yes.' Rose glanced back at the school ruefully.

'Aye,' the groundsman nodded. 'Well, the regulations. Only by car. So they know where you are, like. There's something coming.' He stepped back into his battered lodge.

Rose looked beyond the drive and saw a small cab climbing the long stretch of roadway. Coming back from somewhere, anywhere that wasn't here, she thought. The heavy gates buzzed noisily and swung open; Rose moved wearily to the side. As the cab rolled past, she saw a row of three girls sitting in the back – shining hair, shopping bags and white smiles.

Run, she thought, *run through the gap. He won't be able to catch you. Run to the mainland. Escape.*

No. Rose shook her head, she was more of a fighter than a fugitive. The groundsman reappeared as three seabirds noisily settled on the roof of the gatehouse lodge. In her irritation, Rose's eye caught on something – a moving link across the wildly rural headland on the other side of the peninsula. She squinted and saw exactly what it was – a long string of girls on horseback, looping the gorse bushes as they moved forward in a chain. Snug grey capes around their shoulders, riding crops by their side, grey velvet helmets catching the sunlight.

'The girls are allowed to leave?' Rose heard herself shriek with the wind.

He turned to follow her gaze. 'That's an activity, you know.

Otherwise it's only the Upper Sixth, some days. Get that cab number, but I warn you, it's over two hours to Edinburgh.'

Rose felt deflated and she couldn't hide it from the groundsman. 'I just wanted to go for a walk, to the village.'

'Here, what's your name?'

'It's Rose. I teach Classics.'

'Why don't you try the beach? It'll be a bit rough today, though, with the wind.'

'Yes. That's fine,' Rose said quickly. 'How do I get down there?'

'The walkway's a bit tricky where the handrail's missing, mind – but there's your tunnel.'

'Tunnel?'

'Your tunnel that runs from the school to the beach. A postern; they say William Wallace once used it.'

'Oh, really?' Rose nodded eagerly. 'How do I get there?'

'Don't know. That's not our area.'

'Whose area is it?'

'The porter fellas, I reckon. Couldn't tell you.' He shook his head darkly. 'Look, I don't go up to the school. None of us do. It's a terrible place, but of course you know that.'

Rose drew back. 'What on earth do you mean?'

'You know what I mean.' He pushed his beanie hat further up his head as he looked warily back at the lodge. 'Especially since that girl died.'

Rose's breath caught in her throat. 'A girl *died*?'

'Aye.' The groundsman rubbed his rough chin with his fingers.

'When? What happened?'

He didn't reply; the noise of the wind seemed to roll between them. Rose pulled at her cuffs as her thoughts ran wild. 'I've heard nothing – when was this?'

'Last year, it was,' he replied uneasily, 'You didn't know?'

'No. What happened?'

'You're new. I don't—'

'What happened?' she forced.

'Something to do with . . .' He paused, not looking at her, choosing his words with care. 'She was ill. There was a doctor at the last minute. Of course, they told us lot nothing about it.'

Rose's thoughts tripped over themselves with shock. 'My God. Why didn't she go to hospital?' The groundsman said nothing; Rose's eyes didn't leave his face. 'And she died? Why wasn't it in the newspapers?'

'I woulda thought that you could tell me that. You're the one on the inside.' He motioned towards at the school building, his face twisted in resentment.

Rose didn't answer. Her ears were starting to ring again. With the cold or with alarm, she wasn't sure. She said goodbye to the groundsman, who nodded back in his shambling manner.

She didn't once look at the sea on her brisk return, those words turning around in her mind.

A girl died here.

Surely the man had misunderstood, an exaggerated rumour perhaps? Rose shook her head, forcing herself to stow that away for now. She had too many other things on her mind. She could already see her weekend spent with piles of work spilling over her blanketed legs, pages stamped with the stain of her drained teacups. But she would ask for the cab company's phone number, and – if she dared – the way to the tunnel to the beach.

Rose was late, and she was never late. She climbed the stairs with her anxiety weighing her down; she just had to get to her classroom and teach the Upper Sixth. They would command her attention, forcing her mind away from the student who claimed she'd manhandled her; from the police statement she'd been called on to write; from the death of a girl and its subsequent cover-up; from her predecessor who seemed to hover over everything like a ghost.

'I'm sorry I'm late, girls.'

As Rose walked into her classroom she sensed something wrong, something odd about the girls sitting there so stiff and obedient. The glow of the morning light gave Rose no relief after the stone darkness of the school's lower floors; the room felt strange, as if hers and not hers. And then it hit her: a new Sixth had been added to the row of five.

'Bethany,' Rose managed. For a moment she'd stopped breathing.

'Yes, I'm here, I've returned.' The girl's eyes were fixed on the desk. 'I quit Classical Civilisation last year, but I'm back now.'

The other Sixths' faces were twisted with discomfort and disgust as Bethany stretched her long fingers over a pile of books on her desk. Rose looked at those fingers too, before glancing across at her bureau, at the books in disarray – realising which ones Bethany had taken. She glanced up at her piece of volcanic rock, her skin prickling with fury.

Rose kept her voice steady. 'Bethany, this is very unexpected.'

'I didn't think it would be a problem.' Bethany's voice came out thin and strained. 'I've missed this class.'

'Does anybody know you are here?' Rose asked, thinking immediately of Vivien and her censure. *Please do not speak to the girl or approach her; it will stand against you;* and then worse – *teenage girls have their peculiarities.*

'I've told my housemistress, that's the done thing. She thought it was a very good idea,' Bethany answered fluidly, without looking up. 'Might boost my scholastic options, she said.'

Rose narrowed her eyes. 'This is not a good idea, Bethany, given what you have said about me.'

'That's entirely separate.' Bethany's voice stayed low. 'I don't want to be in C Pathway anymore, and this might change that.'

Dulcie cut in: 'That's nonsense, Bethany, and you know it. It's already been decided for you!'

'I can change their minds,' Bethany shot back.

'Your father's mind, perhaps, but not the Headmaster's!'

Rose looked from Dulcie to Bethany, suddenly feeling an inexplicable sting of pity for the girl. She surprised herself by saying, 'If you wish to learn, Bethany, then you would be welcome here. But I will have to check with the Headmaster.'

Bethany looked up, her face flooded with a relief that made Rose wince.

'So, in the meantime, can I stay?'

Rose checked the discomfort across the other girls' faces and injected some authority into her voice. 'I'm not sure, Bethany. You will have to retract your allegation against me – and halt the investigation if you wish to be in my presence.'

'I can't.' Bethany shook her head and her long hair shivered around her shoulders. 'It's too late for that.'

'Then you must leave.'

'No.' Bethany's translucent eyes flashed at Rose. 'Please, I beg you.'

Rose hesitated, more from panic than anything else – she didn't know how to address this properly, so that Vivien would see her side. She rearranged her features to project a control she did not feel.

'For today, then. But you must remember that this is my classroom. It abides by my rules.' Rose could hardly believe her own words. 'You may borrow those books, but do not touch anything on my bureau again.'

'Thank you.'

Dulcie tutted loudly, pressing her hands around her bodice, brushing her hair away from her shoulders as if to be rid of something. Her searing blue dress outshone the others in their pastel silks – but Bethany, in her usual grey, seemed to draw the energy of the room.

'This isn't your book, anyway. It's Jane's. So I *can* use it.' An ugly smile played about Bethany's lips. 'We did *Oedipus* with Jane. It's an excellent play, I've missed it.'

Bethany's words seemed to crash into Rose's ears, but she couldn't recover fast enough. Instead, Dulcie wheeled around to Bethany and said what Rose could not:

'How dare you, Bethany? How could you?'

'How dare I what?'

'Use her first name like that?' Dulcie's mouth puckered. 'Her name was "Madam".'

'She always said I could.' Bethany pressed Jane's book against her chest. 'She was kind like that . . .'

Rose shook her head senselessly, remembering that wretched handkerchief in the drawer downstairs marked 'BdV', and Vivien's words about Bethany's inappropriate attachment to a previous member of staff.

'You're a disgrace, for heaven's sake,' Dulcie spat at Bethany. 'What are you *really* doing here?'

Astonished by the confirmation of her fears, Rose didn't know how to interrupt.

'*She* said I was welcome!' said Bethany, pointing at Rose.

'Does Clarissa know you've come back in here?' Dulcie's hands were clenched into dainty fists. Tash and Lex shrank back between the two girls. 'If she finds out—'

'I'm not frightened of you, Dulcie,' Bethany sneered, 'or your darling Clarissa – even if she is head girl.'

'Ladies.' Rose stood in front of Dulcie's desk, urging herself forward. 'Please, let's get on.'

'Madam,' Dulcie snarled up at Rose, 'are you going to let her speak so casually about the previous Latin Madam?'

'No, Dulcie.' Rose watched Bethany out of the corner of her eye, adding carefully, 'But I think it's best left alone at this moment.'

Dulcie looked around wildly for the other girls' acknowledgement, but their eyes were pointing away in avoidance, pairs of arms folded together.

'Girls. You can't speak to each other like this, and I believe,' Rose's nerves caught in her voice as she once again remembered Vivien's instructions, 'you are discussing a matter that doesn't belong in this classroom.'

'Oh please, Madam,' Dulcie muttered crossly, 'spare us.'

'Understand that I am not taking sides here. At all. We need to get on.' Rose strengthened her voice to counteract her shaking hands. 'Let's do a written exercise. I wanted to talk about this essay question – why the play is called *Antigone* and not *Creon*. I'll put some pointers on the board . . .'

'What will *I* do?'

Rose hesitated at the blackboard. 'Bethany, why don't you start reading *Antigone* quietly?'

'Yes, and perhaps if there are things I don't understand,' the girl suggested carefully, 'you and I can have extra sessions?'

'No, Bethany, no!' Rose exclaimed, her hand tearing the chalk across the board. 'I'm certainly not available for that.'

'But how else will I catch up?' Bethany protested.

'I'll have to refer that to the head of Languages,' Rose spoke at the board, 'and the Headmaster.'

Dulcie leaned across the desks with a jagged elbow. 'Look, Bethany, don't think we can't see what you're doing. Especially after you've accused Madam of hurting you. We don't mind this Madam, so if you're going to give her a hard time, you can just shove off.' Her chest heaved with exasperation; she pointed a manicured finger. 'And if you make this like before, I'll push *you* down the stairs this time.'

Bethany's face fell. 'I didn't mean to—'

'Girls!' Rose turned around, her face heavy with trepidation. 'Fresh sheet of paper. Compare the two characters, Antigone and Creon. We will work through your ideas afterwards. Now, get on. Bethany, start reading.'

Rose tried not to notice Bethany smiling behind the pages of her book. She didn't want to consider why the girl was there – did she really want to make amends, or was this another tactic to derail Rose? At least this time there were witnesses.

Bethany's deranged smile lasted throughout the lesson, punctured by Tash's nervous glances across her peers, and Dulcie's agitated frown as she scratched out her efforts across the page. Rose stayed at her bureau, planning a well-articulated note to the Headmaster.

At lunch Rose thought she'd timed her entrance to the dining hall impeccably, but she found herself queuing behind the girls at the dessert section of the canteen, resenting the pointed gazes in her direction.

Rose had crossed the dining hall from a side door. She still wasn't used to the enormity of the space, from the hellish racket of the girls' chatter against the clang of cutlery on porcelain, to the high wooden ceiling hanging perilously over them all. There was the uniform grace of the Sixth dining tables: delicate fingers on napkins unfolded across laps, forks laid aside, knives poised over plates. Then the others: the rabble of the Intermediate tables, the excited shout of the Juniors reaching across their slopping meals, and the Asian girls scattered across their odd and isolated pair of tables. Rose didn't like to see their segregation, and chided herself for not yet daring to question it, or find out why none of them had crossed the threshold of her classroom.

Rose's thoughts ticked over quietly, ever preoccupied with Bethany; she wondered whether the girl would call a halt to the investigation, or come up with a new claim. At least she'd dropped her note for the Headmaster with the secretaries.

He was there, in the dining hall. She'd seen him seated with some of the Upper Sixth, his smile broad and holding the whole table. Anthony was sitting opposite him, one leg astride the bench, his thick sandy hair stippled in the light, smiling along with them. The girls were tight in their bodices, hands propping up their chins, eyes bright and listening. In the middle was Clarissa, with her shimmering auburn hair and her chestnut-brown velvet headband. These girls, then, were worth the Headmaster's time, and Rose wasn't? Was it the investigation that kept him so distant?

In the canteen Rose distracted herself by staring at the card stand next to the pudding trays, detailing the nutritional value, calories and 'Allowance Number' of this option. She frowned at the card, never having really paid attention before. The same information stood next to every meal choice around the canteen. Rose squinted at each of them.

There was a clang of a heavy spoon scraping a dish; a Sixth

in front of Rose was scooping out the sweeter pieces of fruit, leaving clean the splodges of meringue and cream.

'Sorry, but can you leave some of that for others?'

'Pardon, Madam?' The girl turned around. 'What others?'

'Me, others?' Rose's cheeks flushed. 'Look, don't take all the fruit for yourself. It's a complete pudding, not just bits.'

'I'm not quite finished, Madam.'

'Alice,' a thick male voice intruded, 'that's no way to treat a member of staff.'

'Oh.' The girl moved aside, opening herself up to the other teacher. 'Good afternoon, Sir, would you like some pudding?'

Anthony nodded towards Rose. 'Where are your manners, Alice? Have you forgotten them since Juniors?'

'But,' Alice continued, 'manners don't apply to the Madams, Sir? Isn't it only for the men and the Sirs?'

'Nonsense, Alice,' Anthony answered hastily. 'Men and women deserve equal respect.' He placed a firm hand on the girl's arm. 'Madam and *all* the other female staff are your superiors.'

'If you say so, Sir.' The Sixth dropped her bowl on the tray with a crack and shook her hair out.

'Apologise to Madam, Alice.'

Rose clutched her tray with dismay. 'Oh, no, that's not . . . entirely necessary.'

The girl rounded on Rose with a poisonous look. 'I apologise, Madam. I hope you'll excuse me.'

'Well done, Alice.' Anthony let go of the girl's forearm and took a step towards Rose, scratching the stubble lining his chin. Her face must have betrayed her thoughts, because he added, 'That was terrible, I know. She's just confused. It's your being new, Rose – and of course the special nature of your probationary period.'

'She's probably heard about this allegation against me,' Rose garbled, 'And you don't need to rescue me, you know.'

'No,' Anthony's face fell a little, 'I do know that. Here.'

Anthony passed Rose an empty bowl, touching her hand with his fingers. Rose took it, glancing away from him. 'Thanks all the same. You'd better get back to the Headmaster. You both seemed quite busy.'

'Busy?' Anthony frowned.

'It's fine.' Rose replaced the bowl and moved out of the canteen, her tray bumping against a girl's back as she did so. With a drop of dread, Rose recognised those black straggles of hair. She sucked in her breath as Bethany whipped around.

'Oh, it's you,' Bethany said with no trace of surprise, her pale eyes entirely opaque. 'Barging into me again. Careful, there's people about.'

'Bethany,' Rose heard a growl in her own voice. 'I was kind to you today. Do *not* speak to me outside the classroom, please.'

'Is that what you're eating?' Bethany leaned over Rose's lunch, her hair dangling into the gravy. 'Better be careful or Matron will count this against your allowance.'

Rose pulled her tray back as Bethany straightened up, tugging her hair behind her ears. A drip of gravy smeared across the grey silk chest of Bethany's dress. Rose glanced at it as she stepped away.

Clarissa streamed past her as she went. She was aiming for Bethany, already pointing at the stain across her dress. Rose couldn't hear their words, but Bethany's head hung low as Clarissa's voice rose with an energetic reprimand.

Rose sat herself on the furthest section of the staff tables, alone, and staring down at the meal now stained by her tormentor. Would Rose ever be rid of her – or at the very least, understand her actions? Bethany seemed to be living some parallel life to the other Sixths, a destructive shadow in harsh relief against her peers' daily glory. On some different 'Pathway' – whatever that meant.

Rose could feel Anthony's stare from the other side of the hall, the crease in his forehead growing deeper. She didn't look up.

Above the main double-door entrance to the dining hall stood another portrait of the Founder – the severe-looking William Hope dressed in scholar's robes, with one hand flat against his heart. Rose's eye caught a small link of Juniors wandering towards the doorway to leave. As they passed underneath the painting, they drew out the skirts of their white dresses, gazing up at the Founder and curtseying low.

'All right, ladies.' Rose took a moment to fortify herself against the Fourths. 'Quiet, please. Let's move on to the next task; look at the translation in front of you. Here Queen Dido is getting ready to go hunting with Aeneas. She's clothed in splendour. In Book One, remember, she was compared to the goddess Diana when she showed Aeneas around her kingdom of . . . ?'

The girls remained silent. Rose watched many fingers tear agitatedly at the paper edges in front of them. Four weeks in, and they'd given up pushing her around with their taunts – which meant that only she did the talking now. Rose looked at her ceramic owl on the windowsill for encouragement.

'Dido's kingdom. Anyone?'

At the edge of the classroom, Daisy swung her dark curtain of hair forward. 'Somewhere in North Africa, wasn't it, Madam?'

'Yes.' Rose's eyes flicked to the girl. 'Carthage. Well done, Daisy. Write that down, girls. I'll put it on the board.'

The silence resumed as Rose scratched out the name with her chalk. At the front, pale little Nessa hadn't yet bothered to write anything, and was staring into the space in front of her. Rose moved forward to stand in that space, her voice stronger this time.

'So, Dido is compared to Diana—'

'Diana. What's she the goddess of, again?' Daisy asked, tugging at the badges on her lapel.

'Hunting,' Rose said carefully. 'Thank you again, Daisy. Hand up next time. Let's at least try to stick to the rules, even if we're not reaching our aims.'

'Oh Madam, did you say hunting?' Freddie's clipped voice came in. She raised her ivory face to Rose; Nessa beside her looked up too. 'We hunt at home. Some people are against it. Are you?'

Rose looked at Freddie's tawny eyes narrowed with a challenge. 'Put your hand up if you want to contribute, Freddie.'

'But why is the Diana comparison important, Madam?' Daisy interrupted, her hand waving in the air.

'Well, Daisy.' Rose looked across at Daisy gratefully. 'Firstly, Diana is a goddess, a virgin goddess.'

'But Dido has a dead husband,' Josie chuckled loudly from the back, her thick black eyebrows raised, 'so she's hardly a virgin, Madam.'

Rose hesitated, momentarily stunned at Josie's unexpected grasp of the topic. 'Yes . . . Dido is a widow. Good. Hand up next time.' So Josie had been paying attention, Rose thought. Were they all paying attention? 'But this is symbolism. It's a huge compliment for Dido to be compared to a goddess . . . even though she's probably *more interesting* than the goddess Diana.'

At the front, Nessa's freckled face twisted up to Rose. 'What do you mean, how can a queen be more interesting than a goddess?'

'Well.' Rose hesitated, noticing the many faces that lifted to hear her answer. 'The goddess Diana exists in Greek and Roman society as an ideal for young women. She's twinned with Apollo, who was a model for young men. So us ladies,' she said, sweeping the entire class in with her arm, 'get animals and nature, a bit of running around – and the young men get art, music, poetry, the *sun* for God's sake!' Rose dropped her arm. 'So, yes, Dido's got plenty more going on if you ask me.'

'Madam,' Freddie pushed her red curls behind her shoulder; the rest of the girls seemed to wait for her to speak. 'You talk as if you know these goddesses personally.'

'Well,' Rose began as she wandered over to her chair to sit down, 'when you study all of these characters as I have, you sort of try to find the things that speak to you. We haven't come very far from the ancient world, and some of the ancient women were really fantastic . . .' Rose looked askance at Freddie as the rest of the class listened. 'I mean, there's—'

'My mother's name was Diana, Madam,' Daisy called out.

'That's lovely, Daisy.' Rose stood up as the class tittered at the outburst. She was grateful for the interruption – Freddie was still looking at her with those bright, analytical eyes.

'And there's our royal princess, of course,' Nessa added. 'Is she related to this goddess in any way, Madam?'

'No, Nessa, I don't think so.' Rose saw the rest of the class shoot each other looks at Nessa's daft comment, Josie's mouth was gaping open with glee. Rose added kindly, 'But it's a nice thought.'

'Dido, Diana, Venus,' Nessa smiled weakly, nudging Freddie next to her, 'I can't keep up with you, Madam.'

'Yes, quite,' Freddie said loudly, tilting back in her seat. 'One powerful queen, another tricky goddess, why's it always women with you, Madam? In History we're always learning about men. *They're* the ones that make the decisions, that do the important things.'

'Oh, I disagree, Frederica.' Rose stepped towards the board, annoyed in spite of herself. 'Women are usually the lifeblood behind the important things. Often they'll be the characters moving everything forward. In these stories, here, in *this* classroom. You'll see.'

'It's Freddie, Madam.' A thin line dented the girl's forehead, her mouth tight. 'Not Frederica.'

'Oh yes, of course,' Rose gave a firm nod. 'So. Dido's appearance before the hunt – let's read it again, and make a note of anything striking.'

But while the rest of the girls leaned over their pages again, Freddie didn't. 'Madam, is it true that you knew Bethany before you came here?'

Rose felt something electric move through her, and answered quickly, 'Not at all.' Her eyes stayed on the page. 'No. And I'd prefer to focus on what we're studying, please. Can anyone spot an adjective and its counterpart in the Latin?'

To Rose's relief, Freddie bowed her head to the page. At least two girls were about to raise their hands. Daisy's arm was already in the air.

The next morning the Headmaster sent his response via the secretaries: the incident had been noted, Bethany wouldn't be attending any more of Rose's classes – but the investigation was still active.

At the beginning of break Rose was trying to leave the

common room just as a crowd of male teachers filtered through the door. She seemed to be forever getting in people's way: never alone in body, always alone in mind. She moved to the side.

A housemistress was considering Rose from across the wide room. She was wearing a patterned dress with slightly outdated leg-o-mutton sleeves that drew Rose's eye. It took her a moment to realise that the woman was striding towards her purposefully.

'You're the new Latin Madam?'

'Yes.' Rose stiffened. 'My name is Rose.'

'And you teach Alexandra Coryn?'

'Alexandra . . .' Rose thought about it. 'That's Lex, isn't it?'

'No, please don't call her by that ridiculous name.' The housemistress's mouth twitched. 'It's just a notion of hers.'

'It's what she wants to be called.'

The housemistress narrowed her eyes at Rose. 'Alexandra is what her parents would prefer. Anyhow, I checked the latest grade for her essay, and I wanted to let you know that you can't mark her that low. It isn't acceptable.'

'I don't know what you mean.'

'Her first essay for this term. You marked it very low, she showed me.'

Rose was baffled. 'Yes, it was badly done. Ever since the return from London, she's achieved very little.'

'If you amend her grade, and see that her half-term report is positive, then I will ensure that she reacts accordingly. This final year is crucial for the girls.'

'Shouldn't it be the other way around?' Rose's cheeks flushed in spite of herself. 'I'll grade her higher when her work improves?'

The housemistress drew herself up straight. 'You have my word that she will improve.'

'Surely this is an academic matter?'

'Alexandra's parents are particularly concerned about the situation – her brother has been such a disappointment to them, you see. She rather represents the family.'

Rose felt her voice rise. 'Her brother? What on earth does that have to do with this?'

'Oh, Mary,' Frances suddenly appeared; touching the woman's elbow, she cut in, 'it's all me, I'm doing the head of department stuff for now, and I told Rose she should judge the girls harshly when she first arrived. Get them to pull their socks up a bit. My fault.'

Rose turned to Frances, amazed at the lie.

'I see.' The housemistress glanced down at Frances's creased dress, then up at her face. 'Thank you, Frances. Well, see that it's sorted in time for half-term.' She nodded at Rose. 'And if there's still an issue, put it in the Punishment Book.'

'Punishment Book?' asked Rose.

'Yes.'

'What,' Rose wanted to laugh madly, 'so they can write lines?'

The housemistress tutted. 'You should know better than to make fun, Madam, what with your being in trouble. And in your first term too.'

A tinge of shame crept into Rose's face. The woman saw it as she moved away, satisfied.

'I'm so sorry.' Frances was already rolling her eyes. 'Mary's the housemistress of Honour, one of the Sixth houses, and they can be rather . . . forbidding.'

'I wasn't making fun.' Rose's voice was bitter.

'Don't worry,' Frances continued. 'You don't need to have anything to do with her, for now. She doesn't teach anything academic, just pastoral.'

Rose followed Mary with her eyes as she considered again that strange use of 'pastoral'. She hoped that her first duty in the boarding house might explain it. Glancing back at Frances wearily, Rose sighed. 'I suppose it's good for the girls to have so many women about. I was taught mostly by men when I was at school.'

'We do need more women in an academic capacity. That's why it's wonderful to have you here.' Frances turned to face Rose. 'Are you all right?'

'Yes,' Rose answered; but even to her own ears, her answer was hollow.

'Look, why don't we have drinks this evening?' Frances was studying Rose under her white-blonde eyebrows. 'I'll bring some wine round to your flat, what do you think? You must be bursting with questions.'

'Oh, thank you,' Rose felt herself wilt with relief, 'that would be lovely.'

6.

Frances thrust two bottles of wine into Rose's chest.

'Congratulations on finishing week four! It's a strange kind of anniversary, but you know . . .' Rose laughed gratefully, feeling the hard glass of the bottles.

'It's a Merlot and a Pinot Grigio.' Frances kicked her shoes off at the door and ran her hands through her hair, her blue eyes bright. 'One each. Wasn't sure which you'd prefer.'

Within minutes they were both settled across the odd pairing of Rose's modern armchair and the school's stuffed sofa, glasses of wine cupped in their hands. Rose chose the red, saying that she regretted her flat being less welcoming than she'd have liked, seeing afresh the rickety floorboards and her small, faded picture frames. Before Frances's arrival she'd rewashed some dusty wine glasses and rubbed them dry with one of her mother's second-hand dishcloths.

'Goodness, no,' Frances lifted her glass to her lips, 'your flat is a lot nicer than mine. Will you work in House Prudence underneath? I do two nights a week in Temperance.'

'I think so,' Rose answered. 'They've said I will eventually help out the odd night.'

'But you'd rather not,' Frances smiled. She poured herself a second glass.

'No, it's just,' Rose continued, warmed by the wine, 'boarding seems so foreign to me. It belongs to children's stories, to Charles Dickens, you know.' Rose tapped at her glass nervously. 'A lot around this place feels wrong to me. I'm probably better sticking to the classroom.'

'Nonsense, working in a boarding house can be fun – as a tutor you just dip in and out, get to know the girls in another way.' Frances put her bottle of wine on the floor and tucked her feet underneath her. 'You'll be great. We all have to try new things.'

'I suppose so. Here's my first question – why do the boarding houses have those obscure names?'

'Named after the Founder's six daughters,' Frances replied. 'Four combined Junior and Intermediate houses, then they split and move into two bigger houses in Sixth.'

'And remind me, the Juniors are . . .'

'There are three years of Juniors: Firsts, Seconds, Thirds. Then it gets serious in Intermediates: the Fourths and Fifths. Those two years are important, from the age of fourteen to sixteen – they're no longer children, they're young women. Then Lower and Upper Sixth are all about refinement.' Frances gave a small bow of her head.

'Right.' Rose frowned. 'And Lord Hope named his daughters things like Honour, Chastity and Temperance?'

'He was an eccentric,' Frances allowed.

'I'll say. Is "eccentric" just an excuse for toffs to do bizarre things?'

'If that's a real question, then you've come to the wrong place.' Frances's eyes crinkled into a smile.

'Oh dear, maybe I have! This term is certainly not going how I thought it would.' Rose hoisted her legs over the armrest of her chair. She was pleased to be able to let her guard down, even if Frances was her superior.

'Well, it'll all be sorted, just you wait. Then there's lots to look forward to, especially after half-term – Open Day, then Christmas. Things ought to be better by then.'

There was a pause as Rose contemplated the uncertainty of this. Frances swirled her white wine around in the glass before pulling it to her lips.

'So, Rose,' Frances started up again. 'Inevitable question – how's your love life?'

'Oh.' Rose hesitated. 'Non-existent?'

'Really? At twenty-six?'

Rose scoffed. 'Well. There was a guy where I used to work, but it was mostly in my head.'

'In your head?'

'Yes. Haven't you ever had that?' Rose laughed; she was happy to acknowledge the truth of it from this distance.

'No,' Frances said firmly, pouring herself another glass.

'Well, I'm past all that now. What about you? Love life?'

'I've never had a serious relationship,' said Frances, sitting up properly in her seat, 'and I'm almost in my forties.'

'You don't look it.'

'Wedded to the job, you could say. And you're lying. *You're* still in your prime.'

God, Rose thought.

Frances seemed to notice. 'What?'

'I'm sorry, it's nothing.' Rose widened her eyes in exasperation. 'Just the comments I've heard here. *In my prime. A fine specimen*. Sometimes I feel like a—'

'Do you mean the old rascals in the common room?'

'Yes,' Rose nodded. 'But not just them. The way everyone speaks here. I know this place is posh, but it's . . . more than that. Outdated, I suppose. Why is it okay for people to speak like that to women – or to anyone?'

Frances hesitated.

'I mean,' Rose was measuring Frances's reaction, 'my mother is a raging feminist, an activist really. Or used to be. So it's been thrust down my throat my whole life.'

'Really!' Frances tilted her head sharply. 'And did any of it rub off?'

'I've always been slightly wary, I think . . . Mum was very forceful when I was growing up. She always claimed that as a baby I suckled on her boob while she marched with the Dagenham women. There were meetings at the house, *Spare Rib* was delivered every week. It's a feminist magazine,' Rose added, seeing Frances's questioning look. 'Don't you know it?'

'No.'

'Well, it is,' Rose frowned, buried in thought. 'My mother spent her whole life rallying against the patriarchy. Me and Dad just stayed out of it. She's calmed down now, with her illness . . . And it's the nineties, the second wave of feminism is over. But I don't actually think it's right, to speak about women the way I've heard here. I don't like it at all.'

Frances was looking away. 'Did you put that on your application, that your mother is a feminist?'

'No, why would I do that?'

'I suppose you wouldn't.' Frances's face became heavy. 'And she has multiple sclerosis?'

'Oh.' Rose was taken aback. 'Yes, she does. Does . . . everybody know, then?'

'Emma mentioned it, I hope you don't mind. And how is she?'

'She's fine.' Rose gazed at a spot on the floor. 'She's deteriorating, but she's battled it this long. People live with it for years . . . I can't think about it. She's all I've got.'

Frances nodded at her wine glass. 'Both my parents are dead.'

'Oh.' Rose looked up. 'I'm so sorry, Frances.'

'No, no, best place for them,' Frances answered blankly.

Rose searched for something to say. 'Well, it can be difficult. I'm glad I've still got Mum, even if I infuriate her regularly. I'm more like my father. Dad was great but distant – we did share some academic things, but then he was busy with his students . . .' Rose went on, her thoughts slightly confused. 'It wasn't easy for us after he died. I do feel very . . . indebted to her. Even in my twenties, I can't bear to let her down.' Rose shifted in her seat. 'But then again, I still wear lipstick every day to spite her. It's always been . . .'

'Yes, I understand,' Frances said in a muddled voice, nursing her wine glass. 'Parents are hard. You must miss your mum. Well, you've got me now, at least.' Frances turned to Rose with a renewed smile.

'That's kind.'

Frances refilled her glass and Rose glanced at her own; she was still on her first. Frances was talking again. 'We should do this regularly. Let's invite Anthony next time.'

Rose hesitated. 'Anthony?'

'Yes, we could learn from him. You know, I had a meeting with him today. It's funny. Even though I'm his superior, he's treated much better than me. Not his fault. He never gets himself into any scrapes,' Frances added derisively. 'The girls adore him too. He and I – there's hardly anyone else of our generation here. Let's include him.'

'At your place,' Rose said quickly, unable to hide the flush across her cheeks. 'Not mine. Or in the village, away from here?'

'Ha!' shouted Frances. 'That never happens. Put that out of your mind now.' She kicked her feet onto the coffee table as she swung her glass to her mouth. Rose looked at the damp blackness on the feet of Frances's tights. Turning away, she asked, 'Shall I put on some music?'

'Pardon?' Frances was genuinely shocked. 'How?'

'I have a stereo.' Rose gestured to her small oblong machine tucked underneath her shelves. 'And the most ridiculous amount of tapes. What do you want to listen to?'

'Oh.' Frances shook her head vaguely. 'You choose.'

'Do you like Queen? In honour of dear Freddie.' Rose bent to rifle through her cassettes as the wind rattled at the windows. Both women turned to look. The night seemed black and unforgiving, so different from the warmth inside. Rose put a Queen album in the player. As the music played Rose hummed along with the tune, just to stop herself from singing out loud.

'What is this again?' Frances asked.

'It's Queen. Don't you like them? Shall I change it?'

'No need.'

Rose tapped the armrest of her chair. 'I wish I'd been at Live Aid. I was at university. We all watched from a friend's house. I phoned in, gave what I could. How about you?'

Frances stood up and moved out of the little room in one movement. It was so abrupt, Rose didn't know how to react. She waited, wondering if she'd said something wrong.

The toilet flushed a minute later and Frances reappeared brightly, her bare legs creamy white under her dress. Rose wondered briefly where Frances had put her discarded tights.

'Sorry, I drink a lot. Goes straight through me. These two bottles are just part of my own personal supply. I drink it like water.'

'Really? But you're so . . . athletic.'

'I exercise a lot, it's a discipline.'

'Oh,' said Rose. 'Well, I can't really handle my drink either. I'm a lightweight. I only drink socially.'

'Dear me, how sad for you.'

Rose poured out a second glass, noticing Frances's almost-empty bottle.

'Tell me a bit more about yourself, Frances. How did you happen to come here?'

'No, no,' replied Frances in a cheery voice. 'I'm your head of faculty – you are the one that has to talk to me. I demand questions! What's been on your mind?'

'Okay,' stumbled Rose, her eyes roving around the room. 'Well, there are a few things that I'm battling with. But one thing in particular – can I ask?'

Frances nodded. Rose leaned forward and placed her glass firmly on the floorboards.

'Is it true that a girl died last year?'

'How do you know that?' Frances's blue eyes flashed with alarm.

'One of the groundsmen mentioned it.'

Frances sat up. 'It wasn't his right to.'

'Frances,' Rose propped her elbows up on her knees, her face growing warm, 'that's not the point. Did a girl actually die? And why on earth wasn't it in the papers?'

Frances grimaced into her glass. 'Yes, a girl did pass away. We aren't supposed to discuss it.'

'Frances,' Rose said wildly, 'surely you can understand that that's wrong.'

Frances looked straight at Rose. 'Not at all *wrong*. It was a sad affair, but it's over now.'

'There must be more to it than that.'

'There was nothing untoward.' Frances shook her head. 'She became ill, and the on-call doctor performed an operation on her in the sanatorium, but she didn't make it.' She took a large swig of her drink. 'Students died like that all the time in the past, of diphtheria and epidemics and things like that – haven't you ever read *Jane Eyre*?'

'Frances, this is not the nineteenth century. The groundsman seemed to think there was something wrong about it.'

'Did he?' Frances's eyes flashed again over her glass of wine.

'Yes,' Rose insisted.

'I don't know why. The sanatorium has two large lead-lined rooms underground, to store bodies, you know, for that purpose.'

Rose shuddered involuntarily as she processed Frances's words, but forced herself to press on. 'So, there was no connection to my predecessor here?'

'To Jane? No, of course not.' Frances became a little flustered. 'Why would there be? Your imagination is wild, Rose.'

Rose tried again. 'I have another question.'

But Frances's face had clouded over. She slid to the floor and kneeled her way over to Rose's bookcases next to the empty fireplace, pulling out a book on Pompeii. 'Curiosity killed the cat, you know,' she finally said, thumbing through the large hardback.

Rose wasn't put off. 'What actually happened to my predecessor? It sounds like the circumstances of her departure were . . . unusual.'

'Good old Jane.' Frances thumped the book down on the floor and stretched back to reach for her wine glass. Rose noticed the muscly strain of her arm as Frances took a long sip. Then she said, 'Jane was unhappy, she was overweight, and a faded beauty.'

Rose laughed, appalled. 'What does being overweight, or beautiful, have to do with anything?'

'Self-regard is important to the Headmaster.' Frances shrugged wearily. 'She tried to stand against some of the decisions here. Just like you're driving at now, although you've no idea what you're up against. They pushed her out. So let her be a warning to you.'

Rose was affronted. 'I'm not trying to stand against anything. I'm trying to fit in.'

'Well, good, I'm glad.'

'She was close to Bethany, wasn't she?'

'Yes.' Frances's face was heavy again. 'Jane got very upset about the girl, too involved. They were over-attached to each other.'

'I knew it.' Rose closed her eyes at the confirmation. 'And now Bethany is looking for some strange connection to me.'

'It was a terrible time.' Frances was shaking her head. 'Not at all *appropriate* for the girls to witness.'

'Bethany frightens me,' Rose said involuntarily. 'They both do.'

But Frances wasn't listening as she flipped the book over, focusing on a photograph of a mosaic decorating the back cover. 'They like role models, here. They chose you.'

Rose moved her glass closer to her chest. 'I'm no role model, Frances – the girls look at me and talk to me like I'm a piece of dirt. And now this terrifying allegation?'

'I'm trying to support you there.'

Rose leaned forward, almost pleading. 'Have you heard anything about it – from Vivien, maybe?'

Frances turned to Rose. 'Has Bethany come to any lessons since?'

'No. She's been banned.'

'There you are then.' Frances left the book on the floor and lifted herself up to the cushions of the sofa. Rose watched her, worrying about the splinters of the floorboards, the dust from the rug across Frances's knees.

'Look, Rose,' Frances sat down stiffly, 'as your head of faculty, I'm your champion. Okay?'

'Okay.'

'As I've said, your focus here will be narrow, particularly this term.' Frances's eyes were a thorough blue as she searched Rose's face. 'But once you're in, you're in. The Headmaster has his own agenda and the school is a busy one. Just work on your classes, and keep your head down.'

'Right.'

'The girls only really care about their Value. You'll see when we write reports.'

'Their value?' Rose frowned. 'As in morals, principles?'

'Yes, their "Value" – their grades, their achievements.' Frances made quotation marks in the air, swooping up her glass from the floor. Rose watched the white wine slip heavily from side to side as Frances ran her hand through her wiry hair. 'Look. While you're settling in, let's have regular meetings.'

'Okay,' said Rose, gratefully.

'Although,' Frances pulled a pained face, 'my timetable is quite tight.'

'We could have a weekly lunch?'

'Yes, perfect. Let's do that.'

Frances was so deliciously drunk when she finally stood up to leave that she staggered over the arm of the sofa. Rose watched her fall out of her flat's front door and scrape a carpet burn on her bare thigh, her dirty tights crumpled up in one hand. Rose offered to lend an arm and walk Frances back to her own flat, and she agreed, on the condition that Rose didn't come inside and witness the mess.

Of course, Rose still had many questions; and in the following weeks she worked hard to get on top of the school's habits, its timetable and traditions. It was as if she hovered over the workings of the system, locked out, and frightened to fall into the chasm of what didn't yet make sense to her. Rose wondered if she was just being difficult, over-curious, as Frances had said.

Bethany didn't come to any other Sixth lessons, nor did Rose see her around the school. The other girls flatly refused to answer any queries about how the girl was – even the dreamy-eyed Tash bowed her soft head at Rose's questions, Dulcie calling them perverse. It had been four weeks now since the allegation. Rose had been dismayed to receive Vivien's latest update: the region's police constable was comparing Rose's statement against the facts, reading through select student interviews, examining photographs of the pattern of bruises. Rose tried the secretaries, but they only nodded at her curtly: she *could* make an appointment with the Headmaster if she'd like to, but there was no convenient time before the half-term break.

So, she played along, kept her head down and stayed in her classroom-office space. Not that she was having much luck there: her Seconds refused to learn any Latin vocab from week to week, and her Fourths jeered unkindly when Daisy asked for half-term holiday work, even though many of them – particularly Nessa – needed it.

Anthony was continuing his small campaign to make Rose feel welcome, with passing moments in the corridor, and a few lunches. His smile caught her off-guard, and lent a lightness to her day. She enjoyed Anthony's cheering company, his unshakeable dedication to his subject, his infectious good moods – so different from the unpredictable Frances, who could be alternately sympathetic and brittle. Things seemed easier around him; their colleagues were kinder to Rose by the association, even with the stain of Bethany's allegation. Still, Rose found she couldn't entirely be herself around Anthony either. She held herself back, worrying about her feelings running away with her. So much at Caldonbrae Hall seemed uncertain and confusing that Rose was desperate for the half-term break to come. It would be a chance for her to examine things properly, from afar.

On the final Friday before the holiday, Rose had been working late, trawling through the piles of exercise books as the beaming light across her classroom faded softly. She worked better in there than in the office.

With her work finished, Rose wandered back to her flat, holding her breath through the darkness of the Great Stairs. She padded carefully down the steps, feeling her way along the bannister, the scattered rain noisily hitting the glass dome above her. Along the main corridor she passed her hands nervously across the walls, vowing never to leave her classroom so late again.

Finally at the top of the staircase by her flat, Rose saw that somebody was waiting in the narrow passageway. The shape in the darkness turned to greet her.

'Madam?'

Rose blinked.

'Madam, it's me,' a voice said coaxingly, 'it's your Bethany.'

Rose shrank away from her. 'No, no!'

'Is it you, Madam? I came up the back way, like before.' Bethany stepped forward, reaching out a thin arm in supplication. Rose squinted at her, seeing how young she looked, thinner than ever in her pyjamas, her long tendrils of hair falling past her elbows.

'No, Bethany!' Rose remembered herself. 'It's Miss Christie.'

'Madam?' Bethany's voice was muddled, and Rose saw that she was grasping a crumpled letter. 'No! Not you! You're a fraud. You're always getting in the way!' The girl's face convulsed as she stood in the doorway of Rose's flat. '*Where* is Jane? I need her to save me from *them*. They won't tell me where she is!'

'Stop shrieking, Bethany! You'll wake everybody up.' Rose moved forward instinctively.

'Get away from me! Where *is* she?' The girl pressed the letter to her heart. 'She won't answer my letters! They returned this one!'

Rose gripped at the bannister of the stairs, her voice shaking. 'I'm so sorry that she hasn't answered your—'

'What's happened to her?' Bethany drew a thin arm across her chest. 'She can't save me if she's not here. What have they done to her?'

'I don't know, Bethany,' Rose replied desperately. 'I'm so sorry.'

'What have they *done*?'

A shaft of light fell across the passageway; the door opposite Rose was opening.

'For heaven's sake, Bethany.' An old woman appeared, her white hair ruffled and her face misshapen with disapproval. 'You're screaming like a banshee.'

'Matron?' Bethany asked softly, frowning through the dim light. 'Is that you? I was looking for my Jane.'

'Thank God you're here, Matron,' Rose shuddered with relief.

'Absolutely appalling.' The woman turned to Rose accusingly. 'This girl needs care.'

'Matron!' Bethany's voice lifted again. 'What have they done with Jane?'

'Calm down, child.' The matron pulled at her grey towelling dressing grown, marked with the school's emblem. 'You even *look* like a banshee, too, Bethany. You're letting yourself down, you know. Now come here.'

'This is Jane's flat! Not hers!' Bethany twisted her face to Rose. 'Make her go away!'

'Oh dear, Madam.' The matron turned to Rose with knitted eyebrows. 'What *have* you been doing to her?'

'I haven't done anything,' Rose raised her hands. 'She just turned up outside my flat!'

The old woman circled the girl's bony arms with her own, drawing her away from the door. 'I'll take her downstairs. This is her old house, you know.'

'I need Jane. She's the only one who can help me.' Bethany's voice was strained as the crumpled letter slid between her hand and the matron's.

'Not in front of Madam, Bethany. In you go. I'll call from the interphone.'

Bethany shuffled through the matron's door with hunched shoulders. The woman swung back to Rose.

'Now, Madam, I'll give the deputy a ring and she'll come along shortly. She never sleeps, that one. Why are you up so late?'

Rose's voice shook still. 'I've been working in my classroom, I came back a few minutes ago.'

'Thank goodness you'd locked your door, or heaven knows where we'd be. You ought to watch yourself, Madam. Now, off you go to bed.'

There was a final click of the matron's door. But in the darkness Rose still saw Bethany's thin figure spread across her threshold, blocking the way to that haven on the other side, Rose's own pocket of identity within the walls of Hope. But this flat, of course, was Jane's old flat. Jane who had disappeared; whom nobody wanted to talk about – except Bethany. Bethany who now apparently needed to be saved. Rose gave another shudder. The girl was right: she'd taken the woman's job, her role, her flat. Her curse.

7.

The week of half-term flashed by in moments, as if in mockery. Rose soon found herself on the train trundling up to Edinburgh again, her head full of black thoughts in place of those boastful prospectus pictures several weeks before.

In London, Rose had met with a trio of teacher friends who'd moved forward without her, sharing opinions about new films they'd seen, articles they'd read, and new classes they were enjoying. Rose's father had always told her that schools were transient – children adapt, teachers come and go. She hadn't thought that her old friends would move on so quickly and she felt keenly the sting of it.

But Rose had to admit that her mother's new clinic was a marvel. She hadn't prepared herself for the enormous relief at seeing it for herself: the modern open plan of the communal seating areas, the clean pastels of the fabric furniture, the long conservatory and curated gardens. Even the little bedroom Rose's mother had been allocated was neat and welcoming. She was happily very mobile, thanks to a new wheelchair for her weakened legs. Her condition was apparently stable: the nurses had written positive reports full of technical vocabulary Rose didn't fully understand. Regarding her mother at least, Rose was grateful. She told her mother nothing of the investigation or the concerns that pursued her, not wanting them to intrude upon their time together. On the penultimate evening Rose and her mother had even managed to fit in an ecstatic game of Cheat – her mother's favourite – along with an older patient named Gerald.

Rose caught her reflection in the glass of the train window and moved out of the light. During the break she hadn't been able to shake off the edge of Dulcie's voice, or Freddie's mocking stare, or the Seconds' sneers over homework. Or, worst of all, Bethany's haunted face. The girls had followed her through every moment: the spray of a new perfume her friend was using, the face of one of the waitresses in a local pub, the turn of a dress in a clothes shop as she wandered past.

And into a London library where Rose had looked up news cuttings about Caldonbrae Hall. After an hour of reading insignificant announcements, she'd given up. The school's name only whispered across the newspaper pages: an alumna's husband's business success; the Headmaster chosen for a keynote address. Each hollow euphemistic phrase indicated some secret privilege. It was then, looking around her in the wide public library, that Rose realised what she was part of. That Caldonbrae was less of a school, and more of an elite institution containing its own churning practices, a forever fortress turning within itself.

She'd also searched for any mention of Jane Farrier across the library articles. Having no success, Rose decided that she'd write to her teacher training supervisor – who naturally kept a keen eye on the academic jobs market – to see if she'd heard of a Jane from Caldonbrae Hall taking up a Classics post in another school.

Rose stared out of the train window at the landscape speeding past her, England's pale green sliding into Scotland's rough wilderness. A desperate thought occurred to her: she could stand up, tug down the latch of the window, stretch out her arm to pull open the door, and leap out.

Instead Rose sat back with a sigh, resting her head on the mottled fabric of her seat as the rest of the carriage carried on. She would return, and she would focus. Focus on what she'd chosen for herself, and the steps she could take during the weeks in front of her. After all, it was her that wasn't fitting in.

Rose drifted along the first-floor corridor behind a group of Sixths for the Monday morning assembly in Founder's Hall. Rose couldn't see either Emma or Frances in the messy midst of the girls, even though at breakfast Frances had welcomed Rose back as spiritedly as the Junior girls now grappled each other.

In the second-floor corridor Vivien caught Rose by hooking on to her arm, her eyes roving over the Thirds as they filed past.

'Elizabeth, lace up your boots!'

Rose jumped; she couldn't help it. A pair of Intermediates laughed as they passed by.

'Didn't mean to alarm you, my dear.' The deputy head spoke quickly. 'I can't let you into the returning assembly, I'm afraid. Not with the ongoing investigation and the sensitive nature of your probationary period.'

A small humiliation burned in Rose's chest.

'Furthermore, an update on your investigation,' Vivien continued, not looking at Rose. 'We are in the last phases of evidence assessment. You will have one lesson observed, you will not be warned in advance. We need to get Open Day finished first – which you won't need to be involved with.'

'An observation?' Rose asked, alarmed.

'Yes.'

The common room noticeboard still boasted the offending page – Rose had checked quickly on her way up. She added desperately, 'And . . . have you got all the facts?'

Vivien drew her sharp eyebrows together. 'To what are you referring?'

'The fact that Bethany came to the door of my flat just before the break, and the Prudence matron had to take her away. The fact that she returned to my class for one lesson, without permission. I have witnesses for all of it. I wrote to the Headmaster regarding both incidents, but there was . . . little acknowledgement.'

'Of course, Rose, there's no need to be cross.' Vivien took a step back. 'We have all that information.'

'And have the governors and parents been made aware of those facts as well?'

'They will get a report at the conclusion of the investigation.'

'And is it clear on which side the truth is being told?'

Vivien turned her head towards a little group of Seconds; she narrowed her eyes at them. 'As I've told you before, Rose, we must give the girls the benefit of the doubt. That is our responsibility.'

Rose's voice throbbed in her throat. She thought of her mother's clinic, her thus-far commendable teaching career. She thought of her father's reputation. 'Is my job still in jeopardy?'

Vivien paused, her eyes continuing to follow the Seconds. 'Not at present. Please return to your office, Rose. And, of course, I must add: welcome back.'

The Headmaster passed the two of them without so much as a nod. Vivien left Rose to join him, but not before she'd bent to challenge the group of Seconds, demanding that one of them tie the bow at her neck a little tighter.

Rose hovered miserably long after the trail of girls and staff had disappeared into the hall. She only turned away when a piano sounded as clear as a bell, an accompanying trumpet bursting like ripe fruit behind the closed doors.

Early the following week, Rose began her meal, just as two English teachers beside her pulled away their trays. She wasn't surprised; she knew things wouldn't have changed since half-term, particularly after Vivien's lukewarm update. At least she hadn't seen Bethany since that night at her flat.

It was the latter part of the lunch hour, and Rose looked across the dining hall at the Juniors and Intermediates that remained.

It was simpler eating alone, anyway. Rose had started worrying that her table manners weren't as particular as the girls'; last week one teacher had commented on the way she held her fork. This feeling wasn't unfamiliar; as a child the neighbourhood kids had steered clear of Rose, thanks to her father's bookish reputation, and tall tales of her mother's 'scandalous' antics. Rose used to sit in her bedroom with her Greek mythology and wonder if she'd ever belong anywhere.

Still, Rose had a new purpose this week. There'd been a slim letter from her old course supervisor telling Rose that she'd heard of a Jane Farrier within a small boarding school near Dublin. Rose had stared hard at the Dublin school's address and Jane's name written out in another hand, her existence somehow fully confirmed. Rose scraped her food around her plate, her thoughts busy with possible queries – should she ask Jane what had really happened for her to leave? Could

Jane help with this dire circumstance concerning Bethany, and prevent Rose from losing the position she'd once held?

Rose took a swig of water from her glass just as a girl in a loose-fitting grey dress approached the table. The girl hesitated, waiting for Rose's reaction, before slamming her own tray down opposite. She lifted Rose's glass of half-drunk water to her lips as Rose's mouth gaped open with dismay.

'No, Bethany!' she cried. 'That's mine.'

Bethany slammed the empty glass back on Rose's tray, wiping her wet mouth with her sleeve. 'I was thirsty.'

Rose looked around her hastily as a few young faces swivelled towards them. She tried not to panic as Bethany seemed to hang over the table. 'That was totally inappropriate, Bethany. Put that glass on your own tray now.'

'No.' Bethany glared at her, her eyes flashing with sick defiance.

'I won't touch it, Bethany. Put it on your tray.'

'No.'

Rose stood up awkwardly, moving her legs over the bench as quickly as she could.

'Yes, please go.' There was a bubble of mirth in Bethany's voice. 'Why don't you just crawl back to the hole you came from? Get Jane back. We don't need you here.'

Rose's fingers were stiff with panic as she lifted her tray, but Bethany was still talking.

'If *you* go, Jane will come back to save me.'

'Save you from *what*?'

Bethany's features twisted. 'She has to save me from Compassion.'

'From compassion?' Rose spluttered, trying to free herself from the bench. 'What do you mean, Bethany?'

'I need *her.*' Bethany's voice was quietly furious as she leaned forward, her tray jutting out in front of her. 'Not you.'

In one movement, Bethany pushed at Rose's tray with her own, lifting it slightly before a sudden snap of force. Rose's tray flipped upwards. For a white second she saw her lunch things rise, clatter and fall, before the great crack of glass and ceramic shards against the floor.

'Don't touch me!' Bethany screamed.

With a hot face Rose bent down to pick up the food-splattered pieces, careful with the sharp edges, trying not to see the dozens of little faces watching. She piled up the bits in the paddle of her hand, keeping one eye on Bethany's grey dress moving in front of her.

'Don't touch me, I said!'

'I'm not touching you, Bethany,' Rose said as calmly and as loudly as she could.

'Just go away! Don't you understand?'

Rose raised one hand in surrender, hoping that her cheeks weren't aflame, trying not to hear the buzz of gossip echo around the dining hall, the youngest ones even standing to see.

A new voice came in: 'Madam hasn't actually touched you, has she, Bethany?'

Rose looked around wildly; Bethany's face darkened as her eyes focused on someone behind Rose.

'You keep saying "don't touch me" but she hasn't.' Frances's voice was resonant, and Rose could feel the woman's strength above her. 'In fact, I believe that the whole basis of this investigation against Madam is your original lie, then some made-up stories and mysterious reappearing bruises. For which Madam has never been the culprit. Am I correct?'

A nearby Junior turned to her table of friends to repeat

Frances's words. Rose saw, too, that Vivien was standing in the canteen doorway, her slim figure bent with attention, her eyes pointed at Bethany.

'You need to think very carefully about what you are doing, Bethany,' Frances continued as the girl turned her head away, those long straggles of hair rippling with the movement. 'Remember, there are repercussions both ways. The governors are now involved. It is very important for you to tell the truth – or there will be consequences.'

Bethany's head snapped back to Frances. 'What would Jane say to hear you, her friend, speak to me like that? And where *is* she?'

'You will refer to all female teachers as Madam, Bethany.'

Rose remained crouching next to the bench. She saw Bethany's agonised face flush with anger before she swept out of the hall, dozens of small heads watching her as she went.

After a moment Vivien stalked over to the edge of the table and gestured for Rose to stand, nodding at Frances too.

'Rose,' Vivien's voice was as sharp as the disapproval on her face, 'I can assure you that the details of this debacle will be included in the investigation.'

'And you won't get an apology better than that!' Frances finished as Vivien followed Bethany out of the dining hall. Even though Vivien's words had been limited, Rose felt a squeeze of triumph as she stood by Frances's side, her ally, her personal Roman sentry.

In the following days, nothing could smother the victorious leap in Rose's chest. She hoped that the girls' gossip after Bethany's scene in the dining hall would spread and extinguish any bad things they might have decided about her.

Rose had gone further and written a stilted letter to Jane at the school's address in Dublin, before slipping the envelope into the secretaries' outgoing post. Her desperate curiosity was almost too much to bear as she framed her ill-hidden questions with a polite enquiry.

Vivien caught Rose in passing and, after another mention of the dining hall incident, she offered her a second chance at running an activity, properly arranged this time.

And so it was on Wednesday afternoon that Rose found herself striding down the peninsula towards the beach with a dozen girls stringing behind her, for 'Swimming'. The shape of the bay meant that the school's private beach was cut off, entrenched within the peninsula's headland and the school bounds – while the main gate stood further down at the root of the crooked finger.

The group had crossed the rippling velvet fields towards the cliff edge and down the zigzag of the rickety walkway. Rose felt a salt sting in the air, but there was no wind. They were at the end of October now and she'd been astonished that the girls would willingly embrace the cold seawater, but Frances had insisted that the activity lasted only two more weeks, the girls did it all the time, and it was good for the lungs.

Rose was delighted to be outside, to breathe and watch the air play with the tops of the girls' heads as they strode down together. Perhaps her luck was changing. She was even more delighted to reach the mess of the beach and its cliffs. Some parts of the reddish rock were slit and shredded, as if they'd been scored through by Poseidon's trident. He hadn't left the beach free, either. The shore's pink-grey shingle was embedded along threads of dark ragged rock stretching into the water, as if the sea god had reached out from the waves and dragged his wet fingers down the shore, back to his watery tomb.

The beach was domesticated by a row of connected wooden huts set into the foot of the cliff. From there a long wooden walkway ran along the beach and down a thread of rock, a jetty towards the sea.

Rose ignored the jetty, preferring to trample on the shingle that scraped under her feet. The grimy rock looked as though it had bubbled up and hardened; half-spheres of pinks and beige nudged up under her feet. It must be volcanic, she thought, like her piece of Vesuvius up in the classroom. She waited as the girls slipped out of the huts in pairs and threes, ticking them off her list. The girls were identical in their pale grey swimming costumes, a few stopping to tighten their white hats underneath their chins. One threw her towel at Rose, the others dropped them on the wooden walkway. She wanted to laugh: they all looked so charming, darting towards the sea, barefoot and careless.

Fresh screams filled her ears and Rose sprang up. Oh God, if something were to happen – she wasn't trained for that. But there were only girls' heads bobbing up and jolly cries of play. Rose let out a sigh and again counted the distant heads. After a splutter of laughter, another shriek and terrible squawking from interrupted seabirds, all the girls were accounted for.

Rose suddenly remembered the sounds she'd heard last night through her bedroom window. A dark husk of voices – all male – merry, but terrifying. She'd been groggy with half-dreams, but through the thick curtains Rose had spied a shaft of light shining out from the main doors open far below, next to the long bright rectangle of the Headmaster's study window. Nothing else – no person, no car. The strands of men's voices had blown away as she'd hurried back to the safety of her bed. Had she imagined them as she'd slept?

Rose watched one of the girls swim to a broken triangle of rocky outcrop further out to sea, its body and hers buried in the water. The girl squared her arms and raised herself onto some obscure dark ledge.

'Aren't you coming in, Madam?' A small girl was standing behind Rose, her toes scrunched around the pinkish shingle. Rose jumped at the button nose and freckled speckles of Nessa's face, Daisy hanging behind her.

'Oh Nessa, you frightened me.'

'Come on, Madam. Paddle, at least.'

'No thanks.'

At this distance, and with the cliff so high above, Rose could only see the very top turrets of the school. She bit her lip. 'Nessa, do you know where the entrance to the tunnel is?'

'Tunnel?'

Rose tried again. 'The tunnel to the school?'

'Don't know what you mean, Madam.'

'Oh.' Daisy looked over to the beach huts. 'I've heard of it. But actually, I've no idea, Madam.' Rose noticed a damp stream of black hair escaping from Daisy's swimming hat.

'It definitely exists,' Rose continued, 'but it should be here somewhere, if this is where you swim, and the huts are here.'

'You're always asking so many questions, Madam,' said Daisy with a shake of her head. 'Aren't we the ones who're supposed to ask the questions of you?'

'What?' Rose hesitated. 'Yes, I suppose so. Off you go, then.'

Rose closed her eyes, trying to hold on to the brief delight of being outside. She listened to the pull of the tide, the dim merriment of the girls, a squawk of a seagull. But as she inhaled deeply, Rose caught the dank reek of seawater. She suddenly thought of that poor girl in some lead-lined room, buried in the bowels of the school, an operation gone wrong.

Rose knew she needed to watch the girls, but she kept her eyes closed for another moment. *Yes,* she thought, *this would be a horrible place to die.*

As she waited in the common room for Frances later that afternoon, Rose looked over at Anthony, busy with a flurry of papers, his knees folded to support them. Another teacher was gesticulating at Anthony as he listened, his handsome face pointed with concentration. He seemed different to Rose; he was wearing thick tortoiseshell reading glasses, and his stubbled beard was growing thicker. She looked away.

The common room was better lit than she was used to, and Rose had tucked up her feet, resting her head on the side of her tall armchair, her hair brittle with the salty sea air. She cradled her glass of wine in one hand, feeling the fire's heat on her other cheek. The afternoon on the beach had been good for her. Sometimes she felt she was watching herself navigate these dark corridors, just like Clarice Starling in *The Silence of the Lambs* – another favourite she'd seen repeatedly last year. Rose had liked Clarice's unapologetic, steely face; that scene where she got in the lift with those tall men, or when she slipped under the garage door because she could.

'So, you found the bar.' Anthony was looking down at Rose, shifting his pile of papers from one arm to the other. He'd taken off his reading glasses; his hazel eyes were weary, but still vibrant. 'How's it going, Rose?'

Rose was suddenly very aware of herself. The salty bite of her lips, her grimy fingernails, the wine glass stem between her thighs. The other teacher patted Anthony heavily on the back as he moved past.

'Yes. Fine,' Rose attempted. 'How are you?'

'Fine, as always. All the better for seeing you.' Anthony leaned his arm on the headrest of the chair opposite Rose. 'Girls behaving for you yet?'

'I think they're fed up of torturing me now,' Rose gave a peaky smile, 'and are moving on to plain disinterest.'

'I've heard the odd snippet of your lessons. You're keeping the girls on their toes. We're lucky to have you.'

'You've said that before,' Rose tittered. 'Is it still true?'

Anthony smiled at her warmly. 'Well, actually, I—'

'Rose,' Frances invaded Rose's line of sight, 'I thought we were meeting?'

'Oh.' Rose turned her head. 'We are.'

'I don't want to interrupt you.' Anthony dropped his arm from the chair, his smile fading.

'Don't worry Anthony, please do join us.' Frances said, annoyed, and Rose bit her lip with dismay as she glanced across at Anthony.

'No, no. Don't mind me,' he shrugged. 'I've got these files to get through.' Anthony ducked his head and moved away with his usual loping grace. Rose's eyes followed him as he went.

'So,' Frances continued crossly, perching on the seat opposite Rose, 'we haven't really seen each other.'

'Well,' Rose tried to sit forward but her limbs felt heavy, 'apart from when you rescued me in the dining hall on Monday.'

Frances smiled all the way to her eyes. 'And how was your half-term?'

'Fine. Too short. Yours?'

'Boring. I didn't leave this place, actually. Too much to do.'

'My God, really? For what?'

'Well, the entire Languages faculty.' Frances's high cheekbones were tight as she pulled a defensive face. 'Open Day next Friday, the Christmas dinner . . .'

'The Christmas dinner?'

'And the carol service and all the celebrations . . . you know how it is.'

'I really don't. It's barely November. And how can there be any carol service if there's no chaplain?' Rose added sarcastically, 'I thought the Headmaster did away with all of that.'

'He thinks it's nonsense. But Christmas is a milestone of the year. And anyway, we all still know the hymns from before his time.' Frances shook her head like a prize horse. 'Right, I'll get a glass of white to match yours then.'

'I hadn't realised we had regular access to booze. Why didn't you tell me before? I need it badly with this investigation still going on.'

'You know that I have my own worthy stock in my flat,' Frances laughed dryly. 'And anyway, they can't hang on for much longer – it's clear where the blame lies now.'

'Yes, but even then, it's on my record – the police statement,' Rose said uneasily. 'The parents' newsletter, the governors, all of that.'

'Please put it out of your mind. It's being sorted.'

Frances went off to get a glass of wine, and when she returned Rose had another question ready for her friend. 'Why did you become a teacher, Frances?'

'Oh.' Frances hesitated before sitting down. 'Why do you ask?'

'Sometimes I wonder at my own choice.' Rose raised a small sigh. 'It can feel like torture.'

'I suppose I sort of . . . fell into it. Academically excellent, or something. And you're supposed to do what you're good at. Languages are like Maths, and my brain is fused in the same way.'

'Have you only ever taught in private schools?'

Frances straightened her blonde fringe with her fingers. 'Yes. But what about you – how did you become a teacher?'

Rose shifted her gaze beyond Frances's head as she spoke. 'My father was a teacher. He was really good at it.'

'Oh yes, wasn't he a prominent academic? A professor, with published works and things?'

'Yes.' Rose nodded again. 'I really admired him. So after he died, academia seemed an obvious path for me to take – and, hopefully, like you, I appear to be half decent.'

'Cheers to that.'

'Thanks. We got all these letters when he died.' Rose's eyes seemed to slide out of focus as she remembered. 'All these people he'd affected. Lives he'd changed, his old students. It was incredible, I can't tell you.' Her breath caught in her throat. 'And then sometimes, when I get stern in the classroom, I can hear his voice in mine.'

Frances didn't say anything.

'Sorry,' Rose said. She blinked and scratched the armrest with her fingernail. 'I've never said that out loud before.'

'No, not at all.' Frances's eyes were soft. 'Do you mind my asking, how did he die? He must've been young.'

Rose lowered her voice. 'My parents weren't young parents.'

'Oh.' Frances waited, then she said, 'I'm so sorry for your loss.'

Rose remembered her wine glass and spoke into it before taking a sip. 'Not as sorry as I am for yours.'

'My dad was great too, a wonderful patriarch. I adored him, but my mother preferred that I –' Frances broke off.

'That you?' Rose prompted.

But after a hard swallow, Frances said, 'I'd rather not talk about it. What a serious conversation! Never mind, I'm glad to know that we both suffer from father issues. And in a place like this, you're not in any danger of meeting any potential boyfriends. So cheers to that, too!' As Frances laughingly leaned over to clink Rose's wine glass, Rose caught sight of the worn and ripped lining of Frances's jacket.

A withered voice interrupted them: 'Ladies.' They both looked up to see John's features twisted into a smile. He had the newspaper's crossword folded under his arm, a pen in his wrinkled hand. 'Shall we? I hear you're very clever, Rose. And I *know* Frances is.'

Rose opened her mouth to decline, but Frances had already forced a pained smile onto her face. John nodded confidently at them both as he stepped towards the armchair beside Frances.

'Excuse me, dear,' the old man said as Rose shifted her legs to the floor to let him pass. 'You wouldn't fetch me a glass of whatever you're having, would you?'

No, Rose thought, *I'd rather not.* But she knew that for her own sake, and Frances's, she had little choice. As she poured the blood-red liquid into a glass at the bar, she wondered how an establishment that promised to educate 'girls of the world' could somehow make its women feel so small.

LUCRETIA

quaerentique viro 'satin salve?' 'minime,' inquit; 'quid enim salvi est mulieri amissa pudicitia? vestigia viri alieni, Collatine, in lecto sunt tuo; ceterum corpus est tantum violatum, animus insons; mors testis erit.

To her husband's question, 'Is all well?' she replied, 'Not at all; for what can be well with a woman when she has lost her honour? The mark of a strange man, Collatinus, is in your bed. But only my body has been violated; my heart is innocent, as death shall be my witness.

(Livy's *History of Rome* I.58.7, written c.29–7BC)

History has remembered Lucretia as a model of propriety, but that obscures the tragedy and significance of her story. One night, her husband's comrades got drunk at their military camp and declared a 'virtue' contest between their wives. While the other women were soon discovered to be mid-drink or mid-feast, Lucretia was spinning alone by candlelight, having dismissed her servant girls to finish the work herself.

The sudden burst of men into her chamber gave her a shock. At the front was her husband, Collatinus, his dewy eyes bright with love for her. The trouble was, many other pairs of eyes were admiring Lucretia, too. She was proclaimed the most virtuous of the wives, and Collatinus the winner amongst men. He grasped his wife in an embrace, not seeing the look of furious lust on the face of Sextus Tarquinius, son of the tyrant king of Rome.

Several evenings later, Sextus came upon Lucretia while she was sleeping, and held a dagger to her throat. He ravaged her repeatedly, claiming that if she screamed, he would kill a slave, strip him naked, then lie him next to her dead body. This threat of dishonour in death was too much for Lucretia to bear, so she suffered her abuse in silence.

The next morning the sleepless Lucretia summoned her father and her husband. Through tears and furious sobs she told them the truth of her rape. The two men were electric with anger, and declared revenge against Sextus to redeem her honour. But Lucretia had the final say. It was too late – she did not wish to be forgiven, nor become a living example of infidelity. Lucretia took out a dagger, and with a sudden movement, stabbed herself in the chest.

Devastated, her husband and father returned to the military camp to tell their comrades the terrible story, far from the ears of the tyrant king's son. In the months that followed, an army was raised against the city walls of Rome, with Collatinus at the head. They drove out the seventh and last king of Rome, bringing an end to his tyranny, and a beginning to the glorious Roman republic.

Lucretia, then, was responsible for prompting a change in ancient Roman history – because she spoke up, and took control of her destiny. Her self-chastisement and self-sacrifice might seem alarming to us today, but her death inspired those that loved her to make meaning out of her shame.

8.

On Caldonbrae Hall's Open Day, Rose kept to the edge of the stairs and away from the visitors milling around the corridors. Emma was handling the parents in such a way that Rose marvelled at her deftness – drawing them into her classroom, softening her voice to ask them where they'd travelled from, how old their daughter was. Anthony, in his easy kindness, had asked Rose if he could be of any use; she reminded him that her classroom wasn't on the designated route, and she wasn't expected to speak to any of the visitors. Still, she'd tidied her classroom and repasted her posters and postcards to the wall, just in case.

It was breaktime and Rose was making her way down to the common room. The corridor walls' white paint had been touched up the day before, the wood panels richly polished; abundant bouquets of flowers had appeared in corners, beside elegantly inscribed signage. In the entrance hall, too, a display cabinet had been erected, stocked with labelled shields and trophies.

Along the first-floor corridor she passed a Nigerian family, guided by a slender Fifth. The elegant mother had a thread of gold knotted through her braids, and her daughter's hair was bound with a matching gold ribbon that shone along with her nervous smile, while the father stood tall and severe in his pristine suit. Rose couldn't take her eyes off the little girl, simultaneously glad and surprised to see her there.

Rose turned away, gripping the bannister of the Great Stairs as she made her way down, nudged by shoulders and elbows, forever uneasy and out of place.

But on the library landing the door swept open. Her eyes were drawn through, surprised to see the long study tables and soft armchairs pushed back. Tall boards were spread about the central space instead, blocking out the bookcases; their titles caught her attention: *Value. Study. Discipline.* A few broad-shouldered bodies blocked a clear view before the door swung closed in front of her.

Rose hesitated as a balding man pushed through the door and held it open for her, his eyebrows raised and smiling. Nodding back at him weakly, she moved into the library as a wave of gruff voices washed over her.

The room was full of men. Three dozen polished gentlemen in a semicircle of expensive cologne, each carrying a sort of thick white brochure. Some with immaculate cuffs and groomed eyebrows, others with the nub of signet rings on the edge of their hands, their cheeks ruddy and worn. They were an array of ages, and all were speaking loudly in their cut-glass accents, patting each other's arms, with a slap and a guffaw thrown in at various intervals.

Rose spied John nodding sincerely at two of the gentlemen as they stared into a page of the brochure; and then nearer, Frances in a tight black dress, her face pliant and agreeable as she motioned an older man towards one of the tall boards.

Encouraged by her friend's presence, Rose crept foward once the man had moved away.

'Frances.'

'Rose.' Frances turned to her with quick shock. 'What are you doing in here?'

'The door was open,' Rose answered simply, glancing down at the brochure in Frances's hands. The open page showed a bright image of a girl's smiling face, with listed words underneath. Rose peered closer – she thought she recognised the girl's thick fringe and pointed chin; yes, it was one of her Lower Sixth. Rose heard herself ask, 'What's happening here? What are these?'

'Oh.' Frances snapped the brochure shut and stood up straight, blocking Rose from the crowd of people in the room. 'It's a particular prospectus, for the sixth-form.' Frances spoke quickly: 'You know how the Sixth is very separate from the Juniors and Intermediates. These gentlemen are prospective fathers. Don't worry, it's not something you're involved in.'

'But,' Rose looked inquiringly over Frances's shoulder as she ushered her towards the door, 'why is this meeting so secretive?'

'It isn't – it's just very formal. And you're very new, Rose.' Frances was slightly breathless. 'Please don't speak to anyone.'

Rose narrowed her eyes. 'Can I have a look at that brochure?'

'No. Listen.' Frances's voice was plaintive. 'You're not supposed to be here.'

'Is it me? Because I'm not good enough or something?'

'No.' Frances's face softened as they reached the door. 'It's not like that – you're just not trained for—'

'Can't you just explain?' Rose urged, her back flat against the door; she gestured at the brochure in Frances's hand.

'No. I can't – please.' Frances closed her eyes for a moment. 'Let's go and have a cup of tea.'

'I don't mean to offend you, I just want to understand,' Rose pleaded. 'I'm really grateful to you, Frances, for always helping me.'

Frances gave Rose a brief, glad look that reminded her of a Junior who'd finally got a question right. At that moment she understood her friend even less than this private Open Day meeting she had stumbled upon.

John was looking over at them, his withered face creased in unhappy surprise.

'Come.' Frances nodded steadily. 'Let's have a cup of tea before you get into any more trouble.' She thrust her brochure on the nearest bookshelf; Rose gave it a long look before they left the library.

In the uncomfortable silence of the lower passageway Rose wondered whether she could broach the subject again, now that they were away from the main stream of visitors. They stepped aside for three passing food trolleys, but one still jabbed Rose's hip as it pushed by.

'Ow!' Rose cried out, holding her side as a catering woman called back, 'Sorry, running late! The girls need their elevenses.'

'Really?' Rose frowned at the exotic-looking food laid out on the second trolley, grimacing at the twinge in her hip. 'Which girls? Why can't they go to the dining hall like everyone else?'

Frances's face was stony. She answered quickly. 'Some of the girls are kept aside today. In Verity and Temperance.'

'What? Why? Surely the Headmaster is proud of *all* of his beloved girls.' Rose couldn't hide the sarcasm in her voice. 'Surely he wants them all on display?'

'These girls aren't strictly students.' Frances's voice was dull as she continued down the passageway. 'Not today, anyway.'

'What? Are you telling me we've got some mad girls locked in the attics here at Caldonbrae?' Rose stuttered, hobbling after her friend. 'And they've got their very own elevenses?'

'No, Rose.' Frances pushed open the door of the common room. 'For heaven's sake, no.'

'Please explain, Frances.'

'There's no need.' Frances turned around at the door, speaking under her breath. 'Be careful what you say in here.'

'Okay, but,' Rose insisted, 'tell me why some girls aren't included in Open Day?'

'Because the management do not wish them to be seen,' Frances said with finality, striding towards the tea service.

Rose almost cried out, 'Why not? And who is it?'

Frances wheeled around with her face set. 'Honestly, Rose, I've just rescued you, *and* deserted my post which I'll probably have to pay for later. Let's just have a quiet cup of tea, all right?'

Rose was stung. 'I didn't ask you to rescue me.'

'Oh, for heaven's sake!' hissed Frances, pushing away from the tea service. Rose followed her with her eyes as the space between them grew. Frances crossed the swirl of armchairs and threw herself into another beside the three Moirai, the toad-like women of judgement settled near the fireplace. The three women sipped their tea, observing Rose through calculating eyes, seemingly enjoying her discomfort.

Rose turned to the tea service, glaring at the boxed array of teabags, her mind thundering with confusion and hurt.

Rose's bad mood followed her through the weekend and into the following week, all the way to her unexpected lesson observation that Thursday.

She couldn't hide her mortification when one of the three Moirai women stepped into the classroom as the designated observer. It was a terrible lesson: the silent Lower Sixth Latinists were docile but ungenerous, their perfect lashes fluttering with frowns of mistranslation. Rose unwisely went further than the curriculum by pushing the three girls into a tricky bit of Livy – real Latin, not from the textbooks, and one of her favourite stories in Roman history: Lucretia. The girls didn't respond as she hoped, certainly not in a way that would impress.

'Okay, ladies. Before the lesson ends – any thoughts on Lucretia?'

'It was a bit weird, Madam. I understood the shorter sentences.'

'I had to look up every other word, Madam.'

'But did you get a sense of the story?' Rose asked breathlessly.

'Well,' tried the girl nearest the front, her thick fringe hanging over her eyes, 'did she stab herself at the end, Madam? With a dagger?' She stared into her page. 'In front of her husband and her father?'

'Yes, Lily.' Rose looked at the girl for a long moment, remembering last week's sixth-form brochure and her strange, smiling face. 'And Lucretia's suicide prompted her father and husband to then drive out the tyranny of the Roman kings.' Rose glanced at the clock as her observer frowned. 'Never mind. Well attempted.' She started collecting the papers from the girls. 'Thank you, ladies.'

As the Sixths wordlessly left the classroom, Rose scanned the poor translations. She hoped that she'd done enough for the observer to report back positively to Vivien; but as she looked up to thank her, she'd already left. Rose didn't dare to imagine what she would recount to the two other Moirai.

A few moments later a girl strolled in and, with a wide smile, clipped the door shut behind her.

'Hi, Madam!'

Rose was slumped in her chair with something like defeat, but still couldn't mask her surprise at the intrusion.

'Don't get up, I'll only stay for a few moments,' the Sixth said as she tossed her auburn curls behind her shoulder. 'I hope you don't mind?'

'Not at all.' Rose stumbled over her words as she sat up. 'Clarissa, is it?'

'Yes. It'll only take a moment.' Clarissa sat down on the desk in front of Rose, her knees together and turned to the side. The front of Clarissa's green dress, although buttoned to the nape of her neck, had a sheer band of fabric that revealed her tight cleavage. Rose pushed her chair further back with her feet.

'I am so pleased to finally speak to you, Madam.'

Rose opened her mouth but reminded herself that this was a student. 'How can I help you, Clarissa? I do have a lesson in a few minutes.'

'This won't take long. Here, Madam, I have something for you.' Clarissa readjusted her green velvet hairband. 'It's a letter of apology from Bethany.'

Rose's face changed as she stared at a white envelope that had appeared in Clarissa's slim hands. The writing on the envelope was small and masculine. Rose took it, opened it, and turned the letter over in her hands.

'Did she write this or did you?'

'Madam,' Clarissa smirked, 'I would never need to write such a thing.'

'I don't really need a letter of apology.' Rose surprised herself. 'I think I rather care more that she's all right.'

'How kind of you. She's fine,' Clarissa nodded brightly. 'She's in the san. The sanatorium, that is. She's not attending lessons currently.'

'Why the san?'

'She is in the best place she can be, for girls in that phase. The nurses are wonderful. Don't worry, Madam, she's not on domestic duties or anything.'

Some dark presentiment moved across Rose's mind, and she read through the few sentences of the letter again. 'Yes, but . . . is she being treated properly in the san? She seemed to be worried about . . . something.'

'And,' Clarissa continued brightly, 'how are you enjoying our little school, Madam? Isn't Hope a splendid situation?'

Rose looked up at Clarissa with the corner of a frown. 'Did they . . . do they teach you to talk like that?'

Clarissa's eyes clouded over. 'I'm sorry?'

'The way you talk, the way you look – your hair, your fingernails.'

'I don't know what you mean, Madam.' Clarissa's pointed chin seemed to stiffen. 'This is who I am.'

Rose looked down again at the letter.

'And how are you getting on, Madam,' Clarissa's voice had less courage this time, 'with the other members of staff?'

'Oh, fine.'

'Madam from German, and Sir the head of History?'

Rose stood up so abruptly that the chair screeched behind her in protest.

'Thank you for bringing the letter, Clarissa.'

Clarissa stood too, and Rose could see she was affronted.

'One more thing, Madam. The deputy head wanted me to tell you not to seek out Bethany. We think it would be better—'

'Who is "we", Clarissa?'

'Oh, the Headmaster, and the deputy head, Madam Ms Johns. As head girl they often include me in their—'

'Do they indeed?' Rose couldn't hide the cynicism in her voice.

'Yes, Madam,' Clarissa answered with renewed vigour. 'And we think you and Bethany ought to remain entirely separate from now on, until the situation is resolved.'

Rose started. 'The situation is not yet resolved? The investigation?'

'I believe not.'

'Even with this letter of apology?'

'No, Madam, it's already gone far beyond that.'

Rose shook her head, mortified. 'And the deputy head didn't think to tell me any of this herself?'

'No, Madam, she's quite busy.' Clarissa's face sneaked out a neat smile. 'But thank you for seeing *me*.'

The head girl left just as the Fourths appeared, parting in a line at the door to let Clarissa pass. Rose had never seen them so obedient. But soon enough, they were throwing their bags about, filtering through the desks. Rose didn't mind; she was glad of their rough bustle after the calculated charm of Clarissa.

As the noise rolled over her, she stole a regretful glance at the pile of unmarked books on her desk.

'Madam, this Latin is really hard.'

Daisy was staring into the page of Livy, the Lower Sixths' work. Her tall figure seemed absurd in her white buttoned dress, her long sleeves too tight around her wrists.

'Oh, yes. It's not for you.'

'What level is this, Madam?' Freddie was now peering over the crook of Daisy's elbow as she passed by. 'Is this Sixth stuff?'

'Yes, Freddie.'

'So, is it possible to take Latin further, then?'

Rose was momentarily astonished. 'Freddie – is that something you would consider?'

'Um . . .' Her ivory face opened up. 'Maybe?'

'Don't worry about persuading me, Madam,' said Nessa, moving her pale hair out of her face as she scoured the page on her own desk. 'I only understand one word in this whole thing. *Nocte,* night. Nocturnal.'

Rose smiled. 'That's great, Nessa.'

'*By night,* ablative,' called out Daisy.

'Oh my God.' Rose staggered out a laugh. 'Well done, Daisy.'

Nessa was pushing the page to the edge of her desk; it almost reeled over to the floor, but she caught it. 'Who is Lucre-t-i-a, anyway?'

'Lu-cree-sha,' Rose said, correcting her pronunciation.

'Okay. Who is she?'

'Is she like Dido, Madam?' Daisy called out.

Rose surveyed the room of bustling girls, anxious to start the lesson. 'Not quite. Not at all, really, she—'

'Is she a real woman or a mythological one?' Daisy pushed.

'She's real, she's part of Roman history.'

'Tell us about Lucretia, Madam,' Freddie said, tugging her blazer over her seat and untucking her cloud of red-gold hair.

Rose glanced at their unmarked books again. 'All right.'

She turned to the blackboard and drew a diagram; she wondered how far back to go, and decided to keep it simple. The room dissolved into silence as she talked. Yes, she thought, maybe she'd find them a more basic translation to top it all off next week.

Rose finally drew a little stick woman holding a dagger to her heart. She turned back to the room, triumphant.

'I don't get it, Madam,' said Nessa. She and Freddie were grimacing at the board from the front.

'Looks like she had a ghastly time, Madam.'

'Yes, Freddie,' Rose sighed, pinching the chalk between the tips of her fingers, 'But through her actions, Lucretia made an impact on Roman history. There's loads of interesting stories about that sort of thing, if you care to listen.' Rose waited for the class to respond, but they didn't. 'We're obviously much more liberated today. But it's amazing that even in ancient times, domesticated women, like Lucretia, could make a difference.'

Freddie's face was fixed into a frown. 'Who is liberated?'

'Women today,' Rose almost laughed. 'Us. We are independent from men, we have rights. We can be leaders without the need for fathers or husbands to take the reins.' Rose continued: 'Look at the Queen, look at – God help us – Margaret Thatcher.'

Nessa glanced at Freddie next to her, who demanded, 'Don't you like Margaret Thatcher, Madam?'

'No, Freddie, I really don't,' Rose said firmly. 'Not after privatisation, and what she did to the North.'

Daisy passed her hand across her mouth. 'Madam! How controversial you are.'

'Madam,' Freddie spoke again, and she was staring straight at Rose, 'in the *Aeneid*, Dido is quite powerful.'

'Oh, you *did* read Book Four over half-term, then?'

'Yes,' Freddie nodded. 'I liked her actually. Although she's always looking "with her eyes", and tearing at her hair and things. She's quite emotional, isn't she? She could buck up a bit—'

'Yes, but Freddie,' Daisy interrupted with her clear voice, 'she dies at the end of Book Four, so what's the point? I did the holiday work, too. But I thought Dido was a bit of a cop-out. At least this Lucretia woman died for something. She sounds excellent.'

'You are harsh. Dido's been a survivor her whole life.' Freddie turned to pull a face at Daisy. 'She saw no other way out, since Aeneas abandoned her by sailing away. She was doing well until he arrived.'

'But really,' Daisy insisted, 'what is the point of her story, Madam? It seems so trivial.'

'Not at all, Daisy.' Rose placed her piece of chalk along the edge of the blackboard. 'Dido's story is self-contained within the *Aeneid*. She's a powerful queen. She founded a city, after the murder of her husband, she escaped the tyranny of her brother. She may have been real, even.'

'And Aeneas ruined it . . . but isn't he supposed to be the hero?'

'Well, Daisy, that's an interesting question! And Virgil leaves us plenty to discuss. Did you know that Dido has more lines of speech just in Book Four than Aeneas has in the entire *Aeneid*? Could it be that *she* has a lot more to say?'

Rose looked out expectantly at her pupils but their faces were impenetrable. Only Freddie seemed to react. 'How many books are there in total again?'

'Twelve. But we're only studying Book Four for your GCSE exam next summer.'

'Who is Virgil?' Nessa asked, looking bewildered.

Rose turned to rub the blackboard clean as Daisy and Freddie shuddered with laughter. She smiled along with them too; for now, it outweighed her dismay.

The following evening there was a strange unified movement across the dining hall, and a silence that followed. Even the air seemed to change, as a figure in a dark grey dress followed a nurse carrying two meals on one tray. The girl was painfully thin, with sunken eyes and a shaven head.

Her hairless head drew every pair of eyes in the hall. Rose squinted to identify the girl as she sat down opposite the nurse.

Bethany.

Rose's face snapped back to her tray, horrified. But still in her mind's eye she saw that shorn head hunched over, the vulnerability of her frail shoulders, the kinks of her bony skull. Those long tendrils of hair gone, a halo of shame in their place.

The Junior tables passed around dark looks, heads turning, leaning into each other's ear with an unkind whisper. The Intermediates' faces were white as they dragged their cutlery around their plates. The remaining Sixth were solemn and obedient at their tables. The indifferent face of the Founder watched them all.

Once the two of them had eaten, the nurse took Bethany's thin arm and guided her away – back where? Rose wondered.

To the sanatorium? To some iron bed, in some clean and empty hospital dormitory?

The younger girls watched the dining hall doors even after Bethany had gone, the wake of her disgrace hanging over them as a warning.

AGRIPPINA

iam in mortem centurioni ferrum destringenti protendens uterum "ventrem feri" exclamavit multisque vulneribus confecta est.	Then, as the centurion bared his sword, ready for death, she, presenting her stomach, exclaimed, 'Strike my womb,' and with many wounds she was slain.

(Tacitus' *Annals* XIV.8, written c.AD116)

Agrippina is a lesson to us all in getting ahead. Of course, she was privileged to be born into the imperial family, but no other noblewoman dared to rise as high as she did.

After the death of her husband in exile, Agrippina was permitted to return to Rome under the emperor Claudius, her uncle. He was a reluctant emperor, easily persuaded by his advisors and his women – in fact, his most recent wife had been executed for conspiracy against her husband. Agrippina saw an opportunity and seduced Claudius, against the wishes of his counsel, who labelled it incest. It was his fourth union, her third, and both had noble sons to raise. Claudius's boy Britannicus carried the stain of his late mother's dishonour, so it was easy for Agrippina to persuade Claudius to adopt her own son, a strapping young lad, as heir to the throne. In recognition, Agrippina's son was given the new name of

'Nero'. Soon after, emperor Claudius succumbed to death by poison. Many suspicious eyes turned to Agrippina, who had high hopes for her teenage son. And indeed, after Claudius' death, Nero rode out into the Forum with the imperial praetorian guard, and declared himself emperor.

Nero was a young and boisterous ruler. He regularly ridiculed his young rival, the righteous Britannicus, before having him poisoned as his father had been. Claudius's closest advisors, too, were poisoned or driven to suicide. At Nero's side, Agrippina made sure their path was clear.

And the Roman public were delighted with her. She was a relation of Julius Caesar, after all, and very happy to be celebrated thus. 'Augusta' was her new honorific title, and her face bloomed across Rome – stamped on Roman coinage, carved on a statue conjoined to her teenage son. Indeed, the success and popularity that the young emperor Nero enjoyed was entirely thanks to his mother, the empress.

But her dominance did not last. The young emperor soon tired of his mother's interferences. Perhaps her plotting had been too ruthless – she'd taught her son too well. His tyranny and extravagance stretched beyond Agrippina's control, and she was forced to leave Rome once again. There were many attempts on her life, arranged secretly by the emperor to seem accidental, but none hit their mark. And so, Nero was forced to throw caution to the wind. His assassins appeared at her countryside refuge under the cover of night. There would be no final escape from death. This time, Agrippina would face it boldly, and command one of the assassins to aim his sword at her womb – the place from where traitorous Nero had sprung – so that through her death, her son might always be reminded who gave him life.

9.

Rose spent the weekend trying to shake off that vision; her pitying worry for Bethany was almost too much to bear. Should she visit her in the sanatorium? Of course not. The school had been carrying out its pattern of punishments for 150 years – who was Rose to question them? Bethany's path, and hers, were now diverging; Rose had to be the one to keep her head down and succeed, rather than follow in the girl's declining footsteps.

And on the following Monday a small reward came: Rose was asked to trial a night in the boarding house. She was glimmering with nerves but Emma reassured Rose that it proved Vivien's good faith in her, and that they were seeing *how she'd do.*

Rose found herself sitting in the tutors' study after a tour of House Prudence, led by the brusque and buxom housemistress. The boarding house, the first she'd seen, was a luxurious rabbit warren, within which she'd completely lost her bearings – short corridors divided by year into identical cubby-hole bedrooms. The dormitories offered perpendicular iron bedsteads beset with soft toys or family photographs, the odd petticoat slung over a chair. Nestled in the innards of the house was one large reception room with a long kitchen and the highest beamed ceiling she'd yet seen, plus two shorter day rooms. There were dim sounds everywhere: the soft plunk of a piano in some other room, and the tick of a toaster's timer in a smaller galley nearby.

By now, Rose's eyes were already tight with fatigue; she wasn't used to the school day stretching so far into the late evening. She stared at a long list of strict punishments within 'Discipline' taped to the wall, a few details written minutely beneath. Below that, Nessa's name was marked with a red dot beside two others. Rose felt a sting of empathy for the girl – she knew what it was to be a name on a board.

A group of Thirds were filling up the long sofa in the study. They were like young gazelles with their soft eyelashes, passing fingers through each other's hair, draping their long limbs over one another. One pointed her little nose in the air. 'Don't look at me, Madam, my spots are out. I'm a mess.'

'You are not. It's all part of growing up.' Rose tried to sound reassuring, but she could hear her own accent falling out of line with their clipped tones.

'It's no good. Bad genes. Everybody says so.'

She was nudged by the girl next to her. 'You're nowhere near as ugly as that First with the ears – have you seen her since her new haircut? She ought to have them taped back. She's so repulsive none of the Fifths want her as a fag.'

The group collapsed into laughter as Rose frowned.

'A fag? Like a cigarette?'

'No, Madam, like a skivvy.' The girl who answered rolled her eyes. 'You know, someone to do your dirty work.'

Rose turned away, disgusted, as a nub of an idea pushed at her. She knew she wouldn't get detailed answers, but at least they would be blunt with their honesty. 'Can I ask about punishments, girls? The Sixth girl, Bethany deVere . . .'

'Oh yes, Madam, awful. We're not supposed to talk about it.'

One of the girls sat up. 'Bareheadedness is one of the last-resort punishments, Madam, but it's never supposed to happen in Sixth, because they need time to grow it back.'

'Before what?'

'Before they leave. But she's in C Pathway, so I suppose it's all right.'

Rose hesitated. 'What does "C Pathway" mean?'

'No, Madam,' the girls looked at each other cautiously, 'we're not supposed to talk about it. It's not decent. And you're new.'

'Still,' the girl perched on the sofa's armrest wasn't bothered, 'it's jolly having *you* here, Madam, we have the other Latin Madam for lessons.'

'Mrs Jenkins with the large bosom, you know.'

'Ah.' Rose didn't think she'd ever noticed Emma's bosom; she regretted the change of subject.

'Could you sneak us in some magazines, Madam? It's not one of our privileges.'

'Oh,' Rose said, 'so you do read magazines, then?'

'Only the designated ones. You know,' one of them shrugged prettily, '*Vogue*, of course, and—'

'*The Lady*?' Rose suggested. '*Horse and Hound*?'

'Ooh, could you get them for us?'

'Mummy says we're really lucky,' another girl chortled. 'Back in the day our grandmothers could only read annuals, and they didn't have a video machine. This place was like a nunnery.'

Rose asked carefully, 'And what about TV, or pop music?'

'Madam, it's frightfully vulgar.'

'Headmaster says television is the enemy of civilisation.'

'Oh,' said Rose.

'In one of my Discipline activities last year, Madam,' one girl added, 'we watched some films and studied female behaviour.'

'And,' Rose kept her voice light, 'these Discipline activities?'

'Yes, Madam. We've already done the basics. Skills. Social etiquette. General deportment – posture, voice and, er . . . ?'

'Manners,' piped up another.

'The basics?' repeated Rose. A few girls nodded eagerly. 'It seems odd you have to learn all these things, when your academic lessons are far more important.'

'Not at all, Madam. Discipline is important, too. It gets more serious later, anyway.'

'Okay.' Rose narrowed her eyes. 'But those things aren't normally taught in other schools. Do you do things like typing?'

'Typing?' one girl snorted.

'No, Madam,' another added helpfully, 'but there are typewriters you can use in the library.'

'No,' Rose urged, 'that's not what I meant. Are you learning things like elocution?'

'No, Madam, there's no need for that. That's only for the foreign girls. How funny you are.'

One girl caught her lower lip in her teeth. 'Clarissa is the most accomplished of all of us, Madam. That's what we're aiming for.'

Her neighbour sat forward. 'Whom do *you* have, Madam, in your Upper Sixth?'

'Oh.' Rose sat back in her chair, frustrated by their flitting comments. 'I've got five girls for Classical Civilisation. Dulcie Hughes—'

'She has lovely hair.' Three girls nodded.

'Alexandra Coryn, Natasha Swire—'

'Oh, excellent, Madam,' one girl squealed out. 'Dulcie and Alexandra are very important. They were prefects in Fifth.'

Rose considered this bit of information; yes, Dulcie would've made a formidable prefect.

'Natasha Swire is a bit –' The girl on the armrest hesitated.

Rose looked across at the girl. 'What?

'Nothing, Madam,' she answered quickly.

Rose tilted her head. 'Tash is probably the nicest of all of them.'

'Yes, but she's . . . odd, Madam.'

'Odd?'

The girl leaned forward conspiratorially, almost whispering. 'Queer, Madam!'

'Clarissa,' the middle girl interrupted loudly. 'Clarissa is the best of them all. That's why she's head girl.'

'Actually,' her neighbour raised her nose in the air, 'I preferred George List as head girl.'

'She was far before your time.' The two girls turned to face each other.

'And yours. I know her, though. My family knows the Lists. We Christmassed together once.'

'Really? When?'

'None of your business.'

Rose was frowning deeply, but she asked, 'As in *Freddie* List, in Fourths?'

'Yes, Madam, all of her sisters have been head girl. They come from a long line of Hope girls – four daughters and then their mother before them, their grandmother and so on. They've all gone on to excellent things.'

'What kinds of things?' Rose was unable to hide her desperate curiosity.

The girl on the armrest swung around to face her friends, bumping them with her knees. 'Goodness, I'd love to know *that* family.'

'Freddie's wonderful; once she let me brush her hair, such beautiful curls. I wish I was in Verity with her.'

'We've got Nessa, though, and they're best friends. Hopefully she'll stay.'

The girl in the middle of the group scowled. 'She won't. Nessa's useless.'

'Okay, girls. That's enough.' Rose didn't want to listen to any more; the dismay that had lodged itself somewhere in her chest gleamed afresh, for Bethany, for Nessa.

As the evening drew to a close, Rose looked at the array of photographs in the House Prudence lobby. Rows of smiling girls, flanking their housemistress and house staff seated in the first row. The younger ones were dotted along the front, their hands folded and beaming. Rose glanced past each picture, decades' worth, seeing that not a single Asian face decorated the groups. She mentioned this to the housemistress, treading on her words carefully as the woman searched her desk drawer for the evening duty sign-off form. The housemistress replied that no, the handful of Japanese girls that attended Hope were spread across Verity and Temperance.

'But why are there so few of them?' Rose urged. 'Why isn't there more diversity in a place like this?'

'Hope only takes Japanese girls, Rose, no others yet. A few joined us last summer, and several others came in September. They are an innovation.'

'An innovation? But that sounds –' Rose spluttered. 'Are they not students, like all the others?'

'Of course they are. You do exaggerate,' the housemistress tutted, casting Rose a disapproving look.

'They're not the ones who were kept hidden on Open Day?' Rose suddenly cried out.

The housemistress shrugged in response. 'They just weren't involved, that's all.'

'That's discrimination!'

'Dear me,' the housemistress stopped shuffling through her pile of papers and leaned forward, 'how dramatic you are, Rose. I shall have to note down your comments for my pastoral team.'

Rose was silenced and left staring at a little gold brooch pinned to the housemistress's dressing gown, the same Caldonbrae grey as the matron's.

In bed that night, it occurred to Rose that Jane must have tutored in Prudence, below her flat, and perhaps worn one of those dressing gowns. Would Rose, too, one day? Her mind strayed to the letter she'd sent to Dublin – there'd been no answer yet. Did Bethany have that same address, scrawled across those tear-stained pages she'd held that night? She'd said one letter had been returned to her; would Rose's be returned, too?

It was unnerving, how much time Rose spent thinking of that poor hairless girl, rattling around in her own tortured mind.

At the end of that Thursday morning, Rose dismissed the class. '*Valētē, puellae.*'

'*Valē, magistra.*'

'*Disceditē.*' With a sweep of her arm Rose gestured the Fourths out and signalled a reminder for Daisy to stay a moment.

Rose turned to clean the blackboard. She felt momentarily stunned that the lesson had gone so well. It was the first time they had got through a whole translation unscathed, and she had only carried them a little bit. Josie had been quieter too, not as acidly unkind with her comments as she'd been previously.

Agrippina the Younger wasn't on the curriculum, but Rose was glad to have introduced her. It was a fun translation and the girls had enjoyed the gory bit: Agrippina's murder by an assassin. Rose smiled at the clean blackboard and turned around.

But it wasn't just Daisy waiting patiently. Rose saw that Freddie had strayed behind too, with Josie and Nessa slumped on the desk behind her. A long slant of early winter light slid across the room and teased the tops of their heads, touching the rough red of Freddie's hair, the dirty blonde of Nessa's and the dark glow across Josie's forehead. The light was lost in the jet black of Daisy's hair but shone out a slice of her cheek and the almond-shaped brown of her eye.

Rose faced the scattered group, slightly apprehensive. 'Girls, I only needed to see Daisy. Can I—'

Freddie sat on a desk. 'I just wanted to ask you something, Madam.'

'Okay.' Rose hesitated. 'And you two?'

'We're just waiting for Fred.' Josie rolled her eyes at Nessa.

'Fine. What is it?'

Freddie looked sideways at Daisy. 'Daisy can go first.'

'I wanted to give you the other translations I did over half-term, Madam. I know it's late, but . . .' Daisy said in a rush, glancing at the other girls. She threw out an awkward arm.

'Well, here they are . . . but don't worry if it's too much. My father helped me with most of it. He was a Classicist, Madam.'

'Oh really?' Rose took the pages with interest. 'And what does he do now?'

'He's a barrister.'

'That's great!'

'We're not very—' Daisy began, but Josie cut in with a sneer: 'At least he's not a *teacher*.'

'Nothing wrong with teachers, Josie,' Rose retorted. 'What do you want him to be, landed gentry?'

Nessa and Daisy glanced at Freddie and Rose realised her mistake. But Daisy piped up again, cheerfully, 'Daddy always says, we've got innate breeding, but no money.'

'Freddie's got both,' Nessa nodded with a smirk. 'When she writes to her royal godmother she has to put a funny mark on the envelope so they know.'

'Nessa!' Freddie was outraged; her cheeks were clashing violently with her hair.

'Oh, sorry.' Nessa looked abashed as Josie snorted with laughter.

'How excellent for you, Daisy,' Rose said, looking down at the translations again, 'to have a Classicist for a father. We'll go through these next week.'

'Separate to class, though?' Daisy's eyes widened with alarm.

'Yes, of course. We'll find a time,' Rose nodded firmly, placing the pages on her bureau. She glanced across at her ceramic owl. Feeling the four pairs of young eyes on her, she didn't know why she suddenly felt so uneasy.

'Madam,' started Freddie, 'you were saying, about today's translation . . .'

'I enjoyed that translation,' said Daisy.

'Yes, me too,' Nessa added. 'I liked it better than that Jupiter and Io story.'

'Yes, I'm sorry about that one,' Rose nodded with regret, remembering that disaster of a lesson. 'It was confusing.'

'Didn't you feel sorry for Io, though?' Freddie turned to Nessa. 'That bit where Jupiter turns her into a cow, and she scrapes her name into the dust with her foot. Bit sad.'

'Yes,' Rose nodded again, 'Jupiter was a bit . . .'

'Sex-obsessed?' suggested Josie.

Rose hesitated. 'Well, he—'

'But Agrippina,' Nessa raised her thin eyebrows, 'I like *her*. Jupiter didn't turn *her* into a cow. And she had her face on a gold coin.'

'Good old Agrippina,' Freddie nodded, smiling. 'Mother of the emperor. She was feisty, even if she got a sword through her womb.'

Rose looked at Freddie and actually laughed. 'She *was* feisty.'

'How many times did she get married?' Daisy asked.

'Three times, I think,' Rose answered.

'They got married at around fifteen back then, didn't they, Madam?' Daisy frowned. 'My father was saying. Our age.'

'Yes.' Rose bent to her bureau, folding Daisy's extra translations into her planner. 'Regrettably. Poor girls had to marry old men. Pliny's third wife was fourteen, and he was forty.'

The air seemed to break as the girls shared a glance. Rose looked up and said with finality, 'Well, I'm glad that you all take an interest.'

But Freddie was staring at Rose full in the face. 'Can we do more of this, Madam?'

'More of what?'

'We're collecting your ancient women.'

'My ancient women?'

'You're repeating yourself, Madam,' said Josie, pushing herself off her desk. 'Not an attractive quality.'

Nessa and Freddie tittered in response, stopping when they saw Rose's bewilderment. Daisy was waiting, too, for Rose's answer. There was a spark of interest in Daisy's face, the same spark that had flashed across the class that morning.

'Girls,' Rose's voice was sincere, 'if you'd like to learn more, I'd be very happy to teach you.'

'Not now, though, Madam,' Nessa frowned. 'It's breaktime.'

'Nessa,' Freddie laughed all the way up to her honey-coloured eyes, 'you're such a clot.'

Rose said nothing more as the small crowd of girls left her classroom, Freddie leading the way.

The following week brought December and Rose couldn't ignore her private disappointment in her first term. So little had been achieved across her classes that a huge chunk of the curriculum awaited her in January, if she ever got there. The investigation hadn't yet been concluded; she'd hoped for a final note from the secretaries, or a summons to a meeting – the long-delayed welcome from the Headmaster. It didn't help that Frances was avoiding her, too, after their disagreement on Open Day. And with Bethany in the sanatorium, her hair gone, her dignity with it, Rose felt that somehow she was the villain now.

On Friday afternoon, one week before the release of the holiday, Rose broached the topic in the Classics office.

'You ought to be pleased,' said Emma, flatly.

Rose gritted her teeth. 'I'm not pleased, I feel completely devastated for Bethany.'

'Careful, Rose.' Emma shook her head. 'You don't want to sound like Jane.'

'It seems so cruel.' Rose grew more ardent after Emma's remark. 'Abusive, even. What do her parents – no, her mother's passed away, Vivien said – what does her father say?'

'He understands that this is Hope's way of dealing with things.'

'I know this place has its *way*,' Rose felt her temper rise, 'but it doesn't ever seem to be one that cares for the girls.'

Emma scoffed at that. 'I'm shocked to hear you say that – given what you've suffered, thanks to her.'

'She's a teenager! She doesn't know any better. She's full of emotions!'

'Well,' Emma turned her face to Rose, 'I'll repeat that next time you complain about your classes misbehaving.'

To escape the conversation, Rose took herself up to her classroom to stand at the arched window. It was a gloomy afternoon, dim with early winter. The sea would have been calm, but for the rocky outcrops that gathered white swirls of foam with every movement. Further out, a flock of seagulls were balancing on the slow swell of the water. Rose watched them as her breathing slowed, her heart beating along with the water's easy tug and pull.

It wasn't just Bethany's hairless head that haunted her – Rose knew that something was wrong with her mother. The latest update had been worse than she'd expected: another flare-up, with a numb tingling spreading through her mother's limbs. Rose couldn't bear for that part of her life, the one thing that felt sorted, to burst. But soon they'd spend Christmas and New Year together: plenty of opportunity to catch up, give her mother hot baths, play cards, boost her moods, all the while avoiding the conversation Rose wanted to have.

She came away from the growing dark of the arched window. Hearing bursts of Emma's teaching voice through the classroom wall, Rose returned to the Classics office.

But at the office door, she halted. In the shadow of Rose's desk chair there was a hunched figure, her shaven head a bare silhouette against the window's dusk. Rose bent her arm to the wall and flicked on the lights.

'Bethany.'

The girl seemed to look beyond Rose, blinking at the sudden brightness. She wasn't frantic this time; her voice was gentle and sad. 'I heard what they did to Jane. I can't bear it. I want to go and see her. They won't tell me which hospital she's in.'

'But – what do you mean?' Rose stuttered. 'She's teaching in Dublin.'

'Dublin? No, no. You don't know? She's in Inverness. They've kept her nearby.'

Rose's breath caught in her throat. 'But – how can that be, is she ill? What hospital?' Bethany's translucent eyes turned away from Rose, so she added quickly, 'Look, I am glad to see you, and I was hoping you'd come back to our class. I will *absolutely* help you catch up—'

'I'm not glad to see you at all, Madam, whoever you are.' Bethany spoke quietly. 'I'm doomed, just like Jane. Well, she can't save me now. She was the only one that could.'

'Bethany, listen—'

'There are things they're not telling you. You don't know *anything*.'

'I can help,' Rose insisted. 'I can help you improve your grades.'

'No. You're probably doomed too. Clarissa told me that you and Madam Miss Manders are just like me and Jane.'

'Frances?' Rose sputtered out. 'What?'

'You two are a disgrace, Madam, just like us.' Bethany let out a miserable sigh. 'No. There's only one way I can see Jane again. I must see her again.'

'Wait. Stay here, Bethany. Shall I get your housemistress, or that Prudence matron?'

'No.' Bethany settled herself deeper into Rose's seat behind the desk, so frail in her grey dress, and without her usual ribbons of black hair. 'I've made up my mind.'

Rose dashed down the corridors and the many streams of steps. Her first thought was to speak to the secretaries, but on the Great Stairs, she hesitated. The glass eye was dark with the weather and seemed to crack above her head. Rose looked up, and turned back.

Emma met Rose at the door to the Classics office. 'She's gone,' Emma said before Rose could explain.

'Bethany? How?' Rose panted. 'I didn't see her on the stairs.'

'Don't worry, I'll inform the Headmaster for you.' Emma's thick curtain of hair fell across her shoulder. 'This absolutely can't go on.'

'Did you send her away? She was very upset.' Rose checked around her desperately. 'I went to get help.'

'As I say, Rose, and I know you concur,' Emma's voice was sharper than Rose had ever heard it as she moved back through the doorway, 'this is an absolute disgrace.'

Rose looked at her empty chair, the leather back pushed and slack with use. Emma switched off the lights and walked away.

The term drew to its final week and Rose witnessed the school change around her. The building looked as though it had been scrubbed clean, the winter sun's low beams giving the outer walls and buttresses renewed radiance. Even the sea darkly glistened with approval, the lawns freshly mown and the sports pitches roped off against the cold bite of the wind.

Inside, the panelled walls of the main corridor were lined with swoops of holly, ivy and festive greenery, and the symmetrical Great Stairs encircled themselves around two identical Christmas trees that reached high up to the oculus above, decorated immaculately with silver-grey ornaments. It was as if the peninsula, bereft as it was of trees and foliage, had found a way of inviting in the wealth of nature for the pre-holiday spectacular.

Lessons had been cancelled on the last Friday. The bustle was reserved for the Founder's Hall Christmas dinner preparations, where strings of girls obeyed their designated teacher in tying together bursts of flowers, wrapping treasured gifts on white tablecloths, or arranging the Christmas crackers around each table. Others were decorating a third tree on the far end platform, itself skirted with boxed presents – for whom, no one was sure.

In time for the carol service the main school was cordoned off too, with only a long, carpeted pathway to the chapel cloister and Founder's Hall remaining open. It ran from one end of the school to another, the boughs of greenery accompanying the route.

The governors and the Sixth parents arrived in their long black cars; a small helicopter perched on the lawns without Rose ever hearing it approach.

When it was time, Rose stood in the quad of the chapel cloister and looked up. She felt so small in this gap between the jagged walls, her feet stiff against the humped and broken paving stones. It was almost dark, but the sky was a mottled white. The fresh air caressed her cheeks in this pocket of open space.

Most of the school had already gathered in the chapel as the last girls streamed along the cloister. Rose hurried behind them.

The chapel was extraordinary to behold: a massive, forbidding church, forged into the rock and the side of the school building like a beautiful barnacle. It was cream-coloured, tall and narrow, with fan vaulting meeting the line of pillars, as if the heavens had sucked them upwards. Above the altar bloomed an enormous rose window, speckled with blue stained glass. At the other end, a soft fugue played out from the unseen organ.

The governors and parents had filled the back rows. The Juniors in their grey blazers were filtering up into the long galleries on the west side of the chapel, the Intermediates joining them too; all had thick silver sashes around their waists and neat bows at their necks. The front rows were evidently reserved for the Sixth, wearing identical arrangements of high-necked dresses in virginal white, silver or pale grey. Two choral groups of girls sat near the altar, ready for their contribution.

There were no Asian girls in the chapel at all, an observation Rose tried to ignore as she found an empty seat near the back, coughing on the incensed air. She set her face forward, not daring to check for that shaven head amongst the spread of white at the front.

The carol service passed in phases: readings led by the Headmaster, Vivien and then Clarissa; carols sung by rows of panicked faces, with one soloist looking more surprised than any of the others when she took up the tune.

Rose ignored her programme and only mouthed the words to the hymns, stiff in her formal academic gown. But when the hollow of the chapel's occupants recited the Lord's Prayer together, Rose spoke the words, too.

There was a blanket of merriment over Founder's Hall that Rose hadn't anticipated. The girls had done their jobs well; each table seemed to breathe with celebration for the feast.

A society dinner, Rose's mother would have called it. The invasion of parents, governors and friends meant that the hall felt almost unrecognisable to Rose; the wealth and influence of these guests was as potent as their perfumes, as startling as the set jaws of the fathers, the dripping furs of the mothers.

Rose heard three mothers badger a Sixth housemistress. 'Couldn't we have another one of those opera trips? Hope has the best boxes, especially at Glyndebourne – let's all go during the season.'

'I think it's Ascot this year,' the housemistress answered the eager mothers. 'It's being arranged.'

'Ladies' Day?'

The housemistress nodded.

'Ooh.' One of the mothers placed an arm on another's as she exclaimed, 'Let's go to Philip Treacy together for our hats.'

Rose was soon introduced to a lord and lady, a member of the Foreign Office, a member of Parliament and a man who was 'top at Sotheby's' and laughingly asked Rose if she were any relation to their 'friends' at Christie's. Rose tripped over their accents, wide and tight as if they carried marbles in their mouths. She wondered whether the haste of the introductions had been deliberate, but intimidation stopped her responses anyway. Each of the guests looked at her with knowing curiosity, an elbow-jerk and a brief mention of her being 'new', before they moved on to the next topic of prosperous conversation. Just as one mother was joking about selling the van Dyck to pay the school fees, nodding in her husband's direction, Rose turned away, and the woman's swaying wine glass spilled over. Rose found her table gratefully, realising that she'd rather deal with the girls' brashness in the classroom than this hall full of terrifying adults.

She'd been seated between Emma and Deirdre from Geography, with a smattering of guests around them. The dishes were brought out by mute ladies that Rose recognised from the canteen. The meal was a gourmet version of a traditional Christmas dinner, colourful vegetables draped over thick slices of goose meat and lashings of gravy. After the puddings were served, an older man with very tanned hands leaned forward to speak to Rose from the other side of her table.

'Fabulous architecture at Hope, don't you think? Every corner another treasure! Aren't you new?'

'Yes, I am. Yes, it's very striking,' Rose said between mouthfuls, the only female at the table not to leave her pudding untouched.

'It's the baronial style.' The man's vowels were hard, Rose couldn't make out his accent. 'Renovated by Lord Hope. He was very stylish.'

'Apparently so.' Rose swallowed, looking at the man's wrinkled face. 'You seem to know a great deal.'

'No, no.' He pushed his plate aside. 'You'd have to ask John, he's the expert.'

Rose looked at him again. 'Forgive me, where are you from? Your accent—'

'South African.'

'Oh. Who belongs to you, then? I might teach your daughter.' *Or granddaughter,* Rose thought, but best to be polite.

'No.' The man let out a brief smile. 'I'm here as a friend of the school. I'm in banking, and I run several charities—' He broke off, interrupted by his neighbour. Rose sat back, relieved. She turned her face to the rest of the hall.

The Headmaster didn't seem to be eating at all. He was amongst several fathers, grouped in intense conversation. Meanwhile, Vivien had abandoned her seat and was now leaning in to a group of mothers at the table behind Rose. One mother with blonde brushed curls smiled up at Vivien as she said, 'Look, I know the waiting list is as long as my arm, but *darling,* my relations in Singapore would just love to have a look at the prospectus if they could?'

Rose turned her head to hear Vivien's measured response. 'We'll see. You won't be able to tell them about the application process – remember they shall have to be approached. But, of course, a family connection *will* help their case.'

On the other side of the hall, Rose saw Frances holding court over her table, her face flushed and smiling, her cheekbones so high that her blue eyes disappeared. The front of her dress was rumpled; she was still wearing her tights, but her shoes were kicked to the side. One mother watched Frances talk, her mouth agape, while a French teacher frowned with disapproval.

'Rose, you look quite beautiful tonight.'

'Oh.' Rose blushed to find Anthony hovering over her, smartly dressed in a dinner jacket. He took Deirdre's empty seat by her side. 'It's because I'm wearing a lot of make-up.'

'No,' Anthony scoffed, before turning serious. 'It's you.'

Rose looked at Anthony, his hazel eyes as warm and merry as the rest of the hall. 'Not networking then?' she teased.

'No, no.'

He didn't offer anything else. Rose suddenly felt self-conscious, and shrugged off her academic gown. 'I don't need to wear this anymore, do I?'

'No, no need.' He helped her pull off the garment, draping it carefully over her seat, leaving his arm there too.

'Where's yours?'

'Back in my office.'

Rose took up her napkin with a smile. 'You rebel.'

'Hardly.' Anthony passed a hand through his sandy hair. Rose watched a father at the next table empty a bottle of wine across several glasses before opening another.

'Anthony, my boy.' An older man had separated from a nearby laughing group and was leaning over. 'Are you coming to the Gun Room?' His dark features were raised in enquiry; he didn't look at Rose.

'Oh, soon, soon. Duty first.'

Rose waited for the man to move away. 'What's the Gun Room?'

'It's . . .' A note of rough anxiety crossed Anthony's face, 'William Hope's old quarters. Silly really . . . a billiard room, smoking room.'

'I see.' Rose nodded jovially. 'And who was that just now, the Marquis of Spain?'

'Funny.' Anthony looked at Rose with a weary smile. 'But don't.'

Rose was surprised. 'All right.'

Anthony seemed to relax, his arm still behind her chair. Rose held her hands together, wondering what to say to him.

An abrupt voice came in behind them.

'Madam, Sir, please go back to your boarding houses.' Rose

turned to see one of the assistant housemistresses, dishevelled-looking in a loose jacket, oddly incongruous with the rest of the scene. 'There's an issue with one of the girls and we need all hands on deck.'

'What?' Anthony turned his head with concern. 'Why was there no alarm?'

'The porters have called it a night.' The assistant was already moving to the next table, appealing to staff, away from the ears of the guests. 'Please report back to your house. All houses, from Honour through to Clemency.'

Anthony bent towards Rose. 'We should go. Which house are you?'

'Prudence. What do you think has happened?'

'I'm Chastity.' He stood up. 'Come on.'

Rose obeyed, taking her gown in her arms as she paced down the corridor. Anthony moved through a short door with a quick but reluctant goodbye, his Sixth boarding house in the same wing as Founder's Hall. Rose's walk was longer, the cool air of the corridor welcome as she followed the short throng of staff towards the Junior and Intermediate houses. Their wine-sodden conversations guessed at the issue that summoned them, but none of their suggestions seemed likely to Rose.

Rose heard the truth when she got to the Junior day room of her boarding house.

'A girl has run away.'

'Where from?'

'Not this house,' the housemistress huffed as she left Rose with the girls.

'Then we have to wait?'

'Of course, Madam.' A First smiled at Rose, showing all her teeth.

An excited hum crept through the house, the girls awake late and talking loudly, the lights over-bright for that time of the night. Rose felt her nerves prickling with frustration. How far could a girl go, anyhow? The peninsula was gated, surrounded by groundsmen, isolated and cut off from the world.

The three dozen Juniors were huddled across the sofas or piled long across the floor, knees up with layers of pyjamas and soft slippers. A few of them were playing cards, smashing their hands over piles at sudden intervals. One or two others were clutching stuffed bears, their hair long and rippling with the crimps of undone plaits.

'Has this happened before?' Rose asked one of the Thirds.

'Only once, Madam, years ago, when my auntie was here apparently.'

Rose thought longingly of her own bedroom, her gown now stiff in her arms, her limbs heavy. She stood up with a sigh.

'Wait here, ladies, I'll be right back.'

Rose left the room to check the Intermediate day room. She opened the door a crack to see a short line of Fifths tugging at each other's bodices, their dresses undone as fingers pulled at strings to further loosen them. The rest of that group were bunched together across the sofas, just like Rose's Juniors.

'Please can we go upstairs and get undressed, Madam?' said a Fourth to another woman in the room.

'No,' answered a bored voice – the assistant housemistress. 'We stay together for now. And you're lucky Matron's not in here. She's got a bee in her bonnet about the way you all looked during the service tonight. Something about scruffy shins and socks not being pulled up, petticoats showing. Apparently the deputy head was furious.'

'Madam, if a girl's run off then Madam Ms Johns has got more important things to worry about!'

Rose closed the door. The peninsula, this late, in the dark – images dashed across her anxious thoughts. The beach, the rumpled rocks there. The churn of the dark water on every side.

She returned to her designated room; the large windows reflected black as soon as she opened the door. Tugging the curtains closed, Rose saw the matron's reflection bustle in and greet the younger girls; they responded in a singsong voice before resuming their conversations.

Rose turned to her; the woman looked worried.

'Matron, who is it that's missing, do you know?'

A girl spoke up between them: 'It's not someone from this house, is it, Matron? One of the Sixth?'

Rose saw her own face mirrored in the matron's eyes and realised that she already knew the answer.

At breakfast the next morning, Rose heard the news. The truth had been confirmed earlier than that, thanks to the helicopter pulling away during the early hours of the morning, after hovering so long over the beach and its forbidding rocks.

They had found Bethany's body around the next bay, slapping against the cliffs with the ebb of the tide. Her limbs were pale and swollen, her shorn head cracked and bruised by the rocks. One of the local paramedics had to climb down to arrange pulling her up. The beam of the helicopter had helped, as well as its ladder, even though it hadn't been created for that purpose.

And now the gossip of it rippled through the dining hall; the breakfast pastries seemed impossibly shining, the jam too sweet, the knives sharper than usual. The Juniors, particularly, tossed the truth around like a delicious morsel of food. Rose couldn't help but feel horrified by their heartlessness as she watched them from the staff tables.

Her colleagues weren't much better with their pointed questions: 'Where is she now, has anybody . . . identified her?'

'Not formally, but it could only—'

Rose felt her own voice rise. 'Are they sure it's her?'

'They've brought her back to the school. She was handed over this morning.'

Seeing Frances in the doorway of the canteen, Rose rushed to her friend, the weight of her conscience propelling her forward. Frances's face was pale, her hair unruly, her upper lip somehow swollen; Rose caught a whiff of stale wine on her breath.

'Frances,' she said in a whisper, 'this is terrible news.'

Frances's voice was hoarse and somehow distant. 'Rose.'

'I can't help feeling that I could have done something. Bethany was—'

'Yes.'

'How did she get to the beach?'

'They don't know.' Frances shook her head. 'The groundsman, the porters, even the games staff, they should have seen her.'

Rose's face crumpled. 'Is her father here?'

'Her father has been contacted. He will be the one to formally identify her.' Frances was looking across the girls with a terrible resentment in her eyes. 'He was . . . disappointed.'

Rose was momentarily stunned. 'Disappointed?'

'They don't know,' Frances said quietly, 'how she got out of the san.'

'But she was in my office last week, Friday afternoon. She got out then. I went to get help . . .' Rose paused desperately. 'But then, Emma had dismissed her. I don't think I did the right thing there.'

Frances's blue eyes honed in on Rose. 'Why didn't you say anything before?'

'Emma said she was going to report it to the Headmaster.' Rose hesitated. 'I'm sure he knew.'

'That wasn't for Emma to – why didn't you raise the alarm?' Frances's face seemed to contort with emotion. 'Why didn't you *do* anything, Rose?'

'I thought—'

Frances pushed past her, using the edge of her tray roughly.

Rose followed Frances with her eyes, trying to piece fragments of their conversation back together, to understand what had just happened and why Frances was so angry. Her gaze fell on Anthony near the door, his coat rumpled and damp-looking, his hair scruffy, his face rent with pity. Rose realised he must have been one of the ones helping outside.

Her eyes pricked with tears. Blinking desperately, she saw the Headmaster come through the door behind Anthony, his expression heavy as he conversed with some official-looking men, pulling at the fingertips of his gloves.

Rose blinked again and thought of a lead-lined room.

Above the Headmaster's small group, Rose's gaze found the tall painting of the Founder and his grim complacency.

'Madam?'

It was Nessa and Freddie, one of whom dropped an envelope

into Rose's hands and said, 'We wanted to wish you a Merry Christmas.'

'Have a good holiday, Madam,' added the other softly.

Rose only nodded as she stared at the envelope, unspeakably white and innocent. The hard corners pinched at her fingers.

LENT TERM

Caldonbrae Hall's Mission Statement:

To support and guide our girls in becoming
enlightened, fulfilled and resilient women,
ready to serve and enrich the society to which
they belong;
and
To honour our pioneering heritage through
rigour and innovation,
in the everlasting pursuit of excellence.

Caldonbrae Hall prospectus, 150th anniversary edition

10.

Rose scoured the papers during the holiday – every headline spread across the lobby tables of her mother's clinic. She checked the deaths and births announcements in *The Times*. She tried *The Telegraph*, the *FT*. She even trawled through the frayed magazines emblazoned with the latest scandals, articles on the Manchester bombing and pieces analysing the declared separation of Prince Charles and Diana. But Bethany's name was exempt.

Rose felt strangely cut off from Caldonbrae Hall. She thought constantly of Bethany's family, her father. Could Rose have done more? Could any of them? Rose caught herself glancing at her new 1993 calendar more than once, staring hard at those early January days, considering how life at Hope might look during that first week back.

She'd tried to focus on her mother, encouraging her to spend more time with the other patients and their Christmas cheer. Meanwhile, Rose had a favourite seat by the library bookshelves to nurse her own thoughts, jolting at the interruption of Bethany's ghostly face every time she closed her eyes.

Rose had been asked to sign a few papers, now that her

mother's care was past its initial phase. She was surprised to see Caldonbrae's name on the documents listed under 'power of attorney', and approached her mother in the conservatory on a bright January morning.

'I'm not sure what it's saying, Mum. Shouldn't the power of attorney go to *me*?'

'Yes, darling, of course,' her mother muttered. 'But they're the ones sorting it out legally.'

'Can't I sort it myself?' Rose added quietly. 'We don't need them.'

'Rose, just sign the papers. I can't tell you the hassle they're saving us.' She shifted around in her chair. 'Don't you have any idea how much this place costs per month?'

Rose mumbled resentfully, 'I assure you I am earning every penny.'

'You mustn't make a fuss over this – I can't even hold the pen properly now with my hands.'

Rose looked at her mother, a pale imitation of the woman she once was, her nervous system undoing itself from the inside out. If Rose told her how things were really going at Caldonbrae, what would she advise? Had her principles evaporated along with her physical strength? Perhaps not, but Rose knew her mother would find a way to cast some blame back on her daughter; any problems were always inevitably her fault.

She spent the rest of the holidays readying herself for the return to school. She carefully repacked the pile of Fourths' exercise books, which she'd thrown in at the last minute before leaving Caldonbrae. It had made her suitcase doubly heavy, but she'd wanted to take something of theirs with her. After poring over the mass of messy pages, neglected and unmarked by Jane, Rose realised they were too far gone. She decided that next term she would give the class entirely new exercise books, with any decent grammar pages from the old books cut out and kept. Rose took comfort in her plan, all the time trying not to think of Jane, wherever she was, and whether she'd heard of Bethany's death.

Rose couldn't bear to look at the Upper Sixth as they filtered along the desks for the first lesson back. She wondered whether they saw the same empty space that she did.

In a letter topped with the school's emblem Rose had been informed that the formal investigation had now been entirely dropped and her dossier updated. However, her probationary period would be extended until the end of this new term, to ensure that everything could be carried out in the proper way. The letter was signed by the Headmaster, but as Rose stared at the scrawl of his signature, she was certain that Vivien had crafted every word. Rose knew that she should feel relieved by the letter; that it was a key part of her professional progression. But she didn't like what it confirmed. False as it had been, the allegation had bound her and Bethany together, and that link had been severed with her death.

Rose's voice sounded dull to her ears, falling flat as it met the faces of the Upper Sixth, drawn either in sorrow or boredom. *Hippolytus* wasn't much help either. They were stuttering towards the end of the play – Hippolytus's body had been fatally trampled by horses and his redemption-seeking father summoned. Rose was reading all the parts, trying not to remember her former students and their eagerness in volunteering to read, half the world away now. She reached the end of a line and put the book down.

'Girls, I wanted to say—'

'I know, Madam, it's terrible,' Tash interrupted, her eyes wide and manic.

Rose breathed out. 'Yes, I'm—'

'I'm devastated.'

Dulcie elbowed Tash. 'Will you shut up about bloody Charles and Diana? You wouldn't stop prattling last night, and at breakfast this morning.'

'I won't! It can't be divorce. Not in the royal family!'

'Girls,' Rose's voice was strangled, 'that's not at all what I—'

'You should ask Frederica List in Fourths,' Lex began, smirking. 'She'll know the truth of it. Isn't she Princess Anne's goddaughter?'

Tash turned her head. 'Freddie?'

'Her name,' Dulcie glowered at Tash, 'is Frederica.'

Rose finally interjected. 'No, Dulcie. She prefers Freddie.'

Lex leaned back with another smirk. 'Everybody knows the royal family are naff.'

'No, you're wrong,' Tash said crisply. 'My aunt says they set the ultimate example for the rest of us.'

Lex laughed. 'Don't they give each other silly Christmas presents, like tweezers and things?'

'Some of the middle royal ladies are old Hope girls,' Tash narrowed her eyes, 'so don't be too hasty with your judgement, Lex.'

'Well, Tash,' Dulcie elbowed her neighbour, 'maybe you can have Diana, now she's been cast aside.'

'Madam,' Lex was still smirking, 'what do *you* think?'

'Well,' Rose said apprehensively, 'if you really want to know, I respect Diana for taking charge of her own life.'

'Oh, of course,' Dulcie scowled. 'Rather like Bethany did, Madam?'

Rose had to steel herself; this wasn't a moment to lose her temper. 'Girls, this is serious.' She sat down on her chair and gave the row of five a sweeping look. 'How are you dealing with this shock? Is there anything—'

'Good riddance, I think. She never belonged here.'

'Dulcie,' Rose said calmly, 'how can you be so—'

'What, Madam?' Dulcie sat forward, nearly slamming her hand on her desk. 'Practical?'

Rose swallowed the sickly burn in her throat. 'Did you girls go to the funeral?'

'No, Madam.' Tash shook her head. 'Of course not. It was a private family thing in Sussex.'

'Oh, how sad.'

'Hardly,' Dulcie snorted.

'Dulcie, I wonder,' Rose said wildly, 'what is it that makes you say such harsh things? One of your peers has died.'

'By choice, Madam.'

The four other girls looked askance at Dulcie. Rose didn't drop her gaze. 'So when they teach you all these *disciplinary* skills for the future, they don't teach you compassion?'

'Madam,' Tash added in a soft voice, 'none of us wants to talk about it. It's done. Besides, *compassion* means something else here.'

Rose tried to breathe away her emotion. She reached for the upturned *Hippolytus* on her bureau; but Dulcie wasn't finished. 'I forget that you don't actually know anything, Madam. It'll be so much easier when you finally catch up.'

Rose sat forward, suddenly furious. 'Why don't you just tell me everything, then, Dulcie?'

'I can't!'

'Why not?' Rose's book slid off her lap.

'To be honest, Madam,' Dulcie's face was brimming with exasperation, 'I'm surprised you're still here. Some of us thought you wouldn't make it back after the break.'

'My goodness, Dulce, you're so unkind!' Tash gasped.

'Okay.' Recovering herself, Rose bent to pick up her fallen book. 'I give up. Let's just carry on with the play.'

For the next few days Rose waited for Bethany's name to bloom from any of her colleagues' mouths, for the girl's story to fall out of a conversation. For that strange question – suicide or accident? – to be answered. For any hint of grief, or remorse, to present itself for examination. But Rose found none; the general severity of the staff didn't seem to reduce itself to sorrow. More than once, she was tempted to let Bethany's name fly out of her mouth, fully formed, just to shock them all.

There was no doubt, either, that Frances was avoiding her. Bethany's death seemed to have stunned her into silence. Grief wasn't unfamiliar to Rose, but she couldn't regret her friend's silence more; there was so much she wanted to talk to Frances about, candidly. During her lunches and passing conversations with Emma – with Anthony, too – Rose had been unable to summon the courage to speak up, but she knew it would be different with Frances.

On her newly allocated Thursday evening duty in House Prudence, Rose was watching the Thirds finger a pile of flap-jacks, the crumbed oats falling across their laps. Rose rubbed one eye with tiredness, aware that she might be blurring her make-up. The girls were chatting, many of them clean from the shower and smelling of lilac soap. Rose was only half listening to them.

'The opera was Wagner, it was lovely – but I had to sit next to Granny,' one girl was saying, raising her eyebrows regretfully, 'and she snored all through the second act.'

Two other girls were looking at Rose expectantly.

'Sorry?' Rose sat up, now alert.

'Apparently she was obsessed with you, Madam.'

The other girl hooked Rose with her eyes. 'Yes, Madam, what did really happen with Bethany?'

Stunned, Rose couldn't reply.

'Did you help them identify the body at the beginning of the holidays, Madam?'

'Did you mind terribly, Madam?'

It was all wrong. When Rose wanted to speak, the girls didn't; when they did, she couldn't.

'It's an ugly business, Madam, now that we're all locked up for the foreseeable. The Sixth aren't even allowed out at the weekend!'

'But aren't any of you sad about it?' Rose blurted out. 'Don't you think it's . . . really sad?'

'My father said she took her fate into her own hands.'

'She's a warning to us all, Madam.'

The chatter stopped abruptly and Rose turned to see one of the house prefects at the door with a stern face, another girl hovering behind her, equally cross.

'Madam! It's past Junior bedtimes.'

'Oh.' Rose stood up. 'You're absolutely right. Let's get on with it.'

The girls hopped off the sofa and brushed the crumbs to the floor, one of them sucking at her fingers. The prefect's friend, another Fifth, was scrutinising the Thirds and caught Rose in the wave of her loud rebuke: 'And watch what you're eating, girls, for heaven's sake.'

'Yes,' added the prefect, 'remember Diet. Especially with Valentine's Day coming up.'

The prefect's friend wasn't finished. 'Did you smuggle those flapjacks in with your tuck?'

'No.' A dash of fear crossed one girl's face. 'Matron gave them to us. As a treat.'

'Because Hattie finally got her menses.' Another girl volunteered, nudging her mortified friend.

'Oh, how ridiculous,' the prefect scoffed. 'And have you lot already had Body Inspection?'

'Body Inspection?' Rose repeated idiotically from the doorway.

'Yes,' the Third hastily answered the Fifth, 'it was straight after holidays.'

'Too soon in my opinion,' the prefect retorted.

'You shouldn't talk like that to each other,' Rose interjected, trying to impose some order over the conversation. She nodded at the Juniors: 'Come on, girls, bedtime.'

There was already a flurry of movement along the Junior corridor as girls dashed in and out of rooms towards the messy gathering in the bathroom at the far end. Showers jetted on and off as the Seconds furiously scrubbed at their teeth or rubbed soapy flannels over their red cheeks.

Rose watched their little routine. So many of the faces were familiar to her from her own lessons – it was strange to see them now, so unmade and vulnerable. She resisted the urge to throw the blankets over each of them, tuck them in, and whisper something, anything, comforting.

'What's Body Inspection?' she eventually said.

A sleepy head raised itself. 'Weights and measures for matron.'

Rose glanced over the heads soft on their pillows, before saying gently, 'I see.'

'Goodnight, Madam,' three voices said in unison.

'Goodnight, girls.'

'Madam, please switch off the light,' replied a little voice as Rose hovered a moment too long.

An hour later Rose was crossing the lobby on the ground floor and heard an adult voice coming from the study, addressing a group of Fifths. By instinct she held her breath and waited, seeing the prefect's figure perched on the sofa's armrest.

'Yes, well, ladies.' Rose recognised the adult voice as Vivien's. 'I hope you're all being kind to Madam. She has much to learn.'

There was a general mumble from the girls, before, 'She got the bedtimes wrong, Madam.'

'All the same, give her the benefit of the doubt, please, Victoria.'

There was a short silence.

'Perhaps she's a good role model to you all. Intelligent, attractive.'

'Hardly,' scoffed one of the Fifths. 'I heard that you wanted someone else, an old girl, but she wasn't available. This was all you could find. It shows.'

Rose felt as if she'd been struck.

'I won't speak to rumours, Isabella, and neither should you.' Vivien's voice was as sharp as her unseen face.

'But, Madam, wasn't she another one of Bethany's?'

Vivien seemed to hesitate. 'Not entirely, Victoria, no.'

'That's what everyone is saying.'

A third voice came in louder: '*And* she's not married, Madam. She's a townie. She's probably got china dogs on her mantelpiece, like my uncle's new wife.'

Vivien made an indistinguishable noise. 'Perhaps she serves as a cautionary tale, then. Alone and working in a school like this, serving exceptional girls like you.'

Rose sucked her breath through her teeth before clearing her throat loudly across the dim light of the lobby.

'And here she is!' cried Vivien, rising to greet Rose at the study door.

Rose glared at Vivien, her cropped hair brushed back, her well-defined features suddenly haggard in the light.

'The big sister of House Prudence,' Vivien attempted.

'No, Madam,' Rose answered, her voice weaker than she expected, 'not a big sister at all. I'm a teacher.'

Vivien gave Rose a broad smile and guided her across the lobby. Rose stiffened at the touch.

'I hope you don't mind too much,' Vivien began. 'Being with the younger girls, the riff-raff. Mind you, Clemency is much worse.'

Rose looked away from Vivien, her jaw tight. 'I don't mind it here.'

A cluster of Fourths were moving towards the stairs and Rose saw Nessa glance back at her nervously, her mouth slightly open at seeing the deputy head there too.

'Ah, yes.' Vivien turned to intercept the look. 'Why don't you go up to your flat, Madam. I'll take it from here.'

'That's very kind of you, but this is my duty.'

Vivien nodded. 'Well now, you must be pleased that the investigation is over? And all that grief at the end of last term!'

'Is it really over?' Rose frowned at Vivien's casual tone. 'I—'

'Yes, and all relevant people have been notified.'

'But Bethany—'

Vivien interrupted sharply, 'There's the staff meeting on Monday to discuss matters.'

'Oh.'

Vivien clasped Rose's hand and readjusted her smile. 'Of course, there is much to talk through, but now is not the time.'

The Monday afternoon staff meeting was taking place in the common room. The Headmaster was sitting adroitly on the armrest of an oversized chair, the rest of the seats dragged across the rugs to face him. The fire crackled behind the wide circle of staff as he spoke of Bethany.

Her father had arrived on the last Saturday of term to have the body driven home, he explained. Rose imagined the long black cars, one longer than the rest. The family had held a private funeral on their estate in the south of England, Mr deVere fully understood the circumstances surrounding his daughter's death – her fragile emotional state – and how the school had done their utmost to serve her needs. Rose turned her face away at that.

The Headmaster continued by acknowledging the grief of some of the girls, and how the staff must band together and maintain a stiff upper lip. The housemistresses and matrons were taking the girls directly in hand, the restrictions and freedoms had been tightened up for the first half of term, but he wanted to maintain some normality around Hope. Cradling her teacup, Rose checked the faces around her, etched with pity. Emma was leaning her chin in her hand, nodding along with the Headmaster's words.

By the time Rose reached the bottom of her teacup the speech was drawing to a close. There was a brief gap, and Rose surprised herself by raising her hand. The Headmaster's brow seemed to stiffen.

'Rose?'

Rose lowered her hand gingerly. 'Will there be a short service for Bethany, a memorial perhaps? For the girls and those that knew her to pay their respects?'

The Headmaster's brown eyes seemed to sear through Rose, though his expression remained solemn. 'A few members of the Sixth arranged that very thing, and it took place last Wednesday.'

'Really?'

His expression didn't change. 'Yes.'

'But it wasn't advertised,' Rose pushed, ignoring Emma's mortified face. There was an uncomfortable shift amongst the staff seated around her.

'As I say, my dear, we are trying to manage this very difficult situation.'

Rose opened her mouth again but the Headmaster had already turned to Vivien, who finished the meeting by warmly encouraging the staff to approach her with any questions. Rose looked away; whatever courage had beaten through her now faltered.

As the other members of staff began to rise out of their seats, Frances sandwiched herself between Emma and Rose and stated, 'I must apologise for my shortness at the end of last term, Rose.'

Rose didn't look at her friend, trying to understand the formality of her apology. 'It's fine. Thanks for saying that. I was so upset to leave this place at the end of term.' She glanced up; Frances seemed surprised by her honesty. 'I felt devastated for the poor girl. And this,' Rose nodded at the room, 'doesn't seem enough.'

'This *is* enough,' Frances insisted, shifting to face Rose

properly. 'We can't do any more than this.'

Emma intervened sharply. 'Yes, Rose. Drop it, won't you? It seems a bit perverse, your questioning it.'

Rose felt the heat rise in her cheeks. 'I don't seem to be able to drop it.'

'But you *must*.' Emma's hair swung forward. 'The girls have associated you with Bethany and that's terrible for your reputation.'

'I know they have.' She turned to face Emma. 'But why aren't we talking about it? Was it an accident, or did we . . . drive her to it?'

'We absolutely did not.'

'But how do you know?' Emma and Frances shared a look as Rose bowed her head. 'And shouldn't someone tell Jane?'

It was the first time Rose had said the name aloud and she felt a strange rush of adrenaline as she did.

Emma's face hardened; she put out her arm as if to block Rose's armchair. 'What's wrong with you?'

'What's wrong with *you*?' Rose shot back. 'That's two student deaths in two years on school grounds. Where is the accountability? And where *is* Jane? This place is all about traditions, honour, rules . . . which means what? Turning a blind eye when things go wrong?'

Emma leaned forward. 'Rose, please watch what you're saying in here.'

'Apparently you wanted to hire someone else.' Rose's chest seemed to thud. 'I was the second choice. Is that true?'

Frances's face was open with dismay.

'No.' Emma shook her head. 'No, it's not like that.'

'And already I'm one term in, a girl has died, and the rest

of the students think badly of me.' Rose was quieter now, talking half to herself. 'I think I've made a terrible mistake. I think this place might drive me mad.'

'Look ahead.' Emma's voice was strong as she gripped Rose's chair. 'Concentrate on what's to come.'

'Emma's right, Rose,' Frances added forcefully. 'There are so many great things ahead. You've got so much to give.'

'Yes. And please,' Emma finished, 'drop it about Bethany.'

Rose looked at her two colleagues as the room moved behind them. Teachers pouring out more tea and coffee, pointing at the noticeboard, laughing at a story from the holiday. She gave Frances and Emma a resolute nod.

But Rose knew she'd now hit upon a purpose: to write to Jane and tell her what had happened. She'd try every hospital in Inverness if she had to. A second letter, this time full of truth. The woman had a right to know, even if it would bring only grief – and it would need to be Rose that told her. She'd somehow bound herself up in this bizarre ensemble of fate, the three of them: one dead, one absent and one very much alive.

11.

Rose's Fourths were unexpectedly thrilled to have a flock of new exercise books on the second lesson back, with everyone's best pages kept from their previous books. Nessa gawped at her own pages, raising her freckled face to say, 'Madam, you really care, don't you?'

'Yes, of course,' Rose answered simply.

But their new delight didn't last long. They soon returned to that heady badgering of Rose, most of it coming from a renewed Nessa, rather than Freddie.

'Madam, apparently Sappho wrote love poems for women and she was a woman?'

'She did,' Rose answered, writing on the blackboard.

'So, Madam, we were wondering, are you more like Sappho or are you more like . . .' Nessa looked around the room for inspiration.

'Aphrodite?' Freddie tried, not looking at Rose.

'Normal,' Nessa said at the same time.

Rose tried to process what they were saying, her piece of chalk hesitating mid-word. She lowered her arm with a shaking laugh.

'I think I'm more like Aphrodite. Not that it's any of your

business,' Rose answered, grateful to the girls for making her smile. 'And, Nessa, there isn't really such a thing as "normal".'

'Oh, of *course*, Madam.' Nessa smirked at Freddie. 'I forget, you're a radical.'

'A townie, rather,' Josie called out from the back. 'Definitely not a gownie.'

'Didn't one woman in mythology fancy a bull, Madam?' Daisy suggested unhelpfully from her side of the classroom.

'Er . . . yes, Daisy,' Rose smiled. 'But that's a story for another day.'

'I enjoy Dido and Aeneas, Madam,' said Freddie, stretching out her arms and almost hitting Nessa in the face. 'And all the stuff about Carthage and the African tribes.'

'Me too,' nodded Daisy, along with a few other girls near her.

'And me,' Nessa added as she admired her new exercise book again, 'even if it is all in Latin.'

Rose halted at her small triumph, glancing at the acquiescent faces around the room.

Daisy continued: 'The Africa stuff is quite similar to colonies in Geography.'

'Oh no, Daisy,' Freddie gritted her teeth and turned back to face her, 'Geography is *such* a bore.'

'Yes, Tweedle Dee teaches us, Madam,' Josie said in her deep voice. '*She*'s a Sappho. Madam Miss Whitaker, with the double chins.'

Rose thought of Deirdre, whom they meant. 'Don't be unkind.'

'Oh, her lessons are all right,' Nessa nodded. 'She's an old girl, Madam. She's just set in her ways.'

'What?' Rose bristled. 'Miss Whitaker? She went here, to Caldonbrae?'

'Yes, Madam,' answered Nessa, surprised at Rose's shock. 'I don't think she's ever left.'

'Tweedle Dee!' Daisy laughed. 'Because once she took us for games, and—'

'That's not why, Daisy,' Josie interrupted loudly. 'It's because of her and that matron, Tweedle Dum.'

But Rose was still working through this new information. 'Are there other old girls, here, too?'

'Yes, of course, Madam,' Nessa nodded. 'Quite a few.'

'But Deirdre must have left,' Rose frowned, 'to study Geography at university . . . and then perhaps get some teaching experience . . .' Nessa shrugged with disinterest. Neither Emma nor Frances had ever told Rose about any old girls – it seemed so unusual to leave a place like this only to return.

'Well, anyway,' Rose sighed, seeing her waiting class, 'Sapphos or Aphrodites . . . I'd much rather you ask my preference for Latin, Greek or Ancient History.'

'No,' intoned Josie, 'we don't care about that. We just wondered, Madam, which one it was – Madam in German or Sir in History?'

Not more gossip, Rose thought as she turned to the board. It was true that along the main corridor Rose was noticing some arched eyebrows in her direction – from the Juniors and Intermediates, mostly, their white sleeves reaching to guard their whispering mouths.

'It's neither, Josie,' Rose finally answered.

'But everybody needs somebody to care about, Madam,' Nessa said innocently, 'Every woman needs a counterpart.'

'Do they?' Rose turned back with a half-laugh on her face.

'Yes, or they end up like the women in your stories.' Freddie swept out her long arm, taking in Rose's mosaic of cards and the tatty posters on the walls. 'Dido, Io, Agrippina. That woman that killed herself, Lucretia.'

'Yes,' Nessa piped up again, 'there's a lot of death and loneliness in these stories, isn't there, Madam? People betrayed or left behind.' Her little face was thoughtful. 'I wonder if Bethany was trying to be like Lucretia. Maybe she wanted to make some difference for the rest of us by her death. Walking into the sea with her dress full of stones. What do you think, Madam?'

The entire class stiffened at the mention of Bethany's name.

'Don't talk to Madam about it,' Josie's sharp voice came from the back. 'We're not to discuss anything. She doesn't *know* anything.'

Rose stared across the girls' faces as a flat silence spread across the room.

'Does it upset you to talk about her, Madam?' Freddie was looking at Rose carefully.

'No,' said Rose firmly, painfully aware of the many rows of eyes waiting for her answer. She knew what she wanted to say, to shout out. But she remembered the Headmaster's solemn face in the common room, and managed, 'I had nothing to do with Bethany.'

'She was a bad apple, Madam, not like the rest of us,' Josie continued, tipping her chair back. 'I want to be a success story. And *she* was not.'

'I think it's really sad,' added Nessa quietly. 'She's just like one of these poor women.'

'Yes, maybe she is,' Rose nodded, without looking at any of them. She turned back to the board. 'Now, let's get on. Clean page in your new books, please.'

*

That weekend Rose found herself pulled down the drive again. The walk was barer than ever as any little patches of yellow and pink flowers had blown away with the winter, but the gorse bushes still shook with the wind. The school building was dark grey against the pearly January light; its windows like a thousand eyes staring out at her accusingly.

Rose refused to be trapped inside like the girls were. Out here was Poseidon's dominion, Zeus's air – even if she was alone.

She'd stopped by Anthony's office on Friday to see if he wanted to go for a walk together over the weekend. It was a brave move in the face of the girls' gossip, hidden under a simple gesture. Anthony's colleague in History, Ashley, thankfully wasn't there, but a girl was in his place, sitting on Anthony's desk and looking down at him in his chair. The two looked surprisingly intimate, and when the girl turned around Rose saw it was Clarissa.

'Oh, I'm so sorry for interrupting,' Rose said, flustered, before adding, 'Sir.'

'Not at all.' Anthony's brow was deep with concern; he dropped Clarissa's hand as he stood up. Clarissa glowered at Rose as she muttered, 'Thank you, Sir.' Collecting her textbook, she fitted some papers in between the pages, and meandered out of the room.

Anthony gave an awkward shrug. 'Clarissa. I'm her tutor, you see. She . . . it's difficult. She tends to have crushes, and this term it's on me.'

'I'm sure it's very common here.' Rose was annoyed to find that she minded. 'I'm always anxious about that sort of thing. They really drummed it into us during training – do not touch the children.'

'Yes, of course.'

'But it must be difficult for a man in a girls' school . . .' Rose wished she would stop talking; her cheeks were starting to burn. She knew that the girls adored Anthony – how her Fifths gushed about him, finding any excuse to bring him up in conversation; how many girls' eyes dragged towards his loping walk down the corridors. How her own eyes followed theirs, too.

'Well, Rose, how can I help you?' He reached forward and gave her fingers a squeeze, his hazel eyes warm. She focused on her hand instead, seemingly disembodied by his, which had clasped Clarissa's just a moment before.

'Nothing, it's not important.' Rose said, shaking her head. 'Have a good afternoon.'

At the far end of the drive Rose stopped at the gates. Bolted closed, as usual. The heavy wrought iron froze to the touch as she pulled her fingers out from her sleeve.

'Madam?' The groundsman called out, in a voice less frantic than last time.

'Hello.'

'You all right?' He stayed near his doorway, his questioning eyes peering at her between his beanie and his beard. It was a different man, Rose realised.

'No, I just . . . fancied a walk. All the cabs were busy, and the porters wouldn't take me.'

The groundsman didn't answer. Rose turned back to look at the monster of the school building as he approached her.

'Admiring the view?'

'No,' Rose answered bluntly, one hand still grasping hold of the gate.

'I can't abide it. Your lot've desecrated this place.' The

groundsman cleared his throat. 'The foundations are significant, but that's all built over now.'

'Significant?'

'To Scottish history. The medieval fortress, far before your William Hope. It was a bonny hiding place during the Jacobite risings. Then it were taken and granted to some earl. Now it's claimed for your English colony.' He rubbed his eye wearily. 'Full of those little heiresses and their godawful beast of a Headmaster.'

Rose wanted to laugh in comradeship. 'What makes you dislike him so much?'

'Bloody English, all your upper class sneering at us. Those awful girls.'

'I don't sneer at you.' Rose's voice became serious. 'And the girls aren't so bad, especially the younger ones.'

The groundsman took a step back. 'What're you doing here, anyway? Aye, you must be the one that got Rick into trouble.'

Rose replied urgently, 'I haven't got anyone into trouble.'

'Aye, he said it were a young teacher. He shouldn'ta told you about that girl last year . . .'

'What? No.'

'Walking all the way out here . . .' The groundsman's voice lifted. 'What do you think you're doing?'

Rose said it before she could prevent herself: 'I wanted to see where Bethany . . . died.'

'What? Are you some kind of sicko?'

'No.' Rose's heart seemed to beat in her mouth. 'But why didn't anyone see her that night? Or spot her on the beach?'

'We can't watch every girl that hopscotches around the place!'

'Yes, but this was late at night.'

'During an event,' he nodded fiercely, 'when we were all called in to be near the building.'

The cold air stung at Rose's face. 'Oh, I didn't—'

'Who do you think you are, missy, asking questions like that?' The groundsman turned back to his lodge. 'Go back where you belong.'

Rose shuddered as he slammed the door of the crumbling lodge, seeing again the school's coat of arms emblazoned above the arch of the door.

The wind drove her on her way back up to the school. She imagined the girls' faces pressed up against the windows, held inside and watching. Then Bethany's thin pale face, her blunt head water-sodden and dirty against those scarred rocks. But this time, Rose imagined Bethany's eyes closed, at peace, and free.

Rose returned to a small white envelope with her name scrawled across it, propped up at her door. Tearing open the letter, she moved into her sitting room. The page was typed, some of the letters slammed over and corrected; its paper was yellowed and misshapen, as if it was once wet but then dried.

Dear Madam,
You'd better be careful. Everyone knows about you, even Hope's governors. So you'd better stop making such a fuss and do your job properly. You don't want to be like the other Latin Madam. You don't want to end up any worse than that either. Remember, we have your mother. Let us take care of her, and let your other Madam take care of you. Buckle down and get on with it, or there will be consequences.
Yours,
One of Us

Rose extended the letter the length of her arm, squinting at it. Then she let it flutter slowly to the floor. She moved to the sofa, holding her knees against her, trying to calm her racing heart.

Should she tell Frances? Emma? Should she just go straight to Vivien? Was it harassment? The letter was designed to frighten her. But the comment about her mother. That they '*have*' her? Rose held herself tighter and wondered which downstairs phone she could use to call her.

You don't want to be like the other Latin Madam – was this what Bethany had referred to, that something had happened to Jane? *Let your other Madam take care of you* – whom were they talking about?

Rose glared across at her stereo, fumbling through her albums in her mind, choosing one that could take her back to herself, away from this. But just as the cracking silence of the flat and the blow of the wind against the glass couldn't be unheard, her thoughts could not be drowned out.

Rose took the letter and folded it very tight, until it was perfectly small and flat. She went to her bookshelf and pulled out *The Bell Jar*. Sliding the letter into the book, she pushed it back hard onto the shelf. Rose hoped the lyricism of Sylvia Plath's pages would absorb the letter's words into their own. One no more deranged and hopeless than the other.

12.

But the letter followed Rose into the new week, and in turn, Rose followed the girls, gazing at the buttons down the backs of their dresses, the dashes of long hair dancing behind them. The girls seemed to merge into each other, under that immense glass eye, ever watching. Which of them had written it? Which of them could be so cruel?

Another surprise waited for her on Wednesday morning breaktime, when two books were returned to her desk, Euripides and Sophocles, from among Bethany's things. But Rose knew they weren't hers at all – they were Jane's copies, come back to haunt her. She stared at the silent pair, as closed and quiet as tombs, and fled her office to Anthony's along the corridor, hoping her beating heart might be soothed by his presence. But he wasn't there – no doubt at the same meeting as Emma, one that Rose's probationary period didn't allow her to attend. She'd protested this, since some important upcoming events were to be discussed: Valentine's Day in a matter of weeks, Affiliates Day at the end of term, and beyond that the great Thirtieth of June. That date seemed so far off to Rose – the end of the school year; a miracle if she reached it.

Rose returned to her office to glare at Jane's books, before nudging them under a pile of unmarked papers. The bell rang and jolted Rose all the way to the end of her nerves. She was due in the library.

Her Thirds were already there, sitting at the wide desks, astride the armchairs. Their round faces were alarmed as they suffered a rebuke from a Sixth.

'And what,' the girl reeled back with crossness, 'are you girls *doing* here, anyway?'

'Research, Clarissa,' Rose interrupted fluidly.

'Oh, Madam.' Clarissa raised her delicate eyebrows at Rose. 'Your class needs to be silent, they're distracting me.'

'This is the designated ensemble area, Clarissa. I checked with the librarian when I booked it,' Rose said firmly. 'If we're bothering you, could you perhaps try sitting further away?'

'No,' Clarissa's voice lifted, 'you don't understand, Madam. My French isn't where it should be – I'm an Elite, after all, and we're in January now!'

'An Elite?' Rose repeated. She noticed that the head girl seemed less made-up than usual, and perhaps hadn't washed her hair for a few days.

'Oh Clarissa,' one of the Thirds piped up, 'you're so brilliant, I'm sure you've got nothing to worry about.'

Clarissa let out an impatient noise and rounded on the girl. 'Of course I have! You don't know anything about it!'

Another Third tried: 'I can't wait to see you all dressed up at the Summer Ball, Clarissa. Have you chosen your dress?'

'What *is* this, anyway, Madam?' Clarissa was glancing down at one of the posters a group was working on. 'I can't even pronounce this – Arachne?'

'Arack-ne,' one girl corrected automatically, her face crumbling soon after. She looked up at Rose desperately.

Rose nodded at her. 'Well, since you ask, Clarissa, we're looking at mortals who've been punished by the gods.'

A Third leaned forward. 'It's really interesting, Clarissa. Look at ours, Actaeon. He was out hunting and by mistake he saw the goddess Artemis – or Diana – bathing naked, so she turned him into a stag, and his dogs—'

'This is nonsense,' spluttered Clarissa.

Rose stopped smiling. 'This is not nonsense.'

'It is.' Clarissa faced Rose. 'Classics never helped any girl I know. They should concentrate on the *real* subjects they might need. Like French.'

The next table of Thirds turned their faces to listen.

'These girls,' Rose said firmly, 'should concentrate on learning subjects they enjoy.'

'I hardly think they enjoy Latin.'

'I can promise they would disagree with you.'

'And *I* can promise *you*, Madam,' Clarissa shot back, her pretty face slipping into a snarl, 'that they would disagree with you, if I have anything to do with it.'

'They can speak for themselves, Clarissa,' Rose answered coolly. 'They have full intellectual freedom.'

But the girls at the table were mute, their eyes fixed on an indefinable space in front of them.

'Is everything all right, dear?'

The librarian had crossed the table in front of them, shaking some crumbs off her cardigan, late after breaktime. She was addressing Clarissa, not Rose. 'You seem quite frantic.'

'I'm fine.' Clarissa seemed to remember herself, and with a measured face she turned to Rose. 'I apologise for my lack of composure, Madam.' She glowered at the Thirds. 'I apologise, girls, I'm not myself. I'll be fine as soon as I sort out this French.'

Once Clarissa had settled at a desk further away, one girl raised her hand timidly. 'Is there really any point to this, Madam?'

'Well, let's see.' Rose's voice was thick. 'Are you enjoying yourself?'

The girl nodded.

'Are you learning something?'

'Yes.'

'Do you find it interesting?'

'Yes, Madam.' A trio of voices answered her this time.

'Well, then. There's your answer.'

That afternoon, Rose took advantage of an available cab. She hoped a mid-week trip to the harbour village might go unnoticed, even though there was the added caution of the girls' going-out ban.

Rose appreciated the muddied stone walls of Kennenhaven, feeling as grey as the grime of the place itself, and as murky as the winter weather. Slamming the cab door behind her heavily, she pushed into the post office.

The secretaries had notified Rose that her mother's chest had weakened suddenly, that they were trying her on a temporary oxygen tank. Rose despaired at the thought of her once-activist mother trawling a heavy tank behind her wheelchair, the slim tubes hooked up around her ears and into her nose. She had to speak to her, away from the school.

Rose blinked in the electric brightness of the post office, so bland and modern after the rafters and arches that she was growing accustomed to. She went straight for the payphone. The clinic's line rang and rang, just as it had done earlier in the secretaries' office. But now there was a sudden nurse's voice. Her mother was sleeping, did she want her to be woken up?

Rose hesitated, tapping the plastic of the handset. 'Better not. Is she okay, though? Can I leave a message?'

Rose picked out a card from the wire rack in the post office. She ignored the sunny images of the peninsula and its grandiose building, too much like those prospectus images she'd been seduced by last summer. Instead she chose a pretty view of the Cairngorm Hills, the sky clear above them. Her eyes went blurry and Rose found that she was crying.

She pulled her scarf tighter around her, even though it was warm inside the post office, dabbing her face with the edge of the wool. Eventually she turned to the desk. 'Can I pay for this and postage at the same time?'

The woman was frowning at Rose suspiciously. 'Of course you can.'

'I'll just write it now.'

The whiteness of the card was dazzling to Rose. She didn't know what to write. She looked back at the frowning woman with a sniff. 'Do you deal with the post from Hope?'

'From Caldonbrae?'

'Yes, sorry.'

The woman shook her head. 'No, dearie. The postman collects theirs, and then ours.'

A short man laughed from behind Rose. 'There'll be a huge difference in the envelopes.'

'Okay,' Rose said. 'I think that's good news.'

The woman fixed Rose with a beady eye. 'You're not one of them, are you?'

'Aye, she is, Morag,' said the man with a grin. 'Hear her accent.' Rose glanced at him, only seeing the blur of his green waxed jacket.

'I am not one of them,' Rose announced.

She scrawled out her mother's card, and added the five envelopes with their respective Inverness hospital addresses. Yes, Rose thought, five letters to Jane, as retaliation for that cruel one she'd received. Surely one would get to her. Picking through the coins in her purse she made enough for the stamps. Thanking Morag with an awkward little bow, she rushed out, wondering if she should walk back to the school, to regain some of her stamina and fight, and prove to the gatekeeping groundsmen that it could be done.

But outside the post office a Caldonbrae car rolled past. Rose hoped that it wasn't John's withered face she'd seen set back into the seat, on his way to the golf course. Better call the cab back, then, to cover herself, Rose thought. At least there were letters now that would freely go ahead, even if she couldn't.

On Rose's next visit to the common room, she didn't check for any heads swivelling towards her when she swung through the door. Had John seen her in the village? Would he try to intercept her letters? She busied herself with the teabags at the tea service, too distracted to choose between Earl Grey and raspberry.

She looked up at the noticeboard instead; there was a new, official document pinned up on the board, in Rose's old spot.

Any comments regarding the standards of
Vanessa Saville-Vye would be gratefully received.
She is on her last warning before demotion to House Clemency.

Rose was struck. What had Nessa done wrong? And could Rose contribute some comments? Nessa had been handing in work on time, and was very willing and charming in the classroom, even if she didn't have the intellectual goods to back it up.

'I'll never understand why you are incapable of using a cup and saucer like the rest of us.' Vivien was beside Rose, smiling, a thick curl decorating her forehead. 'Do fill up your mug, dear, don't let me stop you.'

Rose thought of that letter, upstairs in her flat, pressed between the pages of Sylvia Plath; and of the five envelopes – all gone off from the post office in Kennenhaven. She saw none of it on Vivien's face.

'Rose, I'm so pleased with the way things are going with you so far this term. I know things have been up and down. But we'll be approaching the end of your probationary period soon enough.' Vivien was still smiling. 'There's a lot to go over once that's concluded.'

Rose held her empty mug close to her chest. 'Will I meet the Headmaster, then?'

Vivien tilted her head. 'You've already met the Headmaster, Rose.'

'No, I mean, have a proper meeting. We've never discussed my role as head of department. There's things I'd like to—'

'Yes, I'm sure. But the Headmaster's a busy man.' Vivien gave a dismissive shake of her head. 'I can help with that. You'll take over the head of department duties from Frances, and much more, after your contract is sealed.'

'Yes.'

'We've got you in boarding, and you did one or two Swimmings, didn't you? The Conversation lesson last term was a disaster, so we won't have you on that.' Vivien eyed Rose carefully. 'So, I wondered whether you might like to contribute to another kind of activity this term. Just to give you more of a go . . . Any thoughts?'

'Oh . . .' Rose panicked. 'Perhaps I could help with Valentine's Day? I hear from Emma that it's an important event. What about the logistics?'

Vivien stood back, measuring Rose with a bemused smile. 'Well, really?'

'Yes.'

'It could be a good distraction for you, and help you move things forward. It's soon – on the Friday just before half-term so the girls don't miss out over the break. A good way to round off this half of term, perhaps.'

Rose tried to mirror Vivien's tone. 'Excellent.'

'You don't look particularly certain, Rose.'

'No, no,' Rose insisted, hating the fact that her face betrayed her so clearly. 'I am.'

'Right, that's agreed then,' Vivien nodded, remaining where she was. 'I shall let the secretaries know.'

In embarrassed avoidance Rose glanced back at the notice that betrayed Nessa's name. Vivien followed her eyes and grimaced. 'Ah, yes, I see. Poor little Vanessa, struggling again. She's in your house, isn't she?'

'Yes, she is.'

'She needs to pull her socks up.' Vivien raised her dark eyebrows. 'Anyhow, good to see you, Rose.'

'But . . .' Rose said desperately, moving to block Vivien, 'can I help Nessa in some way? I am eager to settle in and contribute, really I am.'

'I see.' Vivien's eyebrows contracted further. 'Any remedial sessions for Intermediates and Juniors are usually done in house, Rose.'

'But if it's academic . . . perhaps I could help Nessa with History, too, and English?' Rose couldn't ignore Vivien's sour expression. 'Perhaps not, then. But I'd like to contribute some comments to benefit Nessa, if I can.'

'Yes, I see that. Well.' Vivien rearranged her face into a smile. 'For now, anyway, the secretaries will be in touch regarding Valentine's Day.'

Rose watched the deputy head move out of the common room, before turning back to the noticeboard, aching with sympathy for Nessa.

Surely having Freddie always by her side meant that Nessa would be fine? Surely being in a school like this one meant that she'd be taken care of? What did demotion mean – was it so very terrible?

Remember what happened to Bethany, a small dark voice answered Rose.

She wanted to find the housemistress of Prudence and tell her as many positive things as she could about Nessa. She wanted to chase Vivien down the corridor and insist, shout even, that this one – Nessa – would be worth saving.

DAPHNE

inque patris blandis haerens cervice lacertis
'da mihi perpetua, genitor carissime,' dixit
'virginitate frui! dedit hoc pater ante Dianae.'
ille quidem obsequitur, sed te decor iste quod optas
esse vetat, votoque tuo tua forma repugnant.

Clinging to her father's neck with cajoling arms, she said 'My dearest father, let me be a virgin forever!' Diana's father granted it to her at birth. Indeed he yielded, but your beauty itself, Daphne, prevented your wish, and your loveliness opposed your prayer.

(Ovid's *Metamorphoses* 1. 485–489, written AD8)

Daphne was a nymph and the daughter of a river god. Her favourite pastime was dancing around the wooded grove with her friends in the dappled sunlight. Unlike the other nymphs, she didn't like to tempt the satyrs or flirt with any suitors that came upon them, and she certainly didn't want to leave her father's side for any husband. Virginity suited her perfectly well, even if her father longed for grandchildren to play about with in the river.

One afternoon while Daphne was collecting flowers, Apollo and Cupid were arguing. Apollo had been teasing Cupid for his small stature and youth, as well as his inefficiency with the bow and arrow – something Apollo claimed to be better at. A furious Cupid assembled his arrows, picking out his most powerful two: a golden arrow of burning desire, and a leaden arrow of terrible hatred. First, he struck Apollo with the arrow of desire, and then, knowing of Daphne's virginal resolve, he shot his second arrow into her chest.

A chase began, with Apollo begging Daphne to take him as her lover, and Daphne in turn shrieking her refusal as she fled. Apollo grew closer, snapping at her heels. Daphne begged her father to help. He could only answer with his own magic, and as Apollo finally reached out to grab the terrified Daphne, she was transformed into a tree. A laurel tree, with branches for arms and foliage for hair, her heart beating softly beneath the bark.

Daphne got her wish, even if it wasn't her choice. She would stay a beautiful virgin forever, close to her father, her body never ravaged. Later, her honour and renown came through Apollo – the young god grew to worship the tree, and used his power to render it evergreen. He even bound his famous wreath from its leaves, his lyre from its wood, as she stood serene and unresisting.

Perhaps Daphne was ravaged, then, after all.

13.

February seemed to arrive without anyone noticing – no change in the outside cold or in the tight freeze of the pipes thudding through the walls. Caldonbrae Hall was held in an everlasting season of grey. Rose wished she could seek comfort from the common room's hearty fire, but working quietly in her classroom, alone, suited her better.

Rose felt strangely fragile and separate from Emma's cheerful notes of encouragement and even Frances's invitations for more evening drinks. Anthony, too, had resorted to a kind of smiling bafflement towards Rose, from the doorway of her office, or opposite her at the dining table. But whatever might be happening outside it, Rose had started to feel secure in the bright air of her classroom, and the small trust that the girls were placing in her there – even if one of them had written that horrible letter, or might falsely accuse her again.

Rose threw herself into her Valentine's task: distributing flowers. Each girl was to have one white rose from the Headmaster. A wealth of additional requests had flooded in for the luckier girls, too: deep red, blush pink, sunny yellow. Rose had been astonished at the sheer number that poured in via the secretaries, particularly for the Sixth. Overgenerous parents and siblings, she supposed – it wasn't as if they were meeting any young admirers. Rose couldn't help pitying the few Sixth girls who would cradle only a single stem, knowing it to be from their Headmaster.

On the Thursday morning, the Fourths filled the desks with their relentless energy, and Rose was glad to see them. Nessa was struggling over translating English into Latin, more so than the others, who seemed to trick the jigsaws of declensions or conjugations into meaningful sentences. Rose had provided the main verb, so the rest of the sentence just needed to agree. But it wasn't agreeing with Nessa – her brain was frayed, along with her nerves at every mistake she made. Rose leaned over her, remembering the positively shining report she'd given the girl's housemistress.

'Tell me what's not making sense, Nessa, and I'll explain again.'

'No need, Madam. She's a moron,' Josie called out from the back.

'And you're a bitch,' Freddie answered from the front, her head bent over her work as the rest of the class lifted their heads.

'Whoa.' Rose straightened up with her hands raised. 'Girls.'

'Sticks and stones, Freddo,' Josie shouted, her beetle-black eyes sparked with emotion as she tipped her chair back. 'Careful what you say to me. And you, Madam.'

Freddie seemed to jerk into action. Dropping her pen on the page, she turned around in a swirl of red curls. 'Nobody is interested in *anything* you have to say, Josie. So shut up.'

The room shifted awkwardly; even Daisy straightened up with attention. Nessa concentrated on her own page, not seeing the spread of ink across Freddie's neat work from the dash of her pen.

'For heaven's sake, girls, I won't have this in my classroom,' Rose said firmly, 'Don't speak to your peers like that, Freddie. And Josie, don't be so rude to Nessa. I'd like you to apologise. We're all learning here.'

'Be kind to each other?' Josie mocked in a loud voice.

'Josie, I'm warning you.'

'Madam, you're so tragic.' Josie pulled a face. 'Just as well you're stuck in ancient times. When you finally work out what's really going on, you'll never be able to catch up.'

'Out!' Something in Rose snapped. 'Get out of my classroom!'

'No need.' Josie raised her thick eyebrows with the bell's confirmation. 'It's the end of the lesson, anyway, *Madam*.'

Rose attempted the Latin phrase for dismissal but the girls were gathering their books, reminding her that she'd lost all control over the lesson. Heaving her chest with frustration as the room began to empty, she turned to clean the blackboard.

But three of the girls were waiting for her again, the white skirts of their dresses pushing at the desks as the door closed.

Rose dropped her arm. 'Yes?'

Three, not four, Rose observed. The friendship was definitely fractured, then.

'Sorry about the bad language, Madam,' Freddie frowned. 'Josie's awful. You might want to watch it with her, though – she'll only run off to the deputy head.'

'Why would she do that?'

'Madam Ms Johns is her aunt, Madam.'

Rose opened her mouth – of course, she thought those beetle-black eyes reminded her of someone. 'Well, I've got no intention of *watching* it with her, or anyone.'

Freddie looked impressed. She raised her eyebrows at Nessa, who smiled back.

'Your owl has moved positions, Madam, did you know?' Daisy spoke into the pause.

Rose looked over to the window. She saw that Daisy was right: the round eyes of the little ceramic creature were now facing the rows of desks, away from Rose's bureau. 'Oh. How strange.'

'Tell us about a new one, Madam?'

Rose turned back to Freddie. 'A new what?'

'Another one of your stories. A new ancient woman,' pushed Freddie. 'Some of the Sixth were telling us about a play they'd studied with you. *Antigone*?'

'The Sixth talk about our lessons?'

'Some of them,' Freddie nodded.

Nessa laughed for the first time that morning. 'We all talk about you, Madam.'

Rose pulled an anxious face. 'I wish you wouldn't.'

'Tell us about Antigone,' Freddie pushed.

'After that outburst today, I'm not sure I'm in the mood. And I have other lessons to prepare for.'

'It's breaktime, Madam, and you hardly ever go to the common room anymore.'

Rose frowned, caught out.

'Antigone,' Daisy repeated. 'Is she a real woman or a mythological one?'

'She's . . . mythological, I suppose,' Rose replied.

'Oh. I prefer the real ones.'

Rose looked back at Daisy as she sat down a few desks away from Freddie; Nessa was still standing and hugging her books to her slim frame.

'Do you have any pictures of her, Madam?' Freddie gestured forward with her arm. 'Like you had of Agrippina?'

Rose took in Freddie's honey-coloured stare, the interested tilt of Daisy's head and Nessa's decisive settling on a desk. She smiled at the three of them in their white dresses, adolescence fighting its way onto their faces, their figures, their personalities. 'All right then. I don't know of many pictures of Antigone – she's a character in literature, after all. I'm sure I'll manage to find one for you girls.'

Rose spent much of Valentine's Day in her classroom; she was glad to be away from the hubbub downstairs, and was relieved that the half-term break would come the next day. She felt as though she'd been holding her breath, holding in any flicker of temper with every step she took. Rose wished there'd been a response from one of the Inverness hospitals; she knew it would make all the difference if she could just hear from Jane.

She'd handed the distribution lists to the Fifth prefects as the roses arrived in a string of vans, too many to count. Rose thought that the local florists must have raided the whole of Scotland for the heap of perfumed flowers. For her there'd be no cards, no roses – nothing but a bottle of wine for herself and any available friend over half-term. She ignored the squeak of optimism that she might receive something from Anthony.

Rose looked across at her Upper Sixth that morning. Lauren's cheeks were brushed with blush, while Lex had unfastened her silk dress at the nape of her neck, revealing a delicate pearl necklace. All five had recently manicured nails. With half-term looming, Rose had decided to ignore the fourth and final play on the syllabus, *Medea*, and throw a simple bit of mythology at them instead.

But it wasn't going well. However splendid the girls looked, they seemed to have disappeared behind their eyes – caught in this numb, unspeaking phase after Bethany's death.

'Is everything all right, Dulcie?' Rose asked with a mix of concern and frustration; the girl's mouth had been torn with dismay since the beginning of the lesson.

'Yes, Madam,' Dulcie answered automatically, her eyes sliding away from the images in front of her.

'Fine. Let's carry on. This is supposed to be fun.' Rose widened her eyes with frustration. She'd spread open a book of celebrated ancient artworks, along with printed pages of an Ovid translation: the story of Daphne and Apollo. The book's chosen page shone out photographs of the famous Bernini sculpture as Rose continued: 'Daphne here is caught mid-transformation. Look at all the different angles – here, she's a girl; there, she's almost a tree trunk. Look at her fingers, twisting into small branches. Look at the movement in the marble. Look at Apollo, one arm gripping on to her.'

'I still don't understand why Daphne is running away crying to her dad,' Lex huffed. 'Why wouldn't you want to marry a god? Why would you want to stay a virgin forever?'

'But does Daphne get away? Does she go free?' Dulcie demanded suddenly.

'Read the English translation, Dulcie. I suppose the answer is up to you.' Rose tilted her head. 'The transformation is soon complete – but is she free? See how Ovid describes Apollo, touching the smooth bark of the tree, still warm, and Daphne's heart beating beneath it.' Rose stopped short, seeing the girl's reaction. 'Dulcie, have I said something wrong? Do you need to take a moment?'

'I'm not upset, Madam. I'm not upset.' Dulcie expertly

glided a finger underneath her eye as her mouth slid open with emotion.

'What's happened?' Rose felt a flare of alarm at the girl's sudden vulnerability. She studied her for a moment, but then stiffened.

'Dulcie . . . what's that on your hand?'

Dulcie sat up straight and spread out her left hand in front of her. She sniffed resolutely. 'It's my engagement ring, Madam. It's beautiful, isn't it? He wanted to give it to me early.' The other girls turned to look; Lex blinked with envy at the ring, her mousy ringlets falling forward.

'Who wanted to give it early?' Rose asked, her mind buzzing with confusion.

'My *fiancé*, Madam.' Dulcie said it with a French accent, properly.

'Your fiancé? No.' Rose gurgled out a laugh at the absurdity of Dulcie's answer. 'You're seventeen.'

'I'm eighteen, Madam.'

Lex had propped her face up with her elbow. 'It's an astonishing ring, Dulce, there's nothing to be upset about.'

'I know,' Dulcie nodded. 'He just . . . wasn't what I was expecting.'

'It's always a shock to meet them for the first time.'

Dulcie reeled back. 'How do *you* know, Lex?'

'I don't.'

'What's this?' Rose had dropped her book into her chair. 'You'd never met him? Your fiancé?'

'It's fine,' Dulcie said quickly. 'I'm lucky. We all are. We're all Elites, after all. Our Values are very high. I held myself properly, I said all the things we're supposed to say, but it was harder than I thought.'

Rose searched the girls' faces, her thoughts fractured as she tried desperately to piece their words together. 'Hang on. You were trying to impress this man you'd never met . . . your fiancé – and you didn't like him?'

'Not really, but—'

'Then *why* is he your fiancé?' Rose demanded.

Lex gave an exasperated sigh. 'Because that's the way things are, Madam!' An astonished Rose saw Lex's face fall before she turned to Dulcie. 'Oh my goodness, Dulcie! Madam is still in her probationary period – we're not supposed to tell! Why on earth did you wear your ring?'

Tash held her mouth in disbelief, echoing the fright on Lex's face.

'It's my ring,' Dulcie was breathing quickly. 'Clarissa said I could wear it. She said it would be a good idea today, to make me feel better.'

Rose turned her face to the side, unable to believe what she was hearing.

'Madam might as well know, anyway,' Dulcie added savagely, her emotion turning into resentment. She lifted her face to Rose. 'I've been finished for him, Madam. We all have.'

Tash cried out, 'You'll be punished for saying!'

'For whom?' Rose urged.

'Our husbands. In our Pathway, Elite, we've got the best.'

'The best what?'

'Come *on*, Madam.' Dulcie rolled her eyes, heavily and with effect. 'The best pool of husbands. Suitors. Men from the highest sphere. Aristocrats, mostly. Men of influence.'

'Mine's a QC, top of the legal profession,' the fifth girl, Jenny, said. 'He's lovely – I'm lucky.'

Rose was flat against the blackboard, her mind racing.

'We're *all* marrying up or across, you see, Madam,' Dulcie nodded, adding bitterly, 'well, maybe not Lauren – she's American so she can only marry up!'

'Yes, but she's a double deb so she's lucky,' Lex added. 'She met the Queen *and* she'll meet the President.'

Lauren gave a shy smile, in spite of Dulcie's comment.

'*Your* requirements have been very peculiar, though, Jenny,' Dulcie leaned forward sharply, 'you have to admit.'

Jenny raised her chin haughtily. 'You're just jealous that mine's not an old codger like yours.'

'Tash has a lord, although she'd rather a lady, I think.'

'I think we should stop talking now!' Tash cried out again.

Rose's eyes hitched from one girl to the next, the rest of her body tight with panic as the girls waited for her reaction. Finally, she asked, 'Did you pick them, or did they pick you?'

'They choose us, Madam,' Lex said. 'Of course.'

'So,' Rose's throat was achingly dry, 'here, at Caldonbrae Hall, this school . . . arranges marriages?'

'Oh Madam.' Dulcie darkened, shaking her head. 'Trust you to say something so basic like that.'

'Yes, don't simplify things in such a droll manner!' Lex said, copying Dulcie's tone. 'We make alliances.'

'Not so *droll* when Dulcie's clearly upset,' Rose shot back, her face burning with the revelation.

'Well, there you are, Madam,' Dulcie continued, her pointed face full of satisfaction. 'Now you know the main function of Hope. The Founder had six daughters, after all. That must have been a lot to worry about, for a man like him.'

14.

It was as though she'd been watching a film reel, some kind of tasteless farce, or satire.

Rose moved robotically; she dismissed her Sixth early and set her things down in her office. She strode down the length of the third-floor corridor, the clack of her heels on the stone slamming into her ears. Turning the corner, she practically fell into Frances's office.

The weak light flickered to reveal the room's chaos – papers pinned across the wall, piles of files spilling off the desk onto the floor; a battered armchair on the side, and two pairs of worn leather heels at the door. The long wide window, identical to Rose's, showed the wild blur of the seascape.

Frustrated by her friend's absence, Rose switched off the light as she left. She moved as fast as she could, whipping down the Great Stairs two steps at a time. In the entrance hall the depleted display of Valentine roses sat in buckets across the flagstone floor, small pools of water dampening the discarded distribution lists. Above the mess, the great glass eye watched.

In Rose's mind she could see Dulcie's diamond ring flash with spakling light.

Hot tears swelled in her eyes as she carried on down to

the common room. Rose wanted to hammer on the door, to scream as she entered. But the hammering was only in her chest as she let the door slam shut behind her, scanning the chairs, trying to keep her breathing straight. The low room was so dimly warm, the hub of chatter so contented that it ought to have been another world.

The Headmaster was standing near the tea service. He turned, smiling mildly at the small group of staff around him, nodding as he traced a fingertip around the handle of his teacup. Rose moved her hand back to the doorknob instinctively, her cheeks still burning with horror and confusion.

Frances was nestled in a group of laughing women near the fire. Rose let go of the door and moved around the edge of the room, away from the power of the Headmaster's voice towards the strength of another.

Frances's laughter faded as she caught Rose's expression. 'Rose,' she said, sitting up.

'Frances,' said Rose, desperately.

'What's wrong?'

Rose's voice cracked as she spoke. 'It's the girls—'

'Rose,' called out one of the women in Frances's group, 'such a wonderful job you've done with flowers this year. Although . . . perhaps the prefects needed a little help this morning?'

Rose turned her head to glare at the woman.

'Yes,' said Frances, standing up, 'Rose has done a great job.' She stepped aside to block Rose from the group and lowered her voice. 'Listen, I know what you're going to say.'

Rose protested, 'Frances, I—'

'Not here, though. We can talk this through later.'

Rose shook her head vigorously.

'Go back to your flat, Rose. Gather yourself together. Best foot forward.'

'No, I –' Rose whispered at her friend. 'You don't understand.'

'It's all true,' Frances said carefully. 'Everything they've told you is true.'

'But how?'

'You weren't supposed to know until—'

'My probationary period was over.' Rose's voice cracked again. 'But how?'

Frances blinked her clear blue eyes. 'Who was it that told you?'

'The Upper Sixth,' Rose spluttered. 'Dulcie has a—'

'Of course,' said Frances with an irritated twist of her mouth. 'They're on heat this time of year.'

'Is this what it's all been about – the disciplinary systems, their *Value*?'

'Rose,' Frances was firm, 'we can't—'

'And the girls said something about requirements.'

'Yes, yes.' Frances shook her head grimly. 'It'll all come out now.'

'Why are you so calm about this?' Rose finally cried out.

Frances hissed. 'Keep your voice down!'

'Frances?' called out the woman behind Rose, with concern.

But Frances didn't shift her blue gaze, placing a tentative hand on Rose's arm. 'Don't you think, Rose . . . in some way, you already knew?'

'Rose,' the Headmaster's voice sounded behind them, 'I wanted to commend you for your contribution today.' Rose's back stiffened, her every nerve standing on end. 'And thank you for agreeing to stay over half-term.'

Rose found her voice, and turned around. 'Half-term?'

'You will be staying over half-term to aid our Japanese girls who are not leaving for the week, but in fact moving into their new boarding house, House See.'

'But,' Rose glared at the Headmaster, 'I've got my train booked for tomorrow.'

'The secretaries have postponed your ticket. Not to worry, dear. And your mother's clinic knows not to expect you. Yes, your staying here will make all the difference. I expect you're thrilled with how well things are going.' Rose looked down at him, the brilliant shine of his brown eyes, the curve of his jaw. 'Vivien will take you through everything necessary for half-term. Frances, may I have a word?'

Frances followed him silently, and Rose was left to stare at the seated group of women, who stared back at her, nonplussed. Hearing Frances's voice rise and fall with the Headmaster's, Rose left the common room without another word.

Rose stared at the ceiling above her bed, at the plastered mould of the light fitting. The wind was screeching at the window, and the damp of the late winter pressed at the glass as if to taunt her.

Frances had been 'fully engaged' with the Headmaster that Friday, then left early the following morning to visit an aunt in the West Country. Rose had found a hastily scrawled note on her desk, with a promise to see her the minute she returned. So Rose really was stuck there for the next week, with the secretaries' instructions for her, the girls and House See.

Her thoughts were still frantic in their discovery, panicking about what to do next. Rose turned her face to check the time. She saw her upturned book on the bedside table and realised how distant that narrative was, and how very real and alarming her own situation. She couldn't stay here much longer, she knew that. But what about the problem of her mother? Rose couldn't ignore the fact that she had a degenerative disease, and was using an oxygen tank now. If Rose left Caldonbrae, she'd have to take on these new medical expenses herself, an amount she'd never be able to shoulder on an ordinary teacher's salary. She could move her mother back to her previous palliative clinic – but the money from the house was gone. Then, without a good reference from Caldonbrae, and with inevitable questions from a potential school, Rose wouldn't have a hope. No, she might never secure another teaching post again, if the Headmaster had anything to do with it. Not in Britain, anyway. What about her old tutors in Rome? But she'd never be able to afford to live there, work, pay rent *and* pay for a medical clinic. Could she find somewhere to live back in Kent perhaps, and what – look after her mother full time? Register with the local council for benefits?

No, Rose thought fiercely, she'd been taught to work for a living, to pay her taxes, to graft, to contribute and to prosper. She had to stay at Caldonbrae, then – one more year, or for as long as her mother needed her. There was no other option.

Rose had called her mother the evening before, but she wasn't at all fazed that Rose wouldn't be there for the week; even if she *was* feeling frail, she insisted she'd be better without Rose's prattling. She'd received the card, too, but couldn't see what Rose was getting at. How different a person she'd been in the post office that day, Rose thought. How naive, how blind. Rose had simply nodded and hung up the phone, her silence full of words her mother wouldn't hear and couldn't understand.

The half-term week began in House See. Hardly a boarding house, Rose thought, but two corridors of bedrooms attached to a large and bright day room, set within the north wing on the ground floor. The handful of girls did not even fill the newly painted dormitories, but instead stretched themselves across the dark green plush of the day room, basking in the light from the long windows facing the mainland.

Through gentle prying Rose discovered that the girls took up two year groups, Fifth and Lower Sixth, each with its own corridors. But how different the corridors were. The Lower Sixth clutch of girls stroked their hands through their soft hair as the porters moved around them, heaving boxes of plants and ornaments. The Fifths, however, dragged in their own designer suitcases jovially, kicking them down the steps, nudging each other forward to get on with it. Once they were in their rooms Rose caught a group of three laughing girls as one stood inside a billowing duvet cover, its feather duvet trampled under their feet.

Rose soon got to know a few of them; Hanako, a young-looking girl with short hair, was the chattiest of the Fifths and seemed to find everything an adventure. A tall Lower Sixth girl, Ayumi, peeled herself away from her friends and hid her smiles behind her hand as she declared herself the head of the house. She seemed to enjoy passing a daily hour or so chatting to Rose in the day room; she spoke soft and excellent English, and asked to be corrected if she made any mistake. Rose worried slightly about another girl, Shiyo, with a long narrow face, who didn't associate herself with the other Sixths, had very few possessions around her bed, and buried her elegant nose in couture magazines. Shiyo approached Rose on the third morning as the trays of lunch were brought in.

'Madam? Why does no one make our beds each day?'

'Oh.' Rose hesitated. 'I think you might have to make your bed yourself, Shiyo.'

'Please,' the girl wore a heavy frown, 'call me Lisa, I would like to use my chosen English name.'

'Okay, Lisa.'

'Me, I prefer Hanako, Madam,' Hanako called out from her little group as they examined the lunch trays. 'My father says Amanda. But Hanako I prefer.'

Rose kept to a chosen corner of the day room with her planner and various books, only nipping into the small kitchen to top up her tea. The Fifths offered repeatedly to make her one of theirs, but Rose didn't want to inconvenience them. She didn't want anything to crack the softness she'd found in those girls – a softness she hadn't yet come across in her other students. It was so different from the frantic one-upmanship and casual carelessness of the girls in House Prudence, and from the unpredictable energy of the girls in her classroom. Despite her underlying dismay at the girls' segregation, House See's small space was a balm to Rose and an antidote to her painful discovery of Caldonbrae's true function.

'Hanako,' Rose dared one afternoon, 'do you go to lessons with the other girls from Verity, or Prudence?'

'Sometimes yes, Madam. Sometimes no.'

'And why, now, are you being moved in here?'

Hanako nodded. 'There will be more of us, Madam. Isn't this good?'

'Can I see your timetable, Hanako?'

'You are funny, Madam, why?'

Rose gave in to Hanako's smile. There were more questions she had, in order to understand why and how things were as they were. Her own weak conclusions guessed at the girls' slow integration into the Caldonbrae system: just like Rose's own introduction, but seemingly more discreet.

Rose was battling to piece together the truth and place it against the school she already knew. Against her Sixth and their crowing over future husbands, against Bethany who took herself to the beach to die. Was that why she'd done it – was she despairing over this darker purpose? *I'm doomed,* Bethany once said, *and Jane was the only one who could save me.* Save her from the fate of an arranged marriage?

The evenings stretched out late in House See as Rose's questions evaporated into the empty air. Beyond those dark green rooms there was a smattering of half-term staff about, one of whom was Anthony. Their short greetings were regularly interrupted with a summons here or there, and Rose's courage failed her every time she opened her mouth to challenge him. Any feelings she'd been nursing for Anthony now cowered behind this new and ugly knowledge; did he approve? Was he complicit? She certainly didn't dare ask any of the others that lingered in the empty dining hall, or in the scarcely populated common room with its continuous Vestal fire.

On the first morning back after half-term, Rose's lessons had been cancelled without explanation. After she'd endured a long morning of thrumming panic in the Classics office, at midday one of the secretaries guided her into the Headmaster's study for the very first time.

A blast of light from the windows alarmed her, framed by the blackened lines of windowpanes. As she squinted through the dazzle, Rose saw a silhouetted figure move towards her, too tall to be the Headmaster's.

'Good afternoon, Madam!' the head girl gestured with her arm. 'You've been invited to the governors' lunch. The Headmaster sent me to entertain you before introducing you to them.' Stunned, Rose didn't shake Clarissa's hand. Instead the head girl readjusted her velvet hairband, the same maroon as her dress. 'Have a seat.'

'Where is the Headmaster?' Rose paused, glancing around the large study. 'And the governors' lunch – what is that?'

'You'll be meeting a few of Hope's governors. It's a real privilege, and I gather they will be going through the particulars with you. The Headmaster will be along in a moment.'

'The particulars?' Rose echoed.

'Yes, Madam, now that your probationary period is over.' Clarissa sat down on a corner couch opposite Rose, her knees together and turned to the side. Rose sat down too, carefully. No one had told her that her probationary period was over. How did Clarissa know before she did? Checking around her, Rose took in the handsome room, masculine and full of mahogany furniture.

Clarissa leaned forward and asked, 'How was your half-term, Madam?'

'Fine.' Rose gathered herself. 'How was yours?'

'Lovely. My father and I went to the country. We had a lot of people at the house.'

Rose faced Clarissa. 'And are your family pleased with your . . . progress here?'

'Yes, Madam, of course. My Value is the highest in the year.'

'Is that how one becomes head girl, then?'

'Almost.' Clarissa seemed unable to hide her pride. 'We have to be voted in. I won the vote.'

'You must be so thrilled.'

Clarissa's face dissolved into smiles; Rose noticed the wink of light from a pair of neat diamond earrings she wore.

'Yes, I've got the best one.'

'The best what – sorry?'

'Suitor, Madam. Husband. Of all of them.'

'Of course,' Rose scoffed. 'And he chose you?'

'He won me!' Clarissa gushed as Rose looked at her with alarm. 'No, I'm being silly, of course.'

'And were you happy with these . . .' Rose hesitated. 'Forgive me, I'm still learning – the requirements he made of you?'

'You mean the Promises? Most of them were fine, I've managed. Just the French has been hard.'

'And,' Rose said carefully, 'what were the other requirements?'

'We're not supposed to speak of those, Madam.'

'Oh, I see.'

Clarissa shuffled to sit better on the couch.

'But what about the requirements that weren't fine? Were any of them,' Rose asked tentatively, thinking of the risk she was taking, 'difficult or unfair or—'

'It's only a few sacrifices, Madam,' Clarissa interrupted sharply. 'Nothing worth worrying over . . . for a lifetime of happiness and security.'

Rose blinked sadly as Clarissa carried on.

'I'll be married in the autumn. I'm looking forward to it, to having a husband, a companion, my own household. My father is always busy, he's in the army. Madam Ms Johns and the others have been so wonderful. I don't know what I'd have done without them.'

Rose let a moment fall between them, before saying, 'Can I ask you, Clarissa, did you ever have a choice?'

Clarissa stared at her, puzzled. 'What do you mean?'

'You know what I mean,' Rose pressed. 'Did you ever have a choice?'

'I came here as a child.'

'Yes, but,' Rose pressed further, 'did anyone ever ask you if this is what you wanted?'

Clarissa leaned against her armrest. 'I am everything I ever wanted to be, and I can't wait for the future.'

The way she moved, her beauty, her sensuality, it was all so calculated – and hypnotising, Rose thought. 'But you're almost an adult. You could do anything you wanted. In life. You could go to university, have a career. You could be successful on your own terms – there's certainly money behind you. But you want this?'

Clarissa raised her chin slightly. 'Madam, you couldn't possibly understand. Excuse me for speaking so plainly, but look at you. You're a single woman who has to work for a living. You're alone. As far as I can tell you have no connections, no society, no community – except for your mother, who is poorly, I believe. And your position here is one of privilege. You have no understanding of the way things are.'

Rose said bracingly, 'I am free to make my own choices.'

'Only within your societal limits, your financial constraints.'

Rose opened her mouth to reply, but a small lurch of the door made them both turn. The Headmaster appeared, and Rose's thoughts stilled; how long had he been waiting on the other side? How much had he heard?

'Well,' the Headmaster's jovial voice intruded into the space, 'good afternoon, Miss Christie, Miss Bray.'

Clarissa stood up with her wide smile and greeted the Headmaster.

'Clarissa, dear, how many years have you attended our little institution?'

'This is my seventh year, Headmaster.'

Rose couldn't help but shrink at the gentility of his voice.

'And how many years has the system been in place?'

'Since William Hope founded the school in 1842. My mother was one of ours. My grandmother and my great-aunt, too. They were both great Surrey beauties and married prominent and successful politicians.'

'Clarissa, you are a splendid example of what Hope accomplishes.' He drew his eyes to Rose. 'Will you take Madam to the conference room, please. The governors are looking forward to meeting her.'

'You won't be at the lunch?' Rose dared to ask.

'Ah, Rose,' the Headmaster's eyes grew shrewd, 'the governors are far more important than I am.'

Clarissa hovered nearer Rose. 'This way, Madam.'

Rose followed Clarissa down the corridors as if she were suspended in the air, drifting past swathes of girls, seeing them all with new eyes.

Clarissa halted at the door of the usual staff meeting room. Her small hand found Rose's and shook it. 'Thank you, Madam, I enjoyed our little talk. I hope you'll only continue to prosper here.'

The door opened to reveal Vivien in the door frame; she was already talking under her breath: 'You needn't look so horrified, Rose. Of course, I'd rather you hadn't discovered the way things are in so underhand a way.' She gestured to Rose to enter. 'But all the same, get yourself together. This is an important moment for you.'

A conference table was placed in the middle of the arched room, laid for seven, with white tablecloths and polished silver, serving platters already laid out and covered. The fire was lit.

Rose gazed at the glassy eyes of the stag mounted above the fireplace in some strange solidarity. Vivien twisted her figure towards a group of five men, one of whom Rose immediately recognised as a cabinet minister.

The governors stood up for Rose, gruff and formal, with pinned ties and pocket squares, leaning forward in different motions to shake her hand. Rose acquiesced, suddenly shy as Vivien made the introductions, the stone walls of the room somehow growing hot and cramped around her.

'It really is a pleasure to meet you, Rose,' the man closest to her spoke up. He had a quick smile and a very neat beard. 'Goodness me, you are rather younger than I was expecting.'

Vivien bowed her head slightly. 'Rose, this is the chairman of the governors, Lord Carstairs, a descendant of William Hope.'

'By marriage, of course,' he nodded amiably.

Rose didn't know what to say. 'Thank you for seeing me,' she tried.

'I gather that we are now fully inducting you into the system here.' The man gestured for Rose to sit down. 'But first, can we offer you some lunch?'

The other gentlemen broke into bracing smiles as they passed around the dishes, pouring each other drinks. Rose took as little food as she could without seeming rude, her posture tight and startled.

Ten minutes later the chairman touched the corner of his mouth with his napkin; he checked the others around the table as their conversation died down. Then he spoke up: 'Allow me to start, Rose.

'The girls of Caldonbrae Hall are here for a curated education: one that serves a purpose *and* benefits society. This great tradition continues since its founding.' He folded his napkin.

'The system has three main threads: Discipline, Study and Value. You have so far been privy to the first two. The full structure of the curriculum will be explained to you in due course.'

Rose turned an inquiring face to Vivien, silent next to her.

'Your situation,' the chairman went on, 'is rather delicate. We haven't recruited in over a decade, and now we are expanding. Our previous method of recruitment is not sustainable, so we must look at actively seeking out candidates. We have taken a risk with you. You *must* prove us right. I understand that you are an intelligent, impressionable and modern young woman. We celebrate young women here. We need innovators, visionaries, trendsetters.'

Rose couldn't help herself. 'You want visionaries? But surely you can't deny how . . . antiquated the system seems?'

'Not at all, Rose,' the chairman answered genially. 'Our model works. We are a step ahead – other affiliate schools are now considering our model, not just in the UK. You won't find finer or more accomplished girls across the country . . . surely you've realised that they hail from some of the most affluent and influential families in Britain?'

The other governors nodded, busying themselves with drawing their cutlery together, refolding their napkins.

'Now, I gather things have settled in the Classics department,' the chairman's voice grew kinder, 'and your work in the boarding house is appreciated. Now that the situation is stabilising, the Headmaster and his management will need you to contribute to the Discipline and Value threads—'

'Wait,' Rose interrupted, dread seeping through her chest. 'The girls, are they all entirely aware of this . . . practice?'

'Of course. The girls are the prize.' He gestured across the other governors. 'Their parents are, after all, the client, and we the service.'

'And the service provides,' Rose tried to imitate his language, 'a refined and elegant young woman?'

'Yes.'

The fragments of Rose's logic were staggering together. 'But not an intelligent one, with her own mind?'

'Rose,' the chairman glanced to his colleagues who shared his frown, 'girls this young don't need to have their own thoughts. They are in their physical prime, and we guide them to their full potential.'

'I disagree.'

The chairman sat back as his eyes lit up. 'That smells not of independence, my dear, but waywardness.'

Rose leaned forward. 'These girls haven't had a *chance* to piece themselves together. They *do* need to have their own thoughts. You're obsessed with their refinement, their physical potential, but what about their humanity?' Her voice grew fervent as she felt Vivien stiffen by her side. 'My Intermediates, even my Sixths – they don't know who they are or what they want.'

'I believe you're doing the girls a disservice by saying so.' The chairman's face was impenetrable. 'But it is interesting to hear your perspective, I assure you.'

'*I* have earned my independence. I have a career. These girls never will.'

'Rose, don't be so naive.' The chairman let out a laugh to ease the mood. 'Marriage is by far the best career these girls can have; motherhood too. They find their independence within these great unions. These traditions have been in place for generations, and it is not for you to question . . . Please allow us to re-educate you.'

'How is it possible,' Rose's hands were beginning to shake, 'that William Hope's aims can still be relevant today?'

'Lord Hope wanted to ensure that the aristocratic families were connected more fluidly in a changing society,' the chairman mused. 'He was a Whig rebel, and rather against Queen Victoria in her early reign. A woman on the throne, his party losing power.' The chairman weighed up his words with his hands. 'At the time, Hope wanted to ensure that women still understood their place. Freedom in moderation, you know. These principles still stand today.'

'And so,' Rose summed up, her voice brittle, 'Caldonbrae Hall is actually a refinement factory for model women – wives – disguised as an academic establishment.'

'I'll stop you there, Rose, you go too far.' The chairman turned his head with irritation.

'I haven't gone too far at all. The whole country thinks this place provides the finest education a young woman can receive.'

'Which it does.'

Incredulous, Rose gazed around the table at those knowing faces, all waiting for her to submit. With a small burst of desperation she asked, 'Why me?'

The governor opposite Vivien spoke up. 'You came highly recommended, and you are young enough to be malleable. You had a strong record, good roots. Your father was a professor. I myself discovered an Irish landowner in your past. Is that not the case?' Rose stared at the man introduced to her as the Right Honourable Graham, a retired judge with stooping shoulders and a dash of white hair. 'We brought you on to add to the common "breeding, brains and beauty" line at Caldonbrae,' the judge continued. 'With your academic record we can improve the "brains", perhaps for any higher education requirements our suitors might have. We saw potential in you. As Lord Carstairs says, this search and research method is one we may have to adopt.'

Another governor spoke up: the cabinet minister, who fixed Rose with a sudden bright eye. 'You know, my dear, you needn't feel that your background should hold you back. The Headmaster himself is a Thatcherite self-made man, and we have been very pleased with our choice there.'

The judge nodded vigorously in response. 'We've had great success with him. In fact, not one of our Compassion girls in the past eleven years has had to stay on at the school. They were all placed with older gentlemen quite successfully.'

The chairman dragged a finger across his lips as the others spoke. Rose closed her eyes for a short moment, disgusted. He was a descendant of William Hope. Were his daughters among the girls once? Rose thought of Clarissa and her maroon dress. She thought of Nessa and her freckles, Freddie's firm, ivory jaw. Rose knew the girls better than any of these gentlemen did.

'So I'm an *experiment*?'

She saw the chairman nod. 'You are the first teacher without any prior knowledge of the school's inner system, yes. The others – married women like your colleague Emma, or the bachelor gentlemen – sought us out through a private connection. Your old colleague, Frank Thorpe, is an associate of ours.'

Rose's head jerked with alarm. 'Frank? He knows about this . . . system?'

'Of course. He did all the relevant checks for us regarding your appointment.' The chairman pressed his lips together firmly, before adding, 'Now, may we remind you of the need for discretion?'

'Discretion?'

'You have signed your contract and within it, a non-disclosure form. You cannot discuss anything about Hope outside the school grounds. Furthermore, we strongly disapprove of reviewing the school's methods with colleagues. It goes without saying that no criticisms should be heard by our students themselves.' The chairman pushed his plate to the side as his face grew serious. 'As you understand, we cannot now let you out of our community, Rose. There are many alternatives for wayward or disobedient staff, but your best option is to remain here and acquiesce. Your mother's welfare depends on it. *Your* welfare depends on it.' Something electric moved through Rose as the chairman added, 'You do not want to compromise yourself or anyone that depends on you.'

'Please,' Rose's voice was small, 'don't include my mother in this.'

'We shall, Rose,' the chairman said with a frown. 'She is in our care, through your work with us.'

'You wouldn't . . . hurt her, deliberately?'

The chairman spread out his hands. 'I don't wish to be unpleasant, Rose, but we have to educate you on your limits. And you will find that whatever you give here will be returned to you fully.'

Rose's face throbbed along with her heart. Five pairs of governors' eyes watched her.

'Do you understand all that I have said?'

'Yes, Chairman,' Rose finally managed. 'I understand.'

'Now, if you have any further questions, we have arranged for your colleagues Frances Manders and Anthony Rees to go through the finer details with you.' The chairman stood up with finality. 'I am so glad you are on board. Let me assure you that the benefits outweigh any misgivings you might have.

Our fees are steady, and the endowment that Hope receives annually is very generous.'

The judge stood up too, and his dash of white hair quivered. 'You will always be looked after here, Rose. It's very easy to scoff at tradition, but tradition is a tremendous strength. It holds up the values of Hope, and it holds up the values of Great Britain.'

'Hear, hear,' echoed the chairman, now leaning towards Rose. 'Thank you in advance for your loyalty, Rose. Now,' he announced before heaving a satisfied sigh, 'let's have some of that glorious pudding!'

Rose pushed herself up from her chair. 'Th-thank you, Lord Carstairs.' She didn't dare raise her hand to have it shaken; her whole body was vibrating with dread. But they were no longer looking at her.

'I fancy a brandy with pudding, Henry, don't you?'

'Yes. Gun Room?'

Rose waited as Vivien escorted the governors out.

Frances came through the door moments later, her eyes wide and apprehensive, Anthony swinging behind her with a serious face. He looked at the bedraggled remnants of food, before turning to Rose anxiously.

'Are you all right?'

Rose found her voice, and it burned her throat. 'I can't stay here.'

'Don't say that,' Frances answered quickly.

'They're threatening me, and my mother.'

'That's just leverage, Rose, they—'

'I don't understand any of it. I've never heard of such a system. This is a nightmare.' Rose's voice grew louder as she faced the two of them. 'How can you stand it? Why did you come here – either of you?'

Anthony pulled out one of the chairs to sit next to Rose. 'Listen. It's a school with ideals, and it works. The girls are happy – you've seen that for yourself. A school like this one saved me when I was a boy. And if I can contribute to the happiness and success of others, then I will.'

'What do you mean, a school like this one saved you?'

Anthony shook his head. 'Well, not exactly like Hope. I mean to say that I was set up in a boarding school as a boy, as an orphan, in the Midlands. I was taken on as a scholarship student, and it saw me through. I'll always be grateful to these systems; I'd have had no opportunities otherwise.'

The lines in his forehead deepened and Rose saw again that rough anxiety behind his face; it caught her off-guard. 'I'm so sorry about your parents, Anthony.'

'Oh,' Anthony responded, surprised by the comment, 'it was a long time ago.'

Frances coughed, but Rose carried on: 'You get on well with the Headmaster, don't you, Anthony? You are sort of . . . buddies?'

Anthony drew his eyebrows together. 'We do get on well, yes.'

'He's brainwashed you. The governors too,' Rose said forcefully. 'They're trying to do the same to me. Threatening me with my mother's health and God knows what else.'

'They need you to comply,' Anthony urged as Rose gave him an incredulous look.

'Rose,' Frances interjected, taking over, 'there's nothing we can do for you there, it's higher than Anthony or me. But let's get this part over with. I know that you want to understand everything.'

Rose turned to face her friend, separated by this great chasm they would now attempt to bridge. How could Frances have kept this from her, all this time?

'There are three threads at the school, Rose: Study, Discipline and Value,' Frances continued. 'The Junior years commence with Study and Discipline – that is to say, academic subjects, skills and general good behaviour. A basic minimum of accomplishments is expected of all girls – music, dance, games, home-keeping, the creative arts. This continues into Intermediates. Value begins there too, when the girls start to focus their energies in specific areas; working towards their portfolio, and what they can offer.' Frances paused. 'It gets serious in the Sixth, where the girls are introduced at court.'

'At court?'

'To the royal family, as debutantes. An old tradition that's still very much alive, if you know the right people. That's what the Upper Sixth were doing in London back in September.'

Rose raised her eyebrows as Frances continued.

'At the end of Fifth the girls are allocated Pathways. They follow these through the Sixth. The top one is E for Elite, which feeds into the top layer, aristocrats and so on; below that is P for Professional, where the suitors are usually barristers, surgeons, that sort of thing. New money, too.'

Rose thought of that engagement diamond cutting into Dulcie's ring finger with a small red mark.

'Then the third is—'

'C Pathway,' Rose answered breathlessly. 'Compassion. The one Bethany was in.'

Anthony took up the explanation as Frances seemed to hesitate. 'Yes, Compassion, where the girls either marry a senior gentleman – an eligible widower – or they stay on here and teach.'

Rose nodded, her face full of resentment. 'The girls left behind. And Bethany, forever left behind. Is this why she . . . killed herself?'

It was Anthony's turn to hesitate, and a solemn Frances was no help. 'She was a special case,' Anthony began. 'I think she also missed Jane. Jane had been a Compassion herself, and convinced her that it was no way to live.' He paused. 'I'm not aware of the finer details . . .'

'Why didn't anyone help Bethany?' Rose demanded. 'The management – the governors, too – especially if her father was their client?'

'Well, because of Jane,' Anthony said simply.

'What, so, if there's a disobedient teacher, they punish any girl she's close to?'

'As I say,' Anthony shook his head, disconcerted, 'I don't know the ins and outs of that case.'

Rose grew frantic. 'Are you listening to yourself? We let that girl down. Her father, too, was let down. That cannot happen again.'

Anthony sat back, speaking carefully. 'I admire your empathy, Rose. It will serve you well moving forward. Some of us old-timers are so used to the system we don't think twice when it doesn't go to plan.'

Rose looked to Frances, waiting for her verdict, but she gave none.

'Shall I continue?' Anthony pressed on. 'We were talking of the Sixth Pathways. They depend on Value, Study, and of course the girls' families. Once the parent comes to an agreement with a gentleman, the gentleman gives his requirements, called "Promises", which come under Value. The girls need to build their Value as much as they can during Sixth.'

'And what are the "Promises" exactly?'

'They can be anything,' Anthony replied, 'from a modern language . . . to wine knowledge, tap dancing, archery . . . or even poker-playing. There are dozens of options, it's really up to the suitor. Beyond that . . . it's just a question of training.'

Rose's face broke. 'It's so awful. Can't you hear what you're saying? You talk so casually about Bethany, then you talk about the other girls as if they're products, to train and build up?'

Frances's face was still closed, but Anthony said cautiously, 'Understand, Rose, that the girls are extremely happy to be so accomplished by the end of the Sixth – in the arts, in themselves. They've learned how to function in society, how to get ahead, how to . . .'

'Be a wife,' Rose finished bluntly as an expansive silence spread between the three of them. She glanced at a drag of butter across the tablecloth, at the wrought-iron candlestick shedding its rust on the white. 'Sorry. Please go on.'

Anthony's hazel eyes were gentle and tired. 'What else do you need to know?'

'My timetable?'

'Yes, your timetable needs to expand. Study is the academics, which haven't been strong lately. Discipline is taught in the afternoons, by much of the boarding staff and the old girls—'

'And the governor talked about . . . higher education?'

'Well,' Anthony answered quickly, 'this is where I've been involved, and where your old colleague Frank came in. More recently some of the suitors – particularly the Professionals – are looking for university-educated wives, due to the nature of their society. You could help advocate for that.'

'Really?' Rose snorted. 'Won't it be difficult to control the girls once they're at university?'

'Again,' Anthony eyed Rose warily, 'you don't know the depth of our influence. We are willing to innovate, you see. Hope has been negotiating with one of the colleges at—'

Rose's throat rumbled with rage. 'So, there's a new trend for a clever and educated wife? I'm *so* glad. What exactly does my advocating for it mean?'

'I'm not entirely sure.' Anthony glanced at Frances. 'You might be required to tutor a few of the girls, prepare them for interviews.'

'*More* training?'

'Isn't that something that would interest you?' Anthony asked.

Rose hesitated. She had to admit that it would.

'It's a new innovation. The suitors' agreements—'

'The *suitors*, again!' Disdain poured over Rose's every word. 'Tell me, when are these *agreements* made between the Sixth and her future husband?'

Anthony waited a moment before answering. 'They start around the middle of Lower Sixth, some later than others.'

'And when do they get married?'

'Usually the summer after they leave. If not, they live in apartments in London. Hope has many properties all over the city, it's—'

'What if the girls don't even like men?' Rose thought of Tash. 'What if—'

'Rose.' Frances's voice was hard. 'Come now. Don't talk about what's unnatural.'

Welcome back, Rose thought, *coward.*

'Besides,' Frances continued, 'the girls know they are meant to save themselves for their husbands, and their husbands alone.'

Rose balked at that. 'That's . . . just fucking hideous. And what about the girls in House See – are they trained up, too?'

'No,' Frances said firmly. 'They're an international link to improve our teaching and learning. Things might change, but for now, no.'

'But that's just another layer of discrimination, Frances.'

'Is that everything, Rose?' Anthony interrupted suddenly, his face tight with exhaustion.

'No.' Rose thought of Nessa and felt a throb of urgency. 'What about the girls who are demoted by house?'

'Ah.' Frances pulled a regretful face. 'Yes, there's ranking in the Junior Intermediate houses. Clemency is the lowest house, the route towards the C Pathway, unless they get their act together.'

'But in Clemency,' Rose insisted, 'if the girls aren't doing well, what happens?'

Frances wasn't looking at her. 'There's bareheadedness, and then the girls move into the san with monitoring and individual tutoring until they improve.'

'Are any girls expelled?'

'No,' Frances said darkly. 'We can't let them go.'

'So, how can you be sure others won't go the same way as Bethany?'

Frances didn't respond, and Anthony leaned forward heavily. 'Rose. The girls are uniquely happy here. Their futures are decided in the best way, with their consent and their parents' approval.'

'It's not real consent! They've been indoctrinated!' Rose sat forward. 'How can you stand it, both of you?'

Anthony checked Frances's face before speaking up. 'There are many perks to the job. The gentlemen of the staff are promised excellent pensions, and even senior positions in smaller boarding schools if they wish . . . Besides, the connections here are deeply influential.'

'And the women?' snapped Rose.

'Perks for them, too. Look at your colleague Emma,' Anthony insisted. 'Her two boys were sent through boarding school and university, Hope picked up the bill. Her husband was promoted at work and relocated to be near his wife. Now that they are recruiting single women like you, they will be broadening the incentives.' Anthony leaned forward, lowering his eyes. 'I, however, should be happy here until I retire.'

'But,' Rose said desperately, 'Jane was sent to a school in Dublin, wasn't she? Before . . . Inverness? The governors said they couldn't let me go – but they let *her* leave and teach somewhere else?'

'Dublin?' Anthony looked up, confused.

'Jane,' Frances cut in, 'was a warning to all of us.'

'Frances,' Rose pushed, 'why are you talking about her in the past tense?'

'Oh, I don't mean to.' Frances shook her head quickly. 'She's not well, that's all.'

'Yes, I know.' Rose couldn't control her flurry of panic. 'And is she not well because she had some kind of nervous breakdown, or is she not well because the school . . . interfered with her?'

Rose looked at Frances's blank face, knowing she'd find no answer there. Anthony sat back, regarding Rose with careful and anxious consideration. She could see that he wanted her acquiescence, he wanted her to see his side.

But Rose knew she was as far from her two colleagues as she'd ever been. *I can't stay,* she thought, *I can't possibly stay in this godforsaken place.*

15.

Rose's keys were splitting the skin of her fingers as she resisted their force. Someone was smashing them into her mouth, cracking her teeth. It was that cold, pale face with ribbons of lank hair, Bethany, her eyes impossibly blank holes in her face as she pushed the metal into Rose's mouth.

Rose opened her eyes away from the nightmare, sliding her legs apart in the bedclothes, hot and damp in that cold room. She touched her own face, mercifully intact, but her mouth even now felt parched and injured. Moving out of the bed, she went to the bathroom.

Rose's mind was ablaze with thoughts. She'd been trying to make sense of the last few days, to find some string of logic to this massive reinstatement of everything she'd thought to be true. How clear it had always been – how obscene and obvious.

The staff had immediately shifted in their manner towards Rose. She was no longer a wary intruder to tiptoe around, no longer a source of tricky curiosity, but now simply one of them, and ought to disappear into the furniture accordingly. But Rose distanced herself from their knowing acquiescence. Only the three Moirai were still watching her closely, enjoying her anguish, anticipating her next move.

Not only that, but Dulcie had been removed from Rose's Upper Sixth class, and the other four girls claimed to know nothing about it as their lessons continued. With dismay Rose thought of that engagement ring and Dulcie's overspilling emotion, divulging the truth of Caldonbrae's system. Was the girl being punished for that? Was she still in school? *Yes, but only really in house, Madam,* Lex had answered, *since half-term.* Rose had glanced at the empty seat in the middle of the girls as her Euripides book trembled in her hand. Everywhere punishments, everywhere trapped.

Frances was trying to be helpful – even comforting, perhaps, in her own usteady way. The handover of departmental duties would be slow and methodical, she told Rose in her flat one evening. Frances had drawn near to Rose on the sofa, the hot accompaniment of wine on her breath, a strange intimacy that Rose wasn't used to and didn't welcome.

'I'm so glad that you know now.'

'What do you mean?' Rose swung her body away.

'It's easier. I've had to be so careful about what I said.'

Rose closed her eyes with frustration. 'You've been lying to me.'

'I've had no choice,' Frances protested. 'But we are friends, you and I.'

Rose drew back. 'Friends? When you've been concealing this? And you're okay with it? How can anyone here think this is right?' Rose's head fell into her hands. 'The girls have been brainwashed! So have the teachers!'

'Look, I know it is . . . unusual. Hard even, at times. This,' Frances was nodding enthusiastically at something, 'has been my way of coping with it. My moods, they call it. I'm *volatile.*

I've never been as strong as the school would have liked, but,' she sighed with small pride, 'I am loyal to Hope.'

Frances put her hand on Rose's knee, who stood upright in one movement, her anxieties bolting themselves tighter around her like armour.

'Loyal? No, Frances,' said Rose firmly. 'It's not just *unusual*, either. If this got out to the press, or even further, then—'

Frances glanced up at Rose, her eyes musty with alcohol. 'Maybe you're the one to fight it, then?'

'What? How can I?'

Frances shrugged but her eyes never left Rose's face. 'I don't know.'

Rose hesitated. 'What – call the papers?'

'Why not?' Frances drew her glass to her mouth. 'You can try. They'll probably take you in hand. And, of course, they'll be observing *me* as well as you since we're friends.'

'Take me in hand?' Rose exclaimed.

'They are entirely serious about the rule-breaking consequences, Rose. It's not just you, the ones you care about will be punished too.' Frances took a weary sip of her wine. 'They'll hit you where it hurts, and they always know where that is.'

'You're exaggerating. What is this, the mafia?' Rose sat down on her armchair frantically. 'Why didn't you leave immediately when you found out how it really worked? Haven't you worked out a way to escape, in all the years you've been here?'

'It's complicated.' Frances leaned back on Rose's sofa and closed her eyes, 'Besides, I couldn't leave. Things are difficult . . . and . . . I was so enmeshed in the system. You're young. You've only just arrived.'

'I feel like I've been here for ten years.'

'Trust me. You haven't.' Frances frowned as if in sudden pain.

'But surely I can just . . . disappear?'

'You can't. You won't. Please.'

Rose glared at Frances. She seemed suddenly repulsive; the reek of her breath, her yielding drunkenness, her overreaching compliance.

Rose's repulsion had bounded through to her waking nightmare. At the end of the bottle Rose had politely pushed Frances out of the door. But then she'd heard the men's voices again. A car roaring into life, low hollers softening amidst the slamming of doors. Why were they there? What were they saying?

What would happen if Rose rushed downstairs and called the police at that moment?

Nothing. They wouldn't pass through the gate. The groundsmen wouldn't be there, just as they hadn't been there for Bethany that night. It was a dead night, no wind, no stars. Rose could hear nothing now. The muddle of her thoughts that evening blurred into the next, or was it the evening before? Perhaps it hadn't even happened yet. Had Bethany even drowned?

No, she's in my bedroom, Rose thought, *wreaking havoc with my dreams.*

She settled back in her bed as her thoughts turned to her girls. Freddie's analytical eyes, Nessa's desperate little face next to Bethany's. Their voices calling at her, one after another. There was something there – was she still dreaming? Voices like threads of light she could pick up and tie together, bind as tight as a rope.

Her breathing grew easier. The girls' faces softened; their calls were duller.

This was a purpose that Rose could drive towards, she realised, as rosy dawn began to peek through her curtains. Prevent Nessa from following Bethany's path; prepare and send off those girls to university, to set them free.

She nodded her head, and each nod was a silent vow.

The following afternoon, Rose went to the mullioned window to draw back the curtain she hadn't pulled that morning. The room was suddenly drenched in white light; and there it was, propped up against her plumped-up pillow in the mess of her unmade bed: an envelope, bearing the same crawl of her name.

> Dear Madam,
> Apparently you know how things are now. Aren't you the lucky one working in a place like this? You're out in the open now - and doesn't that feel better? Now it's time for you to get on with it and start proving yourself. And keep your mouth shut or there will be consequences. Do we need to remind you?
> Yours,
> One of Us

These senseless demands, these harsh comments thrown out haphazardly. Typewritten again, the same letter 's' jammed and retyped. The same short sentences, the same strange yellowed paper. The same envelope with spidery writing. This time Rose turned the page around to check the back, and caught a whiff of a particular flowery scent she knew she'd smelled before. One of the girls had been in her flat.

'Leave me alone,' Rose said aloud to the empty room.

She crumpled the letter in her hand. Were the governors,

the Headmaster and his staff, the students, all in continuous conversation about her – perfectly timing these nasty actions to strike her down, encourage her to submit?

Rose strode over to her bedroom window, pushing it open. She held out her arm, and let the damp sea air soften the paper in her hand, before the wind took it up and away, yellow becoming grey becoming nothing.

Should she have saved it, joined the letter to the other one, and taken both to Vivien? They seemed so private, so personal, attacking Rose on a childish level. She was embarrassed even to have been upset by them, and wouldn't let Vivien, or anyone, have her tears. No.

Another entirely different letter had been sent, as Emma had told Rose during lunch that day, over the rabble of the girls' noise.

'The Headmaster received a letter about you from the Lists over half-term.'

Rose froze. 'About me? From whom?'

'Frederica List's parents. The Headmaster was saying he hasn't had a letter about academic enthusiasm like that in years.'

Rose let out a gurgle of surprise.

'You might laugh,' Emma continued, 'but they are an important family. Frederica is proving to be every bit as excellent as her older sisters. She'll be head girl in time, mark my words. And to have singled out your teaching like that . . .'

'I'm sure it wasn't anything.'

'It was, Rose. You should be thrilled.'

Rose gripped her fork. 'So, why are *you* telling me? Why haven't I heard this from the Headmaster, or Vivien?'

Emma sighed, exasperated. 'No need to be so cross, Rose.

Honestly, you've been cross all week. I thought a complimentary letter would be good news?'

Rose pushed her food around her plate. Then she asked, 'Is Dulcie still in your Sixth class?'

'Yes, although she has missed a few. She seems very unhappy. I gather she's restricted to house.'

'She's been excluded from my lessons entirely. I think it's because she's the one that told me what was really going on.'

Emma stiffened, not looking at Rose. 'Yes, I was informed about that. It will be good to have you settle in properly.'

'Will it?'

'Listen, if you play your cards right,' Emma nodded, 'you can help make some excellent connections. And the school will take care of you, and your mother.'

Rose searched Emma's face urgently. 'But the girls, Emma—'

'What?'

'They have no say in the matter. They're packaged off to some man they've never met.'

'Some religious cultures arrange unions like that all the time,' Emma retorted calmly. 'Why shouldn't we?'

Rose dropped her cutlery with a clatter and Emma flinched. 'Because it isn't the same at all. It's wrong.'

'Goodness me, you're worried about the girls now.' Emma shook her head furiously. 'What's next, will you want to become *best friends* with them?'

Rose glowered at Emma, hating her thick glasses, hating her dowdy skirt. But she had no other response; no courage to muster, especially with the Founder's forbidding painting gazing down on them.

*

The second hate letter pursued Rose still, even though she'd given it up to the elements. Surely she had the only key to her flat – or did everyone have the same brass ring of keys, with its many little pieces? There might be replicas of her key all over the school tucked into jacket pockets or tossed into desk drawers. Somebody had gone in and out of there, into her very bedroom, and was unafraid to show it. It was a violation, and it alarmed Rose.

In the entrance hall Rose ducked into the porters' office to ask. She tried to suppress the distress in her voice.

'Who has access to the private flats above the boarding houses?'

The porter on duty looked up from his small TV screen. 'The private flats? For staff?'

'Yes.'

'No one, Madam, only the resident of the flat, and then we have a copy of each key here, for emergencies. They can be requested by management, if necessary.'

Rose nodded through the information, even though it explained nothing.

'Thank you.'

The porter gestured towards her own ring of keys. 'You must be academic staff. You've got the key to every internal door in the building there, Madam.'

'Thank you,' Rose repeated numbly.

She ducked out of the office. Who then, and how? Rose still had the offending envelope, having compared it to all the badly written homework she'd collected from each of her students, scrutinising the turn of each letter, desperate to find a match.

As she moved up the short steps to the main corridor Rose

noticed Lisa striding along proudly with a pair of Upper Sixth girls. She walked with great poise, her elegant nose in the air; obviously her couture magazines were rubbing off on her. Rose wondered dimly how things were going in House See.

But at the foot of the Great Stairs Daisy had been stopped by Ashley, Anthony's burly colleague in History. Daisy was as tall as the man was plump, and she looked miserable at his attention. Rose hastened towards the odd pair.

'Rather think you should be wearing an altogether different dress, my dear, this one hardly fits you. Are you sure you're only in Fourths?' Ashley boomed.

'Yes, Sir, I assure you.' Daisy's face burned scarlet. 'I don't know what else I can say.'

The man chortled. 'And what's your surname, young lady?'

'Ayrton.'

'And what does your father do?'

'He's a barrister, Sir.'

Rose now stood at Daisy's side, and spoke up. 'And a Classicist, as it happens, Sir.'

Ashley's eyebrows furrowed at Rose's intervention. 'Middle classes, good to see them climbing. We've picked the right-looking ones, haven't we? I've noticed her wandering about,' he said to Rose as he appraised Daisy further. 'And she's a Fourth?'

'Yes, I can confirm that Daisy is in my Fourths class.'

'Really?' Ashley smiled hoarsely. 'She looks like a Sixth; I'm afraid I've been giving her rather a hard time about it.' Rose saw his eyes linger on the girl's breasts, pushed out by the brace of her bodice.

Rose moved her own figure between the man and Daisy; straightening her shoulders, she blocked his gaze. She was so close to Daisy that she could feel the girl's breath on the back of her neck.

'Did you have any other questions, Sir, or may I speak to Daisy about a Latin matter?'

'Daisy, yes.' The man's rheumy eyes roved back to the girl's face. 'What house are you in?'

'House Verity, Sir.'

'Goodness, well done you.'

Rose set her jaw to respond, but a crown of gold-red hair interrupted the small group.

'Sir, I'm so sorry to interrupt, but I believe Madam Ms Johns was asking to see you.' It was Freddie, talking in a controlled voice, her animated face bright and appealing.

'Was she, indeed?' The man turned his smiling eyes on Freddie.

'Yes, Sir, it seemed important.'

'All right, then, very good.' He patted his lapel. 'Forgive me, ladies.'

Once Ashley moved away Rose was very aware of the two girls close to her, and others moving past them, closer still. She took a step back.

'*Did* the deputy head want to see him?'

'No, Madam,' answered Freddie, 'but he's one of the ones you have to watch out for.' Daisy's face was still burning from the unwanted attention. 'Come on, Dais. Next time just think what Dido would do. Or Agrippina. Don't you think so, Madam?'

Daisy threw Rose a grateful look and joined Freddie as they walked down the corridor.

MEDEA

οἴχομαι δὲ καὶ βίου
χάριν μεθεῖσα κατθανεῖν χρῄζω, φίλαι.
ἐν ᾧ γὰρ ἦν μοι πάντα, γιγνώσκω καλῶς,
κάκιστος ἀνδρῶν ἐκβέβηχ᾽ οὑμὸς πόσις.
πάντων δ᾽ ὅσ᾽ ἔστ᾽ ἔμψυχα καὶ γνώμην ἔχει
γυναῖκές ἐσμεν ἀθλιώτατον φυτόν:

I am undone, I have resigned all joy in life, and I want to die. For the man in whom everything I had was bound up, as I well know – my husband – has proved to be the basest of men. Of all creatures that can feel and think, we women are the worst treated things alive.

(Euripides' *Medea*, 226–231, written 431BC)

Medea's story might have you believing her the villain, but remember that her tale has been written by men. She was born with a strange divinity – powers from her grandfather the sun god, and others learned at home in Colchis, a wild place outside the civilised Greek city-states.

A young Medea was struck with desire for the Greek warrior Jason. He landed on Colchis, challenged with obtaining the Golden Fleece. Medea made herself vital to his quest, her ointments rendering him invincible, her instructions rescuing him from the onslaught of mythical soldiers, and her spell falling over the dragon that finally released the Golden Fleece. Her reward was the warrior himself, a man she adored and revered. But Medea's father was furious, and she fled with Jason to become his wife.

Medea had expected her father to pursue them, and so had taken her younger brother. She killed him and left the desecrated body strewn in her wake. Her plan was successful, as her desolate father was forced to slow his journey to collect the pieces of his well-loved son.

Years later, as a mother, and a wife, Medea's magic saved her again. The wandering family were summoned to Corinth, where Jason had been promised a position, but through a new marriage. Medea was a barbarian, he explained to her mystified face, and would never be accepted in Greece. Their two children, therefore, were illegitimate. This union with the young Corinthian princess, Glauce, was the right thing to do, Jason insisted, for all of them. Medea had no choice but to accept.

But any advantage promised to her soon shattered when she was visited by the King of Corinth, who demanded that Medea and her children leave the city-state, and sever all ties with Jason. Again, Medea accepted, asking for one day's grace. One day was all she needed. She was visited next by Aegeus, the King of Athens, who offered Medea refuge, in return for her curing an ailment. Refuge for her, he clarified – but not for her children.

Medea managed her situation the only way she knew how. She congratulated Jason, and crafted a golden dress and coronet for his young bride. But once the young Glauce donned her wedding gifts, the poison Medea had concocted took hold. The Corinthian princess suffocated to death – as did the King, who infected himself as he grasped her body, in an attempt to save his daughter's life. Jason was furious, and Medea triumphant.

There was still one last act to perform. Dreading the probable fate of her children amongst the Corinthians, Medea decided the only way she could protect the two sons her husband had been willing to give up was to sacrifice them.

Devastated, Jason watched as Medea mounted a sun-fuelled chariot with the two small bodies of her children, and flew away to Athens.

Medea's instinct was survival, and her violence was a defence. Of all of her powers, the most potent was rage, which guided her actions. After all, if she was going to be called a barbarian, she might as well live up to the name.

16.

Rose's understanding was deepening as the days passed, no thanks to the complacent staff in the common room, or the restrained Emma, Anthony and Frances; but thanks to the rows of cautious girls filling the battle line of desks, uncertain how to treat their Madam now that she knew the purpose of their life.

On the Wednesday of the second week back, Rose turned to her four Upper Sixth, their dresses in full colour as a precursor to spring. The girls' faces, however, were pale and bored over their Euripides books.

'Medea is a barbarian?' Lauren asked. 'Did you say, Madam?'

'Yes,' Rose nodded. 'She's from Colchis, not Greece. Uncivilised, therefore, by Greek standards, and very much an outsider. She's married to Jason, the Greek warrior.'

Lex was pulling a face. 'Sounds like she was a bad choice for him. Is that what the play's about, then?'

'Wait till we get to the end,' Rose said carefully. 'You might not like it, but it's really something.'

She was met with an indifferent silence. Rose was prepared for that, and glanced at her owl before taking to her chair.

'Girls, can I ask? Did any of you *choose* to study Classical Civilisation?'

'Oh,' Tash went first, 'my father thought it would be beneficial towards Conversation.'

'Mine was a Promise,' Lex said witheringly. 'Or I wouldn't be here, trust me.'

'Madam,' Jenny sat up, speaking into the gap that was Dulcie's empty desk, 'we're not to talk about Promises. Especially the Coupling ones. It's bad form.'

'Coupling?' Rose asked quickly.

'No, Madam.' Jenny shook her head in warning.

Rose sat back, infuriated. 'I don't care, I need to understand all of it.'

'Madam,' Lex smirked, 'do calm down.'

'I assure you, I am perfectly calm.' Rose remembered the governor's words. 'Well, let's return to Euripides before any other Promises prevent the use of our brains.'

The following morning Rose watched her Fourths arrive, feeling a dim pain in her chest. Daisy was talking in a stream to Nessa, who trailed behind her as they came through the classroom door. 'If you just learn that formula, then you'll be fine.'

'Will you show me again?' Nessa asked Daisy in her soft voice.

'Yes, of course. Perhaps we should put it all over the walls in your new dorm?'

'We can't do that. You're not allowed in Clemency.'

Daisy shrugged. 'I'll sneak in.'

Rose blinked in surprise at the girl's words.

'Daisy!' Nessa exclaimed hotly. 'That's so unlike you. Anyway, Molly would flip if there were things on the walls. She's always tidying up and looking at herself in the mirror.'

'Okay, well, let me know if there's anything else. Clemency isn't that bad.'

'Nessa,' Rose burst out, 'have you moved house, then?' Nessa looked up, mortified, as many swivelled heads stared at her. Rose instantly regretted the question.

'Yes, Madam,' Daisy answered for Nessa, 'but it's all fine.'

Daisy's kind answer didn't stop the other girls from sharing dark glances towards Nessa, as if she had some incurable disease. Nessa made her way to the front row with her face set.

Rose turned back to her bureau. Why hadn't she done more for Nessa – sought her out on her evenings in Prudence, given her a tutorial or two? What could she do now, to help?

Rose cleared her throat, forcing herself into a bright cheer for the lesson.

'Right, ladies, good to see you. Anyone know where Freddie is?' A few heads swivelled towards each other aimlessly. 'Okay then,' Rose continued buoyantly. 'We're going to spend more time with Virgil today, Dido and Aeneas.'

Several girls groaned.

'Exercise books, please, the pages at the back. *Salvete puellae.* Now look at the board, I've written out a phrase from *Aeneid* Book Five. "*infelicis Elissae conlucent flammis*" – have a go at translating it, you've got the vocabulary. Remind me, who is Elissa?'

'Another name for Dido, Madam, queen of Carthage,' Daisy answered easily. 'And I think that *infelicis* and *flammis* are agreeing.'

Nessa was squinting at the phrase on the blackboard. 'I'll never understand, Madam, why two words agreeing in Latin are always miles away from each other.'

Rose laughed, for the first time in what felt like an age. 'Oh, Nessa. It's one of the banes of my life.'

'*Elissae* must be genitive.' A girl in the middle had raised her hand. 'So the sentence means—'

'Wait, I'd just like to check,' Rose interrupted. 'Who else thinks they have it?' She moved quickly along the desks, reading a few pages.

'Okay, go ahead,' Rose said to the girl in the middle.

'It's *they burned with the unhappy flames of Dido.*'

Daisy said loudly, 'That's what I have, Madam, as you saw.'

Several girls looked up with a mixture of confusion and relief to have it done for them.

'Who burned with unhappy flames?' said Freddie, who'd just strolled into the room. 'Sorry I'm late, Madam. I had to see the deputy head.'

'Yes, who was it that burned, Madam?' asked Daisy.

'The city walls burned, or glowed, after Dido built the pyre, remember?' Rose said, turning to the board, suddenly anxious. 'Perhaps it's a confusing phrase, I just thought—'

'Don't rub it out, Madam,' Nessa called out, 'I haven't finished copying it!'

'Sounds thrilling, Madam. I think we all understand everything now.'

Rose turned back to Freddie, and their eyes touched. She'd been avoiding it, but there was the truth of the place painted on Freddie's face. On Daisy's and Nessa's, on Josie's and every girl there – this strange, ugly destiny.

'What's this, Madam?'

Nessa had raised a photocopied print laid out on her desk. Rose nodded at it gratefully. 'All right, girls, yes. Have a look at this image – it's a mosaic of Dido and Aeneas. It was found in a villa in Somerset, would you believe.'

Freddie shuffled along to her seat as the class bent to look at their photocopies, all except one. Josie's beetle-black eyes were darting between Freddie and the teacher. The back of Josie's hair moved, and Rose stiffened as she saw the little rat's face poke out from the girl's collar.

'Why's Dido naked?' Nessa asked.

Rose couldn't take her eyes off the rat at Josie's neck but she kept her voice measured. 'That's a good point, Nessa. What might her nakedness symbolise?'

'She's not described as naked in the Latin, is she, Madam? I thought she had a cloak and things,' the girl in the middle said. 'Purple, wasn't it?'

'Yes. This nakedness here could be a symbol of her purity.'

'It is a bit unfair that she's naked and he's fully clothed!' Nessa exclaimed.

'Aeneas is wearing full armour, yes. Interesting that you find that unfair.' Rose shifted her eyes to the mosaic image. 'It doesn't look quite right, does it?'

'She has a nice bum, though, Madam,' Josie cackled. 'She's been doing her exercises.'

There was a hollow guffaw that swept across the rows of desks.

'You know, Madam, I think it's great that you're so passionate about teaching us,' said Freddie. 'And that you show us things like this.'

Rose looked at her, that permanent half-laugh playing on Freddie's face.

'But it doesn't really matter, does it, Madam?' interrupted Josie at the back, 'now that you know everything. Maybe you can give us a break? You're *supposed* to be helping us build our Value. I need to be spending my time on Musical Performance or Outdoor Pursuits.'

'Oh no,' Daisy called out jovially, 'let's face it. The Value that we *all* need to work on,' her almond-shaped eyes widened, 'is Beauty and Aesthetic.'

The whole class laughed, but Rose didn't.

'Or do you want to sabotage us, Madam?' Josie's voice was sonorous. 'I mean, you're stuck here, while we go on. Aren't you jealous of us?'

Rose stared at Josie; she wanted to laugh hysterically, climb over the desks, shake the girl until she understood. Shake Josie until her aunt Vivien's hard face fell away from that teenage one.

'No, Josie,' Rose managed, 'I can assure you that that is not how I see things at all.'

'It's better now that you know, Madam,' Nessa smiled weakly.

'Did it ever –' Rose hesitated, trying to keep the weight of emotion out of her words. 'Did it ever occur to you ladies that this,' she gestured forward with her arm, 'might not be something you'd want?'

Several girls glanced at each other as Rose bit back her words.

'What,' Josie scoffed, 'that we would reject a life of luxury, travel, affluence, the *right* people? What else could we possibly want?'

'Madam.' There was a pause as Freddie regarded Rose intently. 'What are you trying to say?'

'I think we should be grateful,' answered Nessa earnestly. 'I'm always grateful.'

Rose looked at Nessa for a long moment, and then back to Josie. She didn't dare return Freddie's stare. The room seemed to be waiting for her.

'I'm not sure what I'm trying to say.' Rose gave in. 'For

now, like Nessa, I'm just grateful that we're getting through this literature.'

And with that, the room seemed to lift with relief.

That evening Rose found herself quite subdued as the Juniors readied for bed, chattering about how many Easter eggs they might get, but how they needed to wait until after Affiliates Day and the end of term to really indulge.

The housemistress was hovering around Rose like some anxious spectre, in continuous conversation with the house prefects. Rose couldn't quite forgive the woman who had allowed Nessa the demotion to House Clemency; she spent the bulk of her evening duty upstairs with the girls. Now, more than ever, she wanted to draw the little ones into some kind of embrace as they climbed into their iron bedsteads.

Rose was forced to engage the housemistress during the gap between Junior and Intermediate bedtimes. As the housemistress busied herself at the desk in the tutor's study, Rose tried to give an account of her half-term experience in House See, but the woman didn't seem to think that the two houses could be compared. Rose resorted to staring into the school photographs in the lobby to pass the time. She checked the older black and white photographs, wanting to pull at them for evidence. How far back did the system go? As far back as it could, Rose knew – to William Hope and his six unmarried daughters of 1842.

In a distant room a tune was being stomped out on a piano, accompanied with bursts of laughter. Rose checked the last few decades' photographs; she saw the current housemistress, and matron, and nodded at the date. But then she paused and peered into the very middle of one photograph, leaning in to see better.

'This student looks exactly like Frances,' Rose laughed. 'My God, it could be her daughter.'

The housemistress was in the study doorway. 'Oh, yes, you've probably spotted her, there.'

'What.' Rose frowned with surprise. 'Frances Manders?'

'From the early seventies, is it?'

Rose saw *1970* marked at the bottom of the photograph's cardboard edge, under the swirl of the school emblem. Her voice, when she finally found it, was like an echo from far away.

'Frances was here, at Caldonbrae?'

'Yes, dear.'

'She's an old girl?' Rose was shaking her head. 'No.'

'Oh, yes. In this very house, under me, in fact. She had great potential, good at sport, but ended up as one of the lower Pathway girls. There wasn't anything for her elsewhere, so she stayed on. She's not as revered as the other Compassions here, unfortunately.'

Rose was almost pressing her face into the black and white photograph – seeing the square of the girl's shoulders, the curve of her cheekbones. Yes, it was Frances. Somehow, she wore the same hairstyle, the bushy blonde falling on either side of her face, that wiry fringe.

'She's in House Temperance now,' the housemistress continued. 'Somewhat improved since her school days, I think.'

Rose couldn't pull her eyes away from those long rows of knees and slim plaits, from Frances's immovable, smiling young face.

The next morning, Rose hadn't found Frances in her office, or among the armchairs in the common room. The final possibility was Frances's flat, even though it wasn't permitted.

Rose made her way there, burrowing through the passageways like bronchioles in the lungs of this great monster of a school.

Rose knocked on Frances's door again. There was movement on the other side, but the door remained closed.

'Frances, I know you're there.'

The door cracked open an inch and Rose saw a shard of blue eye. 'Let me in.'

'I'm just coming out. I'll see you in my office.'

'No, I need to talk to you.' Rose pushed at the door and realised that the resistance wasn't from Frances herself, but from the piles of stuff she'd dumped at the door: pairs of mis-matched boots, a clump of dirty tights. Frances was already walking into the kitchen. Rose watched her friend with new eyes, her nerves jangling as she tried to frame the words in her mouth.

'I don't know why I come back here between lessons, I really shouldn't,' Frances announced loudly. 'Sets a bad example.'

Rose saw that Frances was wearing a pair of leggings under her ruched-up dress. She glanced at the sideboard where a bunch of bananas had turned black and six bottles of red wine lined the wall. 'Frances, there's something I want to talk to you about.'

'There always is.'

'I know that you're an old girl,' Rose blurted out. 'I know that you went here. That you're a Hope girl.'

Frances stiffened. 'It's no secret,' she looked at Rose, a wan smile lifting her face, 'and you never asked.' She turned back to clear her kitchen counter, stacking plates in the sink.

'I didn't think I needed to,' Rose answered in her own baffled way. '*Why* did you keep it from me?'

'It comes with its own problems.'

'You should have told me,' Rose garbled on. 'You've been stuck here – frozen in place – all this time. And that's why you didn't recognise my music, or understand any of my film references.'

'What nonsense! How patronising you are.'

'I don't mean to be, I—'

'You do.' Frances squared her shoulders. 'Coming here and standing there throwing these comments around.'

'Can't we talk about this properly?'

'Talk about what?' Frances turned her squinting face to Rose. 'So typical of you to turn this into a drama.'

Rose flinched. 'Oh God, you sound like one of the Sixth.'

'How dare you!' Frances whirled her whole figure around to Rose.

'I don't know what to say to you!'

Frances's eyes were slits. 'I'm the same person, Rose.'

'How can you be?' Rose cried out. 'You've been lying to me non-stop!'

'Do you think I had a *choice*? They're monitoring me, too. I'm volatile. I went wrong!'

'Your whole youth, your life was spent here! And you teach those languages . . .' Rose hesitated. 'Have you even been to Germany, or Russia?'

'Of course I have!' Frances shot back. 'On arranged trips, and—'

'Don't you see? You're a victim, just as much as the girls!'

'How dare you!' Frances yelled again.

'No, I mean to say –' Rose raised her hands in surrender. 'Just tell me what happened to you – there is so much I don't understand.'

'No!' Frances shouted, slamming her hands down on the counter behind her. 'I'm not your bloody case study!'

Rose shrank away as Frances recovered her composure.

'You *are* morbid sometimes, Rose.' Frances tugged a hand through her ruffled hair. 'Why can't you let things be? Oh, I knew it would come to this.'

'I'm trying to understand all this.'

Frances looked madly at Rose, and pushed herself away from the counter. 'Things went wrong for me, okay? I was an Elite. I wasn't even an aristocrat, my parents were upper middle class, but I worked hard. And then I ruined it.' Frances's face convulsed with disgust. 'A younger girl complained about me, she said I *interfered* with her – but I didn't! She was the one that . . . well, never mind.' Her face fell. 'So I was branded. I ended up in Compassion with few choices – I didn't want some old codger on his third wife. So I chose to stay here and help the others. Haven't you ever read *Jane Eyre*? She stays on at Lowood and teaches the girls.' Frances's chest heaved as her voice grew stronger. 'So don't you *dare* pity me. I could have really been something, you know.'

'Yes, Frances, I know,' Rose said gently. 'You already are something.'

'I don't want to talk about what happened. I have such shame about it. There is so much shame about these things . . .' Frances's eyes shot away from Rose.

'There isn't, Frances, not out there.' Rose was shaking her head. 'You don't have to hide who you are, or whom you love. You're extraordinary.' Frances looked at her, momentarily disconcerted, before turning away again.

'I'm not, I'm a disgrace.'

'No.' Rose approached her friend. 'This place is a disgrace. Let's break out, let's expose it somehow. If there are enough of us who want to stand up to the Headmaster, to the system . . .'

'What,' Frances's face was still flushed, 'the common room full of bachelors, or the happy, simple family women like Emma?'

'What about the girls then?' Rose tried. 'I'm sure some of them don't want this.'

'Like Bethany? She got it into her head that she didn't want to be married to her suitor. Poor old Jane didn't help, with her delusions of grandeur, despite her being an old Compassion girl herself. They brought each other down. And me? I can't fight anything – I don't have the tools.'

'You can, I know you can,' Rose urged. 'Let's do it for Bethany, then. And any others like her.' Her thoughts went back to Nessa and her demotion to House Clemency. 'I won't stand by and let any other girls suffer like she did.'

'You're mad,' Frances scoffed. 'You'll *have* to stand by. Look at Jane. They sent her away – said they'd find her a school – but they had no intention of doing that! And now she can't even think straight.'

Rose's ears seemed to hollow out. 'What does that mean, *think straight*?'

'Nothing.' Frances gave Rose a haunted look.

'No, you said the same thing after the governors' lunch – did they punish her? Tell me, what do you mean?'

Frances turned her back on Rose again. 'What do you think I mean?'

'Do you know where she is?'

'Why, do you want to go to visit?' sneered Frances.

Rose looked at Frances. Her stance, her athletic figure. Rose could still see that teenage grin in her mind's eye. The way she laid her hands on her knees when she sat down.

'How did they let you come here?' Frances carried on. 'I

should have stopped it. They all said you'd be an innovation. And they told us about your poor mother, terminally ill,' she added bitterly. 'And then, of course, losing your father so young.'

'I . . .' Rose's thoughts felt sluggish. 'You said you didn't know about any of that.'

'Of course we did, I just pretended not to. I could see it a mile away in your CV. I thought – she has been loved, and she has suffered. She'll know what it feels like.' Frances shook her head harder. 'These girls don't. They grow up here. Day in, day out. They've been handed over by their parents to us . . . Just like I was. You've really got no idea.'

'But,' Rose raised her eyes to her friend, 'some of the girls, I *do* understand, I think . . . and if you know the system – can't we break it, together?'

Frances bristled. 'No, stop talking like this.'

'But Frances—'

'Rose, please leave.'

'Please don't kick me out.' Rose's voice was desperate. 'You're all I've got.'

'You've got Anthony. I've seen him hovering around your office, giving you longing looks across the dining hall since day one.'

'What?' Rose spluttered. 'That's got nothing to do with this, he's—'

But Frances was beyond listening. She threw up her hands in both defence and defiance. 'I've asked you to leave. Do as I say. Leave me be.'

In the passageway Rose stared back at the slammed door long after she stopped hearing Frances's retreating steps.

*

The following week saw the middle of March and, with it, Rose's swimming activity resumed. The weather hadn't improved but the secretaries had thrust the timetable under her nose, so off she set with the crew of girls, across the fields along the cliff edge and down the walkway towards the beach.

Rose was glad to have a distraction from the catastrophic crash of her heart. The day before she'd tried to grab hold of some small, worthy thing she could do to make a difference: the mission the governors had hinted at. She'd approached Vivien in the common room, apologised for bothering her, and asked about any plans for Sixth girls applying to university. Vivien's smug half-smile crawled up her face as she claimed ignorance, before suggesting some other explanation: was it Rose's Sixth – now that Dulcie Hughes had been removed, were there others that needed disciplining? – or was Rose struggling with taking over the head of department duties from Frances? Rose hesitated, before insisting that the governors had mentioned potential Sixth university applicants at their lunch, and the need for Rose's help. Vivien stopped her there and told her to discuss it with Anthony.

Rose's humiliation was still stinging through her chest as she trod down the walkway steps to the beach. She imagined the sea rising in some kind of mystical tempest, washing the school building away with it. One of the Philosophy teachers had mentioned something about a flood in the past. *But the peninsula's always been fine. William Hope used to say that the bad weather regularly cleared away the devil from this land.*

No, Rose thought, *it's the other way around* – the devil has clawed his way across the land, and left his mark. That's why the peninsula looked as broken as it did.

The girls were happy to be reunited with the freezing water;

it offered them a pleasant freedom from the past restrictions. But Rose wasn't watching them, she was sitting on her usual crop of boiled rock, completely transfixed by a wooden door set into the cliff. It stood apart from the little huts, almost entirely absorbed by the cliff.

Daisy and Nessa were stepping across the stones towards her: one tall and robust, the other slight and frail. They were an incongruous pair, and had dressed themselves haphazardly after the swim: Nessa's dress hung loosely around her bodice, while Daisy's was tight around the shoulders, patchily damp, her blazer slung over her arm.

Rose couldn't help but imagine Bethany's body, the threads of her dress tearing away from her lifeless skin. Had she descended the rickety walkway like the rest of them had? Or had she come through that door?

'Hi, Madam,' Daisy and Nessa said in unison.

Rose cleared her throat. 'Hi, girls, you've finished early?'

'Can't we persuade you to paddle, Madam?' Nessa coaxed.

'No, Nessa, far too cold. Freddie's not here with you. Does she not swim?'

'She's not on the list, Madam,' Daisy said flatly. 'She's never been.'

'It's her chest, Madam,' Nessa added. 'The cold water isn't for her.'

'She might as well have a weakness,' Daisy remarked wistfully. 'She's good at everything else.'

Rose turned to face them. She'd spent the last thirty minutes trying not to see the girls fall in and out of the water, not to watch their bodies as they moved: bodies for sale.

'Clarissa's been taken out of school, Madam, did you know?' Nessa raised her head importantly. 'Health problems.'

'Oh, I hope it's nothing too serious?' Rose replied. 'The Sixth did seem unhappy at lunch.' *Health problems?* she wondered. Clarissa was one of her letter-writing suspects – she certainly seemed to dislike Rose enough. 'And . . . you enjoy swimming, do you, girls?'

'It's invigorating, Madam,' Daisy nodded. 'It's one of the Disciplines.'

'Oh yes,' Nessa said, rolling her eyes. 'I forgot that *we* are educating *you*, now.'

'Of course,' coughed Rose, turning away. 'There's a poster in the main corridor. "Deportment." I used to think it was a joke.'

'No joke, Madam,' Nessa said. 'We all have to learn how to behave. I, however, am not very good at it.'

'Oh, Nessa.' Rose didn't know how to comfort the girl, how to bolster her sense of self-worth.

'Diving is a Value, I think,' Daisy nodded to herself. 'The Headmaster knows them all, I need to memorise them.'

'I suppose you ought to know what you're getting into.'

Nessa had a strange look on her face as she gazed out at the sea. 'They say I'm on track for C Pathway, Madam. I don't want that at all. There was this old man staring at me at the carol service, I didn't like the look of him. If you're an Elite, you can have a really good go, but not in Compassion.'

Rose attempted to shuffle off her rock, her heart beating urgently. 'I'm sure it won't come to that, Nessa. I'm sure you'll have a say.'

'Be serious, Madam. It's all very well you trying to be kind,' Nessa said, screwing up her face, 'but that's the way things are.'

'I'm *sure* you'll have a say about your Pathways. All of you.' Rose was having trouble getting up and Daisy leaned towards her instinctively. 'If you think about it, it has to be about consent.'

'Consent?' Nessa narrowed her eyes.

'Yes.'

'We consent,' Daisy said quickly.

'But how can you, already? You've been here since you were eleven. This world is all you know. But right now, at fifteen, you're supposed to question these things. You should be right on the cusp of . . . whatever you want to do.'

The air seemed to break between them as the two girls fell silent. Rose waited, listening to the pull of the seawater against the stones.

'You're not quite right, Madam. Sometimes we *are* the ones in charge, like in Practice.' Nessa twitched her nose. 'So there.'

'What's Practice?'

'Madam, stop asking us questions, it's so frustrating!' Nessa rolled her eyes. 'You're supposed to be the one with the answers.'

Rose bent to collect her clipboard. 'Sorry, girls, I don't mean to upset you at all. Daisy, could you check the names for me again?'

'Where are you going, Madam?' Daisy asked, taking the clipboard. 'We've still got fifteen minutes.'

Rose moved beyond the two girls. 'I just want to take a look at that door. Can you see it?'

She heard Nessa speaking to Daisy behind her: 'I think that Madam doesn't like this place because it's where Bethany died. She was close to her.'

'Was she? I thought Bethany accused her of all sorts of things.'

'Yes, but Bethany was odd, you know that. She got attached to teachers. And they liked her back.'

'I suppose we should have left some flowers today, to remember her,' Daisy said softly.

Rose's eyes hovered along the ragged shoreline. Had Bethany cried out with regret when she drowned? Was it as Rose suspected – had she resented the Pathway chosen for her, and taken her own? And was it only these few that still thought about her – not even Jane, who hadn't responded to any of Rose's letters, probably because she *couldn't think straight*? Rose hadn't yet allowed herself to interpret Frances's worrying comment.

C Pathway, Rose thought, glancing back at Nessa. Compassion. For whom? Frances, Bethany and now Nessa? Rose glanced at Nessa's soft head, her misshapen dress, that strange crossness scrawled over her face. She looked at Daisy beside her, shivering as she dutifully ticked the names off a list.

Rose shook her head and glanced back at the door, tiny and brown against the craggy cliff. It stood out to her so much now, she couldn't believe she'd never noticed it before.

17.

The next day, Rose waited at the porters' desk, tapping on the wood urgently. One of them appeared with a questioning face.

'You can't go out, there's a storm coming,' he said sternly.

Rose regarded the porter with dismay. 'It's urgent. I need to go.'

'Are you sure the Master knows?'

'Yes,' Rose lied. 'I need to go to the village, just for the afternoon. Please.'

'Mind you're back before the storm hits.' The porter had already grabbed hold of a set of keys, and was moving towards the main doors; Rose closed her eyes briefly with relief.

Half an hour later Rose was safely ensconced in a Kennenhaven tearoom, having treated herself to a hot chocolate. The scorched milk film was sitting at the top and she pulled it away like skin.

The mainland village didn't have a police station, she'd discovered. Rose should have known that the local constable had come from somewhere more official than the village. What could she say, anyway – she'd like to report a crime? The abuse of young girls through forced marriages? Except they weren't forced. Rose remembered Clarissa's words: *I am everything I ever wanted to be, and I can't wait for the future.* Rose gritted her teeth to stop herself from smashing her hot chocolate against the wall in frustration.

Perhaps this was what Frances meant when she blamed her moods. Emma had glided over Rose's revelation of her friend's history at Hope. *Yes, well, Frances is a bit of an anomaly.* Yes, Rose had thought – she's very bright, and occasionally thinks for herself.

Something in her wanted to rush to Anthony, to understand how someone as kind as he could have been indoctrinated into such an archaic and dangerous system. He'd passed by the Classics office and mentioned lunch every day that week, looking at her with soft and hopeful eyes, and Rose had agreed once. But she still couldn't bring herself to speak up or challenge his confident compliance.

Rose looked out at the rain across Kennenhaven harbour. Her second option, after the police station, had been just as fruitless. She'd barely heard the other end of the line as the rain drove hard against the glass of the telephone box, the yellow phonebook split open in front of her.

'I need to speak to a reporter.'

'I see. Can I take down your name and your contact details?'

Rose had hesitated. She'd chosen a left-wing newspaper, hoping they'd be sympathetic.

'It concerns a boarding school and some serious . . . malpractice.'

'Oh yes? The great upper classes, eh? Think they can get away with anything.'

Rose nodded vigorously into the phone.

'What's the name of the school, then, and how are you related to it?'

'It's Caldonbrae Hall and I work there. I'm a teacher.'

'Oh, yes, of course. Malpractice? Our editor could be interested in this. I think his sister-in-law was a pupil there. Any of the Montgomery family still there?'

Rose hadn't answered.

'Hello?'

'Yes, hello. I just need to –' She'd frowned with pain. 'I don't—'

'Do you have a story or not?' the voice sharply demanded through the telephone.

'How does it work exactly?'

'Give us your details, then leave it with us. We'll conduct our own report and so on. Unless you want interviewing? If you require payment, that's a separate matter.'

Rose remembered the governors' lunch, the careful glance of the Right Honourable Graham. 'No, I don't want that. I'm sorry.'

'What's your name? Can I take your number?' But Rose had placed the receiver back on its handle.

Rose stirred her hot chocolate again; perhaps she should have tried a smaller paper, perhaps it was already too late. Or perhaps there was still a chance that she could persuade Frances to hatch a plan. Frances who'd hissed at her, *Leave me be.*

Perhaps Rose should've phoned her mother. The woman who'd stood at picket lines and rallies. Surely she would recommend a course of action, a resistance of some kind? Rose realised she hadn't called the clinic since the shock of the half-term break. One lukewarm update had come through:

the oxygen tank was staying, but the woman's spirits were high. The focus on her mother's 'spirits' troubled Rose – what about her vitals, her physical state? Rose didn't want to press the secretary further, and disrupt this fragile, knife-edge status she seemed to have created for herself.

The tearoom booted Rose out ten minutes after closing time. She stood back from the door just as the cold wind picked up and tugged at her hair. She felt desperate – she couldn't return just yet, even though those dark clouds were drawing forward fast.

Rose swung through the door of the pub – The Ship, the walls and floor wood-lined and beer-soaked. The barman threw his rag over his shoulder, leaning his forearms across the beer pulls. He chewed on something before he asked her, 'You're from the castle?'

Rose stared at him. 'Yes.'

'You're not welcome here.'

Rose tried not to see the blistering looks from the other patrons, nursing their pints while scrutinising her mess of hair and the borrowed raincoat that was far too big for her.

'Just one.' She stepped forward to the bar. 'Please.'

'There's a storm coming, you'd better be off back before she hits.'

'I've got money.'

'We don't need your money here.' But the barman's eye hit upon Rose's desperate face, and his expression conceded. 'All right, one to get you home.'

'That place,' Rose said under her breath, 'is not my home.'

After a dirty glass of red wine, Rose could hear the whistle of the wind over the soothing lull of the other patrons' patter. She wondered about asking for another, but the barman was muttering in dark tones about boarding up the windows with the tide coming in.

Rose didn't want The Ship's patrons to see any porter in a Caldonbrae car collecting her, so half an hour later she decided to walk the coastal path. But she'd underestimated the gloom of the early evening, the air that thrust her back, the pushing slats of rain that streamed down her face. Blinking her wet eyes, she could see the terrible outline of the peninsula a mile or so ahead, jagged and black against the hurrying clouds. The sea too, no longer a mirror, just another tossing shade of despair. She'd never seen the grey abscess of the school from this angle before. That beating heart of life and horror in this brilliant, murky landscape.

Rose pulled the raincoat tighter around her, asking for its protection, but the storm was mightier than her. Her sodden Doc Martens trudged her further on as she angled herself against the storm.

This is what it meant, she thought, when they exposed the children to the elements in Ancient Greece; this is what the baby Oedipus was saved from by the shepherd; this is how so many Spartan boys died – and, she remembered dimly, what King Lear had meant when he cried out on the moor, *Blow, winds, and crack your cheeks!*

Rose hurried back down the raggedy hill path towards the village. The rage of the sea was tearing over the stone harbour wall in falling sheets of water, drowning the cars that were parked there. Boats clanked against each other in the chaos on the other side. The seawater was black and uncomfortably near. Rose could taste it – or was it the rain? The two were one; the gods of the weather were furious and fighting together against man.

'Let me in! Please!' She was banging on the door of The Ship, squeezing herself against its entryway as the sea took a breath between each mighty pull. The windows were boarded up now, the danger of the waves too much for the glass front to bear. Rose banged harder. 'Please!'

A sullen face appeared at the door, and Rose rushed through the gap.

The next morning, Rose stood at the wrong side of the main gates, waiting for the groundsmen. The lodge stared back at her, its roof rimmed with seagulls relieved after the storm, wondering what had drawn her back. Rose couldn't answer them; she was battle-worn, and unresolved.

It was a pale dawn, but a residual mist had lifted itself off the sodden ground for the new day. Rose had passed waking hours on a dingy sofa pointed out by the barman while the staff of The Ship took to their bedrooms upstairs. The storm shook the boards at the windows, the waves battering at them in angry resistance. Her terror had kept her awake.

Rose's reappearance this morning evidently rattled the gatekeeper, who rushed back into the lodge to open the gate with an, 'Aye, thank goodness.' He forced her to wait in the warmth of the lodge until he made a call to the main building. The tinny electricity of the light made Rose blink madly as she sat, too cold to yawn away her lack of sleep. Her thoughts stuttered with exhaustion as she heard the drift of the gatekeeper's words on the phone.

A car arrived to take her the short distance up the drive to the main doors. Rose looked at the face of the building on her approach – it seemed renewed, stronger than ever, as if freshly washed by the storm. A few black cars were parked around the entrance, alongside a police car. Rose stepped into the hall as Frances yelped, rushing towards her.

'Oh, Rose, you look a fright!'

The Headmaster was standing on the steps with two policemen. At the sight of Rose, they turned to give the Headmaster a resolute nod, and moved towards the door, passing Rose without so much as a word.

'What's going on?' Rose said into the blonde frizz of Frances's embrace.

'I was so worried, we were about to send out a search party.'

'Oh God, I'm sorry.'

'We thought you might be lost in the storm; the porter said you weren't there to be picked up yesterday. You were declared missing.'

Rose looked over at the Headmaster's grim expression. She was nodded wordlessly into his study moments later.

'Rose, I am glad you have returned.' He closed the door as Rose looked around her warily. No Clarissa this time – just she and him, one early morning in March. This, then, would be their first official meeting. 'I wanted to check that we are marching to the same beat here.'

He sat down at his desk, straightening a cufflink, brassy and shining at the end of his white sleeve. Rose remained standing, feeling nothing, and not worrying about her bedraggled appearance in this raincoat that wasn't hers.

'When you left yesterday, Rose, were you fully intending to return?'

'Yes,' Rose said dully, 'of course, but . . . the storm.'

'I sincerely hope you are telling the truth. You sent no word. As you can see, we involved the authorities.'

'I really do apologise.'

The Headmaster was studying her face. Rose stood opposite him, her eyes rent with resignation.

'I imagine you'll want a warm bath and a rest,' he continued. 'The rabble in the village can't have treated you well. Emma will see to your lessons.'

Rose found her voice. 'No, no. It's still early. I don't want to let the girls down. I just need an hour to sort myself out.'

The Headmaster leaned forward in his chair. 'I should let you know, Rose, that we sent people to check on your mother.'

'My mother?' Rose faltered. 'What does she have to do with this?'

'Well, my dear, she has everything to do with *you*. And if you go missing, we need to keep her situation regulated.'

Rose took a moment to absorb his meaning. 'Is she all right?'

'Yes, Rose,' the Headmaster smiled grimly. 'Thankfully. And I am very glad that you are, too. We need to keep it that way.'

Rose stepped backwards, motioning towards the door. 'I should go.'

'One last thing, Rose. I wanted to be sure that you recognise the reality of your situation.' The Headmaster arranged his features carefully. 'If you had indeed decided to *deliberately* go astray, and taken action with the information you are now privy to, you would immediately lose your place here. You'd have no reference to take forward with you, and there would be no other school to welcome you. Your career in education, certainly, would be over. And any other besides, if our governors were to have anything to do with it.'

Rose had turned her face towards the Headmaster's unlit fireplace. As he spoke, her eyes hovered above the mantel to the school's emblem, so familiar to her now – the winged dove, the collar around its neck. But now Rose stared at that collar, and for the first time she noticed the chain that held it, linking back to the shield, holding the beautiful dove down mid-flight.

Rose glanced back again at the Headmaster, her legs aching with the effort of standing up.

'And as such, these sorts of escapades won't be taken lightly.'

'I just,' Rose said bitterly, 'went out for a walk.'

'There will be no need for that for the remainder of the term.'

'But,' Rose's words seeped out, in spite of herself, 'I need my freedom. I am not one of your girls.'

'I think you need to realise, dear girl,' he replied sharply, his stiff, nipped face tilted towards her, 'that you are fully locked in, professionally and otherwise. I am sorry to have to speak to you in this way, but this goes much further than your mother. You aren't going anywhere with a dossier like yours.'

Rose's eyes lifted to his. 'A dossier like mine?'

'We know all about your father. Though his suicide was kept well hidden.'

Rose stared at the Headmaster for a long moment, no longer feeling the ache in her legs.

'We understand the shame that information, and its cause, would bring on you.'

'You've got it wrong,' Rose burst out. 'The accusation against him was false.'

'It was dropped after his suicide, indeed.'

'Because it was false.' Rose's voice was rent with passion. 'The girl admitted she was lying, she just wanted to get his attention, she said. She was obsessed with him. But he couldn't bear the shame of it.'

'Yes,' the Headmaster nodded. 'I did come across that in my reading. But one *could* see his suicide as an admission of guilt.'

'He didn't do anything wrong. It's the truth!' Rose cried.

'He certainly still has an excellent reputation within the academic community. We would hate for the truth of this information, and his suicide, to ruin everything he stood for, permanently.'

Rose was staring blindly at the man across from her. The thudding in her head threatened to knock her to the floor, but still she remained standing. This secret she and her mother had hidden for so long, now spoken out loud, by this small man on this obscure morning. The threads of her strength were slipping apart. She was a teenager again, in front of a Headmaster, crying at the loss of her adored father who'd taken his own life.

'How . . . how could you?' Rose finally gasped. 'What on earth have I done to deserve this?'

'You, Rose, have been chosen by us. This is a great privilege. I can assure you that your life will be much easier when you fully conform.'

'But,' Rose lowered her face, 'I am an educator. And you are a businessman, running this factory for wealthy aristocratic daughters.'

A muscle worked carefully in the Headmaster's cheek. 'Well, Rose, that is certainly a simple way of looking at it. The truth is, Hope girls will always become the wives, mothers and companions of the gentlemen who steer our country's – our empire's – future.'

Rose's final comment was a whisper. 'If you tell the girls that enough times, they will believe it. But a woman does not exist for the pleasure of a man.'

The Headmaster sat back in his seat and laid his hands out flat on his desk. 'I have no wish to argue with you, Rose. You've had your little adventure, now go and get on with your school day. The girls will be looking forward to your lessons.'

18.

Later that evening, an exhausted Rose was still scrubbing away the dirt of the previous night, as the storm seemed to have embedded itself into her skin. Questions had followed her all day: girls curious about Rose's whereabouts during the storm; frowns from other teachers at her unpunished return.

'Madam, were you actually missing?'

'Do you have a lover in the town?'

'No, no, girls, don't talk like that.' Rose's voice had been brittle. 'I just got stuck in the village, that's all.'

'In Prudence, we all had to huddle in the day room. They bolted up the doors but you could still hear the birds shrieking outside.'

After lunch there'd been a commotion on the second-floor corridor: harsh voices over younger ones, with a rushing push of over-emotion. There was a blocked door, and a row of Seconds lined up against the wall. Freddie and Nessa were berating the younger girls, whose sulking faces were pulled with injustice.

The girlish energy in the air seemed to awaken Rose. 'What's happened?'

'Hi, Madam.' Nessa stood back. 'These wretched beasts have

blocked in their friend, simply because she borrowed this one's ribbons.'

Freddie boomed at the girl that Nessa had pointed out. 'Let her out now, Kitty.'

'I've *told* you.' Kitty rolled her eyes, as her friends beside her stared at the floor. 'She knows not to touch my things. She's a thief! And you Fourths are supposed to turn a blind eye to this sort of thing.'

'Open that door now, or I'll do it myself,' Rose heard herself say, moving to stand next to Freddie.

'Oh,' Kitty laughed, 'will you, Madam?'

'How dare—'

'You don't need to defend me, Freddie.' Rose cleared her throat. 'Kitty, of course I'll break open that door if I have to; but I hope that you'll have the decency to do the right thing. Let that girl go, now.'

Kitty chewed at her mouth as Freddie squared her shoulders over her. 'Open that door.'

'Fine.' Kitty glowered as she motioned her friends to help her unwedge the door. The girls pushed then fell back with their effort.

'Serves her right, Madam.' Kitty threw Rose a look. 'But I'll do as you say.'

The door was released and the girl appeared. Her very red face was blotchy with tears, her twin plaits loose without their elastic, as if the tight hairstyle had been torn at.

'Now, now, Clara,' Nessa said carefully to the emerging girl, as Kitty and her friends scarpered down the corridor, 'you've had a bit of a rough time of it, but pull yourself together and get ready for your next lesson.'

'Are you all right?' Rose frowned.

The small girl's brimming eyes spilled over as she touched her messy undone plaits. 'Yes, Madam. I couldn't find my own ribbons, so I—'

'Better run to your matron,' Freddie patted the girl's back, 'and get some spare before next lesson. If you need any next time, come and find either of us. Doesn't matter what house you're in.'

Rose gave the girl an encouraging nod before she hobbled off.

'Are *you* all right, Madam?' Freddie was facing Rose now, and for the first time Rose saw that they were the same height. There was something in the girl's expression that made Rose straighten up, to stand taller.

'Yes,' Rose answered. 'Yes, I am.'

That evening, as she tried to clear her head of the storm's noise, Rose remembered the strength in Freddie's face. Washing her exhausted body again, she'd been surprised to find a bloom of fresh bruises on the back of her leg, and on her forearm. She walked through the sitting room in her towel, glancing at her cassette player that sat unplayed in the corner.

Rose replaced the oversized raincoat in the alcove cupboard, sure now that it was Jane's, and grateful that it had accompanied her during the storm. Behind it on the rail was Rose's denim jacket, more foreign than ever. In the front pocket there would be a Polaroid of her and two friends on a trip to Brighton, and a treasured piece of shell from the beach. Rose didn't want to think about that trip; she'd never want to look at another coastline again once she left this one.

The phone rang and rang. Finally, a dull voice answered, and Rose requested her mother's room. The lead burden that had lodged itself in her heart was now spreading, blocking out her stomach and choking her throat.

'Yes, darling, all well here.' Her mother's voice was misty. 'I haven't yet received your birthday card, perhaps it's on its way.'

'What?' Rose squeezed her eyes closed in sudden realisation. 'Oh, Mum, I'm so sorry, I forgot.'

Her mother sniffed and Rose could hear the wheeze of the oxygen. 'It's all right. I've never been one for birthdays.'

'Oh God, I am so angry with myself.' Rose butted her head against the wall. 'I'm truly sorry, Mum, I've . . . been so distracted, I—'

'They made a fuss here so it was quite nice. My nurse, Inga, bought me a wonderful copy of Mary Wollstonecraft. Of course, it's not a first edition.'

Rose's eyes were still closed. 'The days and weeks fall into one here. I barely know what month it is. Forgive me, please.'

Her mother was silent with reproof.

Rose tried again. 'Good to hear you're still reading that stuff.'

'What stuff?'

'Your feminist texts.' Rose opened her eyes. 'Oh Mum, it's really good to speak to you. I've been nervous to phone you – I think they might be . . . monitored.'

'Who is monitored?'

'The calls.'

'Don't be ridiculous, Rose. And anyway, the doctor is pleased. He says I'm improving.'

Rose lifted her head and shifted her gaze beyond the window of the House Prudence phone booth. 'Improving? But I thought you'd taken a turn for the worse, Mum. I've been worried.'

'Hardly worried if you forgot my birthday, darling. But I'm right as rain. They said it's a touch of pneumonia but I told them it wasn't. My hands are better than they were. Inga thinks I'm doing very well.'

'I need you to be well, Mum.' Rose gripped at the handset, remembering why she'd called. 'Yesterday, did they do anything different? Was there anyone new there at the clinic?'

'What do you mean?'

'Any . . . visitors?'

'There are always visitors, Rose, I'm one patient of many.'

'But,' Rose felt a throb of urgency, 'have you told anyone about Dad?'

Her mother coughed. 'What?'

'About how he,' Rose blinked, 'died. Did you tell your nurse?'

Her mother was suddenly abrupt. 'Your father has nothing to do with my life here, nor yours at Caldonbrae Hall. He is behind us.'

'He's not behind *me*, Mum,' Rose answered desperately. 'They know all about it here – the accusation, then his . . . death. How can they? It was all—'

'Well, I'm sure they'll be professional and keep it to themselves.' Her mother's voice was growing weaker. 'They have to. What's this about?'

'I'm so unhappy, Mum . . .' Rose faltered. 'Things aren't going well here. There's weird stuff going on, things I know *you* would disapprove of.'

'Sometimes I think you don't realise how lucky you are. You're just not used to enjoying the privilege of a place like Caldonbrae. I am very grateful to them. Now, you're giving me a headache.'

'Mum, you're not listening to me.' Rose's voice grew

resentful. 'You wouldn't believe the way this school works! It's against everything you've ever believed in! *All* the things you taught me.'

'You,' her mother said, coughing again, 'never listened to anything I tried to teach you.'

'Look, I'm sorry.' Rose tried to quell her anger. 'At least it's the holidays in a couple of weeks. You and I can really talk—'

Rose stopped. She'd heard it, an unmistakeable click. She glanced at the plastic handset, drawing it away from her, before putting it back to her ear again. Her mother was still talking.

'Must you come down? They are funny about the guest room.'

'What do you mean?' Rose stuttered. 'I haven't seen you since January!'

'Do come and visit, but not for the whole holiday.'

Rose couldn't ignore the rising panic in her chest. 'But, Mum, I don't have anywhere else to go.'

'Your home is there, now, Rose. At Caldonbrae. And I'm very happy to know you're safe there.' Her mother took a heroic breath. 'Make friends, for God's sake, spend your holidays with them. Meet a nice man, another teacher. I'd like to visit one day, you know. Maybe once I'm fully better, and out of the chair.'

Locked in, the Headmaster had said. Locked in to her flat, the boarding house and God knew what activities. Forever locked in this relationship with Latin or Greek words, combatting unwilling students. Rose looked at her lesson plan and wondered whether it was even important for the Intermediates to learn all these participles – would it matter, later, when their fates had already been decided for them?

When she'd entered her classroom the following Monday morning, her ceramic owl had been turned around to face the window, its height not reaching beyond the metal of the window frame. She didn't know how long it had been positioned like that, or why. It had been moved before, but not in this small, unkind way. Which of her students would do such a strange thing? The same girl that had written the letters, perhaps – some nemesis determined to beat her down?

'Madam?' The classroom door was wide open and framed Daisy's tall figure, but she wasn't the one speaking.

'Hi, girls,' Rose looked up. 'What are you doing here? It's not Thursday.'

'No, I know, Madam.' Freddie pushed past Daisy, her eyes wide. 'But I wanted to ask if you'd be available to give Nessa some extra sessions. She's struggling to keep up with Study.'

Rose tilted her head. 'I'd like to. Actually, I suggested it to Ms Johns.'

'Great!' Freddie's face seemed to burst with relief; she was already at Rose's bureau.

'But she said that it would happen in house?' Rose raised her hands and stood up. 'I can't . . . I mean, I could ask again . . .' Moving her head, she noticed Nessa looking desperate, still hovering at the door.

'The situation is desperate, Madam. Daisy's been helping her a bit, and I've tried, but there's only so much *we* can do.'

'What about . . . you could ask the head of History, too. He might have the right, if I don't,' nodded Rose. 'Mr Rees, you like him, don't you?'

'Perhaps,' Freddie stiffened. 'Actually, I've seen you sitting with him in the dining hall, Madam.'

'Yes, so have I. But not recently,' Daisy added. 'You were always smiling when you were around him, though, Madam.'

'Please, Madam. We don't need to tell anyone.' Nessa finally spoke up from the doorway. 'Could we at least cover three subjects? I'm really failing.'

Rose saw the shared look between Freddie and Daisy and stepped forward.

'Well,' she cracked a smile, 'that must be why we all live together in a boarding school, isn't it? I can spare an hour or two a week, Nessa, for you.'

Nessa blinked with gratitude. 'Could we start before the holidays, Madam? I'm terribly worried. Now I'm in Clemency I have to prove I'm worthy to move back up again.'

Rose felt Freddie shift with agitation beside her.

'Of course, Nessa,' Rose answered. 'Yes, I'll do it.'

Nessa relaxed and the three girls shared a brighter look.

'When, Madam?'

'What about Friday afternoon? When suits you?'

'I have games, Madam, but perhaps afterwards?'

'Okay, so perhaps an hour before dinner?' Rose nodded. 'We should be able to get away with that. Then we'll find another time.'

'Thank you, Madam.' Nessa's freckled nose wrinkled with relief.

'No problem. I think we'll manage at least two sessions before the break.'

Rose looked at her owl again; she hadn't swivelled it back. Daisy spoke into the silence. 'Since we're here, can we meet another ancient woman, Madam?'

'Oh.' Rose hesitated. 'Don't you have lessons?'

'No, Madam, it's breaktime.'

'Is it?' She looked up at the clock over her bookcase. The piece of Vesuvius rock looked back at her.

'Madam, I've always wondered about this one.' Daisy moved past Rose towards the board, to touch one of the postcards on the wall. Rose watched Daisy pull one away from its blu tack.

'Always wondered,' Nessa said sarcastically. 'Madam's only been here two terms. Honestly, Daisy, you're so—'

'Nessa,' Freddie said warningly.

'One more, Madam? It's difficult in lessons, we might not get another chance all together before the holidays.'

'I hate the holidays, Madam,' said Nessa as she edged forward. 'I'm staying here. But I'm intending to improve my Horsemanship so that my Value goes up. Might change my prospects. We've only got another year and a bit – it gets so serious in Sixth.'

'That's useful,' Rose said haltingly, moving around to sit on a desk.

'Freddie's going skiing.'

'Yes, but I hope it's not too sunny,' Freddie said with a shrug. 'I have to be careful with my complexion.'

'I'm going to see my grandparents in London,' said Daisy. 'It'll be boring.'

'Surely not. London!' Rose attempted. 'Must be nice to get away to the city? Do you . . . go to the cinema and things like that?'

'Oh, no. My grandparents are very old-fashioned, and what with the school restrictions . . .'

'Or . . . what about boys?' Rose was talking in a near-whisper. 'Do you girls ever meet up with other young people in the holidays? Any next-door neighbours you fancy?'

There was a brief pause while the girls looked at each other.

'We're not interested in that, Madam,' Daisy said firmly. 'We're better than that at Hope.'

'I've got cousins and things,' Freddie added, 'but the aim is men. Not the games staff, or the teachers. But the suitors.'

Daisy spoke up. 'We're going to learn all about that – how to entice men, what to say—'

'The power of our virginity,' interrupted Nessa, counting on her fingers, 'and what games to play. That's in Sixth.'

Rose stared at the three girls madly. 'No, no. That's not what I meant.'

'Madam, you're so . . .' Nessa rolled her eyes. 'I can't keep up with you sometimes.'

'We all have to be patient with each other, Nessa. I'm still finding out how things are.' Rose straightened up. 'You have a sister, don't you, Nessa? Wasn't she head girl last year?'

'Yes.' Nessa raised her head proudly. 'Sadie. She was married in the summer. My parents were very pleased with the match. I can't wait.' Nessa drew a hand through her thin hair. 'Being married and getting away from here, travelling maybe, seeing things. I hope I can manage. This place is all I know.'

'Nessa, you can manage all of that,' Rose said before she could stop herself, 'even without being married.'

Nessa scoffed. 'Don't be ridiculous, Madam, how would I do that?'

'With education. Sometimes as women, we have to rescue ourselves, instead of expecting someone else to.' Rose sat forward. She realised she felt bolder with the storm still in her skin. 'That's the best thing a woman can do – learn how to rescue herself, without the need of a man; without the need of anyone.'

But she was met with baffled silence.

Rose's eyes fell on the postcard in Daisy's hand: a black-haired woman stirring potions and clutching at a string of red beads around her neck. She changed her voice. 'So, gather round, let's take a look at Medea. This is a painting by Sandys. I think there's a better version in one of my books, hang on.' Rose moved over to her tall bookcase.

'Medea,' Daisy repeated, laying the postcard on the desk. 'Why is she so upset, and what is she doing?'

'She's a granddaughter of the sun, and she's brewing some herbs for a potion, because she's a witch.' Rose opened a thick book on the desk in front of them. 'Not your traditional hook-nosed witch on a broomstick, but a sorceress.'

'A sorceress.' Nessa imitated Rose excitedly.

'Yes, and born outside Greece. Therefore an outcast in Greek times.'

'Ah.' Freddie touched the postcard sympathetically.

The three girls crowded around, their hair falling softly past their shoulders and over the book. Daisy's straight black locks, Freddie's reddish curls and Nessa's blonde wisps of hair touched Rose's hands as she pointed at the oranges and blacks in the painting. *What a beautiful mess,* Rose thought.

'Medea isn't a very popular heroine,' she began, 'maybe not even a heroine at all. She's usually associated with Jason and the Argonauts. But I've always liked her. There's a Euripides play all about her – the Upper Sixth are studying it.'

'Are they?' Daisy asked. 'Lucky.'

'Well, so can you in a few years, if you want.'

The portrait stared back at them in confrontation. Rose smiled; Medea had probably never had so many young-eyed admirers before.

'Anyway, the story within the play,' Rose continued, 'is

that Medea married Jason, after she helped him retrieve the Golden Fleece.'

'Oh, yes,' Daisy nodded with recognition.

'Years later and with two boys, they landed in Greece again. Jason had been offered a position – but he didn't tell Medea how he would obtain it. He was going to marry the princess of Corinth.'

'But . . . what about Medea?' Freddie protested. 'Wasn't he already married?'

'Yes, he was.' Rose smiled again. 'But Medea was a barbarian, so to some, it wasn't a legitimate marriage at all.'

'That's a bit rude!' Nessa's eyes blew wide open.

'Yes, quite.' Rose bit back a laugh. 'And Medea thought so too. But she had to play nice. She told Jason yes, of course, I'll stay here, you go ahead. With her witchy powers she designed a beautiful dress and coronet as a gift for the young princess bride. But when the princess tried them on, Medea's poison took effect, and the girl started to melt and die. Her father, the king, ran in to help, but by clinging to her dress, he absorbed the poison too.' Rose paused. 'It's almost funny the way it's described in the play.'

'Yuck, Madam.' Nessa's freckled nose was wrinkled with disgust.

Rose grinned back. 'Yes, sorry.'

'Jason must have been furious.'

'He was, Freddie,' Rose nodded seriously. 'He was disappointed not to have his promised position in a wealthy Greek city-state.'

'He didn't want revenge?'

'Yes. And the Corinthians wanted her blood, and any related to her.'

Freddie sat forward. 'So what did she do?'

'So,' Rose hesitated and stood up before answering, 'she killed her children.'

'What?'

'Yes, I'm sorry,' Rose said instinctively.

'Don't be sorry,' Freddie leaned back on her arm and held up the postcard. 'I get it. She wanted to punish Jason. She didn't want them to live a barbarian life. What other choice did she have?'

'*Not* to kill her children,' Nessa said loudly. 'Or at least kill herself along with them, too.'

'Interesting to hear what you think.' Rose looked askance at Freddie. 'In the play Medea builds quite a logical argument before she performs the deed. She wanted to free her children from a persecuted life. If their father married a fellow Greek, they would become illegitimate. Those two boys, as men, would have been outcasts in Greece. In Medea's eyes, their deaths are a mercy.'

'But,' Daisy attempted, 'couldn't anyone help?'

'Aegeus, the king of Athens, said he would help Medea only, not her kids.'

'Harsh.'

'Yes, Daisy, many things were harsh for women then.' Rose glanced at the books on her bureau. 'Nowadays people tend to label Medea as the child-killer, but really, she reasons her way out of impossible situations. I admire her. During the play she manages to dupe one man after another with her language and her actions.'

'What happens at the end then, Madam?'

'She goes off to Athens,' Rose said slowly, 'and performs more witchy antics there . . . Stories for another day.'

'I don't think I like her, Madam,' Nessa declared, turning the page.

The three girls reacted in joyful unison as the next page settled. It showed the marble Bernini sculpture, revealed in full through a spread of photographs.

'Oh Madam, this is lovely!' Daisy gushed. 'Don't you have one of these as a postcard too? I've never been able to work out—'

'Oh, the Sixth were telling us about this,' Freddie interrupted as she read the description. 'Daphne and Apollo. He's seized with love for her, and wants to have her for himself, but she's running away from him, because she wants to stay unmarried – is that right?'

Rose frowned at the images, remembering Dulcie's engagement ring in that Sixth lesson. She took in a breath. 'Let's not.'

'No, let's. It's so pretty, this one.' Daisy was leaning in, so was Nessa. 'So that's Apollo grabbing her – isn't he a god?'

Rose hesitated. 'Haven't you had enough for one day?'

'No. Come on, Madam.'

'Why is she running?' Nessa joined in. 'Is she transforming into something?'

'Yes.' Rose fixed her eyes on the cool marble figures. 'She's a nymph, and sworn to remain a virgin and stay near her father. But Apollo is strong and forceful . . . so Daphne begs her father to save her. He's a river god, with his own powers.'

'So he grants her wish, does he?' Daisy asked.

'Yes, and he transforms her into—'

'Is it . . .' Nessa was peering into the page. 'Is it a tree?'

'Yes, Nessa, a laurel tree,' Rose said encouragingly, 'and so Apollo couldn't have her. But he became obsessed with the tree all the same.'

Nessa shook her head, bewildered. 'So Daphne became a tree for the rest of her life?'

'But,' Daisy glanced at Rose before asking, 'why wouldn't Daphne want to be with Apollo? He's a god.'

'He is, but she has free will.' Rose tilted her head. 'She wasn't interested in any young men, she just wanted to be a free virgin nymph.'

Daisy frowned. 'Is this the consent thing you were talking about last week?'

'What?'

'When we were swimming.'

'Oh.' Rose bit her lip. 'Yes, I suppose so.'

'During swimming?' Freddie interrupted. 'Did I miss something?'

'But, guys.' Nessa put in, staring hard at the images, 'can you imagine being a *tree* for the rest of your life?'

'I don't know, Ness.' Daisy's shoulders seemed to wilt. 'Might be quite nice. And near her father . . . it's a very pretty tree.'

'I suppose the point is, girls,' Rose urged, 'she liberated herself from a man she didn't want.'

Nessa wasn't having it. 'But then she couldn't have anyone else, either?'

'Yes, I suppose that's true . . .' Rose answered. 'But hadn't that always been her wish? It's a tricky one.'

Nessa sat up, her freckled cheek touching the sunlight from the window. 'Madam, before she went home, Clarissa was saying that everything you teach us is nonsense. I don't think she likes you very much.'

Rose shrugged wearily. 'I wouldn't pay too much attention, Nessa. She's got a bee in her bonnet, that one.'

Freddie tossed back her head. 'I keep saying, she doesn't even know you, Madam.'

'I really don't mind, Freddie. In fact, being disliked is one of the perks of the job.'

'Yeah, but this is Clarissa we're talking about.' Nessa pulled a face. 'She's like a goddess.'

Rose moved away from the little group. Daisy was still staring at the images in the book, while Freddie turned the Medea postcard over in her hands.

'A goddess, really? I don't think any of us can aspire to deity, Nessa. They weren't actually that nice, and,' Rose added with a stifled laugh, 'who wants to live forever? Better to be yourselves.'

Nessa rolled her eyes. 'I don't know about being ourselves, Madam. Have you seen us compared to the Sixth?'

'Yes, Nessa, your inner beauty and your unbounded sass outdo them on a daily basis.'

Freddie laughed at that.

Daisy perked up. 'Can we be *heroines* instead of goddesses, Madam?'

'Why not?' Rose scanned the faces of the three girls. 'Good idea. You can be heroines.' She nodded. 'You *will* be heroines. Just like the women in these stories.'

Daisy was pleased and Freddie, her face tense with thought, gave her a glance before turning back to Rose.

The classroom door pushed open, knocking them out of their conversation. All four of them turned at the interruption. A distressed Emma took in the wide book laid out, the three girls sitting on the desks.

'What are you all doing up here?'

Rose suddenly panicked. 'We're just discussing—'

'I didn't mean you, Madam. It's breaktime. Move along, girls.'

The girls looked at Rose and she at them. In the next moment Nessa darted to the door, while Daisy closed the book, and Freddie pressed the postcard back onto the wall. Rose watched them as they gathered at the door next to a stern Emma.

'Thanks for the lesson, Madam,' called Daisy as she slipped through the gap.

'It wasn't a lesson,' Nessa said quickly to Emma. She turned to Rose. 'Bye Madam, and thanks.'

As Emma raised her arm like a bar across the open door, Freddie turned her tawny eyes to Rose, but was then gone in a flurry of red-gold hair. Emma trod down the stairs behind the girls; thankfully, Rose could only hear her undertones of rebuke.

Affiliates Day heralded the penultimate day of term, and Rose was glad to get there. It hadn't begun particularly well; Emma had berated Rose in the Classics office about a matter that had come up during a common room conversation.

'Did you tell Vanessa Saville-Vye she didn't have to be a Compassion?'

Rose was staring into her planner, pressing her pen onto the page in front of her. She didn't want to lie. 'Oh. Nessa. She's struggling, you see.'

'My dear girl, you can try all you like,' Emma was standing and gesticulating, like a Roman senator giving a speech, 'but you can't possibly have any say in these girls' futures. It's not for us to decide.'

Rose didn't look up as Emma carried on. 'You mustn't interfere. I hear she's been misbehaving a lot recently, answering back . . . For one thing, Deirdre said she was impossible during

Conversation. Apparently the girl refused to engage in the discourse, or recite the rote responses, *and* said the others shouldn't either! Appalling.' Emma huffed, pulling off her glasses and rubbing them across her chest as Rose looked up. 'I sincerely hope that *that* has nothing to do with you.'

'Well,' Rose responded, feeling emboldened by Nessa's outburst, 'I think that sounds really encouraging. Good for her if she wants to express herself.'

'Well, there's a limit to what they'll take from her, let me tell you!'

Rose hesitated. 'What limit? And who are you referring to?'

'For heaven's sake, Rose. And today of all days.'

'I'm not doing anything today,' Rose said dully, 'they've told me I'm free to carry on as normal.' Still an outsider, Rose thought, excluded from the very system that sought to rein her in.

'Well,' Emma turned back to her desk in a spin of crossness, 'I am. What do you think my meetings have been about? Today is an important day!'

Rose watched Emma resume her work irritably; she wasn't going to ask. Affiliates Day was for educational visitors, the formal proceedings centred around expansion – Rose at least understood that. In fact, she was grateful she'd be left alone, and that Frances was speaking to her again, even if she insisted that Rose looked at her differently now.

'No, no, House See is fine,' Frances had reassured Rose earlier that day, after she'd surreptitiously asked whether the Japanese girls would be hidden away again, now that they had their own house. 'Open Day was market day and Affiliates Day is professional.'

Rose had looked at Frances, sick to her heart. *Market day?*

In her classroom Rose had smoothed out her tattered posters, just in case any visitors stopped by; she nodded briefly at the Daphne postcard that Daisy had picked out the week before, pressing it firmly back on the wall. *Market day.* She hadn't wanted to push Frances any further, especially as their friendship seemed so fragile. Still: *Market day?* Every time her feelings threatened to overwhelm her, Rose had thought of Nessa, of her own mother, and then finally, of Bethany.

Just after breaktime and as an act of appeasement, Rose offered to fetch Emma a cup of tea. She found herself smiling desperately at every visiting face that passed her on the Great Stairs, along the main corridor too, where she passed a group of visitors led by a man with a thick Russian accent. His unlikely set were dressed in suits, two with an emblem pinned on the lapel and another with an insignia stitched to a breast pocket. Rose squinted at a school motto she thought she recognised. Affiliates, Rose thought dimly as other visiting groups bloomed behind them, so this was what the governors had meant.

But on her return the corridors were quiet; and stepping up the Great Stairs – carefully, with her two cups of tea – she spotted Hanako on the library landing, hovering outside the closed doors, clearly upset.

'Oh, Madam!' The girl saw Rose's inquiring face. 'I'm so nervous! They are making me speak.'

'Who is?' Rose stiffened. 'About what?'

Hanako faced the door, her small teeth pulling at her lip. 'I must go in, Madam.'

Rose hesitated, feeling the girl's anguish. 'Then let's go in together.' She nudged the door open with her knee as Hanako's fingers curled around the doorknob.

The library was busy. The Headmaster was addressing a short semicircle of listeners, the tall room rearranged to accommodate them.

'In return the Japanese girls learn English and their families are associated with the prestige of Caldonbrae Hall. It is a very prosperous and successful scheme, which we are now preparing to roll out to other nations. But don't take my word for it – let's hear directly from one of our House See girls, Hanako.'

Rose stopped as an obedient Hanako moved ahead of her, drawn like a magnet up to the front and to the Headmaster's side.

The girl began to speak. Rose anxiously moved over to the librarian's desk to set down her two teacups, teetering in their saucers. She looked over the heads of the seated swarm of smartly dressed men and a few elegant women, all drinking in the exciting prospects of aligning themselves with the great Caldonbrae Hall. Hoping that they might increase their status in society, or bring in some wealth to boost their own institution's assets. Learning how to train crowds of girls across England, Scotland and beyond to become wives. Rose felt her chest tighten with a quiet fury. The entire group seemed to be dirtying the very library itself, their ardent attention polluting the books. Unseen, Rose scowled at the Headmaster and his deputy standing at the front.

But on the librarian's desk, a stack of paper nudged her hand. Rose looked down. Beside her steaming teacups was a pile of brochures, cleanly printed and identical to the ones she'd seen on Open Day. She weighed one with her eyes, it was dense with information. Frances had said they were sixth-form prospectuses. Rose lifted the topmost one and flicked through the pages carefully. There they were: pictures of the Lower Sixth, each of them advertised, labelled and precisely described. *Open Day was market day* – Rose could still hear Frances's statement, loud over Hanako's nervous stuttering. She bit her lip to avoid the scream in her heart.

Pages of girls' faces. Each Lower Sixth's 'provenance' beneath her portrait, then a division of three threads: Discipline, Study, Value, each with a list of achievements. Rose remembered those men in this very room, dripping all over the pictures, poring over the girls for sale. Suitors, Rose thought. Not fathers at all, as Frances had said. As her chest thrummed Rose flicked to the back pages: 'Make an Arrangement'.

Rose looked up suddenly. Hanako had stopped, struggling to find her words, her eyes marred with tears. The Headmaster was approaching the girl, making to circle her shoulders with his arm.

'Leave her alone. Stop this!' Rose shouted out before she could stop herself. Her hands gripped the brochure as dozens of faces turned to her, the Headmaster's first of all.

'Madam?' the Headmaster's face was creased with unpleasant surprise.

'Can't you see she's upset?' Anger bubbled up in Rose's chest and she darted forward. 'And no wonder! This is a disgrace.' The library seemed to hollow out with silence as the listening audience turned to Rose. 'And all of you! You're complicit in all of this!' Rose saw several affronted faces and Vivien's venomous eyes. 'God, me too. And you're *here*, desperate to be a part of it? You're disgusting. You and your private schools should be abolished!' She sobbed as she felt the full weight of the last weeks, the truth of Hope and its system reflected here in the Headmaster's face, in these intrusive visitors, in those printed pictures. 'You and your ruling classes! You're all fucking disgusting!'

'Miss Christie,' the Headmaster called out to her, touching Hanako's shoulder, and regoverning the room. 'Now, that's quite enough. Please remove yourself from the library so that we can get on with our meeting.'

'Leave Hanako alone,' Rose shrieked back across those rows of startled faces. 'Don't you touch her!'

Everything happened in slow motion. Two teachers rose from the back row, moving to block Rose with their figures and an extended arm. Vivien took the Headmaster's place and held Hanako's shoulders, while the man himself moved around the seated group.

'And I'm not one of your Madams, either!' Seeing the Headmaster's approach, Rose glanced up at the tall immovable bookcases of the library; she wanted to throw herself at them, rock them back and forth and heave them over. Over the heads of these greedy and anticipating visitors. But Frances was suddenly at Rose's elbow, her face lit with horror and astonishment.

'Ladies and gentlemen, do forgive us for these unexpected theatricals.' A beat of fear struck Rose at seeing the Headmaster nearing her, at hearing Vivien's sonorous voice. 'We sincerely apologise.'

'Indeed,' the man with the Russian accent responded scornfully, turning back to Vivien. 'Bad form, Ms Johns. Bad form.'

Frances was guiding Rose away quickly. Rose kept her eyes on the Headmaster, marshalling her courage. They met at the library doors.

'Now that you've had your little outburst,' the Headmaster said quietly, his mouth barely open, 'I hope that's over with.'

Rose heaved her chest and realised she was vibrating with fear. 'I won't be bullied by you. I don't know how you live with yourself.' She could feel Frances's tightening grip on her arm. 'This school is a disgrace. And now you want to spread it further, like a disease.'

The Headmaster's gaze was reserved for Rose's face alone. He said smoothly, 'Frances, you know what to do.'

'Yes, Headmaster.'

'No,' Rose snapped at Frances beside her. 'Don't touch me!'

'Rose!' Frances's voice was brittle behind Rose's ear. 'Calm down. There are people here . . .'

'Get away from me,' Rose cried out bitterly.

Rose somehow elbowed her way out of the library, shaking Frances away as the door fell closed. Her head hammered in agony as she tore down the Great Stairs, along the main corridors and back through the passageways, her arms propping her up, her knees brushing against the walls. She felt broken, hot, split apart. But she had no regret over what she had spoken aloud – or what she might have jeopardised for herself. She wanted to tear apart that group of consorting schoolmasters and teachers ensconced in that great library.

Too late she remembered the cups of tea she'd placed on the librarian's desk. Fortunate for the Headmaster that she'd forgotten them – she would have gladly overturned the burning fluid onto her own hands and let them scorch her flesh for her own complicity, before smashing the porcelain into pieces and driving them deep into the Headmaster's face.

SUMMER TERM

'Caldonbrae Hall is highly unique in its founding vision,
and as such,
it is enormously successful in achieving its aims.'
HM (CI) Inspectorate of Schools within
the United Kingdom, 1992

Caldonbrae Hall prospectus, 150th anniversary edition

BOUDICCA

eo provectas Romanorum cupidines ut non corpora, ne senectam quidem aut virginitatem impollutam relinquant. adesse tamen deos iustae vindictae: cecidisse legionem quae proelium ausa sit; ceteros castris occultari aut fugam circumspicere.

Roman lust has gone so far that our very persons, regardless even of age or virginity, have not been left unpolluted. But the gods are on the side of a righteous vengeance; for a legion which dared to fight has perished, and the rest are hiding themselves in their camp, or are considering fleeing.

(Tacitus' *Annals* XIV.35, written c.AD116)

Boudicca is celebrated in Britain today – there's a heroic bronze statue of her in a horse-drawn chariot that stands high beside Westminster Bridge and gazes at the Houses of Parliament. Some irony there, perhaps, when she could be seen as an anti-colonialist Celtic terrorist that fought against the might of the Roman superpower.

Boudicca was queen of the Iceni, a native Celtic tribe of England, and ruled alongside her husband, King Prasutagus. She certainly looked the part, with her tall stature, ribbons of red hair, gold jewellery, and fierce eyes that shot out firebolts

– an exaggeration of the truth, perhaps, to strike fear into the hearts of her enemies.

Boudicca's husband, King Prasutagus, was an ally of Rome during the invasion, and upon his death he left the kingdom jointly to the Roman emperor and to his wife and daughters. But the local Roman governors had other ideas. They took over the kingdom, raped Prasutagus's grieving daughters and had Queen Boudicca flogged. It would have served them better to kill her. The Iceni people were loyal to their queen, and desperate after the seizure of their lands. Led by the furious Boudicca, the Iceni revolted against the Romans. The death toll was so huge that the Roman emperor Nero considered withdrawing all forces from Britain. However, in one final stand, the Roman army amassed its might. They managed to outnumber Boudicca's forces in the Midlands, and win a decisive victory.

At the battleground and refusing to be captured, Boudicca tugged on the reins of her horse-drawn chariot, her daughters beside her. She told her comrades that they could choose to either take their own lives or become Roman slaves. Her own choice was clear – she could only win or die. Boudicca returned home for that purpose, killing her daughters before killing herself. The province of Britain was once again under Roman control.

But the Romans did not forget. The courage of Boudicca and her Iceni was a warning to the superpower that its invading tyranny would not go unchallenged.

19.

'I wish you'd cheer up, Rose,' her mother scowled from her wheelchair. 'I thought you were only staying a week.'

Rose shifted her gaze away from the windows of the glass conservatory. 'The administrator already told you, I'm staying for the whole holiday.'

'Can't you go back to Scotland? I can't have you moping around here like this. What on earth is the matter with you?'

'Nothing is the matter with me,' said Rose in a monotone. 'I'm just thinking.'

That's all Rose had done for the last ten days: think through what had happened, what she'd seen on Affiliates Day and what she'd heard at the meeting with the deputy head the following morning.

'Personally,' Vivien's voice had been arch, 'I see your appointment as a failure. You are not fit to instruct our young ladies. Indeed, to me you seem mentally unwell. But despite my advice to the contrary, the Headmaster's will is absolute, and the governors support him. You *will* mould yourself to our purpose, Rose, and we've set up key strategies to tackle this.'

Rose had entered a disciplinary phase. During the summer term, her lessons were to be monitored by a member of staff on rotation. Her lesson plans were to be handed in and approved before they were taught. She would be accompanied to the dining hall, the common room, the chapel, and all other locations. She would no longer be helping in the boarding house and she could not speak with any girl without another staff member's presence. She would attend only Junior assemblies, none for the elder years. Her progress would be reviewed at the end of the term. Rose wondered if this was how it had been for Jane in those last few weeks before her departure – she'd never know without a response to one of her letters. Perhaps Frances had been close to the truth with her obscure comment, *Jane can't even think straight.* Was that Rose's inevitable end, if she stepped out of line again?

And so Rose had taken up an armchair in the conservatory and stared out at the gardens, as if she had already had her brain knocked out of focus. She was still holding on to the pages of strategies – which she had folded and unfolded many times on the train journey down – staring into the lines of regulations as if they were prison bars across her mind. She hadn't pushed this one into the pages of *The Bell Jar*; it felt too serious for that.

Rose had only been permitted to leave Hope for a stay at the clinic, and its staff was aware of the situation. Rose had seen the nurses glance over as if she were branded with a scarlet letter of disgrace, particularly after she asked one of them whether lobotomies were still legal in the UK.

'You should call your old friends.' Rose's mother tried to clear her chest. 'Go to the pub, like you used to.'

Like who used to? Rose thought. The younger version of herself, gliding happily through lessons at her previous school, nearly a year ago?

'At least have a haircut, it's looking very messy.'

She surveyed her mother, fighting in that frail cage of her body, steadily breaking down. The bond between them was now warped by Caldonbrae's stronger hold, and it pulled away Rose's own fibres of tenderness.

There was no choice. She would have to go back. There was something to be done, with that last inch of fight in her. Rose was grateful for it; otherwise she might dissolve into the fabric of this faded paisley-patterned armchair, here among the hanging plants and semi-comatose patients.

Rose stared at the letter. She wondered how long the envelope had waited there, gathering dust underneath the door frame during the three-week holiday. At least it sat politely outside the boundary of her flat this time, and not propped up shockingly amongst her things.

> Dear Madam,
> Settle down, now that you've been put back in your place. It's your turn to make a success of this. Everything you care about is in our clutches. Everything will be safe if you can behave. The consequences are clear if you can't. Know your place, Madam. For heaven's sake, that's what you're being paid for.
> Yours,
> One of Us

The paper was a better quality than before, as if it had been refreshed by the holiday. But the typed 's' was stamped over again. Rose held the letter away from her, then pulled it towards her and breathed in. It touched a length of her hair with the movement. There was that flowery scent again.

Rose's tweed jacket was still damp from the soft splatter of rain between the car and the main doors, the wet on her face either that or her tears. It had been her oddest journey yet, her soul a soft globe balancing in her chest as she floated from the London Underground to the Edinburgh train to the rural Scotland train to the Hope car. The views of the outside had danced across her eyes but she'd absorbed none of it.

Three days until the beginning of term.

And this letter was here to remind her of the horror still to come. Would this letter end up folded into one of her favourite books, or flung into the sea air, or handed over as evidence to Vivien? Or should she tape it to the bathroom mirror as a daily reminder to arm herself every morning?

Yes, Rose thought as she dropped her handbag on top of her suitcase, that's exactly what she should do. She drew some tape across the bathroom mirror, breaking the strip with her teeth. It pulled on her bottom lip and she flinched. Another clean strip secured the letter. She pulled out one of her lipsticks and wrote underneath, *Bethany.*

The envelope she discarded. She knew the culprit would never reveal herself, and the letters might continue until Rose had plastered them all over the mirror, all over her skin, all over her heart, and driven herself mad.

On the Monday, Rose stood over the row of Upper Sixth wearing their summer silk. They were certainly being difficult today, even without Dulcie. Perhaps they could sense Rose's loosening grip, accented by the designated observer: a Science teacher at the back, busy with his own work.

'It will be very interesting to hear your thoughts about Medea's decision here.' Rose's voice was almost shrill. 'Do you think she made the right choice?'

'What,' Lex pulled a face, 'in killing her children?'

'It sounds like Medea should have signed a prenuptial agreement, Madam,' Tash chirruped and the others laughed.

'Yes, or she should have satisfied her husband Jason properly.'

'Girls,' Rose said firmly, 'I don't want you to think in those terms. We need to look at the ending, and consider what the Greek audience might have thought. Remember that Medea is not only a barbarian, but a woman who manages to slaughter the Corinthian king, his daughter, and devastate the Greek hero Jason, all in one day.'

'The Greek audience would have been pretty shocked, then, Madam,' Lauren nodded.

'And bored,' Lex muttered.

'Bored?' Rose shot back.

Lex smirked, and Tash took up the reins. 'Honestly, Madam, Medea flying off in a chariot, it's a bit much. I mean, where is the tragedy here?'

'Good question, Tash. Think about it, girls. Is *Medea* a good example of Greek tragedy? Does it stand up to, say, *Oedipus*?'

'Maybe the tragedy is that Medea doesn't die.' Tash's eyes were shrewd. '*She* should have died, instead of the children. And poor Jason could've married that young princess!' Her raised voice caught the Science teacher's attention and he looked up. Lex noticed and added testily, 'Does the Headmaster know you're teaching us this, Madam?'

Rose turned to her. 'Yes, Lex, it's on the curriculum. We had this conversation at the beginning of the year.'

'But does he know the story?'

'I haven't asked the Headmaster if he knows the ins and outs of Euripides' plays, no.'

'I'll bet he does,' nodded Jenny proudly. 'He knows everything.'

'Well,' Lex continued, 'just as long as *you* know there's no need to push your feminist agenda, Madam.'

Rose hesitated. 'I don't have a feminist agenda.'

'No, Madam, *of course* you don't,' Lex smirked. The grim-faced Science teacher leaned forward in his chair.

'Oh Madam,' Tash was grinning. 'We all heard about your shrieking on Affiliates Day too. Thank goodness this is our last year – things are sorted for us. I feel jolly sorry for the others, having you around cocking things up any minute.'

The Science teacher let his voice ring out over the class. 'I don't think this conversation is entirely appropriate, Madam.'

Tash jolted in her seat but Lex was already turning around. 'Yes, Sir, I quite agree.'

Rose glanced at her book of Euripides, marked with the same inscription as the Sophocles. *Miss Jane Farrier, Classics 1.* The girls couldn't see, but Rose wouldn't have cared. *Let them think I'm losing it,* she thought. *Perhaps I am.* It was ridiculous to think that she felt closer to Jane – and Bethany – than to anyone in this whole wretched place, but it was the truth.

'Girls,' Rose cleared her throat, 'I want us to think about the ending very carefully, and what Euripides might have been trying to say, within the genre of Greek tragedy. Which *is* the curriculum.'

'Very well, then, Madam.' Lex straightened her shoulders.

Rose ignored the scrutinising gaze of her observer and continued to read the last chorus aloud.

A week later, as the Juniors were noiselessly filing out of the chapel, Rose stepped out of the procession into the small stone quad. She breathed in the light drizzle that fell into the gap; it was nearly May, the outside cold had caught her by surprise.

'Junior assemblies are quite tedious, aren't they?' Anthony smiled, waiting for her in the cloister.

Rose went to join him. 'Are they?'

'. . . I just mean that it's all silly notices – nothing of importance.'

'I'm sorry that you had to accompany me.' Rose pulled a regretful face. 'The assembly shouldn't have been in the chapel, but apparently they needed Founder's Hall for some event.'

'Yes, the Summer Ball.'

'But that's in five weeks.'

'They do like to prepare.' Anthony gave another weary smile. 'It's rather ridiculous, all this, isn't it?'

Rose hesitated. 'What do you mean?'

'Having you accompanied everywhere.'

Rose looked up at him as they moved behind the stream of Juniors. 'Do you think so?'

'Yes, I don't see why you can't be trusted. You've been doing a fine job with your classes – in Prudence too. Affiliates Day was just a blip. This place just takes some getting used to, and it must be particularly hard to feel like you'd been kept in the dark for so long.'

Rose didn't know what to say, but she felt glad of his kindness all the same.

'Rose,' Anthony put a gentle hand on her shoulder, 'it will be fine.'

She nodded in response. 'Is there, a way, to . . . you know . . . get on with this system? I can't seem to—'

'We all have our ways of coping, Rose. It just takes time to . . . settle in. You can always talk to me.'

Rose found herself nodding, more out of compliance than true understanding.

'So,' Anthony motioned forward, 'what's next, a meeting in House See?'

'Yes, Vivien sent word that I'm to observe some kind of session in there, which might be added to my timetable. She said it was an innovation; I don't know how long it will take. Sorry to hold you up.'

'No, no, I don't have first period. If you're free,' Anthony suggested warmly, 'perhaps we could have a cup of tea afterwards?'

Rose nodded again, reassured.

At the top of the passage stairs Rose saw two girls turn in an electric movement towards them. With a bracing feeling, she recognised Josie and Clarissa. The older girl was glaring at Rose.

Anthony moved slightly ahead of Rose, and spoke first. 'Hello there, girls. Time for lessons, I think.'

Rose hadn't realised the two girls were friends; they were years apart. Clarissa looked more beautiful than ever, her cheeks soft with emotion, evidently fully recovered after her illness last term. Josie was a shadow behind the head girl, and neither of them were looking kindly at Rose. Anthony gave them only a passing glance; Rose was grateful for the quiet defence he presented against the pair.

Seeing Josie, Rose was reminded of Nessa. The new regulations specifically restricted out-of-lesson discussions with the girls. She'd got away with a few extra catch-up sessions last term with Nessa, but could Rose risk it now? She wanted to.

Why couldn't she try this small defiance? Everywhere else she'd be entirely obedient.

She had a new question for Anthony.

'I'd really like to start helping the university girls, too. You mentioned that that would be part of my role, as did the governors?'

'Yes.' Anthony stood still at the top of the Great Stairs. 'Give it time.'

'Oh, is it these new restrictions? Are they worried that—'

'It's a delicate situation at this time of year,' Anthony answered gently.

'I see.' Rose didn't see. 'Are you working with any girls at the moment? I'd really like to make a start . . . perhaps I could follow one of your sessions?'

'I'll let you know. But,' Anthony turned along the corridor and Rose followed him, 'as I say, we'd have a better chance to wait until September. Things are coming to a close here, now, soon.'

Rose turned her face away, disappointed.

'Bit of a walk, isn't it – chapel to the north wing?' Anthony said a moment later, as muffled lessons began behind the closed doors of the first-floor corridor.

'Yes,' Rose answered dully. 'There aren't any shortcuts in this place.'

'There probably are.'

'I don't think so. I've studied the map in the library, trying to work out my bearings if I'm going to stay here.'

Anthony chuckled. 'Well, that bodes well. You know . . .' he paused for an agonising moment, 'I, particularly, will be glad to see you settle in here at Hope.'

'Oh.' Rose's cheeks flushed. 'Thank you, Anthony.' She bit

her lip, not knowing what else to say. Perhaps those small buds of feeling might thaw out soon enough, and give her another reason to commit herself to Hope.

Many passageways later Anthony said he'd wait outside House See as Rose went in. She expected the door to slam behind her at the bottom of the steps, but it fell with a soft thud. She knew well the silence of this house, and it soothed her.

Rose looked across at the dark green day room and its matching velvet sofas. It was full of quiet girls, watching each other.

About two dozen students were sitting on soft cushions on the floor; Rose recognised her few Lower Sixth Latinists. The tall curtains were drawn and dim lamps dotted around the room were giving off a sensitive glow. But Rose was mesmerised by the object of the students' attention: several Japanese geisha girls moving about the room, gracefully, slowly, and with furtive smiles. They wore costumes that were beautifully garish and unique, with a thick sash drawn tightly around each waist; their faces were painted white with rosy lips, and their hair tied up in elegant buns.

One group of students was exploring the craft of a tea ceremony, handling powders with delicate cups or pots of hot water. Another group was watching three girls perform an exquisite dance, exposing their wrists as they took small steps in their wooden shoes. The observing girls were as enthralled as Rose, but none noticed the teacher shudder as she suddenly recognised Ayumi.

Rose pulled at the latch on the door and dashed up the steps. She didn't realise she had been holding her breath until she let it out in the hallway, and almost fell into Anthony.

'Are you all right, Rose?' He tried to take her in his arms. 'You're as white as a sheet.'

'I saw –' She took a moment to gather her words as Anthony's hands moved to support her.

A door across the hallway slammed, the main door of House Chastity. Rose looked up at Anthony; whoever had been there a moment before had caused a cleft frown across his forehead. But Rose's thoughts were frantic.

'Anthony! Is that what they're here for – the Japanese girls – as instructional geisha girls? Is that what they mean by innovation?'

'Of course not, Rose, there's much more to it than that . . . they are our *students* first and foremost.' Anthony pressed his lips together and shook his head. 'Look, I don't get involved with that side of things. You'd have to ask Emma, or Frances. What about your session?'

'It's exploitation. Not to mention abuse of their culture. Those girls – some of them are very special; all of them are vulnerable. Is this what they're worth?' Rose breathed, her mind racing with what she'd just seen, and Anthony's stilted reaction. '"Innovation" used to mean a good thing!'

'Oh Rose.' Anthony's forehead creased further. 'It still does.'

Rose stood up properly and Anthony let go of her. 'No cup of tea for me,' she added weakly. 'I'd better just get back to the office.'

Rose managed to draw encouragement from her classes, and from one particular Junior lesson later that week. The observing Music teacher had nodded off in the corner, the Seconds' classroom noise apparently nothing to the clash of the percussion or shout of the brass. They'd met Boudicca, the Celtic tribal queen, and argued over the Roman need – as a superpower – to dominate through violence, with Boudicca having no other recourse but to fight back. Rose had checked their young faces and taught them a new word: subjugation. They'd written it down before starting their creative homework: drawing a portrait of the tribal queen with her traditional torc necklace, fiery red hair, and Celtic tartan.

An hour later in the dining hall, Rose moved her lunch tray behind Emma to let some Intermediates pass. 'I've been meaning to say, I'm worried about my Upper Sixth and their A levels, now that I've got the head of department duties. Will Dulcie—'

'Oh, I wouldn't.' Emma moved towards a spot at the end of a staff table. 'They don't always take them. They'll leave after the Ball, and then return for the Thirtieth of June.'

Rose stopped, her glass of water wobbling perilously. 'The Sixth *don't* take their exams?'

'No, they don't always need to, since their matches are made.'

'So,' Rose asked hotly, 'why on earth have I been teaching them?'

'To enrich their minds, Rose. There's no need to fixate on exams.'

'But . . . what about the league tables? Hope sits at the top of most of them!'

'Oh Rose, you already know the answer to that – our influence extends far enough to modify those things.'

'What?'

'Well, our Fifths *will* take their GCSEs, so some of it is true. But our Sixth have got the knowledge, that's what matters.'

'Yes,' Rose added scathingly, 'my Sixth should be able to discuss Greek tragedy heartily at one of their dinner parties.'

Emma touched her glasses and gave Rose a warning look. 'Honestly, Rose, you're being ridiculous. Frances must be rubbing off on you . . . are things any better there?'

'Frances?' Rose settled her tray heavily on the table opposite Emma. 'I haven't really seen her since we got back.'

'It's only been a week or so. I hear she's been struggling lately.'

Rose felt a bitter sting, and wondered whether she should try to reconcile with Frances, the only person that had even partially understood her. Should she apologise for pushing her away after that meeting on Affiliates Day? Could she then challenge Frances on the dressed-up girls she'd seen in House See, or anything else she didn't yet know? Rose didn't think her heart could handle any more surprises.

Instead, she attempted a new conversation: 'The girls are pleased to have Clarissa back.'

Emma shuffled neatly onto her bench. 'Yes. Poor thing, I was speaking to one of her house tutors this morning.'

'What was wrong?'

'Well, if you really want to know,' Emma set her arms on either side of her tray and leaned towards Rose, 'she had a *termination*.'

'A termination?' Rose couldn't conceal her shock. Emma's eyes widened with the piece of gossip as she picked up her fork.

'Of course, it's completely confidential – it would decrease her Value enormously, if they knew she was no longer intact. In fact, I don't even think—'

'She's been sleeping with someone?' Rose spluttered. 'Not her *suitor*?'

'No, no, that's forbidden,' said Emma, horrified.

'Does she have a boyfriend at home then? Is that why she was away for so long?'

'The house tutor said there might be a cousin,' Emma shrugged. 'Hardly matters now, it's all been corrected. Her father was *very* severe with the Headmaster; he said he wants to pursue it.'

Rose ignored her food and stared across at Clarissa's Sixth table. The girl was talking animatedly at her friends. She seemed fine, but perhaps that was all part of her training. 'She won't be punished, will she? I mean, surely it's a family matter?' Rose thought of the bareheadedness punishment, imagining those auburn curls of Clarissa's falling away around her pretty face.

'She won't be punished. But it really is top secret, Rose,' Emma warned.

Rose felt a nudge of irritation as she turned back to Emma. 'So the system doesn't always work then, does it?'

Emma laid down her fork and peered at Rose through her glasses. 'Well, I don't know what you mean about that, but it's been dealt with.' She paused. 'And after what happened last year, they had to really take care of it, and what with Clarissa being head girl . . .'

'What happened last year?'

'*You* know.'

'No,' Rose said loudly, 'I don't know.'

'Hush,' Emma whispered, leaning forward, 'the poor girl died during the operation.'

Rose's hand formed a fist on the table. 'Oh my God. That was a termination? This has happened before?'

'Actually,' Emma's eyes were narrowed conspirationally, 'that was the first time it's ever happened. It was one of the games staff who interfered with *her*. And now Clarissa with this cousin. We really do have to ensure it doesn't happen again.'

Rose leaned her head against her hand. 'What was her name?' She looked up at the Founder's painting in spite of herself, the tall slim windows letting in slips of sunlight alongside his portrait. 'Emma, do you realise that girl shouldn't have—'

'Good afternoon, you two. *Bon appétit.*'

Rose jolted. Vivien settled herself on Emma's bench, putting herself opposite Rose. The movement was charged and precise, and Rose was hit with the heady scent of Vivien's expensive perfume.

'I wanted to ask, ladies. How is the disciplinary phase going?'

Rose found that her hands were shaking; she gripped her tray.

'Very good, Vivien.' Readjusting her glasses, Emma smiled brightly at the deputy head. 'All seems well.'

Rose could see a touch of pink in Emma's cheeks; she looked down at her plate, trying not to notice the swivelled heads of the Sixth now looking over at them.

'Decent reports from your observers, Rose.' Vivien's mouth was crooked as she scrutinised her. 'I hope you are continuing to *see the light* as it were.'

'Yes.' Rose winced at her own voice.

'I thought I'd arranged for you to attend a session in House See, but the matron tells me you didn't turn up.'

'Oh.' Rose's heart seemed to flutter in her mouth. 'I did, but . . . I was suddenly unwell.'

'I'd like to have you involved with House See. Those girls are interesting, I like that Lisa. I suppose you are our innovation as much as they, and we ought to bring you all up together.'

Rose nodded, not knowing what else to do.

'Well, good. Let's hope that settles that. Because we do rather need your help with the Ball; you'd make a splendid addition to the team, Rose. It's as important for the Lower

Sixth debutantes as it is for the Upper Sixth and their suitors. The Lower Sixth will have their "coming out" in September, so this is a formal preview. Good.' Vivien stood up and directed her last comment to Emma. 'I'll be very pleased to tidy up this little problem.'

After the deputy head had left the hall Emma pulled off her glasses and rubbed them against her blouse.

'Thank you for not repeating what I just mentioned, Rose. About Clarissa's termination.' She tutted at herself. 'I shouldn't have told you. You're already in a precarious position.'

Rose surveyed Emma. 'You're terrified of Vivien, aren't you?'

'No. Heavens, no.' Emma continued to push her glasses against her chest.

'All of you, you're terrified.' Rose felt a sickness rise in her chest. 'That's how this place survives.'

'No, no. You've got me wrong there.' Emma hooked her glasses back on her nose. 'Anyway, thank you for not saying anything. Please do *not* repeat it.' She glanced at the tables around them, before continuing with her meal. Rose, however, had lost her appetite.

20.

The weather improved with the beginning of May, and the seascape changed with it. But for the first days of the month an unbearable white met Rose's eyes at every window: a soft damp mist, unmoving and unforgiving.

The porters told her it was the 'haar' come in from the water, and that she mustn't go for any walks or she'd lose her way from one metre to the next. Of course, they reminded her, she wasn't allowed outside alone, anyway.

On one afternoon, Rose was informed she had an important note from the secretaries waiting for her upstairs. Fearful of bad news about her mother, Rose grabbed the note on her desk and scoured it, still panting from the rush up the stairs from the common room.

Miss Christie. Please go to classroom Rec 2, next period, for Worship. Cover teacher needed. Vivien insisted on you.

Rose sucked at her teeth, tasting the almond biscuit she'd had with her tea. She'd only ever covered a few of Emma's lessons, in her own classroom. There were no teaching instructions, either. Worship? But Hope had no chaplain, and the lesson wasn't in the chapel. Rose checked the clock on the office wall, she was already late.

She met Emma at the door; hopping to the side, she slid past. 'Emma. Remind me where the Rec classrooms are?'

'In the older part of the building, just beneath us and further along. Through that wonky door.'

'Which wonky door?'

'For heaven's sake, you should know your way around by now. It's where that Conversation was back in September.'

'Oh.' Rose thought about it. 'Yes.'

'But, hang on . . . it's Wednesday.' Emma seemed suddenly anxious. 'Rec 2? Have you really been sent to cover one of those lessons? They aren't usually for the academic staff.'

'Really? Look . . .' Rose showed the note to Emma.

'Then you'd better go.' Emma's mouth was tight and wrinkled. 'You'll need your keys for the door. Good luck.'

Rose didn't have time to question Emma's anxiety. She pushed past stragglers in the corridors and found her way to that wonky door, her fingers fumbling to find the right key.

As she stepped into the passageway a cloud of acrid incense hit her in the face. She inched her way down the dark corridor, so much narrower than the ones she was used to, and much less busy than her previous visit. She followed a hollow, authoritarian voice through to Rec 2, a room she'd only passed by last time.

'Sorry I'm late,' Rose said as she nudged open the door, 'I wasn't really familiar with the location . . .'

Rose wasn't prepared for what met her eyes. The deep crimson of the walls was denser than she remembered, the wooden floor a mess of scattered red cushions. But Rose's gaze was drawn to the portly man outstretched on a long velveteen couch, bare-chested and rickety-legged with a pair of socks pulled up over his ankles. His briefs were unbuttoned and split open for the full extent of his erect penis to be seen. Rose blinked stupidly as she saw a figure kneeling at the man's side, holding his penis upright like a fork. It was a woman that Rose didn't recognise.

Rose backed towards the door, thinking she had the wrong room, that she'd caught a pair of lovers together. But seven older girls were gathered behind the woman, observing her as she bowed over the outstretched man on the couch, a heavy book open at her side. Above the woman's bent head a thick sign was nailed to the wall: *No Penetration*.

The woman turned around to lift her face to Rose, her forehead prominent and her eyes deep-set in her face. 'Oh good, Madam, you must be our additional female. I don't think we've met, I'm one of the auxiliary pastoral staff from Honour. I'm afraid we've started without you.'

Rose was rooted to the spot as the woman turned back to the man's figure. Averting her eyes, Rose stared at the girls, whom she now recognised as Sixths. Their faces wore less make-up than usual, and they each had their long hair tied back in low ponytails.

The woman raised her voice to address the girls, reciting some lines she seemed to know by heart. 'Men desire and deserve your full attention. Intuit what he is thinking, what he is needing – if you can become that missing piece, then you will learn to give love and be loved on command.'

'Please, is this –' Rose stammered. 'What is this?'

'This is Worship, Madam,' the woman answered matter-of-factly, not losing focus as she resumed her work. 'It's part of Practice, for Coupling. Our designated volunteer for today is Sir from History.'

With renewed horror Rose saw that the man naked and spread out was Ashley, a ridiculous grin drawn across his face, his pubic hair a glistening mess.

'But . . . what?' Rose was midway between fury and tears.

There was a tickled laugh from one of the Sixth, as several faces gave Rose haughty and judgemental looks. Turning away from them, she noticed a strange metal instrument bolted to the wall: long and wide, man-height, with leather straps.

'Would you like to contribute, Madam?'

Rose's face snapped back to the woman. 'Would I . . . what?'

'Are you a member of house staff, or—'

'I'm a teacher.' Rose breathed heavily, inhaling the thick incense, trying not to look down at Ashley's grinning face. 'I'm a teacher.'

A few of the Sixth tittered.

'Settle down, girls.' The woman turned to face them, then looked up at Rose. 'Yes, Madam, all right. I can see now that you're very young; I had thought you were older and might know a thing or two. Just observe with the girls then, please.'

'No, no. God, I don't –' Feeling something come up her throat, Rose held her hand to her mouth. The muscles in her stomach contracted as she began to retch. The woman's face was struck with alarm as Rose rushed through the door. She ran down the dark corridor, pressing her hands over her mouth, desperately trying to hold in her horror as the Sixth laughed behind her. But out it came, fluid and repulsive against the harsh stone wall.

*

Rose held her burning teacup, tugging at the string of the teabag. Her hands were still shaking. The water turned a blushing raspberry pink against the white porcelain.

Lessons for Coupling, the so-called "innovation" of House See, Discipline and Value, fulfilling requirements – the numerous pieces of information Rose had absorbed now created a rich, horrifying tapestry, whose patterns Rose recognised, no matter how jarring the logic.

She thought bitterly of Frances's clear blue eyes. Her heart leaked desperately to confide in her, but every time she'd seen her in passing, the woman's face was hard and full of complicated thoughts. Emma's had been no less thunderous when Rose had returned, horrified, to the Classics office, so she'd buried herself in the underground lair of the common room.

'Seen the invitation for the Summer Ball – isn't it splendid?' John tittered, suddenly next to Rose.

Rose had seen the glossy invitation, offered up as an example on the noticeboard. The card opened out with the school's emblem and details of the evening, just three weeks away. The ribbons that bound the invitation together were undone and falling down the wall, the same ribbons that the Juniors wore in their hair. Rose wondered if she could tug at the invitation, unstitch the ribbons and draw them tight around someone's neck – the Headmaster, or his deputy, or perhaps even herself.

'Yes, John,' Rose replied instead, 'it's splendid.'

'You won't find my name on the staff list,' he continued with a jerky movement. 'I'm invited to the event. I've been working hard, I've even got some foreign ambassadors on the list, and a head of industry.'

Rose glanced at the frail skin on his hands as he passed the ribbon of the invitation through his gnarled fingers.

'Headmaster needs me, I'm one of the direct agents. Being taken over now by the young upstarts. Still, it's essential that I'm there, everybody knows me.' He reared his head importantly. 'I'm organising the alumnae dinner in July, at the Banqueting House in London, just trying to decide on the keynote speaker . . .' He nodded at the staff list on the board, littered with names. 'Anyhow, you'll be on there, somewhere.'

'Will I?' Rose darted forward to find her own name. Front of house. She closed her eyes for a moment to stall her anxiety.

'I've sorted my own little table, and I've requested an excellent wine.'

Rose saw a few names at the bottom, appointed to monitor House See bedtimes.

'Will House See be . . . closed again?'

'Of course,' John nodded.

Rose wondered briefly if she could while the evening away with Hanako and her friends in that soft dark green room. 'I'd rather be with them. Can roles be swapped?'

John didn't respond, and Rose looked at him sideways. She didn't know if he hadn't heard, or was choosing to ignore her. She tried again. 'What about the younger girls, are they locked up too?'

'The Junior and Intermediate performances take place before the dinner. Then they return to the houses. The Lower Sixth are all involved in the Ball. The ones arranged will be joining in; the few others will waitress and do hair, that sort of nonsense.'

Rose nodded. 'So there's plenty for me to do in the Junior and Intermediate houses, instead of front of house.'

'Well, I gather you're not *supposed* to have any kind of direct communication with the girls – front of house will prevent you from doing so. The Headmaster has a plan for you,' John nodded as he wandered over towards the armchairs. 'Quite honestly, I don't know why. I caught the Seconds thundering down the main corridor yesterday morning, shrieking about some Celtic tribe. I gather that was down to you.'

Rose's cheeks grew warm as she turned away, daring to mutter, 'I imagine that it was.'

The three Moirai moved past her in their stream of never-ending gossip, latched on to one another, three times symmetrical in their beige shirts and skirts, their scowls and their drooping mouths. Rose overheard their comments for the first time.

'One of the governors was asking me about it.'

'Yes, I know they take an interest. Funny how our Classicists are cursed. Perhaps she should consult the famous Delphic oracle for what to do next.'

Rose tilted her head to listen as they wandered towards their swoop of armchairs, with no thought of dulling their voices.

'There is no *next*. She should just get on with it; I don't even know why there's been such a fuss. She and her polyester suits.'

'We have to experiment with new staff. Hope needs a future.'

Rose wiped off the smudge of her lipstick from the lip of her teacup, first with her finger, and then more thoroughly with the edge of her sleeve.

'She doesn't want to take the same route as her father did, does she?'

'True! And making such a fuss about things here – going on and on to the Headmaster about the exploitation of young girls when he did what he did.'

Rose moved quickly as her teacup tumbled to the floor. 'How dare you?' she called across to the Moirai. 'You don't know *anything* about my father.'

'Oh! Well,' one of the women croaked back at Rose, 'we rather do. But word needn't go any further – I suppose it's up to you.'

'He was a great man, he was innocent,' Rose choked out.

'Can't have been if he took his own life, dear,' the middle Moira added. 'Though of course, you're always going to be biased.'

'Yes, you'd better watch out!' The first tapped her temple with a chunky finger. 'You don't want to follow the same route as old fat Jane.'

'Oh no, she won't. I hear the Headmaster wants to dress her up for the Ball and have her at the front, for everyone to see his great triumph.'

Rose couldn't look at them anymore. She turned and tried to move away, stumbling over the corner of the tea service. 'You'll need accompanying if you're going upstairs!' all three called after her.

Out – she had to get out, she thought, as she left the common room and pushed through the corridors.

A trio of Sixths sidled past her in the main corridor; Rose recognised Lex's voice.

'I'd better not get the curse during the Ball.'

'Oh, don't worry,' answered a Slavic-looking girl Rose didn't know, 'Matron's got something for that.'

Lex's eyes hooked on Rose and narrowed with glee. 'Oh Madam, we heard you fainted in Worship earlier?'

'Frigid old spinster,' Lex's friend laughed. 'If she's going to faint, then what good is she here? And isn't she the one that got Dulcie into all that trouble?'

Rose drove on towards the entrance hall and the main doors, carrying the insults with her, ready to give them up to the air.

'Madam, you're not to go out alone!' called out one of the porters. 'Especially not with the haar!'

Outside, Rose felt her eyes blister with the damp and she blinked. No tears today, she was past that. But they'd been right: the haar was thick and frightening, and she wasn't at all wearing the right clothes. The crash of the sea and the shriek of the birds called her forward, but from one step to the next her bearings were lost. The white stillness stopped her breathing, the kiss of the mist penetrating her throat. Perhaps the haar was Bethany's soul, Rose thought, surrounding the peninsula and its occupants in a stranglehold of torment.

Rose wished she could see the long, jagged line of the coast, to remind herself where Hope began and ended. But it was no use; even if she made it down to the gate, Rose knew she'd be caught there, and punished for it. She imagined herself pulling at the rusted iron bars with her bare hands as they stood fast. But even there at the bottom slope of the drive, the school would rise like a ghost out of the mist. What curious god held this monster in its white hands? Not Zeus, or any she knew. *Carry it away,* she almost prayed, and return the castle ruin to the Scots. Wipe away this living stain on education, on womankind.

At lunch the following Monday, a girl slid onto the bench opposite Rose, who jolted with alarm, her fork clattering to her plate.

'Good afternoon, Madam,' Clarissa declared, pulling her tray in front of her. 'I thought I'd join you for lunch.'

It took Rose a moment to recover; she'd barely slept the last few nights, and her thoughts were slow to gather together. 'These are staff tables, Clarissa.'

'Yes, Madam.'

Rose glanced over at the Sixth tables across the way. 'Wouldn't you prefer your tablecloths and silver, amongst your friends?'

'They let me eat here sometimes, Madam,' Clarissa smiled, showing her pearly teeth. 'Madam Ms Johns and the Headmaster, that is . . . and since you're alone . . .'

'I don't need your company,' Rose said flatly. 'I like being alone.'

'Do you, Madam? I see that you get on very well with Miss Manders, and perhaps Mr Rees.' Clarissa sat forward and started on her salad. Her dress was a particularly loud shade of mauve today, and Rose wasn't sure it suited her. Clarissa lifted her fork victoriously. 'But you haven't eaten with them recently, and aren't you supposed to be accompanied at all times now?'

Rose regarded Clarissa carefully. This was the girl who had managed Bethany's letter of apology, who had insisted Dulcie wear her engagement ring for Rose to notice, who seemed to have recruited Josie to her cause. What did she want with Rose, now?

Before she could stop herself, Rose came out with it: 'Have you been writing me letters, Clarissa?'

'No, Madam.' Clarissa shook her head. '*Bethany* wrote you a letter, which I delivered to you.'

'Not that.' Rose narrowed her eyes. 'I'm referring to typed

letters, delivered to my flat?' She searched the girl's face for any sign of recognition.

'No, Madam, why on earth would I bother doing that?' Clarissa took a swift bite of her food. 'I'm far too busy for that sort of thing. It's already been a difficult term.'

With a start, Rose remembered what Clarissa was referring to, and she softened. 'Yes, I'm very sorry, Clarissa, about what happened to you.' Rose couldn't quite form the words for the rest.

'I don't know what you mean, Madam.' Clarissa continued to chew, then she stopped, her skin reddening with horror. 'Pardon me, Madam, but they – they haven't *told* you, have they? Surely not?'

'Well . . .' But Rose couldn't think fast enough to lie. She was suddenly embarrassed. 'Yes, they have.'

'How dare you mention that? How dare you – you of all people!'

'Me?'

'You know nothing.' Clarissa shook her head furiously, trying her best to recover. 'And even if you did, I'm sure you know it's terribly bad manners to discuss anything so intimate in a public dining hall!'

Rose winced at Clarissa's words. 'I—'

'And you know, Madam,' Clarissa shrilled, gripping at her fork, 'it's all jolly well you settling in. And I'm glad you've got Miss Manders. But you should know, your advances aren't welcome elsewhere – it's best to stick to your kind!'

'What – what on earth do you mean, Clarissa?'

'Mr Rees, Madam. We've all seen how you moon over him,' Clarissa hissed.

'Mr Rees?'

'Yes, Madam, he's not for you.'

Rose's face dawned with comprehension. 'I see. Well, you ought to be careful there, Clarissa.' In spite of herself, she added, 'Having already got yourself in trouble once.'

'Well, I can't imagine *why* you think Mr Rees would want you at all. I don't see how you could be attractive to anyone.' Clarissa tossed her shoulders. 'What is *your* value? Nothing – all you can do is speak a dead language!'

Rose hesitated before she responded. She didn't know what she was doing, arguing with a girl, meeting her on her own petty level – is this what she had been reduced to in just over two terms?

Without another word Rose stood up, gripping her tray of half-eaten food. There were things she had to listen to, and things she didn't. And today, she'd had quite enough of Clarissa's company.

But when Rose returned to her classroom she saw that beneath the arched window her ceramic owl had been smashed, its head cracked in two. The eyes were staring out in opposite directions, as deranged as the rest of the broken body scattered across the floor.

She knew it hadn't been the force from the window, unopened for a week. No, the cause was clear. Next to the owl's broken shards was Rose's piece of volcanic rock from Vesuvius. She looked at them both strangely, one of her treasured possessions having destroyed another so easily, and done by a third deliberate hand.

Bending down, Rose rearranged a cracked piece of one eye so that it fit next to the other. She imagined that the round pair blinked at her once more. Athene's wise symbol, and

Rose's daily companion. She left the mess on the floor as her loss cleaved at her chest.

On the way to her classroom, she'd received news from the secretaries that her mother was now bedbound, with the beginning symptoms of pneumonia – they were certain this time – although her vitals were apparently *ticking along nicely.* The doctor was optimistic about staving off the viral infection, but her mother was so weak that she wouldn't be able to speak too long, or at all, on the phone. The cold steel that seemed to have replaced Rose's heart sparked afresh with the information, but she only nodded at the secretaries, telling herself that at least she was due to see her mother for half-term in a few weeks.

In the following days, Rose's Lower Sixth didn't notice the broken owl, nor did the burly Fourths, who suffered one of the more forbidding Maths teachers as an observer. Nessa had worn a frustrated grimace throughout Rose's perfunctory lesson, turning back to the man every few minutes to check if he was still there. Freddie had given up her usual buoyancy and fidgeted instead; Rose even saw her check her watch once. At the end of the lesson the Maths teacher stood stiffly at the door as the girls filed out. Freddie gave a deadened, 'Sorry, Sir,' after deliberately hitting him with her bag, but Nessa hesitated.

'Sir, I just need to ask Madam something. It's a house matter.'

The Maths teacher looked down the length of his nose.

'Women's problems,' Nessa added.

'All right, all right.'

Rose stiffened as he ducked through the door, the last ebb of her energy following him out. She sat down in her chair.

Daisy hung back, too. Rose looked at her strong profile, her black hair brushed back.

'Madam,' Nessa said urgently, 'I wanted to ask you about my extra sessions and how we can continue them.'

'I can't continue them, Nessa.' Rose was weary. 'I'm in a disciplinary phase.'

'Why, Madam?' Freddie punched in. Rose hadn't realised she was still in the classroom. She met Freddie's gaze, but didn't answer.

'Please, Madam,' Nessa continued. 'The situation is really rather desperate for me, I really—'

'Madam! Your owl!' Daisy's mouth was agape.

The damage looked so much worse from here; the cruelty of the rock and its helpless victim lay exposed with all their jagged edges. Seeing it a second time made Rose prickle with distress as Nessa's small face turned back to her teacher.

'I can't help you, Nessa. They won't let me.'

'But Madam—'

'I can't, all right?' Rose's voice was brittle.

'Please, Madam,' Freddie attempted. 'I think we can find a way.'

'What do you want from me? What is it?' Rose gave each of them an excruciating look as she stood up. 'Why are you always staying behind?'

The three girls drew back; Daisy glanced at the other two worriedly.

'What is it,' Rose forced, 'that you expect me to do?'

'Madam, we—' Freddie started.

'No.' Rose swung her gaze to the window and the blank white mist. 'You're all brainwashed. Don't you realise that? You're all . . . too far gone. I'm sorry.' Rose choked out a horrible laugh as she once again surveyed her broken owl. 'This place is a disgrace. It should be obliterated. It needs to be burned to the fucking ground. Just leave me alone. I can't help any of you. I'm sorry.'

The three girls stared back at Rose. If they'd said anything at all, she couldn't remember it. She would only remember the hurt on their faces, the searching bewilderment. Rose pushed past them, storming out of the room before they could see her own drawn, devastated face.

The next day, Rose avoided her classroom and her office any moment she wasn't required in either, preferring to take refuge in a tall and concealing armchair near the common room fire.

Just before lunch, Emma challenged Rose as she entered the Classics office and streamed straight towards her desk. 'Did you come up here alone?'

'Yes,' Rose answered.

'You'd better not get caught out. Any major flouting of the rules in your disciplinary phase and we'll both be sorry . . .'

Rose didn't reply; she didn't dare allow herself to consider what 'being sorry' might entail.

'Anyhow,' Emma frowned, 'you've got a note. One of your Fourths delivered it – she said it's from Anthony, apparently urgent.'

Rose felt a sting of shame remembering her harsh words the day before; she hoped she hadn't missed a visit from Nessa, Daisy or Freddie. She scrabbled to check the note.

'He's always had a bit of a thing for you, hasn't he? And I can tell it's reciprocated.' Emma raised her eyebrows slyly. 'I'm sure the Headmaster would approve.'

Rose blinked with awkwardness and read the note.

Hi Rose, please come to Rec 3 this period, there's a few things I'd like to discuss if you're free. Anthony.

Rose dropped the note. 'It's for a meeting in the Rec classrooms. I can't go back there.'

'Don't be ridiculous, Rose.' Emma sat at her desk. 'It's midday, anyway. And it's Anthony Rees. You're in no danger there. You won't even need accompanying.'

Rose lifted the note again; it seemed such an odd request. Checking the clock, she left the office. She moved down the stairs on tiptoe, anxious with every step, hearing the distant laughter of the girls.

The door to the Rec corridor wasn't locked this time, and the passageway was better lit than she remembered, thankfully without that powdery stench of incense.

Rose paused. She could hear something: a dark sound, hollow and deep. She turned her head. There was a short, rough grunt and she followed it. Yes, it was coming from the door nearest her, a few footsteps away. Drawn like a magnet, Rose moved closer. There was a regulated panting and a soft cry of pleasure. Two sounds now, with parallel tones.

The door opened in front of her. This was no cover lesson, no professional meeting. The two lovers were at the far corner, leaning strangely on the narrow windowsill, the red walls sweating on either side. The connected pair didn't see Rose, whose heart hammered with the same rhythm as their movements. She gasped.

They stopped, poised at the end of a thrust. The girl caught Rose's gaze with a move of her head.

'Oh Madam, you got my note?' Clarissa said deliciously, a sheen of sweat across her forehead, a lock of auburn curls slick against her neck. She had one hand gripping the man's sandy hair, and the other clamped across his shoulder. Her white knees were wrapped around his waist. Rose was too shocked to move.

Clarissa shifted her eyes to address her lover. 'There, Sir, now she's seen us, you can stop pretending to like her.'

The man's head turned and Rose saw what she already knew. Anthony's face, twisted back, was distorted with a peculiar mix of horror and relief. Clarissa gave him a damp kiss on the cheek as he stared at Rose.

Rose lowered her face, hot with shame; she blinked, but still she could see the ugly tableau of the two figures locked in their jerky embrace, like rutting animals caught in mutual desire.

'I can't –' Anthony turned back to bow his head into Clarissa's shoulder.

'Can't what?' Clarissa kissed Anthony hard on the mouth to reawaken him. 'You can, Sir, and you *will*.' She rocked him back and forward with the grip of her knees.

Rose somehow moved her feet away. She hurried down the corridor, choking on the hot sweetness of their deed, trying not to hear Anthony's agonised clamour. She ran as fast as she could, slamming the door to the passageway behind her.

MEDUSA

excipit unus
ex numero procerum quaerens, cur sola sororum
gesserit alternis inmixtos crinibus angues.
[. . .] 'clarissima forma
multorumque fuit spes invidiosa procorum
illa: neque in tota conspectior ulla capillis
pars fuit. inveni, qui se vidisse referret.

Next one of the many princes was asking why Medusa, the only one of her sisters, had snakes entwining her hair . . . 'She was once the most beautiful, and the enviable aspiration of many suitors. Of all her beauties none was more admired than her hair: I once met a man who recalled having seen her.'

(Ovid's *Metamorphoses* IV. 791–793/795–798, written AD8)

Not many people think about the origins of Medusa when they hear her name – we tend to imagine her only as the Gorgon monster: those bulging eyes, that swirling snake hair, her head neatly severed. But her story is one of cruelty, for she was a victim before she became a monster.

Medusa was a famous beauty. As a young woman, her face caught the eye of Poseidon, who ravaged her while she visited Athene's temple. Athene was outraged, and turned her face away. As a punishment for Medusa's dishonour, and for soiling her sanctuary, the goddess did her worst. She trapped young Medusa in a cave on the island of Sarpedon, twisting her beauty and transforming her into a gorgon monster, with living venomous snakes on her head to replace her cascading locks, and a gaze that turned any who looked at her to stone.

Many years later the hero Perseus was challenged to kill Medusa – the now famous and greatly feared Gorgon. Many gods sought to help him in his quest, even the goddess Athene gifted Perseus a mirrored shield to avoid Medusa's powerful eyes. Using the reflection, he cowered from Medusa, steadying his blade as she moved past. At the right moment, he sliced off her head with his sword. That was her end.

After his triumph, Perseus used Medusa's head as a weapon, thanks to her stone-casting stare. He later gifted his prize to Athene, and she placed it on her shield thereafter. As what – a defence against evil, or proof of victory over a monster she herself created?

There was little Medusa could have done to avoid being tossed about for the sport of others. There are some who call her the ultimate example of a wronged woman. Was there a frightened woman trapped inside the monster, or did her soul roll away with the turn of her eyes?

Regarding our female monsters, then, we would do well to exercise compassion and remember the truth behind their stories.

21.

'Valē, magistra.'

'Valētē,' Rose said forcefully, but only because Anthony was sitting in the corner observing her. It was the first time she'd seen him since his exposed secret last week. The girls had looked to their head of History for his regular brightness, a smile as he scratched his beard, or perhaps a joke or two. But the bitter air between Anthony's shame and Rose's disgust snuffed out any hope of that.

'Madam,' Anthony attempted as the crowd of girls shuffled out, 'may I speak to you?'

'No, *Sir*.' Only once had Rose checked his anguished, lined face during the lesson, and she didn't look at him now. 'I don't want to hear anything you have to say.'

Anthony left the room without a backward glance.

At least the outside brightness had returned. Rose had been surprised to see the clear blue of the sea through the window that morning: the haar had gone. Moved on, moved away, drawn its soft blanket back up into the heavens. *And taken my owl with it,* Rose thought mournfully. Her classroom offered up still more surprises – that morning she'd found Bethany's name scrawled across the blackboard in chalk, exactly how

Rose had written it on her bathroom mirror. She'd rubbed it out quickly, before the girls arrived, but she could still see the imprint in the chalk dust.

Rose breathed out in an attempt to rid the room of Anthony before descending the stairs. Emma was already waiting for Rose in the office, her glasses having slipped down to the end of her nose.

'Ready for lunch?'

'It's a bit early.'

'It'll be quieter,' insisted Emma. 'And Frances is joining us.'

Emma waited until they reached the bottom of the Great Stairs before she spoke again.

'I saw Anthony observing your lesson just now – does that make it easier?'

'Make what easier?'

'To be observed by a friend, a colleague you trust, rather than someone who might be—'

'He's probably the last person I'd want to observe my lessons,' Rose said coolly, 'or even have anywhere near me.'

Emma pulled a face. 'I thought the two of you were . . . ?'

'I have no feeling for Anthony,' Rose grumbled, 'other than disgust.'

'Rose!' Emma gasped. 'That can't be true? I think of him very highly, we all do.'

Rose glanced at the main corridor noticeboards, seeing the satirical Suffragette cartoon, which she now realised wasn't an historical reference at all but a true mockery of those women. 'I'm sure you do, Emma. I suppose Hope likes to hide its ugliness.'

'My goodness, Rose. You are so melodramatic. I have no idea what you're talking about.'

A row of Sixth overtook them, among them a dark-haired Intermediate, whom Rose realised was Josie. She checked for the rat about her neck, in her hair, but it wasn't there.

'I don't understand, Emma,' Rose went on. 'I thought we were preparing prize winners, trophy women who had to remain "intact" for their husbands?'

A cloud of reddish curls stalked past and Rose was caught by a fresh sting of shame. She hadn't yet seen her Fourths since her unkindness last week. Freddie didn't return her glance, and Rose's regret gleamed anew.

'Don't talk so crassly in the corridor, Rose.' Emma touched her arm. 'And wasn't that Frederica List?'

'Yes,' Rose said carefully.

'Apparently she's been asking her parents all sorts of questions. Something about the requirements, and whether *she* could choose her suitor. Can you imagine?' Emma scoffed, then hesitated. 'Not anything to do with you, Rose?'

Rose's chest was tight. She resisted the urge to turn around and check Freddie's disappearing red-gold head. 'No.'

'I'm afraid,' Emma continued darkly, 'you might have your wrist slapped about that one, but hopefully it'll pass us by.' She sighed. 'I shall be glad of the Ball when it comes, and the half-term break. Things are always easier afterwards with the Upper Sixth gone.'

Deirdre joined them at the dining hall doors, her voice an excited whisper. 'Did you hear about Clarissa's father?'

'No?'

Rose ducked her head to listen, in spite of herself.

'He's sent through the legal documents – he's suing the school.'

'Suing?' Emma exclaimed.

'Keep your voice down, Em.'

Rose's ears hummed through the canteen, following Deirdre's movements all the way to the chosen dining table. Once they had sat down she resumed her delicious report. 'Yes, although the matter is entirely confidential, Mr Bray wants to pursue it legally. He's furious.'

'Well, the Headmaster will fix it, I'm sure,' Emma nodded sagely.

'At least,' Deirdre raised an eyebrow, 'they've fired the culprit.'

'*Have* they? I thought it was a cousin?'

'No!' Deirdre carried on, 'it was a groundsman. Clarissa didn't know his name, just his face. She must have suffered terribly, poor thing. But he'll go down for it.'

'But,' Rose interjected, 'it wasn't a groundsman at all. It was Anthony.'

Emma turned to Rose in disbelief. 'Anthony?'

'I say, Rose.' Deirdre's face folded with disapproval. 'Have a care, throwing accusations about.'

'It's not an accusation,' Rose insisted, 'I saw them together.'

'You must have been mistaken,' snapped Deirdre.

'No, I wasn't *mistaken*, Deirdre.' Rose almost slammed her fist on the table. 'It was Anthony Rees. They've been having an affair. Anthony . . .' Rose hesitated. 'Anthony must have been the father of that child.'

'Not a child, dear,' Deirdre grimaced. 'A mistake!'

Rose wasn't giving in. 'I saw them with my own eyes.'

'You're absolutely raving, girl. Get a hold of yourself.'

'Watch what you're saying, both of you.' Emma looked around her hastily.

Frances appeared with her tray, her eyes puffy and her

hair more flyaway than usual. She nodded at the table of three women. Behind her, Ayumi streamed past, her skin clean of any geisha make-up, her face pointed with concentration as she made her way to the segregated tables. Rose followed Ayumi with her eyes, before turning back to her colleagues.

'The system here at Hope isn't working,' she stated fiercely. 'No matter what you try. Divorce, adultery is everywhere – even in the beloved royal family! This system – your precious *society* – is corrupt.'

Frances sat next to Rose and faced the threesome. 'What on earth are you so angry about, Rose?'

Rose stared straight back at her. She wanted to push Frances, force her to speak out, to rage along with her, to be her true self, whatever or whoever that was.

'Nothing of significance, I'm sure,' Rose answered instead. 'Excuse me, ladies, I'm not up to this.' She stood up, tearing her tray away from Emma's dismay and Deirdre's condemnation. 'Count me out for the rest of the day.'

'Madam, *valē*,' said Daisy loudly. 'You forgot the greeting both times.'

'Yes, *valē magistra*,' a few girls repeated.

'Yes, sorry,' Rose answered without looking up.

The designated observer moved out of the classroom before the girls had even scrabbled their things together. To Rose's relief, he seemed to take the cold, strange atmosphere with him. It had been another horrible lesson of silent work; she hadn't been able to look any of the Fourths in the eye, her awful outburst towards those three girls wrapping around her conscience still.

Rose pretended to busy herself with exercise books as the class strayed through the door. She checked the arched window, avoiding the blank spot where her owl used to be. It was a bright day, and the warmth seemed to flash against the white of the vaulted ceiling. A good omen, she hoped.

Three of the girls were hesitating by the door. Feeling a dash of gladness, Rose addressed them quickly, just in case they weren't really lingering at all.

'Girls. Daisy, Nessa, Freddie. I need to apologise for last week.'

Daisy was the first to turn back; her dark almond-shaped eyes were misty. Seeing that Nessa had her arms crossed, Rose's eyes darted nervously to Freddie. Her expression was set, and it was one of deep hurt.

Rose waited for the door to close on the last few departing students.

'I should never have said those things,' she chose her words carefully, 'and more importantly, I didn't mean them. They were spoken out of anger, and confusion, and,' Rose sucked in her breath, 'sheer panic.'

'We could sort of tell. You were so furious, I've never seen you like that,' nodded Nessa. 'It reminded me of the way my father gets sometimes.'

'It wasn't about you three, it was about me. Or . . .' Rose screwed up her face, feeling more vulnerable than ever, 'I don't know anymore.'

Freddie heaved her chest but didn't say anything.

'I understand, Madam,' Daisy said, gesturing to the observer's usual seat. 'You're having a difficult term, I think.'

'Yes, well.' Nessa still had her arms crossed. '*I'm* still failing, just as much as you.'

'Nessa, we're going to devise some sort of plan to help you,'

Rose nodded firmly. 'I just wanted to apologise this morning, and say that I have really enjoyed getting to know you three this year.'

Freddie started forward and Nessa undid her arms as she asked, 'What do you mean? Are you going somewhere?'

'Well, no, I—'

'Move!' called a voice from somewhere below. After a few stomps up the stairs, an auburn head appeared at the door.

Rose tried to continue. 'In fact, you three girls—'

'Madam! I need to talk to you.'

The door swung open to behold Clarissa. Rose's cheeks burned at seeing her, and the tremulous confidence she'd felt moments before seemed to abate. Turning her face away, she could see only those white knees in that red room, that sweating triumph on Clarissa's face.

'Ladies,' the head girl addressed Rose's three Fourths as she glided past them, 'may I have the room.'

Nessa and Daisy obeyed wordlessly, tugging their bags over their shoulders, but Rose saw Freddie glower at the back of Clarissa's head.

'Girls, stop.' Rose faced the head girl. 'I don't know what kind of power you have around the school, Clarissa, but in my classroom, I'm in charge.'

The girls remained. 'I need to talk to you, Madam,' Clarissa repeated, with a tilt of her head. 'You know why.'

'It can wait.'

Clarissa placed her hands on either side of her bodice. 'Madam, the accepted response is that you *will* hear what I have to say.'

Nessa looked between Rose and the head girl, and said softly, 'It's all right, Madam.'

'No, it isn't,' answered Rose. 'Clarissa, please go. If you'd like to discuss something, come to my office at lunchtime.'

'For heaven's sake.' The girl's face contorted. 'Why did you *ever* come here?'

Rose shook with bitter laughter. 'You know, Clarissa, I often ask myself the same question.'

'Do you think you're better than us?' Clarissa pushed her hair over her shoulder as the three girls shared a glance behind her.

'No,' Rose replied calmly, 'I really don't.'

Clarissa gave Rose a glare as she stormed to the door, but not before barking at Nessa, 'And you! Sadie's little *runt* of a sister. Stuck in Clemency, gearing towards Compassion, leaning on Madam to help you.' She gestured at Rose. 'Can you sink any lower?'

'Leave my classroom now, Clarissa!'

The head girl pulled at the door sharply; the force of it pushed at Rose's arched window. As soon as Clarissa's head disappeared down the stairs, Rose turned back to her three girls. Nessa's face was hot with humiliation; Daisy's eyes were downcast, Freddie's full of resentment.

'Nessa,' Rose said, clearing her throat, 'I can't apologise enough for Clarissa being so cruel to you in my classroom. She's upset, and you mustn't listen to her.' Rose's voice almost cracked. 'Please don't go, though, you three. I just . . .'

'It's okay, Madam,' Daisy said gently.

'I just . . .' Rose shook her head furiously. 'I have a final woman to show you.'

'Why *final*, Madam?' demanded Freddie. It was the first time she'd spoken that morning, and Rose was glad to hear her voice.

'Well, what with the observations, I didn't know if we'd have the chance again, and there's only one more lesson before half-term.' Rose took some photocopied images from her bureau and spread them across the desks. She checked Freddie's indignant stance and suddenly smiled, genuinely, at her. Freddie smiled back, too, and her arms broke apart.

'Is this her, Madam?' asked Daisy.

Nessa wrinkled her nose, her voice small. 'Why did Clarissa say those horrible things?'

'I really don't know,' Rose answered Nessa anxiously. 'But tell me what I can do about it. How is it in Clemency?'

'Does she know, does everyone know? Am I going to lose my place? I can't go to the san! I won't be bareheaded, I just can't!'

'You won't!' Daisy cried out.

'Nessa, you're not going anywhere.' Freddie nudged her friend into a half-hug. 'Not if we have anything to do with it.'

Rose hesitated. She couldn't form the words to comfort Nessa; she couldn't lie, and she couldn't know what the school might decide for her in the future.

'I just need to work harder.' There was a pleading tone in Nessa's voice.

'You know what, Ness?' Freddie stated, 'maybe you'd be the lucky one, if you get out of here.'

'Easy for you to say, Fred.' Nessa turned to her friend waspishly. 'It's not a problem for you, you're in Verity.'

'Look,' Freddie's animated face was serious, 'I don't care about that. We need to listen to Madam, and you know, read some magazines and newspapers. Learn more about how things really are.'

Rose considered Freddie's comments, and a beat of gladness urged her on. 'Yes, girls. You've got brains and hearts and . . . perhaps you've got your own bank accounts. There is so much more out there for you, girls, and it could all be on your own terms.'

'On our own?' Nessa screwed up her face. 'With no connections?'

Rose knew she was being too outspoken; at any moment someone could overhear, burst in on them. But still, she measured the three girls, standing, listening. 'Come up to the front, and sit down properly.' She pointed at the images as they obeyed. 'We'll look at this ancient woman.'

'Who's this?' Daisy shuffled forward.

'Is it Medea again?' said Freddie. 'Because we were chatting all about her with the Sixth.'

'Which one's Medea?' Nessa asked vaguely.

'The one who killed all the children,' said Freddie.

'Only her own,' Daisy corrected. 'We were trying to tell the Sixth about Dido, you see, Madam.'

'Yes,' Freddie carried on. 'But they didn't care. We love Dido, everything about her. We hate Aeneas.'

'This lady, Madam,' Daisy observed, leaning forward in her chair, 'looks really angry.'

Medusa's famous face in the Caravaggio painting shone out at them, her hot stare angled downwards, her mouth open in agony, her severed head gushing out blood.

'This is Medusa. She *is* really angry.' *As am I,* thought Rose. 'But it wasn't her fault.'

'She needs some of our Beauty and Aesthetic lessons,' Nessa said with some cheer, 'or maybe Grace and Grooming.'

Rose was glad of the lift in her mood. 'She had a tough time. According to Ovid, she was raped by Poseidon.'

'God of the sea,' shot out Daisy.

'Yes – well done, Daisy – in the temple of Athene.'

'Goddess of war, wisdom.'

Rose nodded.

'Raped?' asked Freddie.

'Yes,' Rose bristled. 'I forget sometimes how casually rape is referred to in the ancient world – it is a terrible thing, not okay at all.'

Nessa and Freddie nodded; Daisy tucked a thick piece of hair behind her ear.

'Well,' continued Rose, 'after that, Athene was furious with Medusa.'

'What,' Nessa frowned, 'because someone raped her?'

'In *her* temple. I know, it's very unfair.'

'This kind of thing happens a lot in Greek mythology,' nodded Daisy, 'doesn't it?'

'It's abuse,' Freddie said darkly.

Rose eyed Freddie cautiously, and then carried on, 'And because of that, Athene cursed her, and made her ugly.'

'I wish I could curse some of the girls in our year and make them ugly.' Nessa tossed her head haughtily, with a small smile. 'And the deputy head.'

'Nessa! Really!' warned Rose with an equal smile.

'Wait, I know this story!' Daisy piped up. 'Athene punished Medusa with snakes for hair, and didn't she turn people to stone with her eyes?'

'Yes!'

'But someone cut her head off,' added Nessa as she glanced at the painting again, 'by the looks of things.'

'That was Perseus. He looked at her in the reflection of his shield, so as to avoid her face, and cut off her head.'

'Ah,' said Nessa softly.

'You feel sorry for her?'

Nessa thought about it. 'Yes. Don't you?'

'I do, yes,' said Rose. 'What's worse, is that nowadays Perseus is celebrated for being a hero, and Medusa is remembered for being a monster.'

Freddie shook her head back and her red curls moved. 'That's rubbish.'

'No, it's true.'

'I mean, it's crap.'

Rose and Freddie looked at each other, and the girl pulled an apologetic face. 'It's fine, Freddie, I think we're past swearing now.' Rose carried on: 'Anyway, Medusa is often cast as the angry, irrational woman, conquered by the man,' she paused for effect, 'which is something I thought you ladies could think about.'

'But she was a fighter.'

'Well,' Rose answered, considering Medusa's face within the painting, 'she might have been, but she didn't have the chance.'

'She certainly made a good monster,' Nessa added.

Rose laughed. 'She did.'

'It's terrible that she was raped,' Daisy suddenly said forcefully.

'Be careful, Daisy.' Daisy looked back at Freddie with a frown.

'Freddie, why do you say that?' Rose asked.

'Daisy was punished the other day,' Freddie nodded seriously. 'In Sexual Health, she was asking questions about consent.'

Rose stalled for a moment.

'It's all right, Madam.' Daisy shrugged. 'It was only lines, and a cut to my evening privileges for the week. My housemistress gave me a severe talking-to, but I wasn't listening.'

She raised her head proudly. 'I know my questions were fair.'

Freddie was nodding at Daisy, before turning back to Rose.

'I see,' Rose answered.

'Well,' Daisy added cheerfully, 'are there any other paintings of Medusa, Madam? I like all these women. They do make the classical world seem fabulous and exciting.'

'Hardly!' Nessa spluttered. 'These stories always end so terribly! All the women die, or worse.'

'Yes, you're right,' Freddie nodded, 'there is a lot of doom in these stories, isn't there, Madam?'

'Yes, but girls,' Rose answered firmly, 'they made a difference, in their own way. Look at Antigone, Medea or Agrippina – they fought back, and stood up to power, as much as they could. They're remembered for trying.'

'Yes, but Madam,' Nessa shot back, 'the price they had to pay . . .'

'We've *got* to keep trying, though.'

'These women did their best,' Freddie said, still nodding, 'But it never ended well.'

'But one day something will get through,' Rose continued forcefully. 'We've got to keep trying . . . My mother taught me that.'

Three faces snapped up to their teacher, and Daisy softly asked, 'Your mother, Madam?'

Rose shook her head, her eyes fixed on the images set between the little group. 'We must use the errors of the past to reflect on our own future. Human nature doesn't seem to have . . . come very far.' Her hand balled into a fist. 'And reading their stories, sharing them with you, all of it makes me feel excited to be a woman. A feminist. Look how versatile, how surprising, how clever we are – and have been – throughout history.'

'Madam, you are so embarrassing sometimes,' Nessa scoffed, but her tone was fond. 'Is this the rescue thing you were talking about?'

'Sort of, yes. Why not?'

'But you haven't rescued yourself yet, have you, Madam?' Freddie said quietly. 'You're here, with us.'

The door opened suddenly. Emma appeared, her worn face twisted with crossness. They hadn't heard her mounting the stairs.

'Rose, what on earth are you doing up here? You're not supposed to—'

The girls slid out of their chairs and stood up.

'Yes, sorry, Madam,' said Rose.

Emma held the door open and beckoned at the three girls. Nessa screwed up her face with humour as she collected her things. 'Oh, Madam, she called you Rose! Is that your name?'

Rose watched the three girls leave, Daisy sweeping the long sheet of her black hair behind her as she went. Freddie was last to go. Somehow Rose felt as though she were seeing them for the last time. She fought an impulse to follow them, to run, slip down the stairs, and take them with her, somewhere, anywhere but here.

22.

Rose was quietly furious with Emma – furious that she'd interrupted her meeting with the girls, furious with her for continually assenting, and even more furious when she insisted that Rose wouldn't be able to help Nessa in any way.

'She's a Clemency girl, it's only a small house and they have their methods. If she needs one-to-one tutoring, they'll move her to the san.' Emma turned away from Rose with a scowl. 'And anyway, I came up to tell you that Vivien wants to see you.'

Rose descended the stairs and found Vivien's study door locked. She enquired with the secretaries, and one stood up authoritatively, insisting that Rose would need accompanying. The other secretaries gave their peer an encouraging look, their eyes creased with concern.

'Where are we going?' Rose asked as they walked along the northern end of the main corridor, in the direction of the sports hall and theatre.

'The sanatorium,' said the secretary briskly.

Rose stiffened; she closed her eyes a moment to quell her unease.

The sanatorium was another barnacle of a building, latched on to the northern bulk of the main school and accessed via a high-walled outdoor passage. It was certainly as tall as any boarding house, but far narrower – in her mind's eye, Rose could see its short square placement on the library's blueprint. Infinitely less homely than any boarding house, the interior seemed to have remained Victorian with its high white rooms spread out squarely across each ward, clean trolleys and gurneys scattered about the echoing, empty space. Rose remembered Frances's comment in her first term, that it had been built to house reams of girl-patients during an epidemic.

'Where are we going?' Rose's apprehension weighed heavier as they descended a set of neat stairs.

'Just down here.'

Rose thought fleetingly of those underground lead-lined rooms, buried far below. The secretary guided her through a set of double doors to a narrower room, a sanitised and blank bedroom, where a figure was sitting in an armchair. For a moment Rose felt dizzy; she'd entirely lost her bearings. The barred window behind the seated figure let out east and straight across the sea, where the land fell away and the rocky outcrops stretched out further beyond.

'Here we are,' said the secretary finally.

With a frown, Rose focused on the woman in front of her, wondering where Vivien was. The nurse by the woman's side spoke up,

'How lovely, Jane, we've got a visitor.'

Rose gazed at the woman that had haunted her since September. She was no such ghost – but not far from it: a shaking, deflated figure, rocking back and forth in her patterned armchair. Her eyes were bulging, her pupils dilated and staring at Rose.

'Is that you, Bethany? Are you a woman now?'

'No.' Rose couldn't breathe. 'No.'

'How long have I been here, Bethany?' The woman had wisps of light brown hair, her Roman nose sharp and her skin pulling around her jaw. She grimaced. 'No. I don't know you.'

'Now, now, Jane,' the nurse said sharply.

'She was here, but they let her go. They knew what she'd do.'

Rose's mouth hung open. 'I'm so sorry, Jane.'

The woman clamped her mouth shut and turned away.

'We didn't shave her head,' the nurse insisted, nodding in Jane's direction. 'She's just pulled it out.'

Jane swung her face back to Rose.

'You're not her! Get away from me!'

Rose was rooted to the floor as she heard again Bethany's words trapped in the mouth of this damaged creature. Jane's mouth contorted again: 'They let her out, they knew what she'd do. They let her out!'

'Oh dear.' The nurse pulled a cheery face. 'Time for another dose, I think! Let me call the assistant.'

Rose watched Jane grapple between the slim auxiliary and the nurse, relenting only when the needle of the syringe sank into her neck. Jane made a guttural noise as they eased her onto the bed; her shoulders shuddered as she closed her eyes on the small afternoon interlude.

'Around Christmas, she became very disruptive where she was in Inverness; she'd had some bad news, I understand,' the nurse explained, patting Jane's shoulder. 'She's much better off here where we can keep an eye on her, keep her regulated.'

Rose looked at the nurse, stupefied, before the secretary steered her away.

Vivien was waiting in the small lobby of the sanatorium. It

took Rose a moment to recognise her, as disorientated as she was, and distressed by what she had seen.

'Shall we continue in my study?' Vivien turned to hold the door open for Rose, the secretary hovering behind.

Minutes later Rose was numbly directed to an upright armchair in Vivien's study. Her thoughts were in tatters, so she tried to focus on a piece of artwork on the wall, a watercolour of a country house. It had to be from somewhere other than here. Wherever Vivien was from, Rose thought – the same place that Josie sprang from too, the household of beetle-black eyes, charm and sharp cruelty.

'Did you enjoy your visit?'

'Is this some sort of sick joke?' Rose managed.

'Not at all, Rose. We felt it was important to answer some questions you evidently had.' Vivien moved around her desk. 'No need to beat about the bush. We must discuss these.'

Vivien tossed a smattering of envelopes into Rose's lap. Rose flinched at the snappish movement, but then her eyes saw what they were. Her own writing was scrawled on the envelopes, one with the Dublin address, the others labelled with various Inverness hospitals, postmarks stamped and the edge of each envelope slit open.

'The Headmaster's old friend in Dublin,' Vivien said carefully, 'seemed to think that one ought to be returned to us here at Hope. The rest were returned to us by our many contacts.'

Rose avoided Vivien's gaze.

'I'm afraid the Dublin address was false, Rose, and fed to you deliberately. Please understand that we contrive solutions to every eventuality; this was always going to come back to us.'

As Rose's words failed her, the deputy head continued with:

'Here at Hope, Rose, our influence extends further than you can imagine.'

Rose looked up at Vivien. 'I had no idea—'

'With regard to this issue, let me clear it up for you.' Vivien leaned a long arm on her desk. 'Jane suffered from weak mental health; it was not fitting to post her in any of our contributing preparatory schools. She was taken to a clinic after a breakdown, and now her treatment continues closer to home. Do you understand?'

'But what . . .' a voice urged from Rose's throat, 'why did she . . . have to go?'

Vivien pursed her lips. 'If you must know, Jane became overfamiliar with one of the students. She enticed her, and ruined her prospects. Jane wanted her here, as a Compassion, a teacher. The very lowest order.' Vivien snapped her head to the side in disgust. 'As if Jane could control that girl's path! Oh, it was a dreadful affair, the whole thing, and a sorry end for them both. I hate to remember it. Not that this is any of your business – but I would say, Rose, that it is not a situation I would like to see repeated.'

'Yes,' Rose managed, comparing Vivien's simplified version of events against the uncomfortable truth that Frances had told her. Stories of pain, stories of harm, stories that Hope tore up and tossed aside in its vast carelessness.

Vivien stood up straight. 'These letters will be added to your dossier, Rose, as evidence.' She brought her hands together. 'We *shall* need you to start impressing us, Rose, rather than having us tidy up your mess.'

'But why did . . .' Rose faltered, 'why did I have to see Jane like that?'

Vivien surveyed Rose, her eyes pointed and her mouth

crooked. 'We're educating you on your limits, Rose. After all, this is more than just a school – it's an institution.'

Rose was prickling with vulnerability. She'd made her way to lunch without Emma, not having spoken to her since she'd seen Jane and been horrified into silence. In the canteen she moved efficiently, filling her tray with as little as she could, keeping her eyes to the floor, trying to evade the general clamour of the hall.

But somebody was standing in her path. Between the gap of two parallel tables, there was Anthony. His presence was hovering and apprehensive, and he was touching her.

'Rose.'

Rose stared straight at him, through him. His face was lined and haggard, his beard thick. Rose looked at his fingers on her arm.

'Get away from me.' She shook him off, swinging her tray between them. 'Don't touch me.'

The tables around them seemed to wake with the tension.

'Rose,' he said firmly, trying to take the tray from her. She held on to it, her fingertips white with the pressure. 'I just need to speak to you. You mustn't—'

'Let go of me.' Rose reeled away from him. Her arm flew out to the side, as did the tray. The sudden movement caught the surrounding girls' attention, their faces swivelled to her and Anthony as her crockery clattered to the floor.

Anthony rippled with anxiety, his hazel eyes driving into her face. 'Please don't do this.'

'What do you care? You've already got away with it.' A thrill of nervous anger ran through Rose. 'You must be devastated that Clarissa's getting married!'

He leaned towards her, enclosing his arms around the cage of her body. 'Rose.'

'Get away from me!' Rose was shrinking at Anthony's strength, pressing at his lapel. 'No!'

'Rose, please. You're being hysterical.'

'Don't you dare!' She pushed him, hard, and he staggered. 'I said no!'

Anthony recovered himself. Swooping the alarmed and staring girls into his gaze, he raised his hands in surrender. He hesitated a moment before stepping away, hanging his head like a wounded beast.

Rose shook her head, her chest hammering with uneasy fury. She became aware again of the dining hall and the blur of girls' faces – painted with confusion, horror, surprise. Rose focused on the mess of her tray on the floor, her entire face aflame.

'Hold on a moment there, Madam.'

Rose stopped at the Headmaster's coaxing voice.

'Come along here with me. Best not to have one of your little outbursts in front of so many girls.' The man made to circle her shoulder with his arm but Rose stood up tall over him.

'Come along.'

There were a few desperate looks from her Juniors, as Rose obeyed. She followed the Headmaster through the main door, set beneath the Founder's painting.

He led her to a low room at the end of a passageway, panelled into the rock. Rose had never been there before, and her anxiety beat in her ears as she took in the rough stone walls, the one slim window letting in a peek of light. At the far end a squat wooden door had been set into the stonework, with a worn plaque above it. Rose could just about read the words: *To Postern.*

The Headmaster was talking in a quiet voice, so lightly that Rose had to stretch to hear. But still she stared at that obscure door. It stood next to the square and empty fireplace mounted with its own stag's head.

'I think we need to decide, dear girl, if this is going to work or not. We can't have you shoving about our male teachers like this, writing letters, phoning papers, and bursting in on significant meetings as you did on Affiliates Day. I must admit, I am disappointed. I had been told that your disciplinary phase was going well, and that since the beginning of term you have been almost entirely obedient.'

Rose nodded mutely, seeing in her mind's eye a letter of dismissal, her furniture loaded up, her bags packed and ready.

'I was pleased to hear you had improved, particularly now that your mother is in a worsened state.' The Headmaster was standing in the stream of the outside glow, his slight figure a silhouette. 'I receive updates on her almost daily. It is important to make your mother feel safe and secure. We wouldn't want to worry her.'

Rose turned around fearfully. 'Please . . .'

'You do need to consider what kind of message you are sending our girls.' The Headmaster was shaking his head. 'You have been quite the confusing distraction for them.'

Rose thought of Jane, her strange figure rocking back and forth.

'Here's what we are going to do. Your job here is safe for the time being. You have signed a contract and you have proven your compliance – despite this small hiccup.' He pressed a hand against his chest. 'I now need your loyalty.'

'Headmaster, I—'

'You will visit your mother briefly at half-term, accompanied, and then you will stay here for the summer. You will have an allocated short-trip period for your regulated holiday.'

Rose blinked.

'For the rest of this term, you will not speak out of turn in front of the girls.' The Headmaster's voice gathered strength. 'You will help with the Ball. You will be a positive presence for the governors, the parents, the friends of the school. You see, I am very interested in you, Rose. The girls often speak about you. The Juniors and Intermediates certainly have a positive attitude towards you.'

Rose's words rushed out. 'That's because no one has ever cared about them before, and I do.'

The Headmaster waited a moment. 'Do you perhaps wonder, Rose, why it is that you are so . . . *upset* by the system here? When everyone else is happy – the girls, and the staff?'

She focused on a spot on the floor. *Not all of them,* Rose thought.

'You, my dear, are made for this, if you would only stop fussing. I demand that you expend your energy towards us rather than against us. And I understand that you would like to champion one of the girls?' The Headmaster stepped forward. 'One of our Fourths that's struggling? With your acquiescence, you would gain a voice within the system.'

'A voice?' Rose looked up.

'Yes, Rose,' nodded the Headmaster, his voice low – almost kind. 'I rather thought that's what all this was about? I saw how defensive you were of young Hanako.'

'Yes,' Rose heard herself saying, thinking of Nessa. 'I'd like to help the lower-performing girls . . . help them to succeed – and in a wider context, perhaps look at reprieves . . . and move away from current punishment methods.'

'And you can, Rose, you can from within. But what can

you do from the outside? Look at Jane,' said the Headmaster sorrowfully. 'Where was she when Bethany needed her?'

Rose bit down hard on her lip; she could taste the wax of her faded lipstick mixed with a thin slip of blood.

'And the girls destined for university . . . I would like to be involved with those.'

'Indeed.' The Headmaster tilted his head slightly. 'This is why we need someone like you here, Rose, to keep us on our toes for the new millennium. Work with us, Rose, we could accomplish such great things together. For the girls.'

Rose hesitated, but the Headmaster carried on.

'My first request, which you will answer now, is that you agree to stand as front of house for the Ball next Friday.'

She looked at him through that darkness, his brown hair tinged with light. Rose felt as though she were in a trance. 'Yes, I'll do the Ball.'

'The girls will be so happy, Rose,' he smiled. 'You won't be sorry. My second request is that you decide where your loyalty lies by the morning after the Summer Ball. Beyond that, we shall have to make the decision for you, before it is too late.'

Rose turned her face away, glancing again at that far end door. 'I understand.'

'I believe that Vivien has already selected a dress for you to wear. I can assure you that if the Ball passes seamlessly, and you decide to fully acquiesce, we will enter a new phase of your career here.' Rose sucked in her breath sharply as the Headmaster stepped towards her, drawing her into a handshake. 'You shall have your voice, and your dossier will be safe, as will your girls. Your mother, too. And your father's reputation.'

Rose tried to echo his demeanour, a pained smile flickering onto her face as his fingers tensed around hers with a tight squeeze.

23.

That evening, Rose gently rocked herself back and forth on her sofa. Was it even safe in her flat when somebody else had a key? Should she determine now what she could fit in her battered suitcase – or would she dare to leave at all?

There was a banging on the door and a voice outside. 'Are you all right? Rose?'

Rose was so glad to see her she couldn't speak. She threw herself into Frances's open arms, sobbing like a child, for all the days and weeks they hadn't spoken. Frances touched Rose's dark hair with the edge of her fingers.

Rose sniffed into her friend's shoulder, wet and ugly with her black tears. The smears seemed to stain Frances's flowery scent. Suddenly Rose drew back.

Frances surveyed her friend carefully, her face lined with pity and gladness. Rose sniffed again. 'Oh my God,' she whispered. 'Oh my God, it's you.'

'It's me, what?'

Rose pulled herself out of the embrace. 'Do you have a typewriter?'

'Yes,' Frances answered kindly, still touching Rose's hair, 'but what does that have to do with anything?'

'Can I see it?'

'Yes, but a few of the keys are broken. What for?'

Rose stared at her friend. 'Was it you?'

'Was *what* me?'

'Did you write those horrible letters?'

A glimmer rippled across Frances's face and Rose saw the answer. She turned her eyes away, her voice breaking. 'Oh my God. Why?'

'I didn't want you to leave. I couldn't let you. I thought I could—'

'What?'

Frances's face shifted. 'Frighten you into staying.'

'Oh my God.' Rose drew back into the next room.

Frances followed her, her voice growing slightly manic. 'Rose, you don't understand.'

'I do. All you've ever done here is lie to me.'

'No, Rose. I adore you.'

Rose moved her hands over her face. 'I don't know who you are.'

'No, you do.' Frances stepped towards her. 'You know exactly, Rose.'

'Get away from me!' Rose went to push at her friend, but she backed away. 'You're worse than all of them. Have you been collecting evidence against me?'

'I . . . well,' Frances hesitated, her frazzled hair a mess after Rose's tearful interference. 'They already know everything, they amass all the information in our dossiers—'

'My mother's illness – my father, dying for his reputation.' Rose let out another sob as she faced her sitting room. 'If I don't comply, the Headmaster's going to destroy all of it. *I might as well die here.*'

'No, you're staying here, with me. Things will get better.'

'I can't even look at you. You're complicit, you're a disgrace!'

'I know I am!' Frances cried out. 'I've always been a disgrace.'

'It's got nothing to do with your sexuality.' Rose wheeled round, furious. 'You're a liar. Every minute, you've lied.'

'Please don't say that,' Frances pleaded, stepping towards Rose again. 'I think you're one of the most spirited, wonderful people I've ever met. I wish you were mine.' She looked away with embarrassment, her blue eyes heavy. 'I know you don't feel that way about me, and I hate myself for being so forward with you now. But . . . you remind me of someone I loved very much. She's the reason I lost my way here.'

'What?' Rose spluttered, shocked at Frances's outpouring of emotion. 'Who?'

'She was . . .' Frances was shaking her head, her voice painfully soft. 'She's married now, of course. She's gone. It's just that sometimes I look at you and I think I've found her again.'

Rose seized at Frances's words. 'So, do something for me. Let's come up with a plan to help the girls.' Rose took a stuttered breath. 'Together, we could break the system from the inside.'

'Not this again.' Frances closed her eyes for a brief, frustrated moment.

'But you could work with me. I'm supposed to be helping girls reach university. I've already started to wake up some of the younger girls—'

'Oh, for heaven's sake,' Frances exclaimed, her irritation getting the better of her. 'The university preparation was just a ruse to keep you here. How could you be so stupid? There's hardly any of those girls! One or two in the last five years, and Anthony deals with them all!'

Rose was struck. 'But it was—'

'Another way to string you along. How could you not realise?' Frances cried out bitterly. 'Of course, you could always *pretend* that's what you're doing. We all have to find a way to make this place bearable. Look at Anthony, how he deals with things. I drink, and I . . . you have no idea how much I have to hold back when I'm around you.'

Rose stared at Frances, completely at a loss for what to say.

'Look. I'm sorry I wrote those letters, I didn't want to lose you. I am unnatural. No,' Frances's face darkened, 'I'm worse than that. I'm an abomination.'

Rose shook her head, remembering herself. 'No, I am not having that. You are *not* an abomination, Frances. You're gay, that's just part of who you are.'

Frances glared at Rose, her face twisted. 'Don't say that word . . . it's disgusting. You think you can just say all of this, try to change my mind, turn me against this place?' She punched at her words. 'Hope is all I've known. Hope is who I am. Any other peculiarities of mine . . . are vices.'

Rose stood in front of her friend. 'You don't believe that – you're just frightened.'

But Frances wasn't listening. 'Even the government recognises the abomination of homosexuality – don't you read the papers?' Her voice grew angrier. '"Section 28". We're not even supposed to *talk* about it.'

'"Section 28"?'

'Four years ago now. Homosexuality is censored, it's officially a disgrace, not to be discussed or promoted publicly.'

'Look, Frances.' Rose stepped forward to press her hand against Frances's chest. 'Who you are, matters. Nothing else but this,' she tapped the side of Frances's head, 'and this. No one else's ideas, or their agenda. Underneath everything you've been taught and all you've suffered is a beautiful, thinking human being, who deserves to be loved.'

'Oh, Rose.' Frances had stiffened under Rose's touch. 'You're so young; you're so naive – how can you possibly understand?'

'*You're* the one that doesn't understand, Frances. You know nothing about the outside world!' Rose hesitated. 'You know, we could go on holiday together – I could show you things. You could meet someone! This place, Hope, is not how the world works.'

'It is how *my* world works, and how the girls' world works.' Frances pushed Rose's hands away. 'You can stop being so bloody patronising. I *do* know how things are. You're coming from whatever liberal hole you grew up in, which I have absolutely no wish to be part of, thank you!'

Suddenly Rose was furious. 'You're a coward. I don't understand you at all. I thought I did, but you've been indoctrinated, all of you! And what's worse is I'm guilty too.' She pushed past Frances, across the room and into the hallway.

'Rose, I –' Frances stumbled towards her friend. 'Wait, please!'

'I don't want to hear another word. I need to save the girls from this, and you'll never see my point.' Rose pulled open the door to her flat, almost pushing Frances through it. She hissed unkindly, 'Leave me be. Didn't you say that to me once? Get out, since you can't help me, or won't. Don't you realise that you are exactly what Bethany refused to become?'

Rose pushed the door closed before she could see her cruel words reflected on Frances's face.

On the Thursday before the half-term break, Rose was nervous about seeing her Fourths. She'd cried every night that week, her soul unspooling at the hopelessness of her situation, but the thought of seeing her girls that morning urged her on. They were her target, and she the blazing arrow drawing towards them. Those girls were the only ones she hadn't yet lost, the only thing that hadn't split apart in this strange, distorted world she'd fallen into.

So Rose set the desks out properly, cracked the arched window ajar for some fresh air, and readied her worksheets. A smile was etched on her face, half-forced, but half-true.

The girls filed in quietly, more so than usual; Rose watched them line the desks, pulling out the chairs in unhappy unison. Rose frowned at their downcast faces, the regretful looks a few gave each other. The designated lesson observer hadn't arrived yet, so an interloper wasn't the reason.

And then Rose saw Nessa. She came in behind Freddie, who seemed to be radiating a terrible fury.

Rose hadn't recognised the girl at first. Nessa's fine blonde hair had been completely shorn, unkindly, all around her head. It was badly done so that clumps puffed out behind her ear, along the hairline at the back. Her eyes were baggy, tear-soaked and red. She looked smaller and frailer than ever, her shoulders sloping, her ears sticking out in seeming mockery of her bare head.

Nessa touched her head before bowing to sit, settling in her seat and placing her things around her carefully. Her miserable eyes turned to the floor as a horrible agony sliced into Rose's chest.

The rest of the class were clenched in hurt solidarity, not looking at Nessa's pale face, her little round head, her whole being violated like a beaten animal.

A terrible urgency seemed to press at Rose's throat as her fingers curled tightly together. She'd spoken to the Headmaster about reprieves, but she hadn't yet promised him her loyalty. Was this what it meant to withhold? Had her hesitancy to acquiesce led directly to Nessa's punishment?

'Ladies, what do you want to do today? Please,' Rose implored as her eyes touched on Freddie's impassioned face, 'how can I make this better – tell me what to do?'

In the back row, Josie stretched her arms behind her in a triumphant movement. 'Nothing, Madam, please let's just get on with another one of your darling Latin lessons.'

The room seemed to shift behind Nessa's miserable figure. A few of the girls pulled out their books resolutely, and Rose waited, before turning uselessly to her bureau.

At the end of the lesson, Rose caught Freddie by the wrist, then let go quickly. The girl's hand was stiff with fury, but she turned around, her ivory face hard as she stared straight back at her teacher.

'Freddie, tell me. What can I do?'

Freddie's tawny eyes darted away from Rose. 'I don't know, Madam. I think it's too late.'

'I'll fight for her, Freddie. I will. The Headmaster's waiting for me to –' Rose broke off, shaking her head. 'I'll fight for her. I'll tell him.'

Freddie's eyes were now fixed on the space in front of her, her anguish flaming across her cheeks. 'It's beyond that, Madam.'

'It can't be,' Rose said desperately. 'How do you know?'

'Because if you've already spoken up for her . . . and if it had mattered,' Freddie said slowly, 'then they wouldn't have shaved her head. No. No one can save her now.'

'You're wrong, Freddie,' Rose insisted. 'This isn't the final stage. I can help. I will.'

Freddie's eyes lifted to Rose with a queer, dead look. 'You've done so much already, Madam. I can't tell you.' She added, 'But I worry that you're as powerless as the rest of us.'

Rose opened her mouth to speak, but her response caught in her throat. One of the Fourths had hopped back up the stairs again and was pulling the door open. 'Fred, Nessa's waiting for you. You're her designated guardian, aren't you?'

'Yes,' Freddie turned to the door, 'I am.'

She left with a short glance at Rose, who would remember the dread in her eyes long after the girl had gone.

As she dressed for the Summer Ball the following afternoon, Rose packed her half-term suitcase.

The Headmaster's main request played on her mind. But what choice did she have, really? There was no other decision to make. *Before we make it for you,* the Headmaster had said. And even worse was Freddie's unexpected rebuke: *You're as powerless as the rest of us.*

Rose was being accompanied over half-term; she was leaving in the morning. But what if she made a break for it on the journey back? What if she simply . . . didn't return? Her salary had gone into her account monthly for the last two terms, so she had something to fall back on if she withdrew it fast. Even the banker-governors wouldn't be expecting that. She'd managed to squeeze her favourite things into her mother's battered suitcase: her father's old books, her stereo and a few other clothes, her tweed jacket – wasn't that all she needed? She could even try tonight, before the masses left in the morning – the groundsmen would be busy, just as they'd been at the Christmas dinner. Rose wondered whether she could pass herself off as one of the Sixth if it came to it.

Or could she risk the tunnel, however precarious it might be? She'd seen that door – *To Postern*, and its narrow keyhole. That way might bring a woeful end – as it had with Bethany – perhaps even that would be better than the alternative. Rose knew that if she left Hope for good, she would effectively be signing a death warrant to her former way of life. Everything felt final to her, any kind of freedom difficult to imagine.

Just in case, Rose had written three letters in neat envelopes, marked *Daisy, Nessa, Freddie,* and propped them up on her kitchen counter. If she was going to go, the porters might find them and hand them over to the girls.

Rose stopped, touching one of the envelopes with her finger. Could she really just leave her Fourths behind like that, left to fend for themselves in their final and most significant years at Hope? No, Rose knew she couldn't. She couldn't ignore that spark of resilience that burned in her chest: one last fight, for them. She still had some instinct for survival. Could she continue pacifying Vivien and the Headmaster, while fighting back in her own way – and still keep her mother safe? Her father's reputation?

The agonising indecision held Rose captive. Her suitcase stood in her flat while her small handbag remained with her for the evening: her bank card, her passport. Just in case.

24.

The early summer winds fell still for the Ball, as if the Headmaster had marshalled Zeus himself into compliance. The sea was a gracious sapphire blue; the bay was ruddy green in praise of the school building, whose outer walls and buttresses were decorated by the timid sun and hanging birds.

Inside it seemed as though every door and window were open; the soft sunlight passed over every Sixth's shoulder, caressing her hair in admiration and excitement.

The main part of the school was cordoned off again, with rope looped along the pathway from the chapel to Founder's Hall. The Great Stairs weren't as lavishly decorated as they had been at Christmas, but more freshly done with wild gorse and meadow flowers, drooping with the touch of any passing girl's dress. The Roman clock ticked on, counting down to the final hours of the Upper Sixth's time at Caldonbrae Hall.

The chapel carried the same spray of wild flowers as the Great Stairs, its altar and front pews had been cleared away for the performance before the Ball. The Juniors and Intermediates patiently tuned their violins and clarinets, or stretched out their long bodies to warm up, their soft figures touching the coloured light coursing through the stained glass.

Many of the Lower Sixth were on the other side of the school, laughing easily as they prepared to light the thick strands of candelabras in Founder's Hall, practising the correct course of light conversation, the polite banter for each parent, the secret smile for any unattached man.

The eldest girls remained in their boarding houses, pressing their hair into place or touching at their faces until they were just right. The rooms were filled with flurries of powder and tulle, fragile lingerie over slim thighs, lashings of satin tight around corseted waists; bright fussy eyes and pink cheeks burning with worry, with happiness; matrons and housemistresses joyfully fussing over these princesses of the night.

At the correct time, a young woman took her place at the main doors. Her face was pale and washed clean. She wore no lipstick. Her long threads of black hair were bolted back into a thick plait, which brushed against her long-sleeved red dress and its matching wrap. She couldn't quite stand straight, but stand she did, her full skirt covering a small handbag at her feet. She had a broad smile that didn't match her eyes.

Long black cars would start to arrive, doors open and close for pairs of parents; the women short and tall with tight hair and pastel gowns, the fathers greying and smug-jawed beside. Then, another train of black cars would trundle forward, bearing dozens of red-cheeked, dinner-jacketed men smiling into the evening sun. They laughed as they shook each other's hands or clapped one another on the back, one with a toothy grin, another with an ebony walking stick.

The young woman could taste this mesmerising influence the all-girls boarding school had over its people; she could breathe in its seduction alongside the clear air passing over the lawns from the sea.

As the cars rolled away the gentlemen would greet the young woman in red with a nod, hop up the steps of the entrance hall, and make their way forward.

Forward to the chapel, for a performance. The girls would give a tremendous display of dance and music, throughout which the young woman would stare at the expert bodily movements, so well-rehearsed and well-measured. Soon after, violins or flutes or pianos would entwine with each other, every melody bright and bittersweet. She was close enough to catch the sharp stink of sweat as each girl slipped down the aisle at the end of her piece.

Then forward.

Forward, where the transformed Founder's Hall stood, open and lined with an array of beautiful teenage girls. Holding its breath and waiting for the Headmaster, as if he were a world-class conductor raising his baton at the beginning of a highly anticipated masterpiece.

Rose floated up the Great Stairs once it became clear that there were no more stragglers in the chapel, and no late guests arriving.

She left the main doors to the school open, having little strength to haul them together. The salty air was achingly refreshing, and by now the June sky had sunk to a dull blue.

Her next role was to stand beside the double doors of Founder's Hall. She did so quietly, keeping her eyes away from the merriment behind her: the streams of girls, a crowd of governors, the smatterings of parents; the heave of staff, the swirling glasses of wine – and the suitors, laughing uproariously. There was an interval of prize-givings; the clatter of food being served; the scrape of chairs as bodies moved to the floor; the slow music as they all came together and swayed as one, lit only by the candelabras' flicker. The air seemed to emanate hot waves of pleasure that nudged Rose's shoulder; she turned away with contempt.

Rose stood in the red dress, her handbag under her elbow, her breathing jagged. Wondering if this was her moment to run, or how far she could get before the school's broken fingers would reach out and choke her.

She'd seen Clarissa, the glittering belle of the Ball, embraced and cheered with praise-fuelled speeches. Blaring diamonds were encrusted along the straight neck of her dress, along the plunge of her back seam. Rose didn't look for any agonised glances between Clarissa and Anthony, or any flushes under the attentive glare of her husband-to-be.

She remembered Anthony's devastated face approaching her that morning, his hazel eyes briefly meeting hers.

'I hope you don't think of me as badly as I think of myself, Rose.'

'I think you're a victim of this system, Anthony,' Rose had answered mechanically, 'almost as much as the girls are. You told me that everybody finds their own way of coping, but you've taken it too far.' She took a careful breath. 'Whatever happens to me, I hope I never lose myself like you've done. I hope I'll never be that wicked.'

He had glared at her, his mouth working to answer. But Rose's emotions were thinly patched together, and she moved away before her words could lose their impact, or she her composure.

From where she was standing now Rose could imagine the Headmaster's penetrating eyes raising a toast at each table, Vivien with her taut vivacity talking round every group.

Emma seated next to her husband, pouring out the wine. There was no doubt that Founder's Hall was alive, and the whole school building was animated by its beating heart.

Frances, pink with drink, had given up her anguished avoidance of Rose and stepped through the doors mid-meal. She seemed to linger, so Rose tried to encourage her friend, no longer caring what had passed between them.

'Are you sure you want to go back in there, Frances?' Rose almost whispered. 'You can talk to me out here. Keep me company.'

Frances's face was straight. 'No, the Headmaster demands it.'

'We could run off later,' Rose pushed, 'to the common room bar, or even the Kennenhaven pub? We could slip out with the others.' Rose touched her small handbag, tempted.

'No.' Frances's voice was bitter as she avoided Rose's eye. 'There's no running off, no slipping out. I belong here, Rose. So do you.'

Rose felt crushed with disappointment as Frances turned away. She looked down at the ring of keys spread across her hands, pressing her index finger against one of the sharper ones; her fingertip white, her fingernail red-painted for the event. She checked the double doors, the heavy brass lock. She probably had the right key there, one of these on that mass of metal. She could lock them in. *Right now,* she thought. *Lock them all in, and run.*

But she didn't.

Long after vast trays of pudding had passed her, a Sixth flew out of the hall with her hand entwined in a man's. Rose fell to the side and saw the rushing back of the girl's silvery dress, a flash of pale skin against the slow turn of the man's grey hair and leathered neck. The couple pursued each other down the side passageway as Rose's heart beat in her mouth.

'Madam!'

She swivelled her head around – was it for her? So many Madams – which one was she?

'Madam?'

Rose's blurry eyes focused on Nessa and the two girls behind her. Freddie and Daisy were wearing their best: the white uniformed dresses pressed in tightly at the waist, laced-up boots at their feet. Their white collars were buttoned up to the neck, and their hair was bound into thick plaits that seemed unnatural to Rose. And then there was Nessa. Her small shaven head was a rough surprise above the doll-like shape of her loose nightdress. Seeing her, Rose felt again that keen slice of agony in her chest. The three girls cast a heavy shadow on the wall as they approached their teacher.

'Madam, are you all right?' Daisy tried.

Seeing the three girls there was wrong, incongruous – they would be in trouble for it, Rose knew, and she too.

'Madam,' Nessa whispered, 'you look different.'

'She's not wearing her lipstick.' Freddie's voice was hard.

'You look so *young*.'

Rose couldn't speak. The three of them moved closer.

'You could be one of the Sixth – except, not so pretty.'

'Nessa,' Freddie said, 'don't be rude.'

Nessa touched her head, abashed.

'Girls.' Rose's voice came out splintered. 'Girls, you're not supposed to be here; it's late, way beyond your bedtimes.'

'We need to show you something, Madam.' Freddie held out her hand; there was a stain on her sleeve, a brownish mark that carried an acrid smell.

Rose turned away, feeling wretched in her tight red dress. 'Please! Go back to your houses before they see you!'

'Come with us, Madam. We've come to get you.'

'I have to do my duty, Freddie.' Rose felt a crawling shame move into her chest, having them here, seeing her like this.

But Nessa shrieked, 'You can't leave, Madam!'

'What?' Rose hesitated. 'I'm not leaving.'

'Yes, you are, Madam.'

'I—'

'Josie, Madam,' Daisy said quickly, 'she told us you've packed your bags and you've written us three letters. She wouldn't say what was in them.'

'Josie was in my flat?' Rose burst out.

'Yes, Madam,' Daisy answered. 'She's always taunting us. She's been going in and out of your flat for ages, Madam. She gets a key through her aunt, Ms Johns. She said she'd seen things written on the mirrors, and she was the one that smashed your owl.'

'Josie said,' Freddie continued, 'that she would take the letters to the Headmaster.'

Rose's breath caught in her throat. 'And has she?'

'No, Madam.' Daisy shook her head. 'She said she'd do it after the Ball. The Ball is too important – she said she didn't want to distract the Headmaster with something so hideous.'

'What did the letters say, Madam?' Freddie pushed; she was looking at Rose with that blazing face of hers. 'Are you going to leave us?'

'You can't,' Nessa said loudly. 'We'd never see you again!'

'But Madam,' Daisy spoke more urgently this time, 'Josie also said the Headmaster has a dossier on you.'

'Girls, I'm really sorry,' Rose tried, checking behind her, 'but I'm on duty and you must go back to your houses. If they—'

'I'm in the san, Madam,' Nessa said quietly. 'They've put me in the san.'

Rose's resolve seemed to puncture. 'Oh God, Nessa.'

'We broke her out, Madam,' Freddie carried on, her voice steady. 'There's a reason we're here. We found your dossier in the Headmaster's office, and we burned it.'

'You . . . what?'

'We burned your dossier,' Freddie announced.

Rose was stunned. 'You broke in to the Headmaster's office?'

'Yes, Madam,' shrilled Nessa, her eyes bright and wild.

Rose felt a strain on her heart, and checked the door behind her again. 'Girls, you mustn't do things like that for me.'

'That's not all we did,' Daisy carried on. 'We built a funeral pyre, in his office, you know, like Dido did after Aeneas: *infelicis Elissae conlucent flammis*, like you showed us. "They burned with the unhappy flames of Dido."'

'We started with your dossier, on his desk,' Freddie said carefully. 'But there were lots of dossiers, and then we found some of the old brochures, of the Sixth, the ones that apparently you—'

'The Headmaster's *desk*?'

'We thought you'd approve,' said Daisy. 'After everything you've taught us.'

'Yes, Madam.' Freddie's tawny eyes seemed to spark. 'We did it for you. We're rescuing you, Madam.'

'Yes, and ourselves,' Nessa added sharply.

'It's what Dido would have done,' Daisy nodded. 'And Medea.'

'No, no, no.' Rose couldn't breathe. 'You've got to show me.

Right now.' Her heart was racing as she glanced at Freddie's scorched sleeve. Rose tugged her wrap over her shoulders, and moved towards them. 'Show me, I don't understand.'

She took one last long look at the doors of Founder's Hall, one open, one closed. The three girls led the way down the passageway and along the corridor. Magnetically, Rose followed, hanging behind them, clinging to her small handbag.

The three girls slipped down the Great Stairs with anticipation as Rose stopped with alarm. A great cloud of smoke was rising in a swirl around the double stairway, coming through the boughs of wild flowers strung up there. Rose hesitated as the dry, acrid smell reeked through her nose. She had to squint to see the bottom of the stairs.

Rose stirred into action. Pushing the girls out of the way, she tore down the steps.

On the main corridor Rose saw what she had dreaded: the thick smoke was growing out of an enormous body of fire from the Headmaster's study. It turned in a great ball, tearing at the walls, reaching up to the ceiling.

'Oh my God!' Rose heard Daisy cry out.

Rose moved towards the fire, squinting her eyes to better see the long strips of flame roaring down the northern throat of the corridor, licking the noticeboards, pulling the wood panels, tugging the long curtains at the far end. Coughing, she covered her mouth.

Rose felt the girls move behind her. She twisted back and spread her arms across the three of them, guiding them away with her figure. Three shocked faces reflected the ugly light of the flames.

'Why's it so massive now?' Nessa shrilled. 'We only set fire to that pile of stuff on his desk!'

Daisy opened her mouth: 'Madam! We—'

Rose pushed them back up a few steps of the Great Stairs. Daisy staggered, her soft black plait coming undone in wisps towards the burning smoke.

'We wanted to free ourselves, Madam!' Nessa screamed louder. 'We wanted to be heroines, like you said!'

Rose absorbed the twisted panic in Nessa's pale eyes, Daisy's gawking mouth, Freddie's stiff shock. Her own thoughts were suspended – as unreal and confused as the thick air that billowed around them. Her eyes followed the threads of flame dragging across the entrance hall towards the front door, her designated spot only hours before. The outside air was feeding the fire's strength. She pressed her small handbag into Freddie's arm and dashed towards the doorway.

Outside was cool and eerily quiet. Feeling the sudden blast of the air, Rose heaved her chest for a moment. It was so dark, she could see nothing at all.

'Get outside, you three!' Rose yelled.

'No!'

'Madam, be careful!'

'Move!' Rose shouted again.

'No, Madam, no!' Freddie screamed back; she drew her arms across Nessa and Daisy, just as Rose had done. 'We're not leaving you.'

Rose turned to unhook the iron fastening and pushed at one side of the heavy door. She slammed one door into the door frame, and moved to the other, as her arm lashed with pain.

'Madam, your wrap is on fire!'

Rose unfurled her wrap and threw it into the flames. She looked for the heavy wooden bolt; lifting it with both hands, she slid it into place. It made a heavy, forbidding sound as it sealed the doors.

'Madam, your arm!'

Rose twisted to look at her arm; the fabric was scalding and she could see blistered skin. Ignoring the long wince of pain, she dashed back to the girls. The flames were rushing to the ceiling now.

'Madam,' Nessa screamed. 'Now there's no way out!'

There is, Rose thought, as she ushered the girls away from the stairway to the south side of the main corridor. Nessa was sobbing, her eyes wild. 'How do we alert the others?'

Just as she spoke, the ceiling above the Headmaster's office seemed to slide and cave in, bringing a portion of the upper corridor with it. Nessa screamed at the smash, clamping her hands over her face.

'Oh my God! That's upstairs! The Ball!'

'Nessa.' Freddie hurried her friend into an embrace, who clawed at Freddie's plaited curls. 'Be brave.'

'*Where* is the alarm?' Rose frantically looked towards the locked porters' door across the entrance hall. 'Where?'

'I don't know, Madam!' Daisy cried out.

There was a cracking sound as the heat grew more intense. Rose raised her head just as the glass of the dome above shattered. Shards of mottled glass screamed down the sweep of the stairs in jagged pieces, slicing into the polished wood of the bannister, the rich carpet of the stairs. Rose tugged the shrieking girls out of the way. A tunnel of cold air hit their faces – but the flames stretched out, higher, to reach the life-giving oxygen.

The iron hands of the great clock slid forward, constant and unwavering.

'We need to go,' Rose said urgently. 'We need to move.'

'Madam, what about the Ball?' Nessa screeched from Freddie's shoulder; she clutched at Daisy now, too. 'Everyone is there!'

Rose hesitated; she thought of Frances, up there amongst those wretched people. Anthony too, and Emma revelling in the evening's merriment. 'I'll sound the alarm somehow . . . Or I'll go back.'

'No, don't leave us, Madam,' Nessa sobbed. 'Please.'

'You can't leave us,' Freddie said, her face stiff and staring at her teacher.

'I won't,' Rose said wildly. 'I'm not going anywhere without you.' She squinted down the cool dark of the main corridor's south side, the only way clear. Behind them, the flames cracked at the fallen glass of the dome and shot out a few shards. Rose tugged at the three girls.

'What was that?' Nessa screamed, still clutching at her two friends as they staggered forward.

'Keep moving!'

'I'm so sorry, Madam,' Daisy cried out. 'We didn't mean for it to spread like this.'

'But you must have realised –' Rose immediately swung her gaze to Freddie, who returned her look with confident defiance. For a moment their eyes touched and Rose understood. She swallowed hard, and answered Daisy firmly. 'No, Daisy. This is my fault.'

'They'll figure out that it was us!' Nessa sobbed. 'Won't they?'

But Rose knew the outcome would be far worse than that. She scrabbled at the group of three, trying to get them to walk, run, faster. Time was moving too quickly, and the fire growing. Daisy started to cough, tossing her head as she freed herself from Nessa.

'Come on, girls!' Rose said frantically, 'We'll go to the boarding houses, we'll get them out.'

Freddie was pulling Nessa along, tugging at her nightdress while Daisy moved on ahead. 'Madam! How?'

'The Junior and Intermediate houses. We can do it – they're on the south side. Wake as many girls as we can together, and then . . . to the dining hall.'

Rose flinched at the pain in her arm, but kept moving. The little group dashed across the flagstones of the corridor, the air growing cooler, clearer now, but the corridor was so dark. Turning back, Rose could see the ominous orange of the growing fire at the end of the corridor. She thought of the sanatorium beyond, and Jane, probably drugged and asleep – she couldn't get to her in time, she knew.

There was another smash, and Nessa screamed again.

'And House See,' Rose said. 'We have to get to House See.'

'That's on the other side, Madam!' Daisy cried. 'They'll never get out.'

'They will, they've got windows on the ground floor. We'll go round the outside, the groundsmen will help. Keep moving, girls.'

'But, Madam,' Daisy called out desperately, 'what's in the dining hall?'

In her mind's eye Rose saw the broad map of the school, its blueprint stamped on the forefront of her mind. She saw that wooden door set into the wall. *To Postern.*

'Trust me, girls. Keep moving. We'll do this together.'

Rose checked the ring of brass keys in her hands, hot now from the fire. Daisy dashed ahead and Rose saw the undone sweep of her black hair disappear into the corridor. Nessa pulled away from Freddie and hurried forward, the halo of her shaven head lit briefly as she moved. Freddie tried to stay in line with Rose, but she couldn't. She bent over, coughing, Rose's small handbag tight around her shoulder as her gold-red plait fell forward.

'Madam.'

Rose stopped for her. 'It's all right, Freddie, we're going to be all right.'

'But Madam, I'm so sorry.'

Rose blinked back at the girl's upturned face, those animated eyes searching her own. 'Freddie, it's not for you to be sorry.'

She reached out her uninjured arm. Freddie straightened up and took Rose's hand.

The fire raged for thirteen hours, great tongues of flame melting into the salty air. The heat of the red, orange and white fell into the cold black of the night. The firemen struggled to get to the peninsula, past the gated and formidable entrance. By then the enormous building had no choice but to give up its reign to the body of flames – and by morning it was a stone jaw gaping out towards the sky, with holes for windows and jagged slants for roofs. Even the chapel's great blue stained glass was shattered into hot shards.

In the early hours the younger girls lined the shingled beach and its wooden jetty, safe in the fresh sea air, standing and watching with only the pull of the tide for company. Shaking and sobbing for their termly home, their beloved possessions left behind. The bay swelled with girls from Verity through to Clemency – but no others, because in their haste, nobody had thought to climb higher and wake the matrons or housemistresses in their flats above.

They preceded the small swarm of Japanese girls, who had smashed their own windows and climbed out – to the shock of the groundsmen – dashing across the fields and down the rickety walkway to the beach.

Nobody dared mention Founder's Hall and what must have been happening inside, at the height of the evening's joviality. Even with its one door open, the thick fumes filtering through the passageways and the high square windows of the hall would have granted no mercy, and those who had already embarked on their union would have died in their own tight embraces.

From the beach, three girls in white stood still with shock and watched their blazing achievement.

Once every Caldonbrae Junior and Intermediate girl had come through that old door, soaked up to their knees and smelling of dank seawater, a young woman found the three girls in white and clasped each of them tightly in turn. She took a small handbag from a red-haired girl's shoulder and said: 'Tell them I went back in. It's the only way.'

She slipped past the authorities, giving a silent nod to the groundsmen. Walking up to the shoreline's cliffs, she hurried towards Kennenhaven and The Ship, moving fast to avoid the accumulating open-mouthed local crowds. She clung on to her handbag and her injured arm, and made her way forward, knowing that she must be counted among the dead. The Caldonbrae influence extended further than the people in that hall; and this was the only way her mother could be safe. The only way her three girls would not be blamed. The only way her father's reputation, too, would remain intact.

Her chest tightened with fear to think of the distressed adults and many teenagers battling in vain for their lives in that very building. Her mind stung to think of Frances trapped along with them. Emma and her husband. Anthony, and young Clarissa who knew no better; Vivien's sharp face caught off-guard. All the others too, pierced through by fire. But she wouldn't turn back and look. The shock forced her forwards, faster, trying not to imagine the resentful ghosts chasing behind her. The question was, where would her exile be, and would she have a chance to say a last goodbye to her mother?

The local police soon moved alongside the firemen to count the surviving number on the beach, taking down the girls' names, ages, their home addresses. The girls had muddled, subdued faces, seeking each other out, hobbling over the boiled rock and greyish stones to avoid the irresistible gaze towards the flaming ruin.

The rest of the parents arrived throughout the late morning hours, once the girls had been taken to the Kennenhaven village hall. They grasped at their daughters and sobbed gratefully into their shoulders. Any furious uproar was snuffed out, thanks to there being no Caldonbrae adults to speak to, none to ask or answer. There was no room for the parents' pomposity among the kind Scottish villagers who covered the daughters in blankets and comfort, who claimed the postern tunnel as a miracle.

The newspapers followed, photographers with hanging jaws, reporters with eyes wide for a story. The truth of the fire was hard to discern. The groundsmen restricted access beyond the school gate, tight in their man-band, insisting that the inquirers wait for the local police and firemen's verdict.

*

Two weeks after the event, the smoke still seeped towards the mainland. Smoke that the newspapers seemed to feed on as they ran story after story that discussed more than the fire's destruction.

The number of dead had finally been recorded: three hundred and fifty-seven souls. Just over one hundred sixth-form girls had perished in the blaze, along with the departing Upper Sixth girls' parents. Numerous school governors too, as well as several dozen gentlemen guests. The Caldonbrae staff: teachers, housemistresses and matrons had been dispersed across the building either at the Ball or up in their flats. None had escaped. Due to the antiquity of the building it had burned fast and efficiently, offering very few means of escape, particularly in the north wing, where the bulk of the fatalities were contained. The final number could not be physically counted, but was taken from various accounts and lists from the school's associates, those that knew who had been present. The newspapers remarked that the loss of certain names among the dead would significantly impact many social and political groups of England.

Morag in the Kennenhaven post office nodded at her customers' passing comments as each day went by, her curiosity lessening as theirs grew. Still, the sudden influx of visitors was a good thing, her husband had pointed out, even if they were generally suspicious of outsiders.

'Terrible tragedy, all those lives lost,' one newcomer said, having travelled a fair distance just to have a look at the smoking carcass of the peninsula.

'Aye, yes.' Morag's husband pulled a regretful face.

'Old building like that, no safety. All wood, stone. Fire must've torn through the place. Arson, was it?'

Morag's husband stiffened. 'Don't rightly know.'

'Supposedly started from the Headmaster's study, I read.' The customer hesitated. 'But it was so late at night. The front doors bolted. Could only be an inside job.'

'Nah,' Morag's husband shook his head carefully. 'Never seen such dedicated staff, never seen such happy girls.'

'The papers don't agree. I read the parents are all in uproar, launching their own investigation—'

'It's our lads, our firemen, our police,' Morag's husband interrupted. 'No need to question it. They've done their job well, and there's nothing to investigate. After all, it were a strange sort of place.'

'Do you believe the rumours, then?'

'Nah, 'course not.' Morag's husband cleared his throat. 'All that nastiness? Just printing to sell copies.'

'I wonder.'

Morag wondered when the customer would finish his analysis.

'Aye. Still,' Morag's husband tilted his head to one side, 'at least they found so many of those little ones on the beach.'

'So that part's true! Fancy that.' The customer frowned with interest. 'They say some of the girls were Japanese . . . I wonder what they're doing up here, so far from home.' He waited for a response, but received none. 'Where will the remaining girls go? The papers said something about partner schools.'

'Ach,' Morag's husband shrugged, 'these rich English always land on their feet. They look after each other, don't they?'

'Even so,' the customer nodded, 'sounds like it might not have been a school like we thought it was.'

Morag opened her mouth as her husband hesitated. 'Aye,

you could be right. But sometimes things happen exactly like they're supposed to, don't they? No need to question it. We're people of honour up here, in Scotland.'

The customer nodded sagely as he paid for his newspaper.

EPILOGUE

Ten Years Later

Rose squinted at the newspaper. Breakfast at the cafe was usually tolerable under the shade of the awnings, away from the golden blaze of the Italian square. But the sun was unusually bright that morning, her dark hair prickled with the early summer heat.

Rose hadn't slept well the night before, but she was used to that now. It was her curse to have her dreams forever marred by girls' faces, tinged by hot tongues of flame. They followed her into the daytime, too, bright ghosts living among her waking hours. She saw Frances's broad smile in her colleague at the library, the spirit of those startling blue eyes turned to ash. Clarissa, too, could be found in the pretty face of her landlady's daughter; Dulcie or Lex in the slender movements of the Italian girls on the street. Even the soft brown hair of a precinct policeman regularly caught Rose's eye and she would stop, thinking that at last the Headmaster had come, had found her after all this time, to avenge his dead.

But no one ever came.

The waiter brought Rose her usual Earl Grey, teabag in, and

it grew dark as Rose perused the paper. It was an international newspaper she didn't usually buy, due to the price and the politics, but today, she'd been advised to via a letter that sat on the table, from Frederica List.

Rose had contacted Freddie as soon as it had been safe to do so, from this self-imposed exile in Rome. Initially she'd expected very little, but soon they'd begun sharing letters as regularly as they could. The fire had freed Freddie of Caldonbrae's stranglehold, but it had not convinced her family of any alternative path. She was still trying to persuade her father that at twenty-five, his youngest daughter might have a more independent life than that of her sisters, perhaps even one that involved a work placement or an internship. But she'd refused to use her father's connections, wanting to strike out on her own, and they'd locked horns. From the strict options offered, Freddie had chosen an arts exchange programme in Rome to be near to Rose, insisting to her father in her undaunted way that her old teacher was a surviving peer from Hope.

But Rose was wary of the girl's intrusion on the quiet apology of her daily life. In her letters Freddie made no mention of the event, and seemed to be entirely unfazed by it, not suffering in the same way as Rose and the other two girls. The bud of feminine courage that had once existed in Rose now bloomed ruthlessly in Freddie. And with that blazing face of hers, Freddie had a resilience that Rose admired but also resisted. If Freddie was a Medea, then Rose was a Medusa: her head separated from her body, her eyes staring out with horror.

Daisy had written about visiting Rome too. Rose imagined showing Daisy around the library and introducing her to her academic friends in the city, but she wondered how Daisy would cope after her nervous breakdown midway through her doctorate in Classics. After all these years of never once betraying a sense of trauma from that night, what prompted her collapse wasn't something bad, but something ostensibly good. Daisy had met a nice man, a young barrister from her father's firm, but the closer they became and the more her father approved, the more she realised that he was exactly the sort of man Hope would have chosen for her. It seemed to prove to Daisy that she would never escape, that Caldonbrae Hall really would always live within her; so, she'd broken things off with the man and fallen behind in her studies. This in turn hurled her towards an emotional collapse. But now, after a year of rest, she was looking for a way to make a timid return to her thesis.

Nessa had never once replied to Rose's letters, but she always hoped, nonetheless. The last the girls had heard, Nessa's family had tried to put her in a Swiss rehabilitation clinic, but she had broken out. Freddie blamed Nessa's silence on that escape and her reported non-stop travelling since. But Rose knew that what they had done to free her – to free all of them – would chase Nessa all over the world, her anxieties tempered by foreign winds, her search for any kind of peace her never-ending.

Once Rose thought she might have spotted that small blonde head crossing a piazza; Rose followed, but lost her in the crowd. She would willingly have crossed the world to find Nessa, and bring her to whatever home she needed, but Rose couldn't leave Italy. The truth of who she really was lay only with those three girls, a few people of Kennenhaven, one former university tutor here in Rome and the dark corner of a drawer where her now-redundant passport lay buried. In England's eyes, she didn't exist.

After the fire, her mother had survived another six months.

Rose had called the clinic twice soon after the event, but had lost her nerve and hung up before anyone answered, not wanting to arouse suspicion. She only learned of her death through Freddie again, thanks to a very fond letter that directed Rose to the obituaries in *The Times*. There, her mother's name was bound up in honour due to her Caldonbrae Hall connection, revered as if she had been one of the long-serving members of staff that perished tragically in the flames. Her feminist legacy lost, her name allied forever with the school – and Rose unable to grieve, her own dead name tied up mournfully next to her mother's.

Yes, Rose would have liked to draw the three girls together with her in Rome, return to their easy classroom discussions from before, uniting after ten years for a kind of purge, in some oblique, ancient way. But she didn't have the power to absolve them – all she could do was free herself, choose to live, and encourage them to do the same.

It was Freddie's most recent letter that birthed a new dash of courage. There was a call to arms within those usual lines of mutual affection, and it directed Rose to the newspaper that now lay in front of her.

> Miss Josephine Harrington, aged 25, one of the young survivors of the tragic blaze that destroyed Caldonbrae Hall and left 357 persons dead announces her intention to rebuild the school in a new location. Miss Harrington laments the loss of this world-renowned institution and has plans to reinstall and renew its ethos and traditions for the twenty-first century: 'I shall be very pleased to revive this cherished heart of British society. With the revered Caldonbrae values as our backbone, we shall usher new generations of girls into

> the modern age.' The location is not yet confirmed, but with the mass of patrons supporting her, the task will surely be a glorious one. Josephine's own aunt and the school's former deputy head, Ms Vivien Johns, perished in the accident ten years ago, and will be honoured among other names in this new Caldonbrae rebuild.

Rose studied the photograph of Josie: the girl's newly adult face, her hair shorter and fuller, the set of her jaw, those hard black eyes. Rose couldn't believe how much Josie as a woman resembled Vivien. She read the article three times before scrunching up the page, staining her hands with its ink.

So there it was, Rose's past enemy rising up again. She'd by now learned that she was not only her father's child, but her mother's too, and this enduring anger could not lie dormant. Freddie had a plan that would end what was beginning again, but it depended on Rose. Were they doomed to fight this many-headed Hydra for as long as it kept reappearing?

Rose glared at the ink stains across her hands. Pushing the newspaper aside, she took a final swig of her black tea. As she did so, her eyes caught on a red halo of curls shining in the sunlight on the other side of the square. Rose gave a rare smile as she slipped the letter in amongst her things and left the table.

Acknowledgements

Firstly I want to thank Nelle Andrew, my agent, who grabbed this book with both hands and didn't let go, even when I resisted punching it into its finest shape. The passion you showed in welcoming and nurturing this novel to publication has changed my life.

To my wonderful editors Emma Capron and Sarah Cantin for seeing the potential in this novel, and for helping me craft it into the best book it could be. Thank you also for bringing the classical women to the forefront – they'd all be so proud of us, I think. Your unwavering belief in this story and in my writing astounds me daily, and I am so grateful that I get to work with both of you.

Thank you to everyone at Quercus and at Macmillan who has worked so hard on this novel, and bolstered it up so brilliantly, especially during the horror of Covid-19.

To the Scottish town of Stonehaven, thank you for being so beautiful and atmospheric, how could I not use your wonderful Dunnottar Castle as inspiration? Particular thanks to the people of the Marine Hotel, and the barman who was kind enough to answer all my pestering questions.

To all the fellow writers in my writing classes in Los Angeles who both encouraged and goaded me into finding my voice, and writing what had to come out – thank you. Particular thanks to Nicole Criona, who expertly led us through our vulnerabilities every Sunday in her living room. And to Anna, my sister's friend, who with one phrase sparked my initial idea and nudged me towards my genre. Those months in Los Angeles will always stay with me.

To my dear friend Christina, a fellow educator and a wonderfully curious mind, thank you for being the best sounding board and cheerleader I could ask for. Thank you for your constant positivity and kindness, and for helping me battle through the darkest hours inside my brain.

To my great friends Anna and Marta, thank you for being such discerning and thoughtful snippet-readers, and always listening to my moans and groans along the way. Thanks also to my wonderful friend Jenn for her ever-brazen encouragement and excitement for this writing adventure, which we embarked on together.

To my exceptionally creative siblings. My sister Camille, the greatest champion of self-expression, for her guidance, her pushing and her ongoing support. My sister Loulou, for her certainty in my true purpose and her continued reassurance that this was the right thing to do. My brother Pierre, who always checks on the rest of us and lends his cheering voice at the perfect time. Thank you all for your very valuable encouragement.

To my mother for reading whatever I put in front of her, and giving me her brutally honest opinion thereafter – not without trying to correct my English, even though she herself is French. Thank you for your excellently sharp notes, and for letting me plough through your thoughts for any surprising or improving idea.

To my father, there on the sad height, who always breathed literature and poetry. I'll always be grateful for those piles of books bought for me every summer and every winter, books that I devoured and cherished, even when I questioned the choosing. Many of those books spoke to me and inspired me to write and speak back. He would have been thrilled about this novel's publication, and more particularly, the act of courageous rebellion within its pages.

To all the kids I've ever taught, this novel wouldn't exist without you. Thank you for teaching me more than I taught you.

Turn the page for an exclusive look
at Phoebe Wynne's new novel

THE RUINS

'I was completely transported by *The Ruins*. Phoebe Wynne has evocatively rendered a beautiful, doomed French chateau while creating immersive, almost dream-like atmospherics. I loved this novel'

Sarah Pearse, bestselling author of *The Sanatorium*

PROLOGUE

The Château des Sètes took up the loveliest spot in the area, everybody said so. It was extraordinary in its setting, flanked by the rushing blue of the Mediterranean and the cut of the white rock. The house was tall, wide, and glowing like a cream jewel with its rows of red blinking shutters; it caught every eye that passed it from afar, whether skirting behind the grounds in a car, or from the front, gliding past on a boat.

This evening the house was lit up for the Ashbys' party. As the sea grew dark the stone sweep of the terrace was dotted with lanterns and merry guests chatting over the jazz from the record player. It was a goodbye party, to celebrate the concert and the end of the orchestral week – the children of St Aubyn's school had performed very well, including the Ashbys' only daughter, Ruby. Many of the parents had recently arrived in the area to enjoy the concert, delight in the party, stay the night at the local hotel and take their child home in the morning. Many of them were also there to appraise the château, envious of their own children who'd spent their nights sleeping in tents on the land and their days rehearsing with the full backdrop of the sea.

But the high-pitched wail of a siren pierced the party's buzz.

It accompanied a flash of blue light, then a swirl of red, which swung across the faces of those gathered there.

For a long moment nobody knew what to do at the sight of a police car perched on the edge of the terrace, like an uninvited guest. Adult eyes turned away politely, but the children were all agog.

A uniformed man slammed the car door and his voice rang out. *'Je voudrais parler à Monsieur Ashby. J'ai Monsieur et Madame Fuller dans mon véhicule et c'est une histoire très délicate.'*

The jazz tootled on, but a strange hush came over the crowd. In the back seat of the police car was the shadow of two dark heads. A second, younger policeman emerged from the other side of the car, just as a small voice spoke up from among the group of children.

'Fuller? Did he say Fuller?'

A confident voice answered, a girl with red hair and frowning eyes. She moved to the front. 'No, he said Ashby. My father's here.'

A smartly dressed man approached the first policeman, shaking his hand to draw him aside. The back door of the car opened to produce another man with short curly hair and a furious face, his eyes blotchy and his nose bloody. Behind him, a woman was hauled out. The policeman leaned his arm on the door to get a better grip on her, and she screamed, a sound that matched the earlier wail of the siren. Her white face wore no blood but her eyes stretched wide as she gaped at the three men around her as she was lifted out of the car. The tips of her fingers were soaked red, bright against her pale hair and paler skin. The girl standing in front of the children jolted at the scream, alarmed to hear such a sound coming from a woman – from someone's mother.

ONE

1985

Ruby had both looked forward to the party and dreaded it. She'd been the last to leave the church after the concert, packing up her flute carefully, straggling behind the group of young musicians as they wandered back down and along the rocky path to the house. The way was lit with dim lights and the swinging torch of one of the music teachers, and Ruby breathed in that smell so familiar to her, a deep, damp green pine. The unseen sea was gently roiling, rumbling out a soothing encore after the heroic might of the concert.

Ruby felt a twinge of anguish. She'd so enjoyed hosting the orchestra trip this year. The performance was already over, the party would be soon, and she didn't know when she'd see Bertie again. This was his last school trip, the end to his final year at St Aubyn's, and now he'd be going off to his next school – strict, grown-up and boys-only. Ruby, two years younger, would be left behind. She couldn't imagine what it would be like next term: to scan the dining room empty of him every lunchtime; to never spot him playing board games in the old library, or football on the lawns; to arrive at orchestra rehearsals twice a week without his smile to greet her.

Ruby clutched at her flute case, holding on to the joy of the concert, the thudding warmth of the orchestra in their altar alcove, the beat of the music under the heat of the electric lights. She'd counted every bar with the nod of her head, watching the conductor as he brought her in with a sweep of his arm, nudging the hopeless second flute beside her when she missed her entry. Even with those moments, the concert had gone brilliantly.

But on her way back to the house, her joy evaporated. Ruby felt annoyed that the whole of August lay ahead of her, empty without the daily cheer and discipline of orchestra rehearsals. Of course, she had always loved her summers in France, but she'd enjoyed having her classmates there during the last week. She'd seen her family house anew, proud of the way it looked with all of them in it. But by this time tomorrow the house would be empty except for Ruby and her parents, and their friends, the Blys. Then again, August always seemed to bring the small dread of more guests than Ruby had bargained for.

The party at the house was in full swing when Ruby got there. The elated concertgoers spilled out along the long sweep of the terrace: parents, staff and helpers, all babbling in stiff English. The mothers were draped in pastel silks and linens, glittering with smiles and diamonds or precious gemstones. The fathers were elegantly casual in cotton shirts and chino trousers, tanned faces and wild hair. Congregating away from them was a throng of messy, delighted children grasping at bowls of crisps and glugging out of plastic cups.

Tables were set out, heavy with lavish plates of food which were interrupted by swathes of green foliage or bunches of wildflowers drooping from jugs. Someone's little sister poked her finger into a bowl of chocolate mousse, before sucking on it delightedly. She turned to see Ruby scowling at her, pulling her finger out of her mouth with a laugh, before realising who Ruby was; her face straightened and she scuttled away to cower behind her mother.

Ruby's own mother, Rhoda, petite and auburn-haired, was standing with her friend, Polly, who rested a graceful arm on her pregnant belly, laughing as she recounted a story.

'Well done, darling girl!'

Ruby smiled brilliantly as the parents of one of the cellos swanned over to her. 'Good evening, Mrs Moreton, Mr Moreton. Did you enjoy the concert?'

'Yes, dear.' The woman nodded over-vigorously. 'Well done, splendid.'

Ruby smiled at the confirmation. 'Thank you. Have you seen my father?'

'Yes, he's been rushing around, setting up for the party.'

Ruby looked up at the couple. 'Didn't he come to the concert?'

'No, darling,' Mrs Moreton said lightly, 'your parents have been terribly busy hosting all of this, of course. Do be good to your mother, she's been a wonderful hostess.'

Mr Moreton was surveying Ruby with a tilt of his head, his hand gripping a tumbler of whisky against his chest. He bent to address her. 'I say, you're rather good at that fluting, aren't you? How old are you, dear girl?'

'I'll be twelve in two weeks.' Ruby straightened up. 'I'm not normally first flute, but the girl who is couldn't come. Next year I might—'

'Jolly good.' He shifted his gaze to give his wife a knowing look. 'Toby Ashby's inside the house. He had a rather important phone call, I gather.'

'Well, I hope it wasn't anything bad,' Mrs Moreton said with a toss of her head. 'Better not ruin everyone's last evening together.'

Ruby smiled thinly at the Moretons and wandered over to the swell of children, her eyes skating over the boys' heads to find Bertie. There he was, his sunny face lit with laughter as he jostled with his friends and their cups of Coca-Cola. He'd looked like that when he smiled at Ruby only a few days ago, asking if she wanted to go for a swim together. She'd barked out a 'no' without thinking. He'd nodded before moving away, leaving her utterly dismayed.

Ruby bit at her lower lip, sore and overused this week from so much fluting. Even though it was evening she still felt hot, a slick of sweat under her undone hair. She was cross that her father hadn't seen the concert, cross with that phone call for distracting him now, cross with Bertie for not seeking her out that evening when she might never see him again. Cross that in the morning the other children would pack up their tents lined along the back patch of land, pile into the school coach or their parents' cars, and leave.

Imogen Bly waved Ruby over and offered her a cup of Coca-Cola. 'I'm so sad it's all over.'

Ruby nodded and took the cup, but didn't take a sip. The plastic felt sticky and it looked like someone had already taken a swig.

'At least we've got the next few weeks together,' Imogen continued buoyantly. 'I can't imagine the house without everyone. But it'll be fun, won't it? I do like the bedroom your mother's given me, far better than that awful tent I've been in all week.'

Ruby gave a half-hearted smile. Imogen Bly annoyed her; at home in England, she and her mother, Polly, were always coming by, or they were going there. Polly, who'd grown up alongside Rhoda, two plants shooting up and flowering together – or so their stories went. Ruby and Imogen did not share their mothers' hot relishing of each other. Imogen probably wouldn't have minded being friends, but Ruby was firm in her dislike. Imogen was in the year above, and her beauty and warmth were too irritating and confusing for Ruby to navigate, so she preferred to avoid her at school. Orchestra brought them together, although Imogen played brass – the French horn – and was always gassing at the back and blasting her instrument out at odd moments during rehearsals, just to be funny. But Imogen was well-liked and had won the Maths prize three years in a row, and so Ruby generally tolerated her and her abundant black hair and too-large mouth.

'Yes,' Ruby said, plastering on a smile. 'It'll be fun, there's always something to do here.'

She took a sip of the Coca-Cola just as a siren jolted everyone out of their revelry.

Ruby stared at the woman plastered against the police car, and made the connection quickly. *Monsieur et Madame Fuller*, the policeman had said. Ruby's head seemed to fill with the woman's scream, her twisted figure and her cold face – which Ruby now realised she'd seen earlier that evening.

It had been at the end of Holst's *Jupiter*. The audience had clapped obligingly, but one woman – Mrs Fuller – had stood up and cheered heroically, her great voice whooping around the church, her face swollen with emotion. The conductor hesitated, his mouth slightly agape. The rest of the orchestra smiled at each other uneasily, now woken from the bubble that had been their music. Ruby had appreciated it until the church began to echo with the woman's repeated claps, her unceasing hoots.

The second flute, Annie, had stiffened beside Ruby and let out a small moan. The cheering woman was her mother.

Mr Fuller had tugged his wife down violently. She'd let out a short cry as she fell back to her seat with a flump, her shoulders jagged and her head hanging forward.

The conductor had waited a moment before raising his baton, and the concert carried on.

But now Mrs Fuller was grappling with her husband as he battled to trap her arms and settle her shaking head, his own bloodied and angry face just as horrifying as her blank one. Ruby's father was speaking quick and agitated French at the first policeman.

Ruby felt sure that something terrible must have happened after the concert.

'My goodness, that woman is terribly upset.' Imogen stepped up beside Ruby. 'The policeman said *Monsieur Ashby*. Are they going to arrest your father?'

'No,' Ruby shot back, 'of course not. That's Monsieur DuPont . . . he's the police chief. He's been here for dinner. I didn't fully understand what he said.'

Ruby's chest quivered with unease. She glanced at the second, younger policeman, at his tight, resentful face and folded arms. Ruby had never seen him before. He caught her eye with his severe, surveying stare and she looked away.

A few other men had hurried forward to support Ruby's

father in his conversation with the police chief. Mrs Fuller seemed to be gathering herself to stand, her tortured features twisted, her legs almost giving way. But as her husband grabbed her arm, she screamed again, louder than before. It was as if she were being burned by a white-hot poker; Ruby felt another bolt of alarm at the noise. In the corner of her eye she saw a small dark shape dash into the bushes – the local stray black cat that always lurked around the house. Mrs Fuller's screaming had apparently scared even him.

'Monsieur Ashby,' Mr DuPont interrupted Ruby's father grimly.

'Darling, can't you do something with her?' Ruby heard her mother's voice call frantically. 'Quickly, Toby, darling? We've got company!'

'Yes, Rhoda,' Ruby's father turned his head to answer, 'I'm well aware. Let's put her upstairs in one of the rooms.'

Their guests were moving across the terrace now; the adults seemed to have given up their polite indifference, their eyes fixed on the fascinating debacle.

Mr Fuller somehow managed to fold his wife into the group of gathered fathers; Ruby recognised Imogen's among them. The mass of men seemed to warp her screaming into long, painful groans.

'Oh! How awful, Ruby!' Imogen was ogling the scene delightedly. Ruby heard a rush of whispers behind her as the other curious children joined them, crowding nearer as Mrs Fuller was taken into the house, those heavy groans thinning out as she passed over the threshold.

'What happened?'

'Who is that woman?'

'Is she drunk?'

Ruby took a quick breath as she watched her father finish his intense conversation with the police chief. Toby Ashby stood tall and narrow, touching his glasses with attention, his neat moustache as stiff as his brown hair. Perhaps that's what it was – Mrs Fuller *did* seem very drunk. Ruby had an aunt who spent every Christmas with them, and usually cradled a glass of something from noon till night. She did sometimes grow hysterical and shouty, just like Mrs Fuller here, although never this bad, and never involving the police. Ruby's mother said her sister drank because she was unhappy, and because she was a housemistress in a school somewhere, without a proper life. Perhaps Annie Fuller's mother was unhappy, too.

Ruby heard her father's voice switch to English as he challenged Mr Fuller with a question. Yes, Ruby thought, she could see the resemblance between him and Annie, something in their pink cheeks and narrow squint.

'She crashed the car. She was drunk,' Mr Fuller answered Ruby's father loudly. 'I couldn't get to the wheel in time. She was trying to get to the airport.' Imogen's mouth slid open with interest and she turned to relay the information to the others behind her.

'But couldn't you have stopped her? The trouble is, they're saying there was an accident – a hit-and-run – on the same road, and they're implying that your car was involved.'

'God, no.' Mr Fuller shook his head forcefully. 'We hit a wall, we didn't hurt anyone.'

'Are you sure?'

Mr Fuller hesitated, then answered, 'Yes.'

'Well, there will be an investigation. I'm afraid neither of you can leave the country.'

A glimmer of fury crossed Mr Fuller's face. 'Can't you help us at all?'

'That is what I'm doing.' Ruby's father gestured at the police car. 'It's a mercy they're allowing you to stay here in the meantime.'

The police chief had heard enough, and with a short bow he announced, *'À demain, Monsieur Ashby. Nous vous contacterons dans la matinée. Bonne soirée.'*

Ruby's father gave a grim nod and replied, *'Et à vous, Bernard.'* He turned to catch the younger policeman's eye with a *'Bonne soirée, monsieur,'* but it was ignored, and the man slammed the door on his side of the car.

The gathered crowd of onlookers ruptured and pulled back, giving the police car a wide berth long after it had rolled away into the night, without any swirl of its colourful lights.

'Bloody disaster, Toby,' Mr Fuller exclaimed.

Ruby's father leaned back to consider Mr Fuller. 'Yes, quite.' His eyes hovered over the inquisitive partygoers. 'We need to discuss this inside, Max.'

'Yes, I'll pour a drink first. Can I get you a whisky, too?'

A few of the parents cast dark looks between them as Ruby's father strode into the house with Mr Fuller hurrying behind. Ruby wondered where they'd put Mrs Fuller, where Annie was, and whether she'd witnessed her banshee of a mother, or her bungling confusion of a father.

'Ruby, Immy.' It was Imogen's father, his bulky figure heavy and his face drawn with concern. 'Come along, you didn't need to see any of that. Do you want to go upstairs to bed? Or enjoy the rest of the party?'

'What's *happened*, Dada?'

'Not for you to know, darling.'

'Is it a secret?' Imogen asked excitedly.

'Well, yes, why not.'

'A secret?' Ruby repeated, sceptically.

'So which is it,' Imogen's father demanded, 'upstairs or enjoy the rest of the party?'

'Oh.' Imogen hesitated. 'May we enjoy the rest of the party, please?'

'The party,' Ruby added, quietly but decisively, thinking of Bertie. Her eyes fell on the space where the police car had been, now swallowed by the evening's darkness. 'Is it really a . . . secret?'

'Ruby, you little thing,' Imogen's father continued, 'your flute solo was wonderful. Fancy getting all those pretty notes out of such a sliver of silver.'

'A sliver of silver?' Ruby repeated uncertainly, her eyes lifting to search the man's worn face. Mr Bly – or Lord Beresford, as people were supposed to call him – had always intimidated her. She didn't know whether it was his height, his wide stooping shoulders, or his dark, sunken eyes that seemed to flash at her as he talked.

'Yes, girl. A sliver of silver.' He laughed expansively. 'You're a damn sight more feminine and beautiful than Immy with her bloody trumpet.'

'Dada, do you really mean that?' Imogen turned and looked beseechingly at her father. 'Don't you know it's a French horn?'

He patted the top of Imogen's head reassuringly. Ruby couldn't help smiling at the compliment.

But she wasn't smiling half an hour later when the children's part of the party was called to a halt and she was sent to bed. To her surprise, Ruby's mother accompanied her to her bedroom.

'You're going to have to share your room, Ruby.'

Ruby's mouth puckered. 'What?'

'Little Annie, that woman's daughter. The Fullers. They're going to stay here until your father can sort out what happened in the accident.'

Ruby looked at her mother, wanting to ask her the questions whose answers she now feared. Through the double windows, a bright bloom of chatter rose up from the terrace below. Further beyond she could hear the lively shouts of the others bedding down for the final night in their tents.

Ruby's mother was waiting for a response, but received none, so she continued. 'Their daughter Annie will sleep in here, and you'll be jolly nice to her.'

'Can't Imogen share *her* room?'

Ruby's mother straightened the coverlet and thumped up the pillows. 'No, darling, we're the hosts. This is our house.'

'We've just hosted the whole orchestra for over a week!'

'Yes,' Rhoda's face swung to Ruby's and their irritation sparked together, 'and you did very well out of it, young lady. First flute, ahead of your time.'

Ruby was almost growling. She sat on her bed to calm herself. 'For heaven's sake! Having Imogen here is bad enough.'

Rhoda stood up straight. 'Ruby, it's been quite a trying evening. There are far more important things to be getting on with. Don't make a fuss.'

Ruby spat out, 'Annie can have the metal bed, not mine.'

Rhoda glanced over at the antique metal bed set near the long windows as a sort of sofa. 'Yes, fine. Move your teddies. And find her some sheets, can't you?'

'*What?*' Ruby's mouth curved with disbelief. 'Can't Lisette do that?'

A voice called out from below. 'Rhoda!'

Ruby's mother stepped over to the window's balcony and peered out, a strategic smile placed on her face. 'Coming!' she turned back to her daughter. 'Lisette is busy tidying up, which you know perfectly well. Don't be such a bore, Ruby, and get this done.'

She sashayed to the door, ignoring Ruby's incredulous face, and clicked it shut.

Ruby wanted to slam the door instead. Annie in her room! That little urchin constantly by her side, like she had been in orchestra, the second flute to Ruby's first. Thin and pale and insipid with her wide eyes and sour mouth. And now her mother, some strange creature, so unlike the other mothers, involved with the police and staying in the house.

Ruby scowled as she lifted her teddies off the metal bed, settling them carefully in her wardrobe, arranging them to face each other in mutual embraces. She was an only child, and had been her whole life; why should she suddenly have to share everything now? It was certainly true that the Vaughan Williams' *Greensleeves* duet with Annie had gone very well, in rehearsals and during the concert – Ruby had done all the heavy lifting, of course. But she did have to admit being impressed by Annie's efforts. Perhaps Annie knew how to rise to a challenge, then. Well, Ruby would give her plenty.

Ruby stared resentfully at the metal bed, wondering where to find any spare pillows or where the sheets were actually kept. She'd never made up a bed in her life. Maybe she'd take some pillows from her parents' bed – her mother's side, just to spite her.